A

ORDEAL IN THE FOREST

GODWIN WACHIRA

ordeal
in the
forest

modern african LIBRARY

First published in 1968 by the East African Publishing House,
P.O. Box 30571, Nairobi, Kenya

Printed by the English Press Ltd., P.O. Box 30127, Reata Rd., Nairobi,
Kenya and bound by afropress ltd., P.O. Box 30502, Saldanha Lane,
Nairobi, Kenya.

Contents

Contents

1 FALSE ACCUSATION

The four boys, Kato, Choti, Nundu and Iru, walked home together from school. Home was a small mud and wattle hut which they, together with Iru's father Kingi, had built on a small plot of land about two miles from school. Although Kingi was working on Bwana Milton's coffee farm and used to send a small sum of money to Iru each month, poverty was reflected in the shoddy, uncared for appearance of the hut and its surroundings. No one had taught the boys to appreciate the value of clean and wholesome living, but the hut was regarded as their own and, boylike, they all loved it.

Choti was the son of a poor village carpenter, whose home and workshop consisted of one small earthen-floored hut. During the holidays, he helped his father to make chairs, hoes, tool handles and other simple objects. Although traditionally Choti would inherit the business on his father's death, he loathed it and all the menial work it entailed. He was a schoolboy, and schoolboys in his opinion were too good to dirty their hands. So Choti lived almost completely with Iru.

Kato's father, Mbugu, also worked for the Miltons. He was a cook, and although he lived very well on the perks of the kitchen, basically he too was a poor man and had no land in the reserve. He had arranged with Kingi for Kato to stay with Iru, although he had no idea of the conditions under which the lads lived. He had been prepared to do anything in his power to educate his son so that the humiliations and indignities which he had suffered through working for a white settler would not fall on the boy also. Mbugu had thought: "Maybe if my son is well educated the white settlers will accept him instead of spurning him because of his colour."

Nundu's father, Thia, was a Tribal Policeman who had

1

many wives, Nundu's mother being the first. He had two elder brothers, both of them working for Major Cook on Ranch Estate near Naro. Thia was always away with the Chief, and Nundu was sadly neglected. His mother was fully occupied with the babies of the family, and travelling up to five miles each day during the dry season to obtain fodder for the livestock. The only means of finding sufficient money to send Nundu to school had been the profit that was made by selling the animals, and Nundu's mother thoroughly resented the extra work that they brought.

Nundu took full advantage of these circumstances. He became a thoroughly undisciplined rogue. His neighbours, who feared Thia, did not dare to complain openly, because Thia, being a Government Servant, could easily get them into trouble with the District Commissioner if they antagonised him. Nundu became a thief and a liar. His schoolmates, not caring about his reputation, admired him because he always had money in his pockets. Indeed, he taught many of them to steal. So Nundu, who wanted a safe hideout, also lived with Iru.

Kato was something of a misfit for he had not learnt to steal from his neighbours what was rightfully theirs. The others, therefore, never told him where they procured the extra food, or explained the strange appearance of various luxuries. Kato was, nevertheless, accepted by Iru, Nundu and Choti because he helped them with their homework — thus saving them many times from the wrath of their schoolmaster, Mrefu. He had a natural talent for story-telling and was one of the most popular boys in the school.

But Kato's efforts did not always save them from Mrefu. Often the latter would beat them brutally for little or no reason. So it was that after one particularly bad beating of Kimu, a classmate of theirs, Nundu, who always assumed command over the others, persuaded them to run away from school.

That evening while the children were gathered around

the smoking log fire in the centre of the hut, Nundu stood up and announced:

"Never again will we go back to that school. We will run away and Mrefu will get the blame for beating us. I tell you what: we can all go to my brothers in Naro — they'll get us jobs. I had a letter from my elder brother last week and he told me that there is a shortage of labour on the farm where they work. I've got plenty of money to go by train — look," Nundu pulled a five shilling note from his pocket, the proceeds of his most recent pilfering, "this will get us all there. You can pay me back from your first pay packets. Come on now fellows, what about it?

Let's make ourselves rich and powerful. We'll never get that by staying in this dump."

There was complete silence, but a shiver of excitement and anticipation went through the group.

"Well, don't take all day to decide. Are you with me or against me?" demanded Nundu impatiently. "After all, I don't have to take you with me — remember that."

"Is there any school near the farm?" asked Kato.

"My dear Kato," sneered Nundu, "what on earth is the point of running away from one school to go to another? Anyhow, you can't earn your living and become a rich man and go to school at the same time — unless of course you can cut yourself in half and be in two places at once."

Kato, very much discomforted by this answer, dropped the subject, but asked, "Will we get houses, bedding and cooking pots?"

Nundu, leaning nonchalantly against the centre pole of the hut, exclaimed, "Ah Kato, your head is in the clouds! I thought you were born and bred on a farm. Now listen to me, you will stay with a friend on the farm. Your friend will be one of my brothers who will put us all up, but you'll have to buy your own cooking pots and blankets."

Choti asked, "How much money will we earn?" To which Nundu replied, "That depends on the generosity of the Bwana and his farm headman. Come on now, let's all go to sleep and we'll complete our plans tomorrow morning."

Kato tossed and turned on his banana leaf bed, his mind in a turmoil. "What am I to do, what am I to do?"

But the following morning when Nundu asked them all if they had made up their minds to accept him as their leader and to obey his orders, Kato answered "yes" with the others.

"Now," said Nundu, "listen." The plan was that they were to leave, apparently for school, at the usual time the next day, and hide until three p.m. when they had to go to the station and catch their train.

Next morning, they awoke as usual, and prepared ostensibly for school. They left at the normal time and then branched off to hide in a convenient cave near the station. They had with them their school bags containing their few possessions.

Zuru Station nestled beside a gorge, between the Aberdare Range and Mount Kenya, made by the swiftly running waters of the Abu River. The scene was dominated by snow-capped Mount Kenya, which is called "Kirinyaga". Nundu daringly bought their tickets quite openly and then joined the others in the cave.

When the train arrived that afternoon they threw all caution to the winds and rushed through the bush and up the path to the platform.

Nundu sprang up. "It's here! Come on you chaps, let's hurry or we'll miss it."

"All of you get in the train, and I will throw the bags through the windows — get in from this side so that as few people as possible will see us," Nundu directed operations.

He hurried back, and as he picked up the few bags he heard the guard's whistle. The train started to move out of the station. Nundu raced out, threw the bags through one of the windows, caught hold of the guard rail and hoisted himself onto the steps. His outstretched leg hit the signal post as the train gathered speed, and he swore volubly. His companions watched anxiously from one of the windows.

"If Nundu has been hurt we'll all suffer," said Iru. "He's got a foul temper."

"Yes," replied Kato with unconscious penetration, "in his own way he's rather like Mrefu."

5

"We've got away, do you hear? Got away. Now we are free."

"No, Nundu," said Iru, looking round. "None of us will be free until we have reached our destination."

Their momentous journey begun, the boys gazed out of the windows, fearing to miss any minute detail. They recognised the Church of Scotland Mission situated on a hill which could be seen from the school. The Scottish Missionaries had established a school here specifically for girls, but had as yet not met with much success. As far as the reserve people were concerned, girls were born purely for profit — from bride prices and labour. What was the point of losing good money or livestock by sending their girl children to school? Girls could not take part in the affairs of men. The Missionaries were meeting with passive resistance but were determined to carry out their duty to God, and forged ahead unswervingly. But the people just shook their heads sadly at those "fools of white men" and went their own way.

A few miles further on was a Catholic Mission, this time for boys and therefore full to overflowing. The Catholic Fathers regrettably crowed over their "opponents'" lack of success, and this too did not pass unnoticed by the Africans of that area.

"Nundu, Nundu, isn't that the Catholic Mission up there on the hill?"

"Yes Kato, why?"

"My father works near there. It must be the same one, yes, I recognise its shape. My mother and I used to walk up to the Mission every now and then for medicine when one of us was sick. They have a wonderful hospital there."

"Isn't that the Aberdare Range to our left?"

"Yes, Kato, I expect that's where your father and *Bwana* Milton used to go hunting before the war. It's

7

beautiful, if you are still child enough to like beauty. Men don't bother about these things."

Even so, they all fell silent and gazed in awe at the impressive Range, which was to play such an important part in their lives, in a future they could not see.

Soon the landscape changed completely. Arid plains dotted with thorn trees and red anthills. The only water in view was the River Como, which had dwindled down to a mere stream. Even so, many huts were dotted about its banks, with the customary little shambas around them. Some of the land near the river was completely inaccessible, covered with huge clumps of papyrus grass, the only bright touch of green for many miles.

"The villagers here," remarked Nundu knowledgeably, "are very poor. The ground will not yield a good crop as it is too hot to grow anything successfully. They sell what vegetables they can produce in the market. Poor fools, see them toiling in the sun. I'll bet you many of them haven't eaten a good meal for many months. Look now, we are coming to Maki."

The others crowded even more eagerly around the window.

"Tell us what all that is over there?" shouted Choti excitedly.

"On the left," stated Nundu, "is a small trading centre, like at home, except that the shops belong to our people, not to those cheating Indians. See that bridge over there? That's where we cross over the Como."

They felt the train shudder and jerk to a standstill, and listened to the yells of the people on the ground trying to climb on the train before it left the tiny station.

The train, with a great sigh, heaved itself out of Maki, and in a few minutes the scenery had changed yet again, and they frequently travelled through open-topped tunnels blasted through small hills. The line passed over wild

8

country, covered in high grass and abundant in shrubs and trees.

"Lion country," remarked Nundu. "Not even I, who am so brave, would walk alone here."

The train crossed once again over the Como river, and under the bridge the boys could see some women collecting water to carry to their huts at the top of the hill. The women's life was truly a hard one, full of toil. Their men treated them like animals and sometimes just as brutally. Now, instead of hundreds of mud huts dotted around like beehives, they could see that they were drawing into a "settled area". The fields were fenced with barbed wire and cedar poles. Cattle and sheep in very large numbers were being herded by drovers, and farm roads intertwined leading from one European stone and *mabati* house to another, over hills and down dales. In one place, some men were chopping trees, in another whipping the oxen on their long trail over shambas dragging ploughs and harrows.

"Oh that I too could own all those cattle and all that land," sighed Kato.

"It is ours, we'll get it back off those white men, even if it means war," snarled Nundu. "We'll get it back, you'll see. These Whites will suffer for what they have done to us, and so will their children and their children's children. We will make them creep and crawl in front of us. Wait and see."

"Yes, Nundu, that is what my father says," replied Kato. "You are right, we all hate the white man for what he has done and is doing. He will suffer and we shall laugh."

The sun was setting now, throwing a lovely pink and red glow over the countryside. There is nothing more glorious than an African sunset, but familiarity breeds contempt and it went unnoticed. Nundu stood up. "Look, see those lights, that's Naro Station and town. We shall be

9

arriving in a few minutes. Come on, get everything together, quickly now, quickly!"

The train drew slowly into the station, and the four boys climbed, rather apprehensively, off the train with their bags and pushed their way through the colourful mob.

They followed Nundu through the gates searching through their pockets for their tickets to give to the collector. Once out of the station, they started off towards Major Cook's farm, where Nundu's brothers worked. They were all very tired.

Soon they crept through the fence which ran round the boundary of Major Cook's farm, and after walking through a few hundred yards of long grass, arrived in a small clearing.

"Here we are," said Nundu gratefully. "Heho, Wenye, Heho, wake up, wake up, it's Nundu."

Nundu banged with all his might on the wooden shutters of a hut. Wenye poked his head sleepily out of the window.

"Why, Nundu, what's wrong? Why are you here at this time of night?"

Nundu gave a very brief explanation of their activities, and Heho and Wenye, roaring with laughter, welcomed the four boys into the house, fed them, and gave them some sacks to sleep on.

"Sleep now, little brothers," said Heho, "and tomorrow we will see what can be done".

Major Cook, nicknamed Kiko because he was a confirmed pipe-smoker, was a first world war veteran. About fifty years old, he was a big fat man who lived the life of a recluse in a huge house overlooking the Como River. He was a slave driver and only the labourers who worked well liked him, and he in turn was good to them in his own way. He had no use for slackers, and was at his wit's end to find good men at this time, for most of his labourers had been pressed into the army. He was excessively rich, owning miles of ranch land which supported about five thousand head of cattle, mainly steers. He also cultivated a few acres of land for market gardening, but lacked sufficient labour to increase this venture. The river Como never dried up even in the dry season, and was an unfailing and invaluable water supply as it wended its way right through his farm.

When Heho and Wenye took the four boys to Kiko the following morning, he was overjoyed, and offered them employment straight away. Nyapara, the headman, was introduced and, joy of joys, they were given a house belonging to one of the unmarried absentees. They were offered a wage of four shillings per month plus posho, beans, skimmed milk and meat. Nyapara took the boys down to the vegetable gardens, and told them what to do. The boys started to dig the cabbage patch. They talked very little amongst themselves, but each of them was wondering if they would have to spend the rest of their lives hoeing Kiko's cabbage patch. Their belief in Nundu's ability to make them rich quickly was being rapidly undermined.

Meanwhile, their fathers had been scouring the countryside to find them, fearing them dead. One of Nundu's relatives who had seen the group at the station told the four fathers who caught the next train for Naro.

As soon as they arrived they hurried down the road to Kiko's farm, following the same route the boys had taken.

"Heho, Heho, my son."

Heho and Wenye came running out of their hut. "Father, father, what brings you here?" Between them they told the boys' parents the whole tale, and took them into Wenye's house where they rested. Nundu and his friends came running to see their fathers, and the re-union was very joyful.

Unfortunately, Kiko, who had had a hundred head of steers stolen the previous night, was informed of the strangers' presence by Nyapara, and together they ran down to Wenye's house.

"What are you doing here, you cattle thieves?" shouted an infuriated Kiko.

"Bwana," replied Mubugu courteously, "we have done no harm, we only came together to find our sons."

"You are trespassers, bad men," shouted Kiko.

"Bwana," whispered Kato, "my father never stole a cow in his life. What he says is true."

"Yes," chorused the others, "it is true."

"Nyapara."

"*Ndio,* Bwana?"

"Tell these men that if they agree to work for me we will forget about this incident, but if they refuse I, as the Magistrate for this District, will have them arrested and sent to jail for trespassing."

A chorus of protests was Kiko's answer, and without more ado he sent for the Police to arrest the men and take them to prison.

"Father, come back!" shouted Kato.

"Father," cried Choti. "I'm sorry, I'm sorry."

Nundu and Iru remained silent, absolutely horror-stricken at what was happening. The four men gravely looked at their sons and at each other, and drawing themselves up proudly, allowed themselves to be led away by the Police.

"Kato, my son, my son, what trouble you have brought on your family. May the god of our ancestors forgive you and your companions for what you have done to your fathers this day."

Kiko looked in contempt at the four boys who were

sobbing unashamedly. The older men, Wenye and Heho, were also silent, but the hatred in their hearts blazed in their eyes and they both turned away from Kiko and went to comfort the boys.

"Your fathers, oh children, are obstinate men. All who stand against me will suffer. I hope you have learned your lesson."

So saying, Kiko turned and walked out of the hut, slamming the door behind him.

2 THE 40 GROUP

In the meantime, back at home, the whole place was buzzing with rumours like a hive of bees. The relatives of the missing boys were bewildered by the non-return of their fathers. Mrefu, the brutal schoolmaster, was dismissed and there was general rejoicing.

It was at about this time that the Chief's son, Toga, returned to the village after three years in the Army. He had lost a leg in action in Abyssinia and was a very great hero in consequence. All the young folk of the village were thrilled by the stories of his adventures, and Toga was more than ready to entertain them since his crippled state made his life somewhat dull. His home soon became a meeting place for the younger inhabitants of the village. Gradually an inner ring of acolytes began to appear among them. Muta, Toga's brother, was an attractive personality. This, together with his prestige as a Chief's son, made him a natural leader and mixer and he chose a number of comrades from all walks of life: Karoki, the Court Interpreter's son, heavily built, humorous, intelligent, always top of his class; Kara, the first born son of a shepherd, ignorant, inquisitive and hard working; John, whose parents were Christians and who therefore knew little about tribal life. He was very often laughed at as a result of the elementary questions he asked. Finally there was Njambi, the only girl admitted into the inner group. Though slightly older than the others, she was brilliant at school. She was popular although very shy.

One evening not long after Toga's return the young people grouped around his house rather earlier than usual.

"Muta, go and call your brother and tell him we are here," said Karoki.

Muta, pushing open the wooden door of the house,

called out, "Come quickly Toga, we all want you to talk to us."

"I am coming, brother, but not very quickly. What can a man do with one leg?"

He made his way slowly over the earthen floor, for he still managed his newly acquired crutch rather clumsily. He smiled at his companions, settled himself comfortably under the eaves of the house, and said, "My friends, we will talk tonight of other countries. White soldiers die just the same as black ones. On the battlefield there is no difference, yet here, the white people say they are better than we are. Their god doesn't protect them any more than ours does us. They are the same as we are: their bodies are white, that's all." Toga sighed and continued, "There's something else you don't know. I met people from the Gold Coast who were fighting too; they are educated and behave like the white man."

"Toga!" interrupted a horrified Karoki. "Do you mean to tell us you have met those awful people from the Gold Coast? Didn't you run away?"

"What on earth do you mean? I don't understand."

"But Toga, everybody knows they are cannibals and eat people."

Toga burst into loud laughter. "Ah Karoki, how easily fooled you can be. No, no, it isn't true! The white men spread these stories around because they don't want us to know about our black brothers who are more civilised than we are. They are afraid. I met many Ethiopians while I was in the army and they told me how they ran their own lives without any interference from *Kaburus* until the Italians overran their land. When this war is over their king will come back to be their father once more. There are no colonial chiefs or tribal police in Ethiopia. The people run their own lives and everything is different. If you even as much as mention Hitler or Mussolini they would cut your throat."

15

"Who on earth are Hitler and Mussolini?" cut in Kara.

"Why, Hitler is the leader of the Germans and Mussolini of the Italians. They are not only fighting the British but most of the rest of the world as well. They are really evil and kill anyone who gets in their way."

There was an awestruck silence, until at last Muta whispered, "Toga, surely no one would dare to fight the British Government?"

"Brother, it's only fools like us who fear white men. There will be a fight for freedom in this country in the near future, and then you will see that they are but men."

"A fight in this country?" they all shouted excitedly. "Tell us all about it."

"Not now, it is not yet time. You know the vegetable factory near Maki Station?" he continued, with a quick change of subject. "All the tinned vegetables from there go to the British soldiers and their helpers."

Mary, a close friend of Njambi, broke in at this point to ask, "White men don't eat our food, do they?"

"Mary, on the battlefield, there are no Africans and Europeans, we share everything and are as one. It is only in camp that we are divided into separate tents. Just before I left I gave the last of my rations to a white man who comes from our white highlands. The white men love our food and say it is nicer than theirs. But look, the sun has gone down over the hills and it is time for you to go to your houses. Goodnight to you all and sleep well."

The group broke up reluctantly, chattering excitedly about what they had heard.

It was while the youngsters were still at school that Toga had his great idea. He had nothing to do but sit outside his hut all day dreaming of what had been, was and would be. He hated inactivity and longed for the arrival of his more comfortable wooden leg that his father had ordered for him. He had been racking his brains for weeks to find something that would interest and occupy the young folk. Suddenly he snapped his fingers and laughed out loud. "I have it, I have it," he cried, "I'll help them to form a dance band! We'll have the best in the District and everyone will want to come and dance here." He nodded slowly to himself and his thoughts raced on: "More than that, some of these young men are strong and willing to fight for freedom; they are good material. I must send to Nairobi for Njogu to come down here and talk to them about *Uhuru*. Surely many of the freedom fighters will come from this area, and these young lads will win back our land for us. Yes, the material is here all right. I must call Njogu as soon as possible."

Here his reverie was rudely interrupted by Muta, who arrived suddenly exclaiming, "Why hello, my brother, why so serious?"

"Serious, Muta? No, not I. I've been thinking and I've had a wonderful idea."

Muta looked eagerly at Toga.

"You know, ever since I came back I've been trying to think of something for you and your friends to do to pass away the evenings, weekends and all the rest of the spare time you have, especially now since you are just about to leave school. At last I've found it. We will make musical instruments and start a dance band. Oh yes, I know, father doesn't approve of modern dancing — but what does that matter? We'll take care he doesn't find out."

"You are the best brother in all the world," cried Muta, hugging him enthusiastically. "It's a wonderful idea."

Toga chuckled, well pleased at Muta's excitement. "I can't work, neither can I walk properly until my wooden leg comes. All I can do is think and I've all the time in the world to do that."

"But where can we hold our dances?" asked Muta.

17

"It must be somewhere father can't find us."

"In the ghost valley, you chump. You can place guards and no one will dare go there. You know how all the old folk fear the ghosts: it's the one place where you will be quite safe."

"Yes, that's a terrific idea. Go on."

"If you stop interrupting me," grinned Toga, "I will. I can make the instruments if you bring me the wherewithal. It won't cost much. What I need is a hide for the drums — father killed a goat the other day and you can get the hide from mother, but don't let on what you want it for! Then we'll need two old steel cooking pots and perhaps a round four gallon tin. I'm sure your friends can find these." He rubbed his chin thoughtfully. "Oh, and I must have the wires for my guitar. They got broken while I was away, you know. Could you get them from Nairobi?"

He rushed from one house to another shouting the news. His friends were all as thrilled as he was and promised to bring the necessary materials to Toga's house the following day.

"Remember," Muta said, "if father finds out he'll stop us."

Muta was so preoccupied that evening that he hardly spoke, even to his mother, except to ask for the hide. He was very thankful when she gave it to him without any awkward questions. He tossed and turned on his bed of sacks, quite unable to sleep. "This is a wonderful idea of Toga's," he thought, "but it certainly does bring problems. Toga can't work properly so he'll live in this house indefinitely, or at any rate until he gets married. Where can we practise? If my friends come to stay with me, I have nowhere to put them let alone find a place to hide the instruments where father can't find them. But that is to pray for the rain before the ground is cleared. Toga is a wonderful brother, I'm sure he can help sort it all out."

He turned over again and at last went to sleep, only to dream all night of the band to be.

The following evening after dark, Muta and his friends crept into Toga's house. It was rather cold and they grouped thankfully round the smoking fire, all eager to start on Toga's idea.

Kara had brought a tin from home, and Karoki and Njambi an old cooking pot each. Muta produced the hide for making the tops and bottoms of the drums. Toga had, earlier that day, given a friend some money to buy guitar strings when he was next in Nairobi, and Mary had made some very fine sisal fibre string, about fifty feet of it, for stringing the drums. The young men promised to start preparing the dancing ground, and to learn to play the instruments as soon as Toga had made them. This was the easiest part of the whole project for they had all grown up to the sound of drums. Since custom forbade the girls to take part either in playing in the band or clearing the bush, they agreed to broadcast the news to all their friends.

Finally Kimu, also a close friend of Muta's, but who had been ill for the last few weeks, heard the news and immediately came to assist his friends. The chosen valley was situated only a short distance away from the village and was surrounded by thick bush land. There were many hidden valleys where dances were held, but the one they chose was certainly the best and its high cliff walls would prevent the noise of merrymaking reaching the village. It was extremely fertile and thickly wooded. A rivulet split it into two parts, one being cleared for the dancing floor and the other honeycombed with caves surrounded by huge cedar trees. It had finally been decided that one of these caves was the safest hiding place for their precious instruments. By day this glen was filled with music from the many brightly feathered birds that lived there, but by night the caves echoed with the weird screeches of hoot owls that made their abode in the valley. The villagers regarded these birds with pure terror for even to hear their cries would bring misfortune or even death on their families. As a result, the birds had been chased away from the village and had taken refuge in this valley where the caves supplied an abundance of food. The young people, however, paid no regard to this kind of nonsense and their desire to dance overcame superstition.

Kimu was greeted cheerfully by his friends on his arrival. He found them cutting grass and trees and making an enclosure for the dance floor. He showed them, with great pride, the marks on his stomach, back and arms made by the Witch Doctor when he drove out the evil spirits. They were very deep and the scars would never go. As he had not regained his physical strength, he was given the task of supervisor.

At this time, the European style of dancing to guitars and drums had begun to creep into the area. Visitors from Nairobi and all the big towns had taught the young people the new steps, which were thoroughly disapproved of by their parents as suggestive and immoral. Indeed the Elders

had forbidden the young people, under pain of dire punishment, to take part in dances of such a nature. This prohibition, however, was of little avail since the young friends, well versed in the arts of deception, found it easy to attend any dances in the District whether their parents approved or not.

Toga, meanwhile, was very busy making the rough instruments. The first to be completed, of course, was the guitar which merely required fitting with strings. The drums were made out of circular tins, covered at each end with cured skins tied in the middle by sisal string passed from skin to skin in a criss-cross fashion. It was difficult work, needing a skilled craftsman, and Muta was kept busy piercing the skins with a nail. In this way, owing to everyone's enthusiasm, the band was completed in a week.

Constant eager enquiries as to his progress had been a tremendous boost to Toga, assuring him of the triumphant success of his project which he knew would increase his importance and prestige as time went on.

As soon as he had finished, Kara, Kimu, Karoki and Muta started practising in the evenings, helped by Toga. They needed no special training and had soon converted some Kikuyu tunes into the rhythm of the white man. Muta plucked the guitar strings while the three others beat the drums, one large and two small, with their hands. The sounds produced were not at all unpleasing to the ear and, it now being the rainy season, they had about two months to perfect the tunes. The new dances consisted of complete distortions of the waltz, rhumba and quickstep or even sometimes a combination of all three and surely no European would have recognised them.

As soon as the dry weather came, the opening night was organised. Word spread like wildfire and, as it was the school holidays, young people for miles around gathered in the valley for a night of fun. The musicians met quite early in Toga's house for the final briefing. Muta was far too excited to notice how unhappy Toga looked.

21

"I only wish I could go with you," said Toga. "How useless I am with only one leg."

"Don't worry Toga," answered Muta hurriedly. "Your leg will be here soon and then you'll be able to come with us. Come on you chaps," he said, turning to the others with the careless thoughtlessness of youth, "let's go. Look at the moon, it's a beautiful night for dancing."

They made their way carefully through the bushes feeling very important, for the prestige of musicians was high in the village. When they arrived they were all astonished at the huge crowd assembled.

"Why Muta!" gasped Karoki. "There must be about three hundred people here!"

Muta did not answer: he was thinking just how important he was. "I'm not only a Chief's son," he whispered to himself, "but the leader of a band. What a big man I am now."

They were greeted with cheers of joy from the happy boys and girls and Muta held up his hand for silence.

"Welcome, everybody, to our new dance ground. I hope you will all enjoy yourselves and come back many times. Before we start, I would like to introduce John. He will not only call the dances but it is his responsibility to see that we are not caught." Roars of approval greeted this announcement for it was known that John had gone to the dance in spite of his parents' strict injunctions not to associate with the sons and daughters of unbelievers.

"He has posted guards around this valley to warn us of the coming of our parents or the Tribal Police and he will tell you if you are making too much noise. You must all listen to any instructions that he may give because if you don't this may be not only the first but also the last dance ever held here."

"Thank you, Muta. I've already nominated certain of you to take away the stools; it only remains for me to tell you all that if you see me standing on Muta's stool waving like this," here John suited the action to the word, "you will just disperse as quietly and quickly as possible and hide in the bush till all is safe again. You must co-operate or we will all suffer. Now," pointing to about fifty couples, "the first dance."

The boys took their partners and waited expectantly for Muta to strike up.

"Now!" shouted Muta. "Come on, let's go! One! Two! Three! . . ."

The dance went on into the early hours of the morning. The next day, just as they were leaving Toga's house to go swimming in the river, they met Njogu who had come to visit Toga.

"Stay awhile, Muta," said Toga, "and meet my friend Njogu. He is a taxi driver who lives in Nairobi. He's as keen on dancing as you are, so next time you must invite him."

They gathered round Njogu eager to hear the latest news. Njogu grinned as he began, "My friends, the news is all about 40. All the young people belong to the 'age group of 40'. This means that they are all prepared to lay down their lives for the freedom of their country. It is a kind of password: they were born in 40, educated in 40 and circumcised in 40, and believe me, we will win our battle in 40 too."

"You speak strange words, friend of my brother, what do you mean by them?" asked Muta.

"Listen, Muta, now is the time to fight for freedom. If you and your friends want to fight with us then you too will be initiated into the secrets of the 40 group. We are holding many meetings all over the country; everyone who attends them has vowed death to the white man and freedom for our country."

Muta looked at Njogu in horror. "You don't mean we

are going to kill all the white men, women and children too?"

"Muta," replied Njogu very seriously, "don't you understand what the white man has done to us and our families? Has no one ever told you that the time has come for us to be free to live our own lives without interference of any kind?" He paused for a moment, desperately keen to win this boy's confidence, knowing he had a big following in the area, and then went on, "Listen, Muta, we will kill only those who are stubborn; the others will all go back to their own country and leave us in peace. We must kill those who remain to save not only ourselves but our children and our childrens' children. Believe me, hatred for the white man is universal. They have taken what is not theirs and we intend to get it back. Can we be wrong to want to do this?"

"No, Njogu, I suppose you are right. I've never had much to do with the white man — I think the only one I know is Kamau's adopted father, Father James, and he is a good man. I've heard much about the way our brothers have been mistreated but they were only rumours. You speak with conviction. You must know the truth. What must be must be. What do you want me to do?"

Njogu breathed a sigh of relief. "In Nairobi we have already started to collect money to buy arms and food for our fighters, but we need more, much more. This is where you come in: I want you to hold a dance and tell everyone what I am telling you now. I want all your friends and your friends' friends to join 40 and to contribute anything they have towards our fight for freedom — even their lives if needs be. We want our land back, all of it. We have asked the White Government to return it and since they refused, well," he shrugged his shoulders, "war it must be; the *Kaburu* will get more than he asked for."

Muta hesitated no longer. "We will do as you wish, Njogu; you have fine motives."

"Good!" replied Njogu. "Do so and I will return in a

short while and inform you further."

Muta and his friends said goodbye to Njogu and walked slowly down the path towards the river, each lost in his own thoughts. Muta remembered hearing about 40 just after he had been circumcised a couple of years previously. He recalled with a wave of disgust what had been done to him and all the pain he had suffered. His brother had looked after him then, and he remembered how he used to have many midnight visitors who came and went in secret. Yes, thought Muta, they used to talk about 40 but I never knew who they were, or even what they were discussing. I thought it was money, certainly not a secret society.

When they reached the river bank, they sat down to talk over all they had learned. "I know," said Karoki suddenly, "let's call our dance band 40. It will be a great joke for no one will know what it means and we certainly shan't tell them!"

So "40" it was, and the villagers asked what it meant and scratched their heads over it, but nobody would tell them.

While all this was going on, Toga had seen a great deal of Njambi and became very fond of her. At last he asked her if she would become his wife. Willingly Njambi consented, and so, as custom demanded, Toga told his mother who in her turn informed Njambi's parents. The Chief, because he was so proud of his son who had been the first in the area to join the Army voluntarily, thus improving relations between the Chief and the District Commissioner considerably, very readily agreed to pay the dowry. Muta, Karoki and Kimu threw themselves into the wedding arrangements with great enthusiasm.

Muta, after telling everyone about the wedding, gave the assembly Njogu's message which was received with no little amount of eagerness — the general feeling obviously being, "We will do all in our power to recover what is

25

B

ours — just tell us how." Muta promised that as soon as Njogu returned from Nairobi there would be another dance so that all could hear what he had to say.

But first came Toga's wedding. It was very splendid and all the guests thoroughly enjoyed themselves. The traditional customs were strictly observed. A new hut was built, and the Witch Doctor performed his part. This all took several days.

At last Toga's mother stood holding a calabash full of castor oil to give the tribal blessing:

"May prosperity remain in this house for ever, my daughter. I give this as a token of blessing; may it never be empty. It is for you, your husband and the children that the god of Kirinyaga," she pointed to the snow-capped Mount Kenya, "will give you and this is as necessary to you as is water to a good tree. May Kirinyaga bless you."

Njambi accepted the calabash murmuring the customary reply, and entered her hut which had already been fully equipped by Toga's mother. Toga and Njambi were now man and wife.

This great occasion was marked by a magnificent feast which was attended by the Chief in all his glory. All Njambi's friends crowded round her and the rejoicings continued far into the night.

It was just after the wedding that Nundu arrived for his customary monthly visit. By this time Muta, Karioki and Kimu had left school for good owing to their failure to find a place in an Intermediate School. Their interests were very limited, and so they both regarded Nundu with a certain amount of awe for he, as they saw it, was an experienced member of the outside world. Nundu, like Toga and Njogu, regarded them as potential freedom fighters and lost no chance to regale them with his political knowledge, gained from attending political meetings throughout Naro and even Nairobi District. On this particular visit, however, he was seeking Toga's advice on the military aspect of freedom fighting. They were kindred spirits, as can be imagined, and Toga spared no effort to help him in any possible way.

Toga, who could now walk almost normally with the help of his wooden leg, was beginning to take an active part in the movement. Njogu, who had access to a great deal of information through his influential friends and his travels, was accustomed to passing it on to Toga who, in turn, spoke frequently at the dances his brother held. He was, in fact, the deputy leader of 40 in the area, Njogu being the leader, although few people knew this for he had very little time to spend in the reserve.

The trend of political events was moving so fast about this time that Njogu was compelled to speak to the dancers immediately to find out what support he had. The three men sat in Toga's house for most of the day, discussing the situation, and then ordered Muta to summon his friends for a dance. In this short time Nundu and Njogu had become close friends.

As soon as Muta had summoned his followers to the dance ground, Njogu arrived accompanied by Toga and Nundu. They walked slowly towards the group and took their seats in the centre of the circle.

"My brothers," said Toga, "today is a very great day for us all. You have heard me speak many times of Njogu, but this is the first day that he has honoured us with his presence. On behalf of you all I would like to welcome him here."

Njogu smiled and was greeted by enthusiastic applause.

"Before he talks to you," Toga continued, "I would like to give you a rough idea of who he is and what he does. He is a taxi driver in Nairobi and has been appointed locational leader by the people from our location who are working in Nairobi. He is a great politician and he is going to tell us how we can co-operate with our brothers all over the country to win *Uhuru*, and chase away the wretched white man." Turning to Njogu with outstretched hands, he announced: "Brothers! I give you Njogu!"

Nundu nudged Muta and whispered, "My friend, you haven't got any problems here, have you?"

"You shut up, or I'll break you into little pieces!" They laughed happily at each other and settled down to listen to their leader.

"My brothers," began Njogu, "I thank you for the welcome you have given me. It makes me very happy to see so many of you here all eager to join in our fight for freedom. With such faithful followers, how can we fail?"

A burst of applause interrupted him, and he held up his hand for silence.

"I was born here, in this village, about thirty years ago. When I was a young lad I went to Nairobi to make my fortune. I tried my hand at many things. I worked for Indians and Europeans alike, and it didn't take me long to find out just what they are. I was a houseboy for several years, mainly for the white men and I learned the meaning of the word hate." He leaned forward. "Believe me, I was treated like a dog and still am. I decided to get employment as a turn boy in a big transport company so that I could learn to drive during our long trips from Nairobi to the great lake and back. The lorry driver was a nice man, my brothers, one of the very few. He taught me so well that I learned to drive within a year, and then I started working for a taxi company. I expect you are wondering why I am telling you all this. Well, you see, this was the beginning of my political career. I travelled, and still travel, all over the country and am really very much of a free agent. My clients are the rich, indolent white men and believe me, they speak freely in front of a poor dog of a taxi driver who, as they see it, couldn't possibly have enough brains to understand their language. I say nothing, but just listen. And when I attend one of the many political meetings that are being held these days, I pass on all I have heard. That's why I have been elected a leader by our people in Nairobi, and wherever I go, I hold meetings such as this one."

Njogu paused, and then, seized by an uncontrollable emotion shouted, "All you young people here and all over the country must end the white man's rule! You are the 40 generation; it is your privilege, your bounden duty to do this! Every white man who is in our land must be killed if he will not leave of his own accord. I preach hatred towards our suppressors. They must die and we must have our freedom before '49' . . ."

He was interrupted by a roar of approval from the group who stood up with one accord yelling, "Death to the white man, freedom for our people."

Njogu once more called for silence, mopping the perspiration from his forehead.

"What about the trench digging that is imposed upon us. Do the white men dig these trenches?"

"No!" the crowd roared.

"And yet if you do not dig them, what happens to you? You are fined twenty shillings and all your livestock is confiscated. You do not protest or resist so the white man thinks you are satisfied. Is the white man punished for refusing to dig these trenches?"

"No! No! No! Death to the white man, death to the white man!" was his answer.

"Look at that patch of land over there," pointing to a distant hillside riddled with brown lines. "That is the way to destroy land, not how to preserve it. The white man thinks he is so clever. He thinks that he will prevent soil erosion by forcing us to dig these trenches. Let me remind you how they are made. They are dug with the sweat of your brow, three feet wide by three feet deep. Is that not so? You dig them on all your hills. You pile up the soil that comes out of these trenches on the hill slopes — and

29

then the rain comes and washes it all away. You are not only reducing your life span by this endless hard labour, but you are losing the soil that our grandfathers and our great-grandfathers cultivated and tilled. What do the white men know about this? For generations our forefathers have drawn good yields from this soil — ah, yes, the white man knows that. He knows that he is ruining our land, and why? Because he wants to crush us. Note very well that he doesn't dig these trenches on the land he has stolen from us, yet you have to dig them by law; a law that is enforced by whippings and brute force. Then they steal our only means of livelihood: our animals. We die from starvation, yet they don't care. They say our gods are dead. Can't you see what they are trying to do? It is your duty to spread word round all your friends and prepare to die if needs be for that which is rightfully yours! Only in this way can you serve your country."

Njogu paused for breath and looked round the gathering, well satisfied with the impression he was giving. The young men were again on their feet stamping and shouting, completely carried away by what they had heard. He glanced at Muta and smiled to himself. Muta was shouting with the rest.

"But be still once again," he shouted. "I have yet more to tell you." He waited until the valley was quiet and looked at the young faces gazing up at him.

"What about the traitors amongst our own people? The Chiefs, who collect and help to spend the taxes that we pay? The Tribal Police who assist them? The white men divide our money amongst themselves and these stooges, and what benefits do we get? How many schools have we to educate us and our children? The only schools that you can go to are few and far between; even then, you can only be educated for four years if you are lucky enough to find a place. But the white man's children are fully educated. They have well-equipped brick and *mabati* schools and there are many of them. Our few schools are built of mud and wattle, and what equipment

30

do we have? None! That's where our money goes, the money that we earn with the sweat of our brows and the aches of our bodies. The Chiefs go round collecting the taxes: you have to pay tax for every wife, and they count the number of houses in your compound and you pay so much per house. You are whipped if you don't and sent to the white man's jail. They auction your cattle, your sheep, your goats. You are reduced to worse than mere poverty. These white men are devils come to earth. What medical facilities do we have? None! We walk in rags and live and die in poverty! The white man travels around in big cars and lives in houses so big and so well furnished that you would think they are palaces of the gods. That's where our money goes. May the gods help us to revenge these injustices! They not only try to kill us by taking our money and forcing us to build trenches, but they are trying to wipe out our religious beliefs, the very beliefs that are the stronghold of our lives. These Christians now they say our dances are evil, born of the devil, so when we dance we dance in secrecy. They say that circumcision is evil too and are trying to force us to leave our young men and women uncircumcised. We have told them the significance of the ceremony, told them that if we die uncircumcised we cannot go to join our ancestors. We have pleaded, begged, but to no avail. Now we must fight, fight, fight!"

At this, the youths once more leapt to their feet.

"Let us kill them now! Now! Now!" The cry was taken up and resounded through the valley.

"Be patient my friends, the time is not quite yet. I am your leader, am I not?"

"Yes, you are our leader, but we must kill, kill!"

"All right then, but you must do as I tell you. If we do not co-ordinate our activities with those of the rest of our brothers we shall fail, and this we must never do. Spread the word around. Remember we must not fail!

You must not, in your enthusiasm, be the ones to endanger our cause of freedom and justice. Curb your feelings until I tell you the time is ripe. I must go back to Nairobi now but I shall visit you again in the very near future and tell you what is happening. I know I can rely on you all to do as I say. You, my brothers, will play a leading role; but remember, this must be kept secret from the stooges of the white government or they will send soldiers to kill us all before we are prepared. Remember, death to the white man, but not until I give you the word. Farewell!"

So saying, Njogu turned and walked up the footpath out of the valley, followed by Toga, Nundu and Muta.

As soon as they reached Toga's house, they went in and Njogu carefully bolted the door.

"Are you sure that we cannot be heard here?" said Njogu.

"Why yes, Njogu, as long as we talk quietly, we'll be safe enough, and if my father comes you can hide under that pile of sacks over there," replied Toga.

"Good! Now let's do away with propaganda and get down to business. Muta, have you any close friends that you can really trust?"

"Why yes, Njogu, old schoolmates of mine: there's Karoki, Kara, Kimu and," he paused and said rather doubtfully, "John — but John is a Christian and I don't think he would go with us."

Njogu answered without hesitation, "You must leave John out of this or he will betray us. Go and call the other three and bring them here quickly for I must be leaving soon. Careful now, mind no one sees you."

Muta went out of the hut closing the door carefully behind him.

"He's a good lad," said Njogu, "I'm glad we've got his support. He leads all the young people in the District;

they will obey his least command. I think we'd better leave the business side until Muta comes back. What about some beer? I'm feeling really thirsty. Nundu, here's money, go and buy us some."

Now this beer is made of sugar cane grated on a piece of flat metal, toothed like a saw and holed by a nail, until it looks like cotton wool. After one night tied in a big cattle skin, usually kept specially for this purpose and dampened before use, the cane is pressed by two wooden rollers to extract the juice. The juice is poured into a calabash and sugar and water is added. The calabash is left to stand overnight by a very hot fire. This process produces a very strong beer brewed sometimes on a commercial scale or for feasts. The beer was drunk from a beautifully carved bull horn which was passed from hand to hand.

A few minutes later Nundu came back with a gallon of beer, followed by Muta and his friends.

After brief introductions, Njogu stood up to address his colleagues.

"My friends, I want you all to understand that whatever I say to you tonight must never be repeated to anyone, not even Njambi or John — secrecy and complete dedication to our cause is our motto. If any of you betray that cause you will become an outcast of the tribe. You all understood, of course, the point of my speech today. It was pure propaganda to win the confidence of the people. Note carefully, I mentioned no concrete plans — only ideas. That is the art of making a speech. If I had spoken to the crowd the way I am speaking to you now, I would ruin all that our leaders are working for."

He broke off here for a swig of beer from the horn which was passed to him by Toga, and continued, "I needn't enlarge on the atrocities that are committed by the white man, you know them as well as I do. You must spread the word around all your friends, but remember to be convincing so that you too can gain the confidence that I earned today. Hold many meetings — perhaps one a week — to keep their blood up. That is the way to gain and keep support for the cause."

He paused for another drink of beer.

"However, now I reveal to you that there is already in existence a wholly African organisation with its own headquarters which is planning ways of securing our freedom. But before I dare go any further, I would remind you of the oath-taking custom of our people. I now ask you, how many of you are prepared to take a similar oath of loyalty to this new organisation, in order to make it possible for me to reveal to you some of the secrets in my possession without fear of their reaching undesirable hands? Neither Toga nor I dare tell you anything further until you have taken the oath which ensures us of your complete loyalty. I will be back in a week to know your decision and then we can proceed further. This includes you, Nundu, and I'd like you to discuss this with the others, and decide with them what you are going to do — I mention you specially as you live so far away. I really must rush now and pick up my passengers, I'm sure they'll be ready to go back and if I'm late they will abuse and beat me."

Njogu smiled at the youths, who were too awe-stricken at what they had heard to say anything in reply, and walked out of the hut.

They walked along slowly to the taxi.

"Toga," said Njogu, "you must exert all your influence on your brother and his friends to get them to join our movement. We must have their whole-hearted support — they are our very first disciples in this village."

"I realise that," replied Toga, "but have you anything specially in mind that you want me to say to them?"

"Oh, just remind them continually of all that the white man is doing to us; of the injustices that we suffer. And you can tell them too how big and powerful they will be if they join our cause, for when we win they will be sure of very high posts in our new government as a reward for their loyalty. You can say that with truth, for you know a great deal more than they do! Also, of course, tell them that when the white men go we will have our land back and we will see that our followers get a big share of the best of it."

Toga grinned ruefully, "I'll do my best, friend. Any other instructions?"

"One more thing. Get those boys to collect bits of iron and wood — you know the sort of thing I mean — suitable for making arms and ammunition: we have no guns of our own except those we can manage to steal, so we must quite obviously make our own. Hide all the bits and pieces in the owl caves and set up your workshop there — get the kids to help you."

"I agree as far as the collection of the iron and wood is concerned, Njogu, but I feel that we can't tell them what it is for, or where it is being taken, until I have persuaded them to take the first, second and third oaths as our society demands."

"But of course, Toga, you are perfectly right. Ah, here's my taxi, so I'll say cheerio for now, and see you next week."

Njogu climbed into his taxi and drove off, well pleased with the success of his mission.

During the whole of the next week, Toga indoctrinated the youngsters as he had been instructed. They could talk of nothing else. By the time Njogu came back, they had made up their minds to throw themselves heart and soul into the new movement.

As promised, Njogu returned at the end of the week, but he did not bring the oath administrator with him. Upon being questioned eagerly, he replied, "I didn't bring him with me as I wasn't sure what you were going to decide. Are you with us?"

"Yes! Yes!" they replied with one accord.

"Congratulations upon your decision. You yourselves will benefit from it, apart from your country. I will return again a week from today with the oath administrator, and on that day you will be sworn in as true brothers of freedom. I must rush now, there are some white men waiting for me to collect them — see you today week."

Njogu drove off in a cloud of dust, waving a happy goodbye to his new recruits.

3 CHALLENGE

On that fateful day when the fathers of Nundu, Kato, Choti and Iru appeared in Court, Major Cook, who was presiding as Second Class Magistrate, took his full revenge. He had discussions with the Police Chief and the Court Prosecutor, who both knew the truth, and they had decided to sentence the accused to a stiff term of imprisonment — five years each, except for Nundu's father, who had a previous conviction and was therefore sentenced to seven years' imprisonment. It was made quite clear to the accused *in camera* that if they confessed to the alleged crime and agreed to work for Major Cook they would be released. Quite naturally, they refused to confess to a crime they had not committed, much to the relief of Major Cook who, after sentencing them, put in a claim to his Insurance Company for compensation for the loss of the cattle. He therefore benefited highly from the deal, and had no further thoughts for the men he so unjustly imprisoned. Six months later, the Police found the cattle in a *manyatta* about a hundred miles away from Naro, and agreed to classify them as unidentified to protect Major Cook. They also agreed to treat the matter as extremely secret, for they all knew what a great wrong had been committed, and what might happen to them if it came to light: even in colonial days, such practices were not knowingly connived in.

News of the convictions travelled swiftly to the various families, who were stupefied at the white man's way of justice. They were furious too, but were too cowardly to do anything more than weep bitterly and store even more hatred away in their hearts. Nundu was more pleased than upset for he did not regard his father with great affection. He also saw how an incident of this nature could be used as political propaganda and thus further his already good reputation with the Nairobi political leaders. Nundu would never miss a chance to better himself, and he was becoming a self-centred, conceited brute. Wenye and Heho nursed their bitter hatred and quarrelled many times with the youngsters who had brought such trouble on their families.

On the evening of the conviction, a sad group gathered in Wenye's hut. Nundu swore that he would take revenge on Major Cook, even if he died in the process and he made his friends swear likewise. Kato, in keeping with his character, was very reluctant to do so, but was swept away by Nundu's persuasiveness as he had been before and, once again, was to live to regret it.

The next day they walked sulkily down to Cook's vegetable garden, and sat in a little group under a thorn tree, each absorbed in his own thoughts. It was Choti, who by now had become Nundu's right hand man, who broke the silence.

"Well, Nundu, you are our leader. What can we do?"

"Yes," chipped in Kara, "you are the one who talks about how great you are. Well, your greatness has got our fathers into this mess: are you great enough to get them out of it?"

"I hate you, Nundu!" spat Kato. "I love my father, and you have done this to him. You don't love your father. All you want is to go and talk about it at your political meetings. You want only to glorify yourself."

Wenye immediately sprang to the defence of his brother.

"Look here, young man," he snarled, "you may speak to Nundu like that, for although he is as big as you are, you are much stronger and could beat him up easily, but don't forget, you've got me to reckon with if you hurt him, and Heho here too. Is that not so, Heho?"

Heho nodded his head in agreement.

Silence fell over the group once more — the silence of sheer desperation. Apart of course from Nundu, who was planning the best method of inciting the people by telling them what had happened. Suddenly, they heard the noise of Cook's Landrover approaching.

"Quickly! Quickly! Kiko is coming," shouted Nundu.

They all got up and began working industriously.

"It's lucky he's not using his saloon car," whispered Heho, "or we wouldn't have heard him coming and he'd have sacked us all."

"Does that much matter?" queried Wenye.

"Of course it does, you fool," hissed Nundu. "Don't

you remember what we swore last night? It'll be much easier to kill him if we are living on his farm, won't it?"

Major Cook stopped with a screech of brakes beside the workers.

"*Jamboni wote*," he said, sensing the tension that hung like a cloud over the group, and hoping to break it.

No one answered him, and he stood there feeling foolish. He coughed and cleared his throat and made comments about the weather and the vegetables — anything to break the tension. But to no avail. They knew what he had done and would never forgive him. He stood in the shamba for a few minutes, trying desperately to find some way to ease the situation, then turned towards his Landrover and drove off.

"I wish I could get rid of them," he thought. "I daren't sack them for the shortage of young men to work in the shambas is so acute and will be whilst the war continues. There's one consolation, however; I've got my own back on their fathers for defying me. I've got the insurance money too, even though the cattle have been found. I wish someone would steal some more cattle, for the Insurance Company pays me far more than the slaughterhouse or a private buyer would." From that time on he tried to avoid the group as much as possible, issued all his orders through the overseer and visited the garden only on market days.

It was just about this time that Mrefu the schoolmaster came to act as a clerk at Naro Station. He was now completely absorbed in the affairs of the 40 organisation, and was delighted to be near his old pupils so as to whip up their hate and bitterness against the whites for whose overthrow he now lived. To establish his hold over them, he pretended great contrition for his past conduct and his first visit was ostensibly made to apologise, almost abjectly. He told of his dismissal and said that the Education Supervisor, who happened to be a missionary, had called him a savage brute. "He was right, you know!" went on Mrefu. "I'm utterly ashamed of myself and only hope you chaps can forgive me."

It was excellent tactics, though with the happy-go-lucky nature of youth, the boys had almost forgotten why they'd run away from school. They light-heartedly accepted him as one of themselves, and though Wenye and Heho were rather more hesitant, they soon saw that Mrefu's hate of the whites was as great as theirs, and this fact was enough to admit him to their intimacy also.

*   *   *

One evening, about four years after the imprisonment of the boys' unlucky fathers, Cook entertained two Police Officers to dinner. Afterwards they sat on talking and drinking whisky until, their brains being rather fuddled by spirits, they began to talk of things better left unmentioned. Mwangi, Cook's servant, knew a great deal about his Bwana and understood most of what he said. He had long been in the habit of listening on every possible occasion, hoping to pick up bits of news that might aid the organisation of which he, like almost all the local people, was a member. On this night he was indeed lucky. "Nobody'll ever find out about those cattle now," Cook was saying. "I must admit I got a fright when they were found, for I couldn't repay the Insurance people."

"Oh, well," said one of the Police Officers, "we fixed that for you O.K. Couldn't let these black apes put one over on us, could we?"

The horrified Mwangi dashed straight to Nundu with the news!

Nundu saw a glorious chance to enhance his own importance and increase the general hatred for Cook. He called a meeting at which Mrefu was also present. When all were assembled, he stood up and with hypocritical melancholy said, "My dear friends, a terrible thing has come to my knowledge! Mwangi has reported to me a conversation

41

in which Cook admitted that he had known for months that the cattle for whose theft our fathers were imprisoned had been found in Manyata. Mwangi says that Cook did not report this because he could not repay the money the Insurance Company had paid him. Our fathers have suffered all this time for nothing! What are we going to do to avenge them? How are we going to make this villain pay for what he has done? We are men, not beasts, and men cannot sit down calmly under such injustice. Our fathers must be cleared of this vile charge. We know and Kiko knows that they are innocent."

At these words curses and howls of grief and rage broke out on all sides. In their fury those present wanted to go at once in a body and tear out Cook's black head regardless of consequences. It took some time before the tumult quietened and Mrefu could make himself heard.

When at last he managed to get their attention he said,

"Children! children! This will not do. I know the grief, rage and pain you suffer for your fathers and believe me, I share your anger. But it is much too serious a thing for us to act on hearsay. I can hardly believe that even Kiko could act so foolishly. First you must see him, call him all the bad names you can think of, and find out if this is really true. Mwangi may have misunderstood and you always must be sure of your facts. Then, if you find it is so, force him into telling you what he's going to do to make up for his great sin."

The others nodded their heads in agreement, but Nundu was visibly scared.

"I . . . I . . . I . . ." he stammered. "I can't do that, not possibly."

His friends looked aghast. "You, you our leader, *you* are afraid!" said Choti, cut to the quick to find that the hero he had idolised had feet of clay.

"Nundu! You don't know what you are saying," shouted Kato. "You outcast, you dog, if you don't see Kiko tomorrow, I'll kill you." He swung round and glared at

Wenye. "Don't threaten me again, you brother of a swine, for if you do I'll kill you too." He seized a panga which was lying against the wall and swung it threateningly at Wenye. Mrefu, seeing how serious the situation was becoming, laid a soothing hand on Kato's shoulder.

"Listen, *mwanake*," he said, "just let Nundu speak; he's your leader, he'll decide what to do, not you . . . Well Nundu?"

Nundu, who up to that moment had been sitting huddled against the centre pole of the hut, had used the time during which the others had quarrelled to size up his own part in the affair. He could see himself losing prestige and becoming a mere nobody. Choti's remark had shocked him, for he knew that Choti regarded him with adulation. If Choti had changed, so could the others, he felt. Kato had already done so. He felt a moment of blind panic, pulled himself together, and stood up. A hush fell over the group as they waited for him to speak.

"You lot of fools," he said scathingly. "I, your leader, am a big important man. Why should I be scared of such scum as Kiko?" He spat into the corner. "There, that's what I think of him. You'll see, I'll go to him first thing tomorrow morning. Me, afraid? *Me?* You blind idiots. Why if I had a gun, I'd kill him." He stopped and looked round anxiously to see what impression he had made. They all gazed at him rather dubiously, but Mrefu once more stepped into the breach. He clapped Nundu on the back.

"That's the stuff, brother, I knew you wouldn't fail your friends. Come, let's go and find some beer to wash the dust from our throats."

All ill feeling dispersed, the friends shook hands and went out of the hut. Confidence in Nundu was re-established. Nundu breathed a sigh of heartfelt relief as he followed them.

"Tomorrow," he thought, "is another day. If I start thinking about it, I know I'll run away and if I do that I'll not only be the laughing stock of the neighbourhood,

43

but I'll ruin my career. What do I care about my father, or their fathers for that matter? I only want to be a big man, the biggest man in the country and nothing and no one is going to stop me." Thus Nundu boosted up his ego and his fast ebbing courage. He drank himself into a stupor that night to prevent himself dwelling on coming events. A weapon in his hand and he was the bravest man in the world, but words were a poor alternative for weapons.

They all trooped reluctantly down to the vegetable shamba the following day. Nundu was petrified with fright, for he knew that if he abused Kiko he might be thrown into prison, and if he didn't impress his friends sufficiently, his whole life and future expectations would be irreparably ruined. Kato, however, who lived his life in a state of indecision, was wondering if what Mwangi had said was true. It would be terrible to accuse Kiko if it wasn't. They'd all be sacked and they'd lose not only their homes, but all means of livelihood. Choti eyed his hero speculatively. "I'll see what he is really made of now," he thought. Wenye and Heho were also deep in their own thoughts, and it was Iru who spoke first.

"Well, great man," he sneered, "you've got yourself into a fine position haven't you? Us too! Well, you've got to get us out of it — and our fathers. Listen, I hear Kiko's Landrover! Brace yourself my friend, you'd better make a good show of it!"

Nundu swung round and watched the dust raised by the approaching Landrover. He grinned cheerfully at the others who were waiting expectantly, hoping that they could not hear the frantic pumping of his heart. "You are all scared, that's what's wrong with you! I'll meet this *Kaburu* face to face, never fear. If he discharges me I don't mind. After all, if our fathers ever find out that we had information like this and didn't use it to help them, they will never forgive us. We've no means of getting in touch while they are so far away. Quick, start working, he's just rounding the corner. Act naturally."

Kiko slammed the door of his Landrover with a flourish and walked along to the group, closely followed by *Nyapara* — he was too frightened to face his employees alone and *Nyapara*, apart from his other duties, acted as a bodyguard.

"*Lete mboga hapa*, Nundu," he ordered. "Load them into the vehicles."

Nundu threw down the beans he was carrying, stalked up to Cook and spat on the ground beside his feet. His friends nudged each other. "That's the Nundu we know," whispered Choti in glee.

"Ssh, let's see what's going to happen now!" replied Kara.

Cook stood stupefied for a moment and then roared, "Scum! Black trash! What do you think you are doing? How dare you!" He spluttered in sheer rage.

Nundu leaned nonchalantly against the Landrover. "Bwana, our fathers were imprisoned unjustly. You know that. I have discovered that the cattle were found six months after our fathers were imprisoned. That was four years ago and you still haven't done anything about it."

Cook slashed Nundu's face with his whip, and Nundu cowered on the ground in front of him.

"I'm sorry, Bwana, don't hit me! I was only trying to help our fathers. Please, Bwana," kneeling at Cook's feet and putting his arms around Cook's legs, "please, please release our fathers, and please forgive me for behaving like that. I, I . . ." Nundu bowed his head, shivering with fright and quite unable to continue. The others looked horrified and both Kato and Choti were certainly sneering at his cowardice, but Nundu by this time was too petrified to care. The habit of years was too much for him. The whip came down on his back with a mighty thwack.

"You snivelling worm! How dare you approach me in this fashion? Who do you think you are, you bastard son of a hyena?" yelled Cook, who inwardly was also shaking with fear, wondering how on earth the secret had come to light. "There is no truth in such a tale! If you ever dare to mention it to me again, I'll wring your neck! Get up off the ground, you troublemaker, and get back to your work, or I'll have you arrested too." He stopped, realising the possible repercussions to himself if he had Nundu arrested, and watched Nundu stand up and compose himself.

"Bwana," he said quietly. "I approached you in the wrong fashion and for that I am sorry, but you had no right to hit me and call me those names. I know that what I have heard is true, and believe me, one day I will kill you." He swung round, picked up his load of beans and

threw them on the Landrover, shaking this time with blind rage.

Major Cook looked as if he was on the verge of an apoplectic fit. "Get back to work! All of you! Do you hear me?" He turned back to Nundu. "I could have you imprisoned for threatening me but," he shrugged his shoulders, "you are a little man with a big mouth that makes idle threats. Why should I bother? You are just scum like all other black men." He stood silently and watched the men load his Landrover with the vegetables for market. He didn't notice the hatred and loathing on their faces, and he wouldn't have cared if he had for he considered them little better than animals. No one dared say anything, but their minds were working furiously. Nundu, of all people, had cowered in front of a white man; he who was always bragging and boasting about his greatness. But he had made up for that by threatening to kill Kiko.

Cook watched them working for a few minutes. As soon as the Landrover was loaded to capacity, he drove off, thankful to get away from the scene. Who had betrayed him? he wondered. He was quivering with fear and swore vengeance on whoever it should prove to be.

That afternoon, Nundu stood apart from his friends, thoroughly ashamed of the impression he had made. Choti began provoking him.

"Well, brave man, what did you learn from Kiko?"

Nundu looked straight into Choti's eyes until Choti was forced to turn away. "Listen to me, all of you," he said. "You are all cowards. What help did you give me? What could I do with a man who had a whip and used it, unless you came to my defence? You let me down, not I you. But I will kill Kiko and I swear that on the graves of my ancestors." They looked at him with a certain amount of respect, knowing that a promise of that nature made by Nundu could never be broken. Nundu continued, "If any of you start asking me futile questions I'll beat the daylights out of you. I'm sick to death of being let down by other people." He rolled up his sleeves and clenched his fists. "Well?" he queried.

Wenye interrupted. "Nundu, we are not looking for a fight with you, we are only criticising the way you behaved in front of Kiko. If you wanted to fight, why didn't you fight him? At least you threatened to kill him, and we all know you will do that, but you can't yet so don't start bragging. It was you who decided to approach Kiko, just to make a good impression on us and show us what a big brave man you are. Now your head should be down to its proper size. I've never seen anyone with such a big head as you. Just shut up! We are all sick and tired of your behaviour."

Nundu, too subdued to make any retort, stalked out of the room and slammed the door. The others, although sympathetic with his plight, could not help laughing. He'd made such a fool of himself. But this time it was very serious indeed and they realised that they would have to leave him completely alone to regain his temper before anything further could be done. When Mrefu came up to visit them that evening they told him the whole sad tale. "Kiko treated Nundu like an animal this morning: the white man has truly brought shame on our families," said Heho. "I am only scared that Nundu will get himself into such a frame of mind that he'll try and kill him. Nundu is unarmed and Kiko has several guns apart from that beastly dog and a nightwatchman."

"I wouldn't worry too much," replied Mrefu. "Nundu will cool down, and then we can start planning a real battle. Don't laugh at him. He has made a big mistake and has made a fool of himself in front of you. Believe me, he is your leader and always will be, and he'll be a good one, but even the best of leaders make mistakes."

Mrefu spoke the truth, for Nundu, although intending to make an end of Cook, calmed down within the week and soon became his normal self again.

4 CLOSING RANKS

Meanwhile Cook was at his wit's end to know what to do. He sent *Nyapara* down to Naro with the vegetables, shut himself in his bedroom away from the curious eyes of Mwangi, and paced up and down desperately trying to find a solution to the completely unexpected situation that had arisen. "How on earth could this have come to light?" he thought. "Whatever will happen to me? I couldn't care less about their fathers," he snapped his fingers in disgust. "The point is, if this does become known, I'll be put in jail myself. I've spent all that insurance money and have none to replace it. If those fools have the sense to go to the proper authorities, I'll be put in jail for sure, not only because of the insurance money but because I told those men that if they would work for me I would leave them alone. They knew that I knew they hadn't stolen the cattle, but was only trying to intimidate them."

He went out of his bedroom and started wandering up and down the house like a lost soul. "I wonder if that swine really means to kill me? Well, even if he does, I've always got Rex — he's a fierce dog if ever there was one! I've got my revolver too!" He patted the weapon affectionately. "Yes, my friend, you'll look after me. I'll shoot the lot of them with you if I have to. I must get in touch with all my friends; they are white men and they'll stand by me whatever I've done. Anyhow, they know all about it and they regard these swine as apes too. Why, they'll perjure themselves in court if need be. We'll never let a black get the better of us. Heavens!" as a new idea suddenly struck him, "If they find out, they'll auction my farm to get their money back." He sat down on the chair beside the fire and buried his face in his hands.

Mwangi, meanwhile, had also become very disturbed, for he had peeped through the keyhole and watched

Kiko's peculiar behaviour. He, like house servants all over the world, was very quick to sense a disturbed atmosphere. Being a clever man, he associated this performance with the information he had passed on to Nundu, and when Kiko refused to eat any supper, he was petrified with fright. "Suppose Nundu has split on me," he thought. "Kiko might kill me! Oh why, why did I go to Nundu's house that night? What a fool I was. Now I've involved myself in something that is none of my business at all! Oh dear . . ." His thoughts were rudely interrupted by Cook bellowing for a drink.

"Bring the whole bottle, fool!" he shouted. "And plenty of water, *upesi! upesi!*"

Mwangi hurried into the sitting room with a bottle of whisky. "Fool!" Kiko yelled, knocking the whisky out of Mwangi's hand. "It's gin I want, don't you know that by now? Fetch gin, plenty of it, and then come and clear up this mess. If you break my bottles of whisky then you'll have to pay for them."

Mwangi rushed back with the gin bottle, cleared up the broken glass and ran out of the room, leaving the door ajar so that he could watch Kiko and see what he was doing.

Kiko half filled a glass with neat gin and swallowed it in one gulp. "Ah! that's better." He started to read the papers, then got up and strode round the room, sat down, poured himself another stiff drink and picked up his papers once more. "No, no," he said, "it's no use. I've got to do something." His face had turned scarlet with rage and drink. Mwangi, who was still peeping through the crack in the door, prayed fervently that Kiko wouldn't want him again. He watched Kiko drink yet more gin, and then sit down at the desk and scribble letters, many letters, taking great gulps of gin at short intervals.

"I wonder if he's writing a note to the Police to come and take me away," Mwangi thought. "I'm sure he must know that it was I who told on him. Why, I've never seen him look so furious before. He seems to have lost all his self-control and he's acting like a madman. Perhaps he's writing up a case against me. Why, I've worked for him for ten years and I've never seen him like this."

As soon as he could, Mwangi rushed down to Nundu's house to tell him what had been happening. "Did you betray me, Nundu? Did you betray me?" he gasped.

Nundu pushed him aside contemptuously. "Of course I didn't, you fool. Get out of my house, will you, and stop panicking over nothing. I'll never betray you. Get that into your thick head and get out!"

Mwangi rushed back to his own house almost sobbing with relief. Nundu, who was still in a violent rage, did not realise the significance of what he had been told. It was not until he calmed down that he grasped just how successful he had been and, sad to say, he became as conceited as ever.

Meanwhile Cook, who was engaged at the Club on Tuesdays and Fridays, had written to Brigadier Frank Jones, the Chief Inspector at Naro Police Station, suggesting a meeting on the Wednesday evening. His tense state of nerves and odd behaviour terrified Mwangi who realised it was connected with what had happened the previous day. He felt that he couldn't rest till he knew what was going to happen at the Club. He knew that if he reported Cook's conduct, Nundu would be less likely to betray him as being a valuable source of information. Immediately, therefore, he rushed down to the Club to tell Nono, one of the Club stewards, to keep him up to date with the situation and arranged for him to listen in to the conversation that was going to take place between the Europeans when they met at the Club. He told Nono exactly what had been happening, and Nono was only too pleased to oblige.

Major Cook arrived at the Club that Wednesday

evening rather earlier than his friend Frank. Nono almost
ran up to him to serve him, because all the stewards vied
with each other to serve Cook as he was the Chairman
of the Club. Nono, apart from being very curious, was
determined to keep his promise to Mwangi and so was
the first man to reach the table. Cook ordered a double
gin and relaxed on the large settee to read a magazine
until Frank arrived. Nono brought the gin and, as was the
custom, he leaned against the wall a few yards away as
one without a thought but to be ready to bring Cook
anything he might require. His success in being the first
one to serve Cook gained him this benefit, for
once a customer entered the Club the steward who
had served him first stayed close by all evening until that
particular customer had left.

About ten minutes later Frank arrived, and after
exchanging greetings, sat down beside Cook.

"I'm sorry I'm late. Bob," Frank said. "I'm terribly
tired; had to finish my monthly report today and I admit
I almost forgot to come."

"It's O.K., old chap," answered Bob. "Thank the lord
you've come." Beckoning to Nono he yelled, "Boy!
Kuja hapa!"

Nono rushed up to the table, almost dropping his tray
as he tripped over his white *kanzu*.

"What'll you have?"

"Double brandy, Bob. I feel I need it."

Nono hastened to the bar, his bare feet slipping on
the highly polished floor.

Frank laughed. "My goodness, that boy can move
fast; he must be terrified of you!"

"He is," answered Cook complacently. "They all are!"

"Maybe, but he isn't a good boy at all. He is one of
the chaps who is going to appear in court charged with a

breach of the Liquor Licensing Act. Three days ago one of my askaris found them with two bottles of European beer."

"Any spirits?" asked Bob, who was busy trying to light his pipe.

"No, luckily for them; only the beer," replied Frank.

Bob nodded his head, still struggling with his pipe. At this juncture the brandy arrived. "Cheers old man!" "Your good health Frank!" They clinked glasses and drank deeply.

"Now, Bob, tell me what it's all about."

"Frank! I'm fed up with these brutes, and something very serious has happened." Nono was trying to catch every word that was spoken. "Look, let's go into the private room where we can talk without being overheard."

"Well, if it's as serious as all that, perhaps we'd better. Hey, you!" shouted Frank.

Nono hastened to the table. "*Ndio Bwana?*"

"Take these glasses to the private room."

"*Ndio Bwana!*" Nono picked up the glasses and followed them to this room. Whilst they were standing beside the window looking at the progress of the new extension to the Club, he placed the glasses on a table and stood beside the door — ostensibly to obey any orders that might be issued. He was in a good position to hear every word that was spoken.

"Now look, Frank," said Bob, "things are getting seriously out of hand. You remember the cattle *shauri?*"

"You bet I do. I also remember that the chaps you imprisoned were innocent, and I've been waiting for repercussions all this time. Has the thing blown up at last?"

"You bet it has!" replied Cook grimly. "You know those chaps are the fathers of my garden boys. Yesterday, one of them . . . " He stopped and looked at Nono. "Boy, *lete* gin *na* whisky *ngine, upesi!*" Nono picked up the glasses and hurried out, furious that he might miss the really relevant part of the conversation.

"Sorry Frank, I must have another drink before I go on. This thing has come as a serious shock. I'm so frightened I don't know what to do."

"Now just calm down, old chap, and tell me all about it as lucidly as possible," replied Frank, who by this time was looking extremely perturbed. "Ah! here come our drinks. Better now? O.K., carry on."

"Well, one of them approached me yesterday morning and asked me if it was true that the cattle had been found. He was very sure of himself, so sure that he spat at me!"

"Spat at you?" exclaimed Frank in horror.

"Oh, don't worry about that. I slashed him over the face with my whip and had him cowering at my feet. The only thing was I didn't like the way he pulled himself together and announced very solemnly that he was going to kill me."

"Well, Bob, you can't put him in jail for threatening you because of what he might say. Do you think he meant it?" queried Frank.

"Doesn't matter if he did. I've got a gun and I always carry it with me. You know, if they have the sense to make an appeal the sentence will be quashed: my insurance company will demand back their money, which I can't pay — you know what the economic situation is at the moment — and apart from that, I exceeded my powers and imprisoned them on false charges, fully knowing what I was doing." He buried his face in his hands, unable to say any more.

Frank absorbed this information in stupefied silence. "My God, Bob, we are in a mess," he said eventually. "For heaven's sake let's have another drink. *Lete* gin *na* whisky *ingine*, boy, treble this time!" Nono seized the glasses and again hastened to the bar. He had understood every word and didn't intend to miss anything. His mind was seething. What a weapon he had in his hand to use against these despicable white men! He would see Mwangi the very next day and tell him all about it. He rushed back with the drinks and put them on the table beside Cook and Jones.

"How the hell did they ever find out about it?" asked Frank. "Have you ever spoken to anybody about it, have you ever written any of it down on paper?"

"I swear I haven't!" answered Bob desperately.

"Well, these black rats can't understand our language; they haven't the brains for that." He shook his head sadly. "My god, what a mess we're in. It must be one of my askaris who has betrayed you — I mean one of those who found the cattle. They speak their barbaric language. That's the only way I can think that the secret has leaked out. Let's have another drink. Boy!" Nono again went to fetch their drinks, noting that by this time both the white men were getting very drunk and their speech was rather slurred, thus making them rather hard to understand.

They both finished their drinks at one gulp and ordered some more. Frank leaned over the table. "Listen Bob, you can count on my support. If any of these fools comes to me I'll shut them up very effectively. You are my friend, my good friend, I'll stand by you — we all will, you know that. I'll sack the askari that betrayed us. It won't take long to find him, and if no one will confess, I'll pick one at random and sack him. That'll put an end to it. We'll teach these bastards that they can't get the better of a European. We're their masters and intend to remain so. Cattle can't fight their masters and succeed . . . agreed?"

"Yes, old chap, agreed. I'm with you all the way on that one. An animal can never turn into a human being!"

"That's the spirit, old man," replied Frank drunkenly, "I'll see you O.K. Let's have one for the road. I'll sack an askari — any askari — that was near *Manyata*. *Now*, let's talk about something more cheerful!"

Cook arrived home in the early hours of the morning. It was quite obvious to Mwangi, who brought him his early morning tea, that he was suffering from an enormous hangover. When Cook got up, he still looked very worried and unhappy, but as he treated Mwangi normally, Mwangi's fears were eased for he knew he would have been sacked if the *Bwana* Frank had blamed him for the leakage. As soon as he had a free moment, Mwangi rushed down to the Club to find Nono. He absorbed eagerly all the information that Nono imparted and determined to visit Nundu that night to pass it on.

Mwangi hurried down to Nundu's house at about nine that night and poured out his story. Nundu, seeing a chance to rehabilitate himself, listened eagerly, then hastened over to Wenye's house.

As usual the whole group was there, gathered around the smoking fire, airing their political views and swearing at the white man. Nundu was greeted with a certain amount of reserve, but was allowed to take his place amongst them.

"Brothers, hear what a great victory I have won against Kiko!"

Mrefu nodded his head wisely. Yes, Nundu hadn't failed them, not really — he was going to be a fine leader. They listened agog to his tale and cheered wildly when he had finished. Mrefu said, "We have made our point. We cannot lose now. Let fate take a hand — it will."

A week later Frank Jones sacked an askari on the pretext of having disclosed Government secrets. Nundu seized his chance of striking yet another blow against Kiko. He waited until Kiko had gone to Nairobi for a couple of days — for whilst Kiko was away *Nyapara* was empowered to employ anyone who came seeking a job — and went to Naro Market to seek out the askari. He found him, as he hoped, a very embittered man at having been treated so unjustly and persuaded him to visit Wenye's hut and become a member of the gang. He was promised employment on the condition that he used all his spare time to teach Nundu and his friends the secrets of Police work and how to handle weapons. He very willingly agreed, and so the following day Wenye introduced him to *Nyapara* who employed him to work in the vegetable gardens. The trap was being surely and stealthily sprung.

Meanwhile, Major Cook was elected Chairman of Naro European Club for a further term of four years. This was a post normally held by the eldest of the settlers in the District. Lord Monckley, who was the Member of Parliament for that area, had previously held the post but had resigned due to ill health. Major Cook was also hoping to become the Member of Parliament in his place at the next elections and was therefore busily planning to seize a chance to take another step up the ladder to make himself the most powerful man in the District.

The Club was situated near Naro, and had a great reputation. Members came from miles around, but it was reserved strictly for Europeans whose numbers had increased now that the war was over. The only Africans admitted to the Club grounds were the employees or "boys" who, as far as the members were concerned, mattered nothing. They were given very little pay and ordered around like animals. It never occurred to the European that, during his highly confidential conversations about the political situation and other subjects, the silent figure standing against the wall near the table understood most of what was said and was really acting as an agent for his own people, thus building up the clouds of hatred and vengeance hanging over the country.

Cook's neighbours knew all there was to know concerning the cattle incident. They were determined to stand together, come rain or hail, for apart from the fact

57

C

that they would never let a "black man" get the better of them, they were getting very badly frightened due to increasing political agitation and, in some cases, violence against Chiefs and African Government servants, who were having their huts burned down by their own kin. There were rumours that there would be a country-wide African uprising, and the African population, as compared to that of the European, was alarmingly high. Who cared what Cook had done if he could protect them and advise them as to the best course of action should these rumours bear fruit?

At this time Carey Milton, who after studying in the United Kingdom had joined the Administration, was posted to Naro as a District Officer. As was usual on such occasions, a party was organised by Major Cook, as Chairman of the Settlers' Association, a post he had only just attained — and as Chairman of the Club. All the residents of Naro were invited to meet the new District Officer, and Major Cook saw yet another chance to gain more popularity by making a political speech at the party. By this time he was being openly tipped as Monckley's successor. Monckley had been a Member of Parliament for ten years and had lost much of his fiery spirit during this time due to ill health and old age, and thus most of his following had fallen away. The fear of an African uprising was growing like a disease and the settlers were all beginning to look to the Major for guidance.

The bar and lounge at the Club had been cleared and rows of chairs had been set facing the platform at the top of the room. As soon as the three hundred or so guests had arrived, Major Cook made his entrance followed by Carey and they took their places on the dais. The Club door was locked to keep out would-be eavesdroppers, and the party-cum-meeting commenced. A hush fell over the group as Cook stood up and cleared his throat.

"Ladies and Gentlemen, we have gathered here tonight to welcome our new District Officer, Carey Milton. He, as you probably know, hails from the White Highlands and I hope you will all give him much needed support in these days of strife. He has a hard job," he paused and shook his head, "a very hard job. These are troubled times. Why? because of the natives who are trying to ruin our country. You all used to look so happy and now all you do is worry about the rumours you hear. I can help you, if you'll let me! But we must discuss the true facts of the situation. We must stand together. You read the newspapers and every day there are reports of increasing unrest. It is time the Government did something to protect our homes and our families. We . . . ."

Here he was interrupted by a roar of approval. "That's the stuff, Bob!" shouted someone.

Cook struck an attitude and cleared his throat again. "We must unite ourselves as one man. We must show these kaffirs just where they get off." He thumped the table. "They are hardly fit to be slaves. They are uneducated, filthy, ignorant of even the basic necessities of human beings. They speak in barbaric languages. We are civilised. Are we going to let kaffirs such as these get the better of us?"

"No!" someone shouted, and the cry was taken up and resounded round the room.

"We have spent our lives here. We have invested our money here. We have built our homes, planted our crops here. Are we going to let it all be taken away from us? These reports of unrest are real. Why, they are burning Chiefs' houses because the Chiefs work for us. They call all their fellows who work for Government disloyal and treat them as butchers. Once they have finished with them, they will turn on us."

He paused for a sip of water and looked at the expectant gathering. "Well, Bob," said someone, "what are you going to do about it?"

Cook leaned forward. "Listen, this is what we are going to do, and I'm sure Carey here will agree with me. We are going to demand that Police posts shall be built on all isolated farms. We are going to demand, not ask, *demand* that the Government declare an Emergency. We are going to arm ourselves to the teeth. We whites must stand together; a building divided against itself must always fall. We have not only the weapons, or soon will have, but the brains to deal with this situation. A man with a black skin hasn't got any guns, any brains or any guts. What can they do against our army, our Police force? There are many things to be planned and done."

Cook looked round, well satisfied with the impression he was making. He didn't notice the group of African bar stewards standing at the back of the room, and wouldn't have worried if he had. "I have said enough for the time being, but I am going to suggest to Monckley that we hold weekly security meetings at this Club to review the situation. If Monckley refuses, why, we will just go ahead. May I now call upon our new District Officer, Carey Milton?" Cook sat down amid much applause, mopping the sweat from his brow. It had been a great strain but worth it. Now he was at the top and had every intention of staying there.

Carey stood on the dais smiling at the audience. "Ladies and Gentlemen, thank you all very much, and you, Mr. Chairman, for the cordial welcome you have extended to me. I was born in this country and you may rest assured that I will not stand by and see it being ravaged by savages. The Government knows this: that is why I have been posted here. We will never submit to rule by primitive peoples. Our Government is with us and I, as their representative, will stand by you and support you all and will represent you in Nairobi. But I am no politician and do not intend to be one. One thing you cannot do is mix politics and the Civil Service!" He was interrupted by a ripple of laughter. "So, I'll just say thanks again, and I am here to listen to all your problems and help you. Thank you."

After the speeches the social evening began, and Cook

and Carey made the rounds. A few minutes later, Cook felt a tap on his shoulder. He swung round. "Monckley!" he gasped. "I didn't know you were here. When did you come in?"

Lord Monckley looked at him rather suspiciously. "Just at the end of Carey's speech," he answered. "I meant to attend the whole meeting, but my car broke down and I was delayed. You never invited me, you know: rather a *faux pas* old chap, don't you think?"

Cook's face went beetroot red. "I sent you an invitation by post — must have been delayed somewhere," he stammered, falling back on the first excuse he could think of.

Monckley slapped him on the back. "Never mind, I'll find out soon enough just what you did say about me. Two can play at this you know! Would you mind introducing me to your companion?"

Cook made the necessary introductions and soon slipped away from Monckley, feeling a fool. "I must be more careful what I say in future," he thought. "Anyhow, Monckley can't do much to me now, I'm too powerful." He dismissed the subject with a shrug of the shoulders. He stayed at the Club until everybody had left, gloating over his success.

At this time the daily newspapers were reporting yet more unrest and political agitation. All the settlers noticed a change in the bearing of their employees. There was a definite air of hostility: Cook could hardly believe that they were the same men. They were rude to him and very often disobeyed his orders. They did not salute him when he passed, or doff their caps as was customary. They didn't even stand up when he came near. Monckley had noticed the change too, for they refused to make way for him when he passed in his car, and they no longer watered the dusty ten-mile stretch of road which he used on his monthly visits to Naro. During these visits, it had been laid down that all the natives should use the cattle tracks — this order they were now ignoring completely.

The wind of change was starting to blow very strongly. Vernacular newspapers were published and these were sold all over the country. Huge political meetings were held which worsened the situation. Very few of the European settlers could read the vernacular — or even speak it. Why should they? They were uninterested in native affairs or the native mind.

Cook, as well as the others, was extremely worried by the publication of these newspapers. He couldn't make head or tail of them, but whenever he went to Naro he could see small eager crowds of Africans standing round men who seemed to be reading the news out loud. On one of his visits, he stood aside and watched one of these groups. "They are getting so agitated," he thought. "Mwangi buys these newspapers. He seems to understand what they say, but he won't tell me what's in them however much I threaten him. I should have learned this barbaric tongue and then I would know what is going on." He climbed into his Land-Rover and drove thoughtfully back to the farm. Some of the labourers on the road jeered at him, but he could not understand what they were saying. As soon as he reached his house he poured himself out a stiff drink and sat down in the armchair beside the fire, the European daily newspaper dangling from his hand.

"I think it's about time we called another meeting," he thought. "I didn't dare go too far with Monckley around, but if I can get his co-operation then it will be easy to supersede him. It was only last week that some fools burned down the houses of a headman and the Chief about fifteen, no, ten miles from here. They seem to be doing it all over the country. Last month when I was in Nairobi I met a huge convoy of lorries on the road filled with singing and drum beating natives on their way to a political rally. Yes, I remember, I tried to pass them and they spat at my car and beat their drums louder. Some of them pointed at me, others laughed with such a look of hatred on their faces. They do seem to hate us Europeans, I can't understand why." And he really couldn't, so blind was he and all his kind. He poured himself out another drink, the paper lying unnoticed on the floor beside him. "After all, what do they know? They drink all the day, they are quite uneducated, they beat their wives, they are uncivilised and primitive and yet they want freedom. What on earth can the word freedom mean to them? I must convene another meeting as soon as possible, but this time, I'd better ask Monckley. Damned nuisance he is." He bent forward and picked up his paper. The headlines caught his

eye. "More Huts Burned by Bandits near Nairobi . . .
Government Proposes Heavier Penalties for Lawlessness."
"No, this is too much. I must ring Monckley at once." He
picked up the telephone receiver and gave the number,
impatiently waiting to get through. "Monckley? Cook here.
How are you?" and not waiting for Monckley to answer
he rushed on. "Look here, old chap, I've got today's
newspaper in front of me and I think the whole situation
warrants an urgent meeting of the settlers. We could do a
thorough review and invite Frank and Carey. I mean,
all of the settlers here are in a terrible state and something
has got to be done. What do you think?"

"Good idea," Monckley bellowed down the 'phone.
"I've been in touch with many Government Officials and
the Chief Native Commissioner, and although what I have
learned is confidential, I could certainly advise my
constituency. Make it Friday evening, 6.30 at the Club."

"Fine, Monckley, I'll arrange it all. See you Friday,"
replied Cook, who then slammed down the receiver. "Old
fool," he sneered, "What does he know about politics, or
about what we feel? I'll show him who is the boss in his
constituency!" He sat down and wrote chits to the various
settlers to inform them of the meeting — very few of them
were on the telephone.

Lord Monckley arrived earlier than was expected on
the Friday and drove up to Cook's house. "I want to talk
with you first," he explained. "Let's go down to the Club
and have a drink together before everybody arrives."

Monckley and Cook went into the private room, followed
by the ever faithful Nono who did not intend to miss the
chance of hearing these two talking.

"*Lete* gin *mbili*, boy," said Monckley peremptorily. "Now
listen Cook, the Government is concerned over the safety
of all its citizens. We are doing our utmost to make sure
that the situation is kept well in hand. We can't stop
agitation resulting from political meetings — this is a

free country! But we are trying to find ways and means of silencing the agitators. I can assure you that you'll see the results in a very short time."

"Well," Cook said doubtfully. "I hope you are right. Do you really know what you are talking about?"

"Who the hell do you think you are?" snarled Monckley, who was very taken aback to find that Cook no longer treated him with the respect that was his by right. "Listen, Major Cook, a house divided within itself will fall. You said that the other night, remember?" Cook spluttered, but before he could say anything, Monckley continued, "I'm with you all the way, not you personally but my people. It's still my constituency. You are their spokesman — all right, but don't go too far, Major Cook, I'm warning you. Now let's have another drink, a drink to friendship. What do you say?"

Cook sat silent for a moment, trying to control his inward fury. He looked at his opponent who had certainly got the better of him in that round, and grinned. "O.K. Monckley, let's do just that; but, er, I wouldn't threaten me too much: I *am* their spokesman you know. We've got a meeting here tonight and you are the most important and necessary person here. Let's go for a walk. People will be arriving shortly, and they must see that we are the very best of friends! That is essential to our cause."

Nono watched them leave the Club and stroll along the golf course. "White trash," he muttered to himself as he helped to put the chairs in position. "We'll show them, very soon. Lucky I understood what they said. I must listen very carefully this evening and report to Nundu as soon as possible. He is very pleased with me and so is Mrefu. That matters a lot for they are powerful people." He grinned. "I shall get a large portion of land for all my work for the Cause. I shall be a rich man. These white men are such fools!"

Cook and Monckley strolled back to the Club, arm in

arm, to greet their guests. As soon as the lounge was full, they walked through the rows of chairs up to the dais amidst cheers and clapping. Major Cook stood up and waited for silence, and another chance to enhance his popularity.

"Ladies and Gentlemen. It is with very great pleasure that I welcome here on your behalf our Member of Parliament, Lord Monckley."

Cook waited for the applause to end, a grin of satisfaction on his face. "Thank you." He turned to look at the rows of expectant faces. "I see you are all still worried and unhappy. Why? Because of the way these natives are behaving. You know as well as I do that they no longer show us any respect, they no longer stand up, or doff their caps when we pass by. They even spit at us. They are getting completely out of control. We want some Government support: we want the Government to help us."

A roar of "Hear, hear!" echoed throughout the lounge.

"How can the Government help us? By declaring an Emergency, by calling in troops, by setting up Police posts on isolated farms. If they don't protect us and our families we may all be killed. These swine don't listen to our orders any more. They've started burning Chiefs' houses — the few loyal to our Government. When they've finished with their own people, they will start on us. They will take our land, our homes, our livelihood. Why, all the work that we have put into our shambas will be wasted, apart from the money that we have sunk in the country. These primitive people really think that they can run our country. I tell you, my friends, that if they tried and succeeded, which God forbid — " here he broke off hurriedly and turned to Monckley, "That, sir, is why you are here tonight — to represent our cause to the Government. In two years our homes will have reverted to the jungle. There will not be one trace of civilisation left. Has it ever occurred to you how horribly we might die so that they can attain their so-called freedom? We have given them many things: schools, hospitals, clothes. We are teaching them the civilised way of life, yet they reject our teaching and say they want their country. *Their* country! We have made it ours . . ." A burst of clapping interrupted him. "My friends, if the Government acts in time we shall be safe, but if it doesn't," he shrugged his shoulders, "they will kill us all. We have the weapons but they have the numbers. We live on isolated farms far from any help." He thumped the table. "The Government has got to do something!" Everyone cheered and stamped their feet.

"The last time I spoke to you things were not so serious. Events have now speeded up to such an extent that the plans I mentioned have to be carried out now before we are all dead! I convened this meeting mainly because of the newspaper headlines. These savages, I reiterate most strongly, can do nothing against our Army and Police Force, but these must be organised by our Government in order to protect us all. They can be organised, but we must have your assistance, sir; you must present our case to the Government immediately and save our lives."

A burst of frenzied clapping interrupted him.

"I think that I have taken the stand long enough tonight. I would remind you once more of our slogan — 'Stand together! A building divided against itself must fall'." He stood waiting until the cheering and clapping had subsided, thus allowing his audience to give full vent to their feelings and showing Monckley just where he did stand in Naro, and then continued: "I now call on Lord Monckley," and noted with much satisfaction that the reception given to Monckley was rather half-hearted.

"Thank you, Mr. Chairman, and Ladies and Gentlemen. I am very honoured to address you tonight. I know that you have all heard rumours that I am retiring from politics due to ill health and intend to return to England. These rumours are not true — there's life in the old dog yet! I intend to help you all, and help you I can in my capacity as your Representative. I would ask you, Mr. Chairman, to remember that."

Did a snigger ripple through his audience?

"Major Cook, I feel, has rather exaggerated the whole situation."

"Oh no he hasn't," came a shout from the back of the room.

"I beg to differ," replied Monckley. "You seem to forget that I have heard these same things, but I also know what the Government is doing. I know exactly what is happening and I can assure you that things have been painted far blacker than they really are."

"Prove it! Prove it!"

"Prove it? But of course I can prove it, but maybe not to your satisfaction for I can't reveal any Government secrets, you know. As you see from the papers," continued Monckley, "the Government intends to inflict much heavier penalties for lawlessness. The Bill has been passed through Parliament. and now these ignorant folk will get a maximum sentence of ten years' imprisonment instead of three. That will act as a deterrent. The Government will not allow these insurgents to get the better of us. After all, how on earth could these black men, who know nothing at all, defeat a Government that is composed of British Civil Servants? They are the best in the world. We have found means to silence the agitators, but I can't tell you what they are. You'll see the results very shortly, I can promise you that. No one is going to be killed. They will hurt themselves, oh yes, but not us. I stress that the situation is not out of hand and that I am with you all the way. I, in turn, will keep in close touch with the Government and our own District Officer here, and I assure you that I will support you, support you all" — with a sideways glance at Cook. "If I have your support, then we can stand firm together. Now, has anyone any questions to ask me?"

There was some rather desultory clapping, and then questions were fired at Monckley from all over the room.

"Sir, just what is Government doing to protect us and our families?"

"But, my friend, I've told you all I can. Just rest assured that it is doing everything possible."

"I'm sorry, sir, but how can you expect us to be satisfied with such a vague answer?"

"Yes," someone else shouted, "if he had his family here and his home, he'd feel frightened too . . . well, sir?"

"The trouble with you all," replied Monckley, "is that you have heard vague rumours, seen a few strange things, and you have added two and two and made twenty five. You are getting panicky. I reiterate that you need have no fear. I shall most certainly inform my colleagues of your feelings and try to get permission to give you more information."

"When is the Government going to declare an Emergency?" shot another questioner from the back of the room.

"There is no need for an Emergency at the moment. The stringent measures, many of them secret, that the Government is taking, will obviate the necessity of there ever having to be one," replied Monckley, uncomfortably. Cook sat silent, looking on with glee. Monckley was finished!

"Sir! Your answers are very vague. Can you give us nothing to go on? For instance, what about calling up our boys into the Police Reserve and posting them on isolated farms?"

"There is no need for that, the situation does not warrant it."

"Lord Monckley!" came a strident voice, "you are a Nairobi man, yet you never visit your shamba here. You have got completely out of touch with us and our feelings. You should get out of that car of yours and walk amongst these natives. They would become a very valuable source of information for you and then you would see just how they are behaving. We demand that you go to Nairobi and ask the Government to declare an Emergency."

"I'm sorry you seem to think I'm out of touch," replied Monckley. "I'm not, you know! I have boys of my own, and I see that their bearing is different. But of course, as your Representative, I will bear your request to the Government."

"I suggest that the Government works out a plan whereby if anything did happen, we could all gather in one place and stand firm together. We are outnumbered by these murderers and you know it."

"Look," countered Monckley, "there is no smoke without fire — that I agree. But you know as well as I do that if there was even the slightest possibility of an uprising, the Government would send for British troops. They have not done so, therefore there is no need."

"Well, what about sacking the troublemakers from our farms?" asked somebody else.

And so the questions went on and on, Monckley desperately trying to keep his prestige, satisfying no one and in fact increasing the fear that was rampant not only in the hall that night, but throughout the country.

It was Cook who finally brought the question time to an end. He stood up and immediately everyone fell silent. "Ladies and Gentlemen," he said, "I'm sure you will agree that you've pestered Lord Monckley with enough questions tonight. He has assured you that everything will be all right and, although opinions differ on that subject, I am sure that he will go back to Nairobi and present our case there. Don't worry, I'll keep in close touch with him! Now, I call upon our District Officer, Carey Milton, to make a few comments upon this evening's discussions."

Carey came up to the stand and was greeted by enthusiastic applause. "Lord Monckley, Mr. Chairman, Ladies and Gentlemen. I, as I said before, am no politician, and it has occurred to me that what has been discussed this evening has a great bearing on politics. However, the relevant point is that you are all very seriously disturbed about recent events and want to know how the Government intends to deal with them. That I leave to our Hon. Member here, as it is entirely out of my province. However, I too am extremely perturbed, and you can rest assured that I will do all in my power to help you to keep this District white and clean. No natives will be allowed to take control here. This is a White District and a White District it will remain. The Africans must be kept to their reserves. Any administrative trouble you have, just bring them straight to me. Thank you."

He stepped down off the platform amidst applause. He was well liked by the settlers and his extremist views were thoroughly approved. Although a young man, he was truly "one of them".

Cook then called upon Brigadier Frank Jones to speak. "I think he has something very important to say to you all."

"Lord Monckley, Mr. Chairman, Ladies and Gentlemen. I too feel the same way as you do. I also have listened with keen interest to this evening's proceedings and Carey and I, from the administrative side, and Major Cook, and of course Lord Monckley, are at one and intend to co-operate and work together to smother this threat to our land. I admit that I am not too happy about all this, and I have a proposal to make to you. I have already discussed it with Major Cook and Carey — Lord Monckley was not here at that particular time — and this is it: as this meeting has dealt so much with the security aspect of the affair, I suggest that you elect a committee consisting of five members to assist me to deal with security and to acquaint me with all your fears. As Major Cook has said, our lives and those of our families are at stake. The situation is serious and must be faced."

He returned to his seat amidst roars of approval. After a very short debate, the gathering nominated Frank Jones, Carey Milton, Lord Monckley, Major Cook and Captain Whimper (a very old settler in the district) unanimously to the Committee. They promised to lose no time in starting work immediately.

Committees such as these were being formed in European Clubs all over the country. They dealt with recruitment to the Police Reserve, security precautions generally, expelling troublemakers and sending them back to the reserves, and co-ordinating their activities with each other to exert pressure on the Government to silence the political agitators once and for all, even if it meant shooting them.

5 OATHS

As soon as the meeting was over Nono went to Nundu to report, and was given a chicken as a reward. Nundu realised just how important this information was, and determined to tell it not only to his own small band but also to Njogu, who was due to collect him at the end of the week to take him to the reserve for the oath-taking ceremony. He had seriously been considering letting his friends into this secret and asking them to take the oath with him. He decided to try them out that evening, knowing that Njogu would be only too pleased if he brought more supporters with him. Time was getting short and action was needed. If he reported on Kiko's speech and the resultant committee that was formed, that would be the deciding factor and he had no doubt at all that he could persuade them to follow his leadership.

That evening he summoned his friends, including Mrefu, to meet outside his house. Many meetings had been held here and it had become the custom to light a fire outside the hut and congregate round it, for the huts were really too small and too hot for meetings to be held inside. As soon as they had all arrived Nundu stood up and gave a report on the Club meeting of the previous night. They looked at him horror-struck.

"What shall we do, Nundu? The white man must hate us so much that he will kill us all," said Kato. "We all know that there is unrest everywhere and incidents occur throughout the whole country. We attend every political meeting we can and read the papers, but where is it all leading? What organisation have we that can conquer the white man?"

"Why, the dreamer is a dreamer no longer! That is the first time I have heard you ask such a practical question," said Nundu. "Truly things are not very happy these days. Apart from the whites playing at politics, we have the problem of Kiko. We all hate Kiko for what he has done to our fathers. We must speak with one voice, and be united against the *Kaburus*. I had hoped, and our great leaders also, that we could win back our country peacefully, but we can't. You know that now."

"But Nundu, you are talking of war, of a fight between blacks and whites! We have no weapons, no military training. Even with such hatred in our hearts what can we do?" said Choti.

"What I am going to tell you now is a secret between us and you must swear to tell no one. But there is one thing which I must ask you first — will you follow my guidance and leadership without question? You will? Right, we are united and therefore I can tell you something I have never mentioned before. I have a great friend in Nairobi, a taxi-driver called Njogu — one of the great leaders of the day. He, together with others, is organising a movement against the Europeans. This is a reality, not a dream. He is calling here on Saturday to collect us all and take us to Toga's house where he will tell you all about it. There is to be an oath-taking ceremony there and if you all take the first oath, which I will do at the same time, you also will be active members of the Movement and learn what is expected of you. Many of our people have sold us to the white man, including the chiefs. That is why their houses are being razed to the ground. If you take the oath you will no longer be the white man's stooge but a worker for freedom. Imagine, when we attain our goal, we shall get our land back. We will own the white men's houses, their cattle, all their property — we shall rule our own country and chase the white men out. Our country will belong to its own people once more and we will live in happiness and peace as our forefathers did. Believe me my friends, this will entail much work, much fighting; but to succeed we must have unity among us and the will to sacrifice our own lives if need be. Remember now, this is a strict secret. Are you going to betray me and, through me, your brothers in the fight?"

"Don't be so silly, Nundu!" said Heho. "How could we possibly betray you? Our hatred is as great as yours and we are with you all the way. The fact that our fathers were imprisoned and suffered at the hands of the whites, who look like the frogs that live in the banana trees, gives us all the more incentive. But even if our fathers had never been jailed, we would still be with you and long to join in the fight for freedom. This chance you have now offered us and we certainly won't turn it down. Lead the way. We will follow." Turning to his companions, Heho continued, "Is that not so, my brothers?"

They all agreed without hesitation, and also agreed to take the oath. Nundu was well pleased. He was becoming more powerful daily and well he knew it. It looked as if his dream of becoming a rich man was really going to come true, and when the time came, he would kill and kill so that he led not just this small band but a huge gang which would be the most renowned in the country. He was becoming possessed of a blood lust now beyond that of a mere bully.

Njogu arrived about mid-day on Saturday and immediately went into Nundu's hut, locking the door behind him. Nundu reported all he had heard and told Njogu that his friends were ready to take the first oath and were willing to accompany him. Njogu, extremely pleased, clapped Nundu on the back. Their discussion lasted for two hours. When they came out of the hut, Nundu was a much wiser man. Also his heart was swelling with pride for had not Njogu entrusted him with secret information that he was not entitled to know until he had taken his fifth oath? Needless to say, this was not so, but thus did Njogu influence Nundu. Being an older man and experienced in the ways of life, he knew exactly what to do with a young lad looking for an outlet for his hate and a chance to prove his capabilities as a leader. After the introductions were made, they all climbed into Njogu's taxi and set out for Toga's house.

By this time the arrangements for the ceremony were well under way. Muta had spent nearly the whole morning searching the village for a black lamb. There were many black lambs, but it was difficult to find one completely black from tip to toe to sacrifice at the ceremony. His companions had been carrying the sugar cane stalks and various other items needed down to the owl caves. Earlier in the day, Muta had gone into the bush to cut branches of various trees. He was accompanied by an old man who, with the help of others, was going to perform the ceremony later in the evening. Njogu and Toga went down to the caves, together with some Elders of the tribe, to complete the preparations.

They built an arch four feet wide just outside one of the cave entrances under which all the would-be oath takers had to pass before entering the cave. It was composed of tall sugar cane stalks and two banana trees standing, one on each side, between the arch and the cave. The tops of the banana leaves and cane were tied together with *Thurura*, a ground creeper similar to a pumpkin. In the cave itself were stools, one for each oath-taker, arranged around the sides with one in the middle for the oath administrator. Another similar arch was constructed in the centre of the cave, the difference being that the branches of four trees were added: *Muthima* meaning loyalty and truthfulness; *Mugere* signifying the number of days the battle would last; *Muir* to act as a warning to the irresolute; and at the top *Mukeria* as a symbol of success, happiness and eventual victory. After they had finished, one of the Elders went to call the group and Toga slaughtered the black lamb and caught all the blood in a calabash which had been cut vertically to resemble a bowl. The lamb's blood symbolised that of the human beings which would be spilt on the battle fields and was a very important part of the ceremony. The meat Toga put aside for eating raw after all had taken the oath.

Meanwhile the young men assembled outside the cave with very mixed feelings — one or two of them being extremely frightened. Nundu and Muta had agreed to remain until last so that they could make sure none of their followers ran away at the last moment. Nundu and Muta kept a very watchful eye on Kato and Karoki — the weakest of the group. As soon as one of them had entered the cave and had taken the oath, he was forbidden to divulge any part of the proceedings to an outsider.

Karoki was the first to enter. As soon as he reached the inside of the cave he was met by the oath administrator.

"What is your name?"

"Karoki."

"Are you wearing any ornamental metal?"

"Yes."

"Take it off and remove all your clothes," (this was to ensure that he became once more pure and innocent as on the day that he was born). "Drink this blood," giving Karoki the calabash bowl containing the lamb's blood. "This is to signify that you will never give up the fight for freedom until the last white man has either left the country or been killed. You will never leave the forest until we have attained independence."

The Administrator waited until Karoki had sipped the blood and had handed the bowl back to him, and then continued, "Now, walk round the arch seven times. The first time you will say nothing, but after that, each time you

"Now, walk round the arch seven times. The first time you will say nothing, but after that, each time you approach me, you will repeat what I say to you and eat a piece of meat." The following promises were made as the rounds were completed:

"I must obey my superiors at all times without question."

"I must never reveal the secrets that I learn to anyone who has not taken the oath."

"I must make any sacrifice requested of me."

"It would be better for me to die than give away what I know."

"If I am told to do something which will benefit my country I will never give up until I have done it."

"I will never make an enemy that is not already my enemy."

Karoki, shaking with terror, then took his seat and watched the others come in, one by one, take the oath, and come and sit down beside him. As soon as the oath-taking ceremony was over, they cooked and ate the remainder of the lamb's meat and drank honey and cane beer. Then they returned two by two, symbolising the end of the ceremony, to their homes to await their first lecture on moral behaviour, and other information necessary to the success of this secret organisation, on the next day. This lecture would be given to them by one of those who had taken the oath previously.

Once they had all taken the oath, they were content to remain as followers, except Nundu who had been promised by Njogu that he could go to Nairobi weekly to take further oaths to become one of the leaders. A week's delay between each oath was imperative, but it was extremely unusual for a new initiate to climb the ladder so quickly. It needed influence from a top man — in this case Njogu. Njogu had also arranged with Toga for Muta, Kimu and Karoki to be indoctrinated as quickly as possible, so that they could take the necessary second oath to enable them to assist Toga to make guns and ammunition.

Meanwhile Nundu, without saying anything to his companions, went to Nairobi the following Saturday to take his second oath. He met Njogu who took him to a hut just outside the city where the same arches had been built. The second oath was the same as the first except that he had to swear to help in every way possible to make the guns. He looked excessively happy when he returned, but although pestered with questions by his friends, he said nothing.

The third oath he took a week later, again in Nairobi, repeating a ritual he knew practically word for word, and swearing in addition that he would never reveal, even at gun point or by torture, the hideouts of the forest fighters, and the various gun smithies and armouries that were being formed in different parts of the country. Njogu talked to him after he had taken this oath and told him all that he had a right to know. The two friends arranged to meet yet again the following Saturday so that Nundu could take his fourth oath.

His friends could not understand why he left the farm so promptly every Saturday afternoon and returned on Sunday evening, but Nundu, true to his oaths, said nothing. They continued to hold their meetings outside his house and Nundu, who wanted them to help make and distribute arms, lectured them on the oath they had taken and explained to them what the second oath entailed. He was growing a much wiser man and knew that he would wear their resistance down to taking another oath soon enough.

The fourth oath, which followed the same procedure, gave him permission to study guerilla warfare, gun making, war tactics and map reading. Njogu told him where the instructors were and who they were, but advised Nundu to learn from Toga and assist him in every way, for Toga, apart from being a friend, was one of the best instructors in the country.

Nundu was overjoyed the following week when he had taken his fifth oath. He was now an oath administrator himself. He was qualified to learn all the secret signs and symbols whereby the leaders could identify each other, and also to pass on messages. He was told who the leaders were in each area, how to contact them in secret and co-ordinate his activities with theirs. He was lectured on how to command a company of forest fighters; but again Njogu advised him to learn all he could from Toga. He was admitted into the most prominent and active group of oath administrators in the country through Njogu's influence.

Nundu, in his enthusiasm, forgot all about his work on the farm and travelled round with Njogu to see what the other leaders were doing. He visited many oath administration centres, and learned how to distinguish the various trees which were essential for use in the inner archways. He also visited gun smithies in Nairobi and watched the men at work. Njogu took him to his house in Nairobi and showed him a list of all the people in and around Naro who had taken oaths, and what status they had reached. Nundu was amazed to find that Mrefu ranked very high in the movement and that Toga and Wenye, of all people, were also prominent on the list. "Why," he thought, "there was I leading them all and egging them on, while Wenye, my own brother, and Mrefu, my old schoolteacher, knew so much all the time. How secret they kept it, and what a fool I made of myself! No wonder I kept finding them talking to each other in secret. I thought it funny that they sent me away if ever I came near them when they were talking, but took it for granted that they were just normal private discussions. Well, I know now and we will make a grand team. They'll be surprised when I show the secret sign on my return! I too can keep secrets!" He realised with a start that he was long overdue at work, took his leave of Njogu hastily and caught the next train back to Naro.

The train slid lazily over the rails, and Nundu was lulled into a false sense of security. He lounged back on the seat, his heart bursting with gratitude at the help his friend Njogu had given him. He felt that he could never thank Toga enough for introducing them. He day-dreamed for a couple of hours, seeing himself in battle, his company the most renowned, and eventually carrying out the coup d'état that would finally defeat the white man. He dozed awhile, and woke with a start when the train jerked to a sudden stop at a station about four miles from Naro. Reality was four miles away! "I must tell Kiko I fell sick at home," he thought. "Kiko hates me and will sack me if he can, especially after that committee meeting they

held at the Club the other day. Yes, I'm certainly an
'undesirable' to Kiko, and they decided that all suspected
employees on every farm should be fired. Maybe I've given
Kiko the excuse he wants to get rid of me, for I'm sure
he won't believe my excuses. He's never forgotten the way
I treated him in the vegetable garden that day. Maybe
he'll beat me, and I haven't got any guns to fight him
with — not yet. Am I frightened of him? I never used to
think I was frightened of anybody." He shrugged his
shoulders. "Well, he can do what he likes. I can reorganise
my gang. I've already reorganised my life, so why not?
He can't put me in jail for being late back to work — or
can he? Look what he did to my father. Whatever he does
to me now will just total up towards the final score. One
day soon I'll kill him, but I can't yet; that would betray
our Cause. I must have a gang behind me when I attack
him. I wonder what he will do to me?"

As soon as the train stopped at Naro Station, Nundu
hurried back to the farm, having by this time persuaded
himself that Kiko would try to kill him before he had a
chance to hit back! He went straight to Wenye's house and
was told that Kiko had already been looking for him.

"You fool, Nundu," said Wenye. "I know what you
have been doing in Nairobi. Why on earth did you stay
away so long? Why lay yourself open to Kiko's vengeance?
Anyhow brother, congratulations. I'm so glad that we can
work together at last. You'd better go and see Kiko straight
away, then come back and tell me all about it. We are at
one now, and have no secrets from each other."

Nundu raced up the valley that separated the huts
from Kiko's house, and found Mwangi cleaning Kiko's car
outside the garage.

"Nundu, where on earth have you been? Kiko's been
looking for you everywhere," gasped Mwangi. "He roars
like a lion these days, and is very free with his whip. I'm
scared to go near him. He's off to the Club again for one
of his secret meetings — Nono tells me all about them."

Nundu interrupted. "Listen, Mwangi, go and tell him I'm here. I've been terribly sick you know and just couldn't get back to work in time."

Mwangi looked at him in horror. "Why, Nundu, he won't believe that — even I know it isn't true, but that's beside the point. I'm too terrified of the man even to speak to him."

"Fool!" whispered Nundu. "Of course it's true. What are you so scared of the man for? Go and tell him I'm here, quickly!"

At that moment the front door swung open and Kiko, dressed in a dinner jacket, strolled onto the verandah. He glanced at Nundu, and said casually, "Who on earth is that oaf there?" and turned away to look at his potted plants, knowing full well that it was Nundu who was standing beside the car, but playing for time to decide the best course of action.

"Bwana!" Mwangi stuttered. "It's Nundu. You . . . you sent for him . . ." His voice trailed away into a petrified whisper.

Cook swung round, his face ablaze with rage. "You black swine, don't you know this is my house? Get out of here! No one is allowed to approach my house. I will see you in the office tomorrow morning. Get out! Do you hear me? Get out!"

Nundu shrugged his shoulders, turned away from the car and strolled across the lawn in front of the house. Cook, with a bellow of rage, unleashed the huge black Alsatian dog that was chained to a verandah post, and shouted, "Get him, Rex!" Nundu looked round and saw the dog streaking over the grass towards him, growling fiercely. He knew by repute that this dog had badly mauled more than one man, and with the agility of youth ran to the nearest tree, caught a lower branch and swung himself into it, the dog's huge teeth just grazing his legs as they flashed past him. "That will teach you to come to my house," shouted Cook who by now was doubled up with laughter. "Down

Rex! Leave him alone now." And, as he watched the dog trot back to him, he continued, "Black man, come to my office in the morning. You're lucky you're not dead." He stooped down to chain the dog up again, patted him and walked to his car, still chuckling with glee. Mwangi was nowhere to be seen, for at the first sign of trouble he had run into the kitchen and slammed the door behind him. He knew only too well that if he had tried to help the dog would either have killed him, or Kiko would have made sure he suffered for it later.

As soon as Cook had driven away, Nundu climbed down from the tree, shaking with terror at his narrow escape, his face streaming with sweat. He stood silent a moment, shook his fist at the departing vehicle and turned to walk back to his house. "He treated me like an animal," he thought. "He not only set his dog after me to chase me like a buck but he hardly deigned to recognise my presence. I suppose I shall have to go to his office tomorrow, but if he had wanted to sack me, surely he would have told me so now. He behaves as if he were a god and I was a devil. I learn more of the truth about these white devils every day. Anyhow, if he does sack me, I shall stay in Naro. He's right, I'm lucky to be alive to be sacked. I've never had such a narrow escape in all my life — what a beastly death it would have been! I've got plenty of other work to do now, although it would have been better if I could have stayed on this farm and used it as my headquarters. Still, I'm lucky to be alive and I'll make him pay." Nundu went straight to his own house, still deep in rather jumbled thought. He lay on his sacks unable to sleep. It was Mwangi who disturbed him about an hour later, to apologise for the way he had behaved.

"I wanted to help you, Nundu, please believe me," he begged, "but I'm so terrified of the man." Nundu looked at him pitying him for his fear.

"Listen, Mwangi, come with me. I want you to come and tell my friends what happened — be a witness for me. That's the way you can make up for your cowardice."

83

They went together to Wenye's house — Nundu knew he would find his friends there for they always met in Wenye's house when he was away. They gathered round him eagerly and for once Nundu let someone else take the limelight for, after all, Mwangi could tell what had happened far better than he. When Mwangi had finished, a silence fell over the group and they all gazed at Nundu.

"Well, brother," said Wenye, "you are truly lucky to be alive. What do you propose doing now? You will be sacked tomorrow and I advise you to pack your things tonight; but that is really beside the point. You are our leader — you must stay near us. What are you going to do?"

Nundu looked at his little band and grinned. "I was foolish to stay away so long in Nairobi as this farm has become a very convenient headquarters for us. Never mind, I intend to ask Mrefu to put me up. I'll work from his house. It's a pity he's not here tonight because we could have fixed the whole thing up now, but I'm sure he won't refuse. Never fear that I will desert you. From now on any meetings we hold will be in Mrefu's house. Nothing, no — not even Kiko's wrath, for who the devil does he think he is? — can stop us. We will stand steadfast and firm. A rock does not crumble, remember that. We are bound to get a few setbacks, and this is one of them. In a way, though, it will be better for me, for I can organise more easily and with less danger of being discovered from Mrefu's house. What do you all think?"

They agreed without hesitation that Nundu had chosen the best course, and parted most amicably, promising to hold a meeting at Mrefu's house that weekend.

The next day, Nundu was summarily dismissed and ordered to get off the farm within the hour. "I warn you, brute, that if I see you again on my farm I'll put you in the same cell as your father. He's still got a few more months to serve. Now, get the hell out of here!"

Nundu just looked contemptuously at Cook until he

was forced to look away, and then turned and walked out of the office. He collected his luggage, looked rather nostalgically towards the shamba where he could just make out the figures of his friends working, then walked down the footpath off the farm.

He arrived at Mrefu's house about half an hour later and was greeted warmly.

"I knew you were coming, old chap," said Mrefu. "That's why I am here waiting for you! I heard all the news through the grape vine and as soon as I saw you coming I rushed out of my office to give you a warm welcome. We are brothers in the same cause, and you may not only live here for as long as you wish, but you may work from here too. No one will know — a clerk is still above suspicion." Nundu, laughing heartily, was thrilled at his reception.

"Thanks, Mrefu. As soon as you have a moment to spare this evening I'll tell you all about it — I mean what you haven't heard on the grape vine! It's funny that a few years ago I hated you so much and you hated me, and yet now here we are intending not only to work together, but to live together also."

"That, Nundu," replied Mrefu, "is true brotherhood. Now, my friend, I must hasten back to the office. Make yourself at home; what is mine is yours. I'll see you later."

It did not take Nundu very long to settle down and organise his activities. He was directed from head office to start administering oaths in the whole of the Naro area. He had to work, of course, in complete secrecy and relied only upon those who had already taken an oath to help him.

His first move was to administer oaths on Cook's farm in the dead of night. The arches, of course, had to be built, but it was an easy task to remove all traces before daylight. He persuaded his own gang to take the second oath, thus making them more valuable to him. They now spent their spare time indoctrinating others and, during the weekends, they went to Toga with the scrap metal that was being collected to learn to make guns and the arts of guerilla warfare from him. After most of the labourers on Cook's farm had taken the oath, he moved on to Lord Monckley's farm and so on throughout the district. He had contacted Njogu through their own secret service to ask if he could set up a gun smithy in the district, but the committee in Nairobi decided that it was far too dangerous to make guns in such a heavily populated European area; and so Nundu was directed to make arrangements with the railway staff for the scrap metal — which was being collected so rapidly that Choti and his friends were unable to carry it with them on their frequent visits to Toga — to be secreted in the guard's van and dropped off the train during the night at a certain spot near Toga's house. From there Muta and his gang collected it (having also been persuaded to take the second oath) and took it to the owl caves. Apart from these activities, Nundu was still reporting weekly to Nairobi on the meetings being held in the Club. He was proving himself to be a most useful spy, and his name was becoming a by-word in the organisation.

Toga, meanwhile, was also making a name for himself because he had proved so adept at making guns. He was now known as Director of Munitions in his area. Apart from the arduous duties which this work entailed, he also was an oath administrator and had sworn in hundreds of members. Muta, Karoki and Kimu by this time had taken their third oath and were proving themselves invaluable to Toga. They had learned the art of gun-making very swiftly and the owl caves were being filled rapidly with the arms and ammunition these young men were making. They too held political meetings and Muta, who addressed these rallies just as persuasively as Nundu, brought many converts to Toga to be sworn in. They were filled with the desire to start fighting, a desire that had rapidly spread throughout most of the country and indeed isolated incidents of cattle slashing and house burning were already beginning to take place. The regrettable effect was that many were forced to take the oath against their will, for the leaders were getting impatient and were sweeping all obstacles out of their paths relentlessly so that the war could be started. These two gangs co-ordinated perfectly with each other and were the best organised throughout the area.

Nundu was elected Field Officer in charge of operations for his organising ability was brilliant. It was he who was to give the word to start the fight in the area when he was so directed from Nairobi. It was hoped that once the word was given all the various companies would operate with one accord and the guerilla warfare training was highly intensified. Weapons and ammunition from the various depots were being secretly distributed and hidden in the eaves of the houses on Cook's farm, and in various other places, ready for the great day.

Meanwhile, the settlers sensed the disturbed atmosphere and the feeling of anticipation that seemed to be everywhere. The hatred between blacks and whites became even more obvious. Kiko had seen Nundu in Naro many times and, on the odd occasion on which he met him, he had been seriously frightened by the look of hatred in Nundu's eyes. He had heard through some of his loyal employees that Nundu had been visiting his farm at night and he was extremely suspicious. Kiko did not realise what Nundu was doing, or that when he sent out search parties to try and catch him, his employees were hiding him, but he realised something was very wrong and brought the matter up at the next committee meeting. Just before the weekend, Nundu was summoned to Nairobi by Njogu and so was not present when Kiko's last desperate blow was struck against him. He suggested at the Club meeting that Frank Jones should hunt for Nundu, charge him with vagrancy and throw him out of the district altogether. These meetings were being held by badly frightened men who were only too eager to grab any straw of hope that was offered to them. Apart from the behaviour of their workers which was becoming daily more disturbing, the newspapers were reporting new outbreaks of violence, cattle slashing, house burning, and even one or two odd cases of white men being brutally murdered — those who were living on the most isolated farms — and no trace could be found of the murderers. It was therefore unanimously agreed that this should be done and so Frank Jones spread a cordon of Askaris over the farms and in the town, thus beginning the biggest man hunt in the history of the district.

Mono, who had been listening avidly to every word, as usual rushed straight to Mrefu's house to warn Nundu. When he found that Nundu was away, it never occurred to him to tell Mrefu what was the matter, so he just bided his time hoping that he could warn Nundu of his danger before the Police caught him.

6 FOREST FLIGHT

When Nundu returned in the late evening a couple of days later, he was still completely unaware of the trap that was awaiting him. He had succeeded in getting a lift home in a car instead of travelling by train, and so did not see the askaris waiting at the railway station. Mrefu was not in the house when he arrived, so Nundu, using the spare key he always carried, entered the house and hid the suitcase he was carrying. This suitcase contained several secret documents including the record of all who had taken the oath in his area. This done, he hurried out of the house, locking the door behind him, and set out in the bright moonlight towards Major Cook's farm to find his brothers. He had met his released father in Nairobi, where he was seeking employment, and had an urgent message from him for Wenye and Heho. As the tension increased so did Nundu's responsibilities. Although he accepted them eagerly, motivated by his ambition to gain power and prestige and indoctrinate his people with the blind hatred that gripped him so relentlessly, he very seldom had a moment to call his own. Thus, on that evening, he strode along the main road instead of walking through the bush, hoping that as it was midnight, everyone would be safely in bed.

"I wonder if I'm wise," he thought, "to walk along this road in such bright moonlight. I can see everything — it's almost as bright as day. Must be careful to plan our raids on the wane of the moon. This light would be fatal to the success of any attack. I'm glad I've got those papers safely hidden. They're dynamite. But I must find a safer place to hide them in." His reverie was rudely interrupted by the noise of a car engine behind him; he swung round and was almost dazzled by the twin lights which shone on him. A shout came from the approaching car. "Stop! Stop! Who are you? Where are you going? Stop I say!" The car

89

halted with a screech of brakes. Nundu, with the swiftness of a leopard, merged into the bush on the side of the road. He had acquired the mastery of this art during his activities as an Oath Administrator, for there were many alarms, some false and some real, whilst he performed the ceremonies, and an Oath Administrator could not afford to be caught.

Nundu sped along the uneven ground, unheedingly catching his legs on thorns and tripping in holes. He had recognised the voice and the car, both of which belonged to Major Cook. He stopped for a moment to regain his breath and wipe away the sweat that was streaming into his eyes. He listened attentively. Suddenly he heard the baying of a hound and the sound of Cook's voice egging it on. "My God," he thought, "he's set his dog on to me again." Frantically he grabbed a couple of large stones, realising it was useless to run any further. In a few seconds he could see the animal five yards away, and hurled the stones at it. The howls turned into yelps of anguish as the stones met their mark. Nundu, giving the dog a cursory glance and seeing that he had smashed its leg, fled on even faster. Cook, realising that his dog had been badly hurt, swore volubly, ran back to his car, seized his rifle and fired about ten shots in the direction of the noise. Nundu heard the shots but, being a fast runner, was soon out of range. Cook's voice yelling, "You black bastard, I'll teach you!" faded away in the distance as he scrambled down the escarpment into the valley.

A few minutes later he was pounding on Wenye's door. "Quickly, brother, let me in, let me in!" he gasped. The door swung open and a very astonished Wenye greeted him.

"Why, Nundu, what on earth is the matter? You look as if you've shaken hands with death."

Nundu pushed him aside, ran into the hut and sank down beside the fire, gasping for breath. Wenye hovered over him anxiously. "What is it Nundu, please tell me — here, have some water." The others grouped round agog to hear the news.

Nundu seized the gourd and drank deeply. "Ah!" he breathed, "that's better. Yes, I came nearer to death just now than I have ever done before. That man Kiko's a swine a beast! Why, I've no words to describe what he tried to do to me." He stopped and looked at his friends. "I was on my way down here, walking along the road because it was so late that I thought everyone would be in bed. As you know, there is a full moon, and because of that I did not see the car lights and get off the road in time. He set his dog on me — I've fixed that dog once and for all — and when he heard his dog yelping, he fired about ten shots at me and his language had to be heard to be believed. Don't look so worried, brothers. I'm all right, even if only just."

"Kiko will set the askaris on to you, you must get away from here at once. What a terrible thing to have happened, but fate was certainly on your side," said Wenye, who was too deeply shocked to say more.

"Yes, Wenye, I must get away from here, but first I must tell you why I came." He looked round the silent group. "Cheer up fellows, I'm alive and kicking! That's all that matters. I tell you, that dog is sorry he ever chased me. Never fear, I swore to kill that white frog, and kill him I will. He won't get another chance to try and kill me first, that I promise you. Wenye, Heho, I saw our father in Nairobi."

"Father!" said Heho, "How is he, is he . . . ?"

Nundu cut in impatiently. "Look, I have a message for you both from him, but I must get away from here. Time is running short. Walk a short way with me and I'll tell you all about it. We'd better take the bush path in case the police are looking for me." He looked at his companions. "I'm sure you will forgive us. Now don't tell anyone I've been here and don't be afraid for me — I can look after myself. I'll contact you as soon as everything has settled down a bit." He turned and walked out of the hut followed by his two brothers, leaving a very frightened and unhappy group of young men behind him.

"Just a minute, brother, I'll scout ahead and see if the path is safe," said Heho. He crept silently up the path and returned about five minutes later. "All is well, Nundu, let's go."

"My brothers, we must make this short and sweet," said Nundu, "for I'm sure the askaris will be out and I don't want them to find you with me. You understand your work is most important here and I'd like you to stay on this farm for as long as is humanly possible. You must not risk betrayal of the Cause through being seen with me. Father is very well, but very, very poor. He is looking for work in Nairobi, but work seems to be hard to come by. Our two younger brothers have gone to High School, but he has no money to pay their fees. I have no work at the moment..." he grinned. "Well you know what I mean! Can you pay for their education? I'll send small sums of money to our mother and our sisters every now and then, which will help a bit." Perhaps there was something unselfish in Nundu after all, even if buried deep.

"Surely, Nundu, we'll do all we can to help," whispered Wenye. "But don't talk so loud, it may be very dangerous for us all if you do."

"Sorry! Anyhow, Father is almost blind now; he has been ever since he came out of prison and it's very hard for a man with poor eyesight to find a job. I gave him a little money and promised to send him some more next time I'm in Nairobi."

"Look," Heho interrupted, "here's the boundary. I'm sorry Nundu, but we must leave you here. We'll help the family all we can — don't worry about that."

They clasped hands. Wenye looked up at the moon which was gradually disappearing under a large bank of clouds. "At least it is dark again, brother. Now, be very, very careful. If you find no one on the road, go back to Mrefu's house and get some sleep, but I think that's a forlorn hope for Kiko is sure to have set the Police on to you. Please be careful," he begged.

"Now don't you two start worrying your heads about me. I'll be all right. Farewell for now; I'll contact you as soon as I can."

Nundu stood and watched his brothers disappear into the blackness of the night, his heart beating like a drum. "I'm alone now," he thought. "I mustn't panic. I'm sure Kiko hasn't set the Police on me, not yet. Anyhow, I'll walk along the boundary fence and keep off the road for as long as I can; surely that will be all that is necessary." He glanced fearfully around him. "I only wish I wasn't so tired. If they do chase me, I'll never get away — my legs feel like lead." He crept along as swiftly as possible, alert for any strange sound that might come from the blackness around him. "If they're after me," he thought, "I must run. I know they'll fire at me, but surely it would be better to try and avoid badly aimed bullets than let myself be caught and treated brutally by Kiko's stooges. I would die a beastly death if they found me. I must run, but oh! I'm so tired. I must keep awake."

The silence of the night was rudely shattered by shouts in front of him. "Stop! Stop! Stop! If you do not stop we will fire." Nundu stopped dead, then started to run blindly away from the sounds, sobbing with fright. He heard the sound of rifle fire very near him and soon bullets whined over his head. He could also hear the shouts of his pursuers, who were rapidly gaining on him. By this time, his breath was coming in short gasps and he had given up any hope of being able to evade either them or the bullets when suddenly he stepped into an antbear hole and fell headlong. He landed on some small stones, groped for one and cautiously threw it a few yards away to mislead the askaris. He ducked swiftly into the hole and a few seconds later heard one of them say, "Ssh, what was that over there?" and a regulation size boot landed squarely on his head. He clenched his fists grimly to prevent himself screaming in pain, felt the boot move away and heard the sound of heavy footsteps fade away into the distance.

He stayed in the hole for about half an hour, until the silence of the night was unbroken by distant rifle fire, and then very cautiously crept out, stood up and peered into the blackness, his ears alert for any foreign sound. He stealthily made his way across the boundary fence and silently walked through the bush about a hundred yards from the footpath that led to Naro. He heard some askaris walking along the path and crouched down to avoid detection. He heard them discussing his escape and complimenting him on his tactics. His heart swelled with pride at his achievement, and it was all he could do to maintain caution until he reached Naro Township. He walked down the deserted street ready to dodge back into the shadows should anyone approach, then strolled along the station platform towards Mrefu's house. To his amazement, he saw that the light was on and his fears of discovery flooded back. He stopped in the shadow of a godown to see if there were any signs of activity in the hut. Carefully he made his way round to the shutter and peeped through a large crack in the wood. To his great relief he saw no one and hastily unlocked the door and went in, locking it behind him. He immediately turned out the light and unlatched the shutters so that he could jump out should the askaris seek him there. He collapsed, utterly exhausted, on the bed and was almost asleep when he heard footsteps approaching. He sprang up and ran to the window and breathed a sigh of relief as he heard a key turning in the lock and turned to face Mrefu.

"Why, Mrefu, what have they done to you?" Nundu gasped, for blood was streaming down Mrefu's face, his clothes were in shreds and he could hardly walk.

Mrefu sat down on the bed and looked up at him. "The Police, they came here to look for you. They searched the whole house in vain and then they took me to the Station for questioning. I told them nothing and so," he shrugged his shoulders, "they beat me up."

Nundu gasped in horror. "They have made a terrible mess

of you. Here, lie down and let me bathe your face."

"No," Mrefu snapped. "It's too dangerous for you to stay here — they may come back. You've got to get away fast! Don't worry about me, I'll be all right. Please, Nundu, please listen to me," Mrefu begged, for Nundu was already filling a basin with water.

He looked at Mrefu who continued, "Look, Nundu, the Police are determined to get you and they will stop at nothing." He surveyed himself ruefully. "If they do, I don't know what will happen to you — look at me. They questioned me about all your activities here and in Nairobi, with special stress on your suspected visits to Cook's farm, and every time I said I didn't know what you did in Nairobi and Naro, they hit me, hard." He grinned. "And a lot of good it did them too! You look a bit dishevelled yourself. Has anything happened to you?"

Nundu briefly recapped the night's events to Mrefu, and they looked at each other in stunned silence. It was Mrefu who eventually spoke. "Nundu, my friend, this is no time to talk of the hatred and sorrow in your heart, for I see your eyes blazing with fury. Those fiends may come back here at any time and if they find you I dread to think of the consequences. You have become very valuable to the Cause, so you can't go far, but it is not safe for you to stay in the town any longer. Listen, I have a solution. You know the thick forest by the side of the river Naro in the valley only a few miles from here? Well, to a casual observer, that forest seems impassable and no one tries to enter it. It is a well kept secret by the very few that there are several caves in the middle of that forest — you did not even know of them yourself! That is where you must go, where you will be safe from the eagle eyes of your persecutors. I can assure you that I will look after your personal needs and arrange for your trips to Nairobi — probably in the guard's van of one of the various trains that go daily. The details, my brother, we can thrash out later on. For the moment, pack yourself some food and let us go, for we must slip away before dawn and we haven't much time left. Oh, by the way, let your hair and beard grow; that way you will be less easily identified."

Nundu, blinded by tears of gratitude, was too overcome to speak. He just nodded his head and silently put some food into a sack. He turned and gazed at Mrefu. "Mrefu, I . . . I . . ."

"Come on now, brother, things might be worse. Hurry now!" interrupted Mrefu.

"If only I could tell you what is in my heart," replied Nundu. "But there is no time even for that. May our gods bless you, Mrefu. Listen, I brought some secret documents back from Nairobi for you . . ."

"For heaven's sake," interrupted Mrefu in horror, "take them away from here before the Police find them. I'll read them in the cave. If they are found here, we're all done for." He seized the papers as if they were hot coals, stuffed them into the bag and hustled Nundu out of the house.

Dawn was just breaking when they reached the forest, so Mrefu showed Nundu where the caves were and hastened back to Naro, reaching his home just before the early birds emerged from their houses. That evening he visited Wenye and Heho to explain what had happened. They listened to his tale eagerly, for they had heard the shots the previous night and were convinced that Nundu was dead. Both they and Mrefu were visited by the Police many times after this incident, but they denied any knowledge of Nundu's whereabouts.

Meanwhile, the Naro Security Committee had demanded the resignation of the Governor and the introduction of martial law so that they could deal stringently with unrest in the country. The fact that Nundu had successfully evaded the askaris did not improve the situation and indeed the intimidation, arson and violence directed against Civil Servants had caused the settlers to declare themselves prepared to take the law into their own hands. The Major had changed from a drunkard to an excellent organiser and an active leader of the area, and his hatred for the coloured man grew even more intense, especially after the maiming of his dog. The newspapers brought more alarming news daily and the incidents of European farmers being hacked to death by pangas were no longer so isolated. Many hundreds of cattle had been hamstrung or slashed so badly that their owners had to shoot them. Reports of houses and stores being razed to the ground were so common that they were no longer news headlines. The situation was severely aggravated by the fact that a new Governor took office at this time, thus shattering the fragments of confidence that the settlers had in the Government even though they themselves had demanded the change. Many of them sent their wives and children back to their home countries and stayed on themselves to try and sell their farms. This was to no avail, however, as security had deteriorated to such an extent that no one would even consider buying property. The White Highlands were no longer an earthly paradise, but a place of terror and intimidation where the only law was that of the jungle. The British Government could not bring itself to take the drastic action the settlers were demanding: that was to allow the settlers to shoot all the trouble makers. And so things went from bad to worse.

A few weeks after the new Governor took office, a State of Emergency was declared and news pamphlets were circulated widely declaring that all political agitators who had been detained would be brought to trial. All the Africans were taken by surprise at the untimely arrest of their leaders and the Declaration only served to remind them of the white man's intention to hold them in servitude for ever, which inflamed their desire to be free from the yoke of colonialism. They had discovered that their beloved leaders were far better educated than most of the European population in the country, and in their leadership they saw hope: hope for a bright future, a future in which they would regain their human dignity and aspirations, a future that would bring them freedom, prosperity, happiness and all those things which the European had denied them since he had taken over the country. The white man represented only despair, hatred and a continued life of darkness and utter misery.

The immediate result of the Declaration was soon very obvious. All the Policemen patrolling the countryside and towns carried rifles. The settlers and their sons wore pistols strapped to their belts and were extremely gun happy. No movement was allowed between one town and another (this rule excluded all Europeans), and all African transport buses and lorries had to remain where they were when the Emergency was declared. A strict curfew was enforced and no African was allowed out of doors between the hours of 6 p.m. and 6 a.m. The orders were to shoot the natives on sight if they infringed this rule. Many of the Africans, especially those in the reserves, had no idea what this curfew implied, or even what the word meant, and as a result the ignorant were either shot or arrested and beaten mercilessly before they were put in detention camps.

This curfew had the opposite of the desired effect, for apart from the unnecessary killings, it also caused a violation of tribal custom. Many of the youngsters, who were accustomed to group together in the evenings, either round the fire or at dances in various hidden places, or otherwise occupying their time, were arrested and beaten by the security forces. This forced them to stay at home with their parents — an unbearable situation as custom forbade elder boys to sleep with their parents. They shared a communal hut with their age group, only visiting their parents occasionally, with their friends, for social evenings. Apart from this, they were no longer allowed to gather together at any time and families were not allowed to entertain even their closest relatives. Each family was therefore completely isolated. The communal system of living, so dear to the African heart and so essential to their very existence, was forcibly prevented. The fire of hatred blazed even more strongly. especially amongst the younger men who regarded this move by the European as a confrontation and challenge which could not be disregarded. Many secret meetings were held in the dead of night and scouts were posted round the meeting places to give warning of the first sign of danger. Luckily for Toga, the security forces had not discovered the owl caves, and he and his band intensified their efforts to supply more arms for the Cause, and recruits to the Cause poured in. The newspapers carried ever more sensational headlines, for now European women and children were being murdered as well as the men. The utter injustice of the Government and the brutality of the settlers towards any man with a black skin was beginning to cause a blind hatred which hit anywhere and anyhow. The African was more determined than ever to wipe out the cruel oppression at any cost. The Government's action, especially in arresting the leaders, caused the whole freedom movement to snap out of control.

A month after the Emergency came into being, a law was passed whereby all troublemakers and all the members of the tribe to which they belonged should be repatriated, forcibly if necessary, to their own reserves. The Europeans were so frightened that if an African as much as glanced at them he was reported to the Police and immediately sent back to his tribe.

The first sufferers from this particular law were Wenye and the rest of Nundu's band. Cook was only too eager to wreak vengeance on the men he feared so much — so they were rounded up like a flock of sheep and locked in a hut on his farm until the following morning when they would be transported back to the reserve. Askaris guarded the house to prevent them escaping.

They looked at each other miserably as they heard the key turn in the lock. They had not resisted arrest for fear of retaliation and so had escaped being beaten and put in one of the many detention camps that had been set up all over the country.

"Cheer up, fellows," said Wenye. "At least we are in one piece."

"How lucky can we get?" sneered Choti. "We should be the happiest men in the world!"

"Oh snap out of it, Choti," said Wenye. "Stop feeling so sorry for yourself. We are all alive and we can therefore still go on fighting. The question is, what shall we do?"

"We have lived in this area for more than ten years," broke in Kato miserably. "Now Kiko will take us back to the reserve tomorrow. I haven't got a penny to take back with me — how are my brothers and sisters going to eat now that I've lost my job? I know we only got twelve shillings each month from that bastard, but we sent it all home. We are all in the same boat and our families will starve. Perhaps our brothers and sisters will die from lack of food. We have made this farm what it is with the toil of our bodies — what have we done to him that he should treat us this way? First he imprisons our fathers who were behaving honestly and decently, and then he does this to us." He buried his face in his hands.

"What about Nundu?" said Wenye. "It's a miracle that he's still alive." And his dark face grew even darker with worry and misery.

They all fell silent and gazed hopelessly at each other.

"Hasn't he been allowed to do enough?" spat Heho. "What is the use of us behaving like a lot of women? The mistake we made was to leave Kiko alone; we should have killed him a long time ago."

"As far as I am concerned," interrupted Iru, "I don't think I could possibly go back to the reserve. I'm useless and I would rather die here than go back and starve with my family. Why, this curfew is stricter in the reserve than it is here. Why should I go back to die like a trapped rat waiting for the water to boil? I won't do it, I won't go back, do you hear me?" His voice became hysterical.

"Keep your voice down," snarled Choti. "You'll have those swine coming to take us to detention for subversive talk if you don't look out."

"I won't do it," reiterated Iru stubbornly. "I'm going to escape tomorrow morning and I'll join Nundu. We'll fight these swine from the caves. I don't care what you people think."

"Perhaps it would be better for us to be killed trying to escape than to die in the reserve," remarked Wenye. "You've got something there, brother, at least we could take some of them with us! Gather close and let's discuss it."

They looked at each other and with one accord grouped closely around Wenye, hope dawning on their faces.

*   *   *

Meanwhile Mrefu, who because of his age had become by tradition one of the senior members of the Organisation, held full sway amongst the Naro African population, unbeknown to his employers who valued him highly. The railways were now the only transport available since all the local buses had been halted by the Declaration of Emergency, so his employment gave him an influential position. Futhermore, he was sufficiently educated to be useful, especially in writing reports. His dominating personality and courage together with a gift for restoring peace between warring factions, and his teachers' training, gave him the position of guide, philosopher and friend to the youths, thus making him a natural commander. Nevertheless, his employment on the railway — useful as it was — had one outstanding disadvantage: it rendered him highly immobile. Nundu had already established a base in Naro Valley and this was regarded as an outstandingly courageous action. A meeting was called to discuss tactics in view of the mass arrests which included most of the prominent leaders of the organisation and the raising of funds for their defence. They discussed the best way to make use of the young people expelled from the White Highlands as well as those in the Reserves. Another item on the agenda was the setting up of a unified command and a declaration of total war against the whites. This meeting lasted for a marathon session of forty-eight hours and before the delegates dispersed they had settled details of propaganda, supplies of food, war material and the command in all areas. It was further determined that delegates should report at regular intervals to their Headquarters.

Mrefu arrived back in Naro at about midnight and immediately hastened down to Nundu's hideout to brief him as he had been instructed. He walked silently through the forest and had almost reached the caves when a black figure hurtled out of the trees and threw him to the ground. "One move and you are dead," it whispered, and Mrefu felt a gun muzzle pressing hard on his forehead.

"Just a minute," he said, "who are you?"

"Shut up and come with me," was the reply, and Mrefu was forcibly hoisted to his feet while the figure peered through the darkness trying to establish his identity. They looked at each other and then Mrefu hooted with laughter. "Why Choti! What on earth are you doing here?"

"Mrefu, why it's Mrefu! I'm sorry, brother, we weren't expecting you tonight — we thought you were still in Nairobi. If you'd whistled as you approached I would have known you for a friend."

"I'm very pleased to see that you take precautions, even if you are in the middle of the forest!" chuckled Mrefu.

"Well you see, there is a big oath-taking ceremony on at the moment and we always take special care when there are strangers in the forest. Not all our people are as loyal as they should be, you know."

"That's true, Choti," replied Mrefu. "I suppose you are holding the ceremony in the clearing. Much safer than taking them to the caves. But, what on earth are you doing here? You were still working for Kiko when I left."

Choti laughed. "We are all here now. Go and make yourself comfortable, and as soon as the ceremony is finished, we'll join you and tell you all about it. You won't have to wait long — we've nearly finished."

About half an hour later, everyone had come back to the caves and they all grouped eagerly around Mrefu to hear his news.

"Before I tell you anything," Mrefu said, "I'm dying with curiosity. Why are you fellows here?"

"Well Mrefu," replied Wenye, "it's like this. We were arrested a couple of nights ago and locked in a house on Kiko's farm to await transportation to the reserve the following morning. It was the day you went to Nairobi. Anyhow, we decided we weren't going to give that swine Kiko the satisfaction of seeing us led away like cattle to the slaughter. You should have seen his face! It was positively evil with satisfaction at what he had done. First we planned to kill him, and then we thought that was more Nundu's affair than ours, so we decided to join Nundu. They left four askaris with loaded guns outside the hut, so we couldn't escape overnight. We had no weapons as you know. Well, the next day, they unlocked the door and Kiko ordered us out. We pretended to be terribly cowed so that they would relax their guard. We were loaded onto a small lorry and taken into Naro to join many of our brothers who had been treated the same way. They prodded us hard with their rifles — why, our bruises still show — and called us horrid names, but still we kept silent and didn't even look up. You should have heard the things Kiko said; truly I don't know how we managed to retain our self control. As soon as we stopped, just outside the Police Station, we were ordered to get off the lorry and join the others a few yards away. There were about thirty askaris there and many white men who were waving guns threateningly. We jumped off the lorry and then ran for it. They fired many shots — you probably saw that Iru was limping slightly when he came in; his leg was grazed with a bullet — they yelled and shouted, but all the same here we are."

"You did a very brave thing," commented Mrefu, "but are you sure that they will not follow you here?"

"Certain," replied Choti. "You see, they set the Police dogs on to us. We ran with all our might, even poor Iru here, who was absolutely gasping with pain, and as soon as we reached Naro River, not more than a hundred yards ahead of the beasts who were just far enough behind us to be on the wrong side of the ridge, we plunged into the water and hid in the reeds. Those dogs yelped at the side of the river — made our blood curdle with their howls — and apart from askaris, Kiko was there egging on about twenty *Kaburus*. They were out for our blood all right. They searched for hours. They crossed the river and tried to find our tracks, but all in vain." Choti laughed. "I tell you, their language made even my ears burn! But that water is very cold. I'll never hide in the river again! They went away eventually, but they left three askaris there so we had to wait until dusk. Our limbs were almost frozen solid by that time but the water dulled Iru's pain. That's about all! As soon as darkness fell, we made our way up stream and we didn't leave the water at all until we reached the caves. That is why they will not find us."

"I cannot congratulate you enough on your ingenuity. I'll commend you very highly to our leaders in Nairobi when next I go. Bravery like that deserves a medal. You're all very brave men," said Mrefu, who was too astounded to say more.

"I too am very proud of them," said Nundu with his usual self-important air. "It will be an honour to have them fighting by my side. But dawn is nearing, and you must leave us soon or you yourself will be caught. What news have you for us?"

"Well, as you know, I have just come back from Nairobi. At a leaders' meeting there, all aspects of the Cause were discussed and I have been directed to appoint you, Nundu, as my deputy, I'm sure you are overjoyed, but please don't interrupt me. I must keep my job obviously, and so my hands are very much tied. You can take over all the duties with which I cannot cope. I'm sure there are no objections from any of you for you all hold Nundu in high esteem. He too is a very brave man. I will inform all our sub-leaders of this directive and I am sure that none will object. May I be the first to congratulate you?"

Nundu was too overwhelmed with joy to speak, but his companions were certainly at no loss to find words of congratulation!

Mrefu watched them awhile, and then broke in, "Time is flying and so must I. Nundu, will you walk part of the way with me?" Nundu readily agreed, so they set off down the forest path.

"Now, Nundu," said Mrefu as they picked their way through the undergrowth, "listen very carefully. Njogu has been sacked. His employers found out that he was using their taxi for his own convenience but that doesn't matter much for he has now bought a car of his own. He has been ordered to organise the volunteeers in his own area and co-ordinate his activities with mine. Now, I am going to depend on you entirely, for this co-ordination will take the time that I haven't got. I've got to keep my job; you realise that. Now we have decided on points along the railway line at which supplies can be dropped. These will be at the 50, 75, 105 and 158 mileage posts. The supplies will be dropped at certain times and they will have to be collected immediately to avoid discovery. I want you to start a recruitment drive. Recruit women to carry the goods — teach them to mix the ammunition and guns with maize, beans — any food. They won't be suspected for carrying baskets of food, will they? Get hold of the young children and the very old men who herd cattle and sheep. They can watch the roads and warn us of the approach of security forces. You can use them as scouts, but don't forget that they must have some-one very responsible always available to report to because they in turn will have to alert our leaders. You will need some of your young women too; they can entertain and feed our liberation forces as they move from place to place. But see, we are nearing the edge of the forest and dawn is breaking.

I have much more to tell you, but perhaps you have enough to go on with for the present. Farewell, Nundu, and good luck. I'll be back as soon as I can." So saying, Mrefu left the cover of the trees and hastened up the escarpment side.

By this time, all the inhabitants of every area who had not yet taken the oath voluntarily were being forced to swear allegiance because leaders did not intend to give them the chance to betray the Cause. Nundu and Njogu, who was regarded as having a "master mind", were both ordered to see that this was carried out relentlessly. The danger of betrayal was too great for them to do otherwise. Their meetings were continually hampered by the movements of the security forces, and they had to move under cover of darkness and hide in their supporters' huts during the daytime. Sometimes it took as much as three days to cover fifty miles, which was extremely frustrating. The security forces swooped on many villages and not only ransacked them, but took away all the young girls they could find for their enjoyment, beat the young men almost to death and hauled them off to the detention camps. This of course made many of the youths run away to seek protection in the forests and the leaders hastily formed them into groups of ten to twenty men, with about three girls to a group, under the leadership of a commando. There was a highly developed sense of urgency attached to all these moves as the trial of the African leaders had now entered its fourth month and the results were anxiously awaited. If the verdict went against them, the plan was to overthrow the Government by force and implacably dispose of all the remaining Europeans. A few more Europeans, in fact, had been killed, very brutally.

The European population regarded the trend of events with horror. It was obvious that the Emergency, instead of helping the situation, had made matters worse. Club meetings were intensified. Many more wives and young children were sent to England. The settlers formed their own bands of Security Forces to defend themselves against the terrorists. They grouped together under strong guard in hotels, big houses or in club buildings. The young men were issued with weapons and joined the police. The British Military Land Forces and bomber planes had arrived to defend the land against its own people by birth and stop the rebellion at any cost. The whole country was in a state of blind panic.

Nundu worked swiftly, devoting almost all his time to oath administering. As soon as any man had taken the four oaths, he was himself appointed an administrator in his own right for the two oaths which were needed to ensure loyalty from volunteers or conscripts.

By this time, Cook's Security Committee had decided, in the interests of security and economy, to put all the members of the rebellious tribe into one village and judge each case according to its merit. A result of this was that Nundu, his brothers and his friends were forgotten as their disappearance had eventually been regarded by the settlers as a victory by the Committee; indeed, things seemed much more peaceful after their departure and Cook felt that he could once again sleep in peace.

Nundu started a propaganda movement of "whispering". It was quite brilliantly devised and consisted of exaggerating all the news in the papers, and circulating various rumours. This method of adding petrol to the already fiercely burning flame became so effective that he set up a specific organisation for this purpose and members visited him at two-day intervals with fresh information and tactics with which to feed the masses. It benefited him personally for his informers kept him in touch with everything the Club Committees said and did, usually only an hour later, and he convinced all the people in Naro beyond any shadow of doubt that the Europeans would be utterly routed and that an African Government was ready to take over.

Rumours of outside Powers taking charge in the country were rife. The Europeans blamed any country but their own for the mess that their part of Africa was in and were convinced that the African was being trained in the arts of sabotage and guerilla warfare by outsiders. Many Europeans prepared for a war on a national basis rather than a local

Kikuyu uprising. Guards were provided for all the Administrative Officers and the Governor, his aide-de-camp and Government House were guarded round the clock. Those isolated in the lonely parts of the country made their own arrangements to screen the workers and repatriate them. Many Africans were cruelly beaten. Some Europeans were sent intimidating letters threatening their lives, and others had been personally attacked by Africans carrying primitive weapons. It was soon apparent that the European and his stooges were the major target, and not one of them could believe it possible that the so-called primitive slave labour had the brains or the initiative to organise themselves and stand together so firmly. A life of contentment had turned into a life of misery and fear.

Major Cook had by now slipped back into the old army routine with great joy, for he had been ashamed of his farming occupation compared to his old army life. He was only too eager to seize the opportunity of becoming an active Major again. Although he was younger than many of them, the settlers had approached him many times to ask for his advice, much to his pride and joy, and he thrilled with power when he threatened his workers with pistols and made them cringe. Life had become just one eternity of self-glory. This was soon shattered, however, when the settlers, finding him to be big-mouthed and nothing else, rallied back to Lord Monckley, petitioning him to lead them through this reign of terror. They gave Monckley unreserved support, thus preventing him from retiring from the field of politics, much to his cynical amusement. Cook never really recovered from that blow, but he began campaigning to lead the settlers in the battlefield instead of in the Legislative Council.

Many European patrols made reconnaissance trips through Naro town. On one particular occasion the patrol met about fifteen people, all youths, who had travelled, as it became known later, from Nairobi to bring directives to Nundu in the valley. These young people, who looked extremely innocent, were challenged and when they refused to stop, Kiko ordered the patrol to shoot them down. To

108

his amazement, before the patrol had time to cock their guns, a heavy automatic rifle was fired at *them* from the bushes and instantly, three men fell to the ground. The African youths seized their chance and fled, leaving a stupefied patrol behind them. Although the attackers were pursued quite relentlessly, together with the youths, the Police failed to find any of them. This incident was the first of its kind in Naro District for, up until then, not one European had been killed there. Kiko convened an urgent meeting of the settlers the following morning. As a result the farm on which the incident had occurred was raided and every man arrested and taken to the Police Station into the eager hands of Frank Jones.

They were beaten ruthlessly with rubber hoses and kicked with nailed boots, and when they still refused to talk, they were given severe electric shocks and made to lie in icy water all night. Many were castrated with a pair of pliers, but to no avail. They refused to speak. Two died at the Police Station and the others were returned to the farm, many of them very near to death, but not one was cowed and not one hid the hatred in his heart. The information wanted was who had killed the settlers' sons and where they were hiding. Where the weapon had come from was still unknown and Naro Town was thunderstruck. This incident started a spate of atrocities against the African workers of a like nature, and many more fled to the forests.

Nundu received those who fled with great joy, regardless of whether they had taken any oaths or not. Nothing could have helped him more with his recruitment campaign than this incident. He administered oaths and formed the oath takers into subgroups under his command. They were directed to terrorise the whole area each night and force their people to accept the movement, take the oath and join its ranks.

The situation deteriorated yet further and Kiko hastily convened a committee meeting at which many decisions were made. He then summoned the settlers to a general meeting to inform them of the resolutions passed. Lord Monckley promised to attend. He had now regained his former power and his constituents rallied to him eagerly and, as he was a first world war veteran, he was consulted on all security matters.

When Cook and Monckley entered the club hall it was very apparent that the Naro European Settlers had lost hope, for out of all the settlers in the area only about half had arrived and no wives or children were present. The few huddled together listlessly in little silent groups, fear written over their faces. They watched Cook and Monckley mount the rostrum apathetically, giving them no sign of recognition.

Cook cleared his throat rather loudly and looked down at his comrades who were still huddled together, but had, with some semblance of order, seated themselves at the back of the room.

"Ladies and gentlemen," he said, "I know very well that you are all anxious to get back to your homes. I know too that you are all wondering what is happening to your families or, if you have sent your wives and children away, to your houses, stores, livestock. I'll therefore make this very short and get to the point straight away. We called this meeting to bring you up to date on the movements of our Security Committee. It was decided that security outposts should be set up next week, for Frank Jones has promised to find the money and men. I know I've said that before, but we were hampered by lack of funds. Now, our Member of the Legislative Council here has promised to find us the necessary funds even if he has to foot the bill from his own pocket. We are starting to build these outposts next week for Frank Jones has promised to find us the men. Our District Officer is going to provide us with artisans and so we are well away." He stopped, expecting applause, but was met with stony silence. "You people have a great deal to be grateful for, you know. After all, we know what kind of things have been happening all over the country, but we have organised our security forces so well that very little has occurred in this district. The terrorists are too scared to touch us. They caught us once on patrol, but never again. We are safe from them and will continue to be so whilst we stand together. Don't give up hope — that would be fatal. Now, I call upon Lord Monckley to verify what I have said." He sat down amidst some rather desultory clapping which changed into definite applause as Monckley stood up.

"Thank you all," he said. "I'll not keep you long for I too know how anxious you must be and how impatient you are to get home; how scared you are of what you might find when you arrive. I only wish to reiterate what Major Cook said. I am in full support of this project and will find all the cash necessary, even if I have to pay myself. This District is very well organised, in fact, from the security side, it is the best in the whole country. We've had very, very few incidents here, and while we keep up to scratch, it will remain that way. Courage, my friends. I am now going straight back to Nairobi to raise the money to build these outposts: can I do more?" He sat down, well pleased with the clapping that followed.

The settlers immediately left the Club and hurried to their various homes. The Police had warned all the residents of the area to be particularly careful not to leave their families alone at night for it was feared that the terrorists might kill them. No more drinking in the Club until the early hours of the morning for them; in fact, none of them left their farms unless it was absolutely necessary.

The members of the Security Committee surveyed each other ruefully as they settled down to the real business of the evening — to decide where the outposts were to be built and the number of soldiers and arms to be stationed at each one.

"They are like frightened sheep," Carey remarked. "Oh, what a terrible state things have got into. If we let

111

their attitude prevail we'll never get anywhere. Shall we proceed?" The others nodded their heads in agreement and sat down, rather dispiritedly, to settle the details.

By now, circumstances had compelled a great number of people to go into hiding: in the forests, bushes, valleys, anywhere where the security forces would not find them. Some lived in complete isolation and refused to open their doors even to their closest friends. By this time the British soldiers, or "Johnnies" as they were called, had arrived in their thousands to assist in the implementation of the emergency laws. The people were very puzzled by these troops as they did not seem to speak the same English as the settlers. Even the educated African was unable to understand their varied dialects. As a result the Africans thought that they had nearly defeated the settlers who were so determined to stay in the country that they had sent for help from other European nations. In these troops they saw the determination of the European to exterminate the African as the Australians had practically wiped out the Aborigines. This quite obviously aggravated an already dangerous situation, for the ordinary people turned to the educated African for advice and assistance, and when they were told that "foreigners" had invaded their territories, their desperation knew no bounds. The "Johnnies" shot many Africans on sight and raped young girls and women of all ages in various villages, and the people quite naturally thought that their country was at war. Even those who held moderate views were severely shaken, although up till now the idea of war was but a key word in political speeches, it became clear to all that it was a reality — the white man was out not only to conquer but to despoil and ruin a people who had very high moral and traditional standards. Bitterness swept through the country like wildfire and many young men found themselves unable to sit idle and witness their mothers, sisters and families being molested and humiliated in their presence. Yet more fled to the forests.

Karoki was one of these young men, for although he

had already taken one oath, he shrank from shedding blood and was therefore not a wholehearted supporter of the Cause. He, his sister, his elder brother's wife and his mother were cultivating their shamba in the reserve when news was brought of the Johnnies' approach. Quite innocently, they continued with their work until they suddenly found themselves surrounded by soldiers threatening them with rifles. They watched in horror as the soldiers herded the rest of the family out of their hut and razed it to the ground. Karoki watched his grandfather, an old man of about sixty, being kicked and beaten because he was too old to move as fast as the soldiers wished. He watched his father try to help his grandfather, and whimpered in despair as he saw a rifle butt descend on his father's head. They dragged both his father and grandfather to the middle of the circle, laughing and joking. Karoki bent desperately over

them and screamed in horror, for his father was dead. He was kicked in the face and forced to stand back. He struggled impotently as he watched his womenfolk being forced to the ground and raped. He heard their cries of shame and misery, as he heard the soldiers' jeering laughs. One of them hit him over the head to quieten him, and he sank into merciful oblivion. When he regained consciousness, he saw his mother and sister weeping over the body of his father, their clothes ripped to shreds, and his grandfather writhing on the ground. He swore then that he would kill all white men, and ran to the forest determined to revenge the horrid murder and the shame and indignity that this affair had brought to his family. He was torn with grief, and the forest was his only outlet.

Njogu, who by now had left Nairobi, was the man in charge of this area. The idea that anyone should perpetrate an outrage of this nature astounded him and he immediately went to Nairobi to seek guidance from his leaders. He emerged from the meeting triumphant because he had been authorised to form a permanent company in the area, and sub-groups of commandos, all of which he was to lead. As it was possible that his company would fight in the same forest as Nundu's, he was advised to co-ordinate his activities with those of Nundu even more closely. When he arrived home he confided in his closest friends and since many of them had suffered in the same way they followed him without question. They left for the forest hastily before the security forces discovered their movements. Their preparation was made in complete secrecy and still only the foremost leaders knew exactly what was happening. Only the old people and the youngsters, apart from their mothers and those who had not already taken the oath, missed them, and it was taken for granted that they had gone secretly to Nairobi and other big towns. It was still not known by the masses that the so-called terrorists were forming armies in the forests.

Life in the forests was hard and demanding. The organisation promised to give its members warm clothes. The supply of these, and also food, was being arranged between the central and local leaders; but even so, they could build no houses or fires, and they were forbidden to wash with soap in case the wild animals scented their presence. Events were moving more rapidly than ever. Both Nundu and Njogu had been forced to form bands of commandos of which they were the leaders. This necessitated complete and absolute co-ordination of their moves. There was no time to waste in duplicating activities, especially those concerning the supply of food and ammunition. Toga meanwhile was still busily organising his gun factory and Njogu and Nundu with this in mind arranged to hold a sub-divisional leaders' meeting there on the following Saturday night and the whole of Sunday. The holding of a public meeting on Sunday was a particularly clever idea, as not even the Security Forces molested people whom they took to be going to a place of worship, so although many people were expected to attend from distant villages and localities, as well as some dignitaries of the liberation army from Nairobi, Njogu was confident that the Authorities would let them through. Many churches were scattered over the country and they were all surrounded by a maze of footpaths — a very convenient cover.

Nundu and his group moved at night only. Apart from the danger of discovery by the Security Forces, there was the even more intense danger of betrayal by one of their own kind and so it took them four days to reach the owl caves. It was widely broadcast on the grapevine that some of the *Ihii* were in the district — naturally only the foodbearers who brought baskets of ceremonial food and gourds of sugarcane beer, and the group's closest relatives, knew where they were. Stringent measures had been taken to ensure complete secrecy and not even those who had taken the first oath were informed of Nundu's whereabouts — the Government was offering large bribes to informers, for it was only too eager to seize and perhaps hang any "terrorists."

115

When Nundu's mother heard that he was nearby, she immediately hastened to see him. They had not met since he had gone into hiding at Naro, and she wept bitterly many times at the dangerous course her beloved son had taken. Nundu, on the other hand, was very reluctant to see his mother for he knew how much worry he was causing her and he was ashamed of himself. She called at Toga's house on Saturday afternoon, laden with food. Immediately Toga sent for a young man to escort her to the hideout. They walked across the valley over the footpath that looked abandoned, although much used, and she shivered with fear as she passed through the eerie patch of tropical forest and approached the caves. When they entered, she looked around in amazement and wonder, for it was almost as if she had entered a small village, so many inlets into the rock were there. The innermost caves were used by Toga and the surroundings were kept carefully camouflaged to prevent detection. Nundu and his band used one of these caves to hide in and they were provided with blankets so that they could sleep comfortably and safely to compensate for their many sleepless nights. Nundu had ordered the scouts who were guarding the caves to report to him immediately if there was any danger, and gave strict instructions that he was not to be disturbed by visitors. On seeing Nundu's mother, the scouts were very perturbed for they feared Nundu's wrath, but eventually she persuaded them to take her to him. He was lying half awake when she entered and for a moment the mother thought her guides had been mistaken for she did not recognise her son. He had grown a long, shaggy beard which, together with a shock of hair, was matted with dirt for he was unable to wash. His body, clothed in animal hides, reeked of sweat and, above all, he had become considerably fatter and had grown several inches in stature since she had last seen him. He was a terrifying figure even to those who knew him well. His mother started to sob bitterly.

"My son, my son, is it really you?" she cried. "What have they done to you? You have almost turned into a wild animal and I hardly recognise you. Are you happy, are you well?"

"Mother, do stop crying. Of course I am well and happy," replied Nundu impatiently. "How are you, my father, my brothers and sisters?"

"They are well, my son; do you not miss us? Do you not want to come back home?" his mother replied.

"No!" said Nundu shortly.

"Nundu!!" she exclaimed in horror. "Do you know what you are saying to me, your mother? What has happened to you? How can you prefer to live as an animal when you have such a happy home; when we are all begging you to return?" She fell on her knees, grasped Nundu's legs and gazed up into a stranger's face. "Nundu, Nundu, come home. Forget all this. Don't you realise that if they catch you they will beat you and kill you? Have you no respect for our love and need for you?"

Nundu pushed her aside and snapped, "Oh Mother, leave me alone, will you? Don't you understand that I am your son no longer? Now go back the way you came. It is dusk now and no one will see you. If you tell anyone where you have been, I shall die all the quicker and my men with me. Go, woman, go." He turned away abruptly.

The elderly woman, blinded by tears, groped her way out of the cave and was sympathetically shown the way back to Toga's house.

As soon as darkness fell, those summoned began to congregate, each muttering the password as he entered the caves. Young girls appeared bearing a great variety of foods and a large quantity of freshly roasted meat. Many of the youths present had been assigned to sentry posts, strategically situated, to enable them to give the alarm should security forces approach — it was the most highly intensified watch yet made. It was an ideal night for such a meeting, for the moon was hidden behind great black clouds, the rain poured down, and the ghostly hoot of the owls echoed over the drip, drip of the water. Lightning flashed, thunder roared, and the latecomers shivered as they hastened into the dry musky warmth of the caves. The freedom fighters were easily recognisable, and indeed one could almost gauge the period they had been in hiding from the length of their hair and beards. They assembled in the largest and innermost cave, satisfying their hunger and talking quietly. When they had all arrived, Njogu clapped his hands. Immediate silence fell and they sat down by the craggy cave sides with a discipline equal to that of any army.

Njogu, who was both Chairman and host, held a roll-call. When he was completely satisfied that no unauthorised person was present, he declared the meeting open.

"My comrades in arms, brothers and sisters. We must first of all thank our god of Kirinyaga for bringing us safely together here today. I call upon Mzee Koi to lead us in prayer."

Mzee Koi stood up and ordered all present to face Mount Kenya. "Oh God of the black man and the God of Kirinyaga, bless all those who have come to attend this meeting. We thank you, oh God, the greatest of all, for our safe journey. We pray to you, oh God of all black men, to guide and protect us during this meeting and to see us safely back to our homes and hideouts. Oh be stronger than the god of the white man! Defeat him and give us what our ancestors and forefathers have demanded for so long — our land and freedom. Oh greatest of great gods, our God of Kirinyaga, bless us."

The old man then sat down near Njogu who rose to address his audience. "Now, you all know why this meeting has been convened. It is too dangerous for leaders to be known by their own names any longer — the security forces are very brutal to those whom they capture and if we are betrayed by weaklings, it will mean death to the Cause.

118

We have therefore decided to adopt animal names and I can assure you it is a very necessary precaution. I would now like to introduce to you two very high ranking officers — here is Simba, whose duty it is to assist us with the proceedings and report back to High Command in Nairobi, and from Naro we have Kifaru, who will address you later.

"It is common knowledge that the white settlers have intensified their torture of our people in the so called white areas. They have formed bands of soldiers; some of these men are but youths; they were born on our forefathers' land. But things are going rapidly from bad to worse. We have now thousands of white soldiers here from over the seas. Neither they nor the others know or understand our customs — the customs that have been handed down from generation to generation. They are enforcing the Emergency laws and care not who they kill, maim or rape. These laws have disrupted not only our normal lives but the life, the very heartbeat of our Nation. Why, even I, who am educated, cannot understand these strange laws or understand the foreign languages these strangers speak. You all know the way they have attacked our leaders, the spate of untruths that have been written in the press, spoken on the news, read from the Church pulpits. Yes, my friends, from the very house of the white man's god comes invective and hate. Many of our beloved leaders have been educated both here and overseas. They speak English, understand it. They can read, write, organise — why, the majority of them are far, far better educated than many *Kaburus* out here! You know I speak the truth when I say this. But these mad dogs have arrested our revered leaders. They have passed judgement on them. The white man's Government has had the audacity to snatch away from us those who are our stronghold; those whom Kirinyaga has sent to lead and guide us through these terrible times. It has thrown them into prison and it has been recommended to the Supreme Court that they should be forbidden to return to their people ever again. This recommendation, oh my brothers, will succeed, have no doubt about that, for are not those

119

who passed judgement also going to ensure that this recommendation be accepted? It is therefore useless for us to appeal. How can black men be treated fairly by laws enforced by white men? Our beloved leaders will therefore be exiled in the country that is theirs, ours." Njogu stopped a moment, shaken with emotion; horror and sorrow were to be seen written on the faces of his listeners.

A deathly hush filled the caves as each and every man and woman present absorbed the full implications of Njogu's statement.

Njogu brushed the tears away from his eyes and continued. "The whites who call themselves police, security forces and so on, have no regard for our human dignity. They are subjecting us to a fate worse than death. We are facing harsh reality now. When one white man is killed they slaughter a hundred of our people, they wound and disable at least five hundred and those left alive are thrown into detention camps where they are herded like sheep. The Johnnies rape our wives and daughters in front of our eyes whilst the white government looks on in approval. The stooges of the Government, the chiefs, headmen and tribal police have assumed such powers that they shoot on sight if they are refused any request they may make. How many of you have had relatives who have been shot because they refused to let these worms touch their wives and daughters, refused to give them access to their personal property? Why, if you do not stand when one of these men passes by, even at a distance, you will be arrested and tortured in the Chiefs' camp by askaris. Believe me my friends, in the towns conditions are far worse." He held up his hand for silence as a roar of anger echoed through the cave. "Please be silent, for you know how sound carries. The atmosphere is laden with resentment and hatred, but for the moment this hatred must remain dormant or we will all be seized. In the towns people are being killed at random; in most cases just because a white man doesn't like a particular black face. The conditions in the reserve are indescribable. So many of our people are illiterate and

120

they are being subjected to laws which they could never understand. All the small people of the Government, the chiefs and headmen, have made life intolerable and we are suffering untold indignities never experienced before. They are protected. They can do any wrong — even shoot those concerned in boundary disputes, and they receive no reprimand. The tortures they use are too ghastly to describe. The white man's Government expects us to tolerate this. We are not mice, we are men. Which of you here is prepared to let this state of affairs continue? Why, I would rather die than live under these self-elected overlords." He stopped, again overcome by his feelings, and realised that most of his audience were weeping. "I have said enough," he sighed. "But I must tell you that it is for these reasons that we have decided to take action against the enemies of our people, our children and our children's children. I pray to Kirinyaga that you will follow those of your leaders who remain with you and abide by their decisions. I now have the honour to invite our brother Kifaru of Naro to speak. He will tell you all about the events in Naro."

Nundu summed up very briefly the experiences he and his group had suffered, and exhorted the meeting to follow its leaders. Then Simba, from High Command, emphasised the support of all the commanders and committees and reiterated that the liberation hour was near at hand and that it was their duty to hit and hit hard.

After a debate lasting many hours, it was resolved to elect committees to deal with supplies, information, propaganda, security, scouts and disciplinary action, and to elect Kifaru (Nundu) as Chief of Staff and Njogu as General. The committees were empowered to cope with details and to pass their recommendations to the General and Kifaru who would make the final decisions. These two, together with Mrefu, formed the Supreme Command for the area.

Njogu declared the meeting closed in the very early hours of the morning. After the old man had once more

121

E

prayed to Kirinyaga, the delegates were asked not to go in big groups, to avoid detection. They dispersed in small groups at ten-minute intervals except those who had been elected Committee Members, whose duty it was to stay and complete the business in hand throughout Sunday.

By 6 p.m. on Sunday evening, the discussions were over and the Supreme Command had passed the final drafts. It was decided that the railway personnel be bribed to transport supplies along the line, and if possible they should be persuaded to take the oath. Women and girls were to use their baskets to carry food to the edge of the forests and leave it at pre-arranged places hidden in the undergrowth or covered by branches. From there the *Ihii* were to collect them at night or at any other convenient time. Any messages for the *Ihii* were to be left with the food. Singing groups were to be formed to popularise the freedom songs with the young people. The success of the Freedom Fighters and the weakness of the Government Security Forces was to be broadcast and propagandized in an exaggerated manner both in the towns and in the country. The imprisoned leaders' names, together with the Supreme Command officers, were to be praised so that their names became a byword. It was to be stressed to the general public that they were not to listen to the radio propaganda of the whites and their agents, nor were they even to touch the many leaflets which were in circulation. Agents were to be planted in the Security Forces and government offices who could pass on essential information to their leaders with regard to the movement of Security Forces and troops. The innocent-seeming elements of the people were to be recruited — the old folk and young children. They were to report immediately any suspicious moves by the whites, recruit more to the Cause and guard against any false codes or names being invented to confuse the issue. As soon as there was any danger of discovery, the *Wazee* were empowered to change the codes and inform the Supreme Command immediately. Special greetings were only to be known by members. Passwords were invented and certain ways of knocking at doors. If any member of the movement betrayed his oath or rank he would be guilty of a dire crime which was punishable by the disciplinary committees; the more serious crimes by shooting or public hanging. A disciplinary committee was to be formed in every gang.

Nundu, extremely proud of his *nom de plume*, Kifaru, and Njogu, now known as General, and the members of the Committee, left the caves at dusk and they went to Toga's house for refreshment. As a necessary precaution they scattered themselves in pairs throughout twenty huts and Nundu promised to start his journey back to the forest at 1 a.m. with his colleagues.

One of the tribal policemen in the village, in civilian clothing, had noted with grave concern the unusual activity in the village. When, on his way to the chief's camp, he spotted two fierce-looking young men, he suspected immediately that they belonged to the Movement and ran to the Chief's house to report. The Chief ordered a thorough search of the whole village and commanded his men to shoot on sight anyone who ran away. Twenty askaris therefore made their way towards the village in a small lorry. As soon as the lights were seen the people, who were merrymaking, realised something was very wrong. Soon the askaris arrived and wasted no time in beating the women with rifle butts to extract information. Screams echoed over the valley and Kifaru and his company picked up their guns and fled down the footpath away from the village, hastily loading their weapons as they ran into the valley. Soon they heard footsteps behind them, but they ran all the faster for they did not dare to shoot fearing the consequences on the kind people who had sheltered them. Their pursuers drew relentlessly nearer and suddenly Kifaru ducked as a bullet whistled past his head and powerful flashlights shone over the group. They flattened themselves on the ground and gazed back up the path. Suddenly they saw two whites and five Police Constables running towards them. Nundu, who went blind with hatred whenever he saw a white man, immediately fired and the whole group opened fire, taking

123

their pursuers so much by surprise that they were dead within a minute. Kifaru and a couple of his group ran back up the path, took the dead men's guns and then they all ran towards the big trees which flanked the main road so that no one would see them. They did not dare journey along the main road so they took short cuts, and as the first rays of the sun filtered through the trees, they had managed to cover thirty miles. Since they knew no one who lived near the path which they had followed, they decided to rest awhile, hiding in the papyrus grass growing by the river. They were completely exhausted and unable to go any further, although the forest was only about seven miles away — so near yet so far. They were all gripped with a terrible fear. What had happened to Njogu, for he had not accompanied them? Was he dead? Had he been arrested? Even these tough men were unable to be philosophical about the fate of a dear friend and a revered leader. Tracker planes, flying very low, occasionally spraying the countryside bordering the forest with machine gun bullets made their blood turn cold — how were they going to reach the forest in safety?

7 REVENGE

Lord Monckley kept his promise to donate money to finance the erection of Security Posts around Naro — his constituency — at strategic points which had been chosen by Frank Jones. The District Officer, Carey Milton, who had full powers under the Emergency Laws to control the movement of Africans, authorise the carrying of guns, detain all and sundry and allocate work to those whom he detained, recommended that as many of the police posts as possible should be built along Naro. It was essential for Major Cook to have one on his farm because of its isolation: it bordered the forest reserve and was therefore considered the most dangerous spot in the District. The District Officer and Police Chief agreed to co-ordinate their work. The Chiefs and Headmen were empowered to assist them in their interrogation of suspects, and these suspects could be used by the Administration for hard labour which was most convenient. Home Guard groups were formed in the area under a Headman controlled by the Chief, and the members of a blissful European community were sure their security arrangements were becoming so stringent that nothing could harm them. As a matter of interest, the Government eventually did step into the breach and aided the settlers financially to build the outposts.

These outposts consisted of a main office and a control room, with a police cell, police sleeping quarters, a canteen and four watch towers — one in each corner surrounded by a seven-foot cedar and barbed wire fence with poles at six inch intervals with the wire turned over at the top for a width of three feet to prevent intruders climbing over. The whole camp was surrounded by a moat approximately ten by fifteen feet, and a drawbridge stretched across it at the main entrance which was only lowered in the day time. All the outposts were built in this fashion, and even the chiefs, who were beginning to fear for their lives, adopted this mode of construction. Most of the commanders of these Police Posts were settlers who were working in the Police Reserve which was another "Europeans and Asians only" body. In the Administrative posts, tribal police were on guard, and Sergeant Majors were in command, with the chiefs' consent, of the patrol area. The patrols were normally pre-arranged between the forces to avoid duplication and possible confusion for if they met each other at night the result could only be a battle between friendly sides.

When the Police Posts were completed, there were as many as six hundred detainees in Naro. Their work which was mainly to thatch and plaster the mud walls and, when the building was finished, erect the fences and dig the trenches, was used as brute labour. Rifle butts, rhinoceros hide whips and an occasional shot in the air were all in the order of the day.

The detainees, performing this type of work for the first time, were regarded with curiosity amounting to horror by their free comrades. They were fed once a day with stiff maize meal porridge with sometimes a handful of boiled beans thrown in. This was supposed to give them enough strength to work nine hours a day. Their friends were too scared to come near them, especially after witnessing several brutal beatings. More and more people were detained and camps sprung up like mushrooms — to the bewilderment of the populace who really had no idea what it was all about. Nundu took advantage of this to spread the rumour that the white man was going to exterminate all the black men, especially the educated ones but excepting the stooges who were now cynically called "good boys". The irony of the situation was that, of the many hundreds who were being detained, only a few were hard core freedom fighters or had even participated in the liberation movement. They were arrested in most cases if their employers bore a grudge against them or feared them. The detainees were interrogated most cruelly, the settlers using the same methods of persuasion as they did when two of their sons were killed. Some of them went even further for many of the prisoners were secretly taken into the forest and executed by a firing squad. One very popular method of decimating the Africans, which was used mainly by the younger white men and regarded as a type of sport, was to tell the man concerned to run into the forest, in fact forcing him to run, and then shooting him down with automatic weapons. The bodies were left for the vultures and hyenas to devour — thus even a proper burial was denied them. Many of the detainees died either from hunger or from their beatings. Others were eventually sent to the reserves where they had never lived, for they had been born on the farms and lived on them all their lives. When their fathers were murdered however, there was nothing else to do with them. Those who were not sent to the reserves lived as slaves working either in the police lines or in the detention can 's, and the camps that were used as transit posts before they were transferred to bigger prisons. The settlers were becoming very apt at interrogation and the torture and misery, not only for the newcomers but for the inmates, was intensified and no breathing space was given to them.

Nundu had stamp d his name on the pages of history by this time. Who had performed braver actions than he? He had shot two police officers, white men too, had killed the five askaris in the reserve and had taken all their guns. Truly he was revered by all who knew of his feats. As far as the Europeans were concerned, the security of the area had deteriorated so much after this latter incident that the Government ordered the soldiers to move into the area round the forest, fully equipped with tanks and all the necessary paraphernalia, supported as well by the tribal police. Policemen in their thousands had been moved into the area for patrol purposes for the Government was determined to capture the terrorists and it did not mind what sort of condition they were in when brought in.

Njogu, who had managed to slip out of the village in the furore, knew very well what would happen as a result of the death of the askaris. Before he left, therefore, he ordered all the young men to leave the village and go to the forest during the night before the Europeans could organise themselves. It was only a ten-mile journey, but if the British Johnnies met them, they would suffer dire consequences — maybe even lose their lives, or suffer disablement through torture.

Meanwhile Nundu had decided to travel through the valley with his band, their weapons hidden under their clothes, and ducking for cover when they heard an aeroplane approach. Thus a ten-mile journey took them half a day, and no one was more relieved than they when they eventually reached the forest boundaries. Those of his company, who up till now had home-made guns, exchanged them for the automatic weapons they had stolen from the dead askaris. His followers were very proud of themselves and of him. Nundu was positively crowing, for he knew how famous this incident would make him. Once they were safely within the forest, he decided that two of them should hunt for an antelope as they had not eaten for twenty-four hours. He therefore ordered Wenye to stay with him, and the others to climb a small hill nearby to watch for possible pursuers. Wenye and Nundu turned and were just about to disappear into the thicket when a loud cry made them swing round.

"Shut up, you fool! Do you want all the Johnnies in the forest to hear you?" snapped Nundi.

"Nundu, Nundu, come here. Look, look!" whispered Iru, the tears streaming down his face.

Swearing under his breath, Nundu climbed the hillock followed by Wenye, and stood aghast. The horizon in the direction of the owl caves was scarlet with the reflection of flames, and in their imagination they could hear the shrieks and cries of the occupants of the hidden village.

"Swine! Cruel, cruel swine!" muttered Nundu impotently.

"They are burning them all to death," gasped Heho. "Oh why did we shoot those askaris down? Poor, poor people, and they were so friendly and sympathetic to us!"

As was usual in any emergency they looked to Nundu for guidance. Nundu whispered: "Let us pray to Kirinyaga for their safety. There is not much else we can do at the moment." He then spoke words of fearful invective as if they were torn from his very soul.

They all knelt down, facing Mount Kenya, and prayed for the safety of the people who had shown them such hospitality and who were now being tortured and perhaps burned to death. They also prayed for Njogu and Toga, not knowing if they were safe.

"Well, I suppose we'd better find ourselves some supper," said Iru, "although I don't think anyone feels like it."

"What's that?" asked Nundu listlessly. "Yes, I suppose we've got to eat to keep ourselves fit. Iru and Wenye, you go. I've no heart for the hunt today. Use the new rifles — Toga does his work well, but they far surpass his guns. Oh no!" He stopped dead as a thought struck him. "What has become of Toga? He can't get around quickly with that false leg of his, and if they've burned all the thicket round the caves, they must have discovered the owl caves. I'm going back."

"Don't be an idiot!" said Wenye, the steadying influence in the band. "What good can you, one man, do against perhaps thousands? No, your job is to stay here and lead us. Truly, our hearts are breaking, but to throw you, and through you, us, into certain death will not help the Cause. I'm sure Toga had the good sense to get out. Anyhow, we'll hear all about it in a few hours or so." He laid a brotherly hand on Nundu's shoulder. "Steady yourself brother. We'll pay them back, and in the meantime Iru and I will find a nice fat buck to eat and then I'm sure we'll all feel a lot better."

They constructed a camouflage for the fire, so that the spotter planes would not see the smoke, out of four poles with "v" shaped tops planted firmly in the ground. They huddled round the fire in a miserable group, and kept alternate watch over the camp during the night, except for Nundu who, with his prerogative as Commander, relaxed undisturbed. As soon as dawn broke, they removed all traces of their presence and started to walk in the direction of Naro, about thirty miles away, through the dense forest, following the elephant and buffalo paths. Besides the weapons they were carrying, they had large chunks of meat which had remained from the previous night's kill. They hoped to reach Naro in time for supper if all went well, but just as they set off, they heard the sound of aeroplanes flying very low and they were forced to duck back into the undergrowth. They hugged the ground face downwards, for they knew that, even in the darkness of the forest, their eyes and fingernails could be spotted. Just before the planes eventually gave up the search in the late afternoon, they heard a few shots about three miles away up the path on which they were hoping to travel. They therefore had to change course yet again, and the short cut to Naro grew longer and longer. As a matter of fact, these shots were fired by Europeans who had just joined the Police Force and were using the outskirts of the forest for target practice, but Kifaru knew nothing of this and he and his band shivered as they heard them. Unfortunately for the little group, this forest abounded in wild game and they were forced to seek refuge in trees many times. They were continually meeting elephant, rhino and buffalo, who chased them, but they did not dare to shoot for fear of revealing their whereabouts.

Dusk found them still far from Naro and so they decided to rest awhile until the moon rose to give them sufficient light to make their way through a part of the forest that was completely strange to them. After a further three hours' walk, they reached the outskirts of Naro with barely enough time to slip into the valley before dawn.

They decided even so to see Mrefu before they went back into hiding in order to arrange for their normal food rations to be supplied again, for they had been away from the valley many days. His house, luckily, was unguarded and he welcomed them with open arms, although very

130

apprehensively, for he too feared detection. The tears of joy streamed down his face to find they were still alive. Njogu had sent somebody immediately after the village had been burned to Mrefu to find out whether Nundu had reached Naro, and since the band had been in the forest almost three days, they were feared dead. It was felt by all who knew him that if Nundu had been killed their organisation would topple for there was no one who could equal his courage and tenacity.

"I had feared you dead, Nundu," said Mrefu. "Thank God you are here, and your band too, all safe and sound." No one had told him that Nundu's new name was Kifaru.

"Oh Mrefu, my father, I am here, but we cannot stay for dawn is nearly breaking. We are all right, but you must remember to call me Kifaru now. I am Nundu no longer."

The older man embraced him, and with an effort pulled himself together. "I will hear all your experiences and deeds later on this evening, for then I will come to visit you at the caves. Meanwhile, what are the papers you are holding?"

"They are for you, Mrefu. They are the report of the conference, and you must read them immediately for we have to take action on them without delay. Can you ask the women to start supplying us with food again? Tell us, are Njogu and Toga safe? Did they escape the anger of the white man? What news of the village?"

"Yes, they have survived and they are waiting at the caves for you."

"Thank God," Nundu breathed a silent prayer of thanks. "Then we shall want food for . . ." He stopped, and there was a rather embarrassed silence. This was caused by the old tradition that it would bring ill luck if people

131

were counted numerically. Mrefu cut in:

"Dear brother, let me recap briefly for you. Just after you left the village, the white soldiers swooped on it and razed it to the ground. Many of our women and children, apart from the men, were burned to death — especially the old people who couldn't move fast enough to get out of the huts in time. Njogu and Toga escaped, and truly Njogu is a brave man. Toga lost his wooden leg in the house — it was burned in the flames. Njogu dragged him out and somehow they managed to get here undetected."

"But Mrefu!" interjected Nundu, "Toga's house was in the Chief's compound. How come that it was burned?"

"The Johnnies burned everything in sight. The Chief arrived in time to save the rest of his compound being burned, but he knows Toga's work — they have discovered the owl caves, and so it was too dangerous for Toga to stay there. The others escaped too — I don't know how they did it. You'll find them all waiting anxiously for you at the caves. You know, apart from the fire, the Johnnies let loose with rifles. I think most of the villagers have been exterminated — if not from the flames and smoke, then from the wild bullets. They beat many too; but I have said that already. My mind must be wandering with grief. All the survivors, and they are few enough, are now living under banana trees — the women and children that is — the men, yes, even the old men who can barely move — have been taken to the detention camps. The suffering in that village is indescribable. Njogu fought bravely. He fired many shots at the oncoming Johnnies, but what could one man do against so many? Mind you, if he hadn't, Toga would never have escaped. He took them completely by surprise and that is how they got away — lucky are those that did. No medical care has been provided, and the few that have been taken to hospitals, if they live, will land up in detention camps." Mrefu broke off, the tears streaming down his face. "That's why they were taken to hospital . . ."

Nundu gazed at Mrefu in horror. "The tale you tell is too ghastly to imagine," he whispered. "I swear that we will avenge the sufferings of our people." He shuddered uncontrollably. "But, my brother, we must leave, or the same tale of blood and horror will be told of our people here if we do not. Read the documents and bring them to us tonight. Please, my brother," he begged, "if you are in danger flee with us; do not let them touch you."

Mrefu pressed his hand and they stood silently together, watching the others leave at three-minute intervals. After the last man had gone, Mrefu and Kifaru embraced, drawing comfort from each other and Kifaru sped out into the darkness.

Later that evening, Mrefu arrived at the caves and they gathered silently around him to hear the rest of his news. "Troops moved into Naro only yesterday," he said. "The new posts are occupied by either the despicable Johnnies or the Police, led of course by white soldiers. I have learned through my intelligence reports that they have started practice firing across the valley with a huge gun to intimidate the population. My brothers, it is a gun that no one dreamed ever existed. Why, I am told the ground shakes and the echoes reverberate in the hills when it is fired. You will see terror on every face. . . ."

"Have you not seen this terrible weapon yourself?" interjected Kifaru.

"Brother, I have not, neither will I, for it is guarded by hundreds of Johnnies and no one can approach safely. But if you listen you will hear it and that is enough. Apart from this, I hear that some of them are teaching our girls to be prostitutes by giving them money to sleep with them."

Kifaru buried his face in his hands to hide the very unmanly tears that were so close to manifesting themselves.

Mrefu touched his shoulder lightly. "Listen, brother, we have somehow got to keep our emotions under control and view these new events with a business-like approach, or we shall never get anywhere. It isn't easy to do, but then, neither will it be easy to defeat the white scum." He paused a moment, and then said thoughtfully, "I think we can prevent this outbreak of prostitution, but maybe we could also use it to our advantage."

"Mrefu! What are you saying?" shouted Iru in horror.

"You can't mean that you are going to encourage our innocent girls to become whores?" whispered Choti. "I only wish that Toga were here, for I know how strongly he would oppose you. But it is a filthy idea, do you hear me. . .?"

"Oh, shut up all of you!" snarled Kifaru fiercely. "This is no time to prate about morals." He turned to Mrefu. "What is it you have in mind?"

Mrefu shook his head sadly. "I too hate the idea as much as you do, but remember that the Cause and sacrifices for the Cause must wipe out every other objective. We can use these girls to our great advantage. They can make up to the soldiers and gather information from them; steal or buy their guns and ammunition. They can get plentiful supplies of food too, for we all know how vulnerable a man is if he is attracted by a woman."

"That is true," shouted Kifaru exultantly. "By this means, we can surely defeat them."

"I still think it is a despicable idea," murmured Choti sullenly.

"So do I, Choti," Iru replied, "and I want none of it."

"You fools!" spat Kifaru angrily. "Have we a lot of old women here? Perhaps," he sneered unpleasantly, "you are stooges of the white man. All right, go back to them. Go and see what they will give you."

They all gasped in horror at the implications of this spiteful remark, and as always, bowed under the strong influence of their leader.

"So be it, Kifaru; what you wish, we will do."

"So you are with me again?" laughed Nundu, well

pleased. "You'd better be, or by the god of Kirinyaga I will kill you where you stand."

Arrangements were, therefore, made to implement this decision, although only Nundu approved thoroughly of what they intended to do.

At this time, Nundu was a very unhappy man for he was suffering from a very strong internal conflict. On the one hand, he blamed himself for the razing of the village, and the terrible suffering that followed. On the other, he felt that maybe he wasn't responsible, for the soldiers had already started pillaging and destroying long before this particular event took place. He pushed all these thoughts away and, heedless of the presence of his companions, jumped up shouting, "Oh damn them all! Damn them!"

They looked up in surprise. "Why, what is the matter?" asked Choti.

Nundu explained the turmoil within himself, the words spurting out as if he was almost out of his mind with the great burden of guilt that he was carrying. He drew solace from his friends, who eventually persuaded him that he was not to blame, and they decided to take revenge by attacking a police post on Kiko's farm, in the dead of night and, if possible, to slaughter Kiko and raze his house and stores to the ground.

"After all," said Chui, "this man is notorious for his anti-black feelings and activities, and he must be made to pay for his evil deeds. We could start taking revenge in no more appropriate place."

They all gathered close around the fire and started to work out strategic plans for the attack which was to take place within a fortnight. More ammunition had to be purchased. Some of the girls who had joined the Movement had to be briefed, for they had a very important part to play. They were to study the movements of the soldiers and inform the gang in detail of the location of the various posts. Special stress had to be laid on the timing of patrols

135

and sentries. The buildings were to be attacked by two different groups, each group led by a steady man with an automatic weapon. The rest of the men were to be armed with daggers and stones to be thrown on the roof tops, and they were all to be instructed to shriek in an endeavour to throw the posts in a panic. Every bullet was precious and therefore no shooting was to take place unless it was absolutely essential. They hoped that a surprise attack coming from three different quarters would obviate the necessity to use precious ammunition, especially if the victims could be reached without it. Presuming that they succeeded in routing the soldiers, everyone was then to collect as much ammunition and as many guns as possible. The penalty for loss of a gun was death from a firing squad, for the group could not afford to lose even a pistol through careless fighting. It was agreed that Mrefu should organise the women and pass on their information to Kifaru. From then on they held intensified meetings to inform each man exactly what part he was to play.

On the evening of the attack, Nundu checked orders yet again, and their guns and supplies of bullets which were solemnly blessed by the Witchdoctor. Fate was on their side that night for Mwangi, Kiko's houseboy, had sent a message through a young girl who lived on the farm to the effect that Bwana would definitely be at his house that evening. They formed themselves into three groups and prepared to set out on their grim mission. One group was to attack from the front, only firing if fired upon. The second group was to guard the main farm entrance to prevent the entry of more security forces after the alarm was given. The third was to swoop on the police post. This was to be done simultaneously, for the element of surprise was the greatest weapon they had. The attack was to begin at exactly 1 a.m., and of course it was Kifaru who would give the command. As they had to carry sufficient petrol with them to pour over the roofs of the buildings, they summoned two young girls to help carry the *debes* over the six-mile journey and hide them as near the farm as was considered safe, and from where they could be easily taken to the buildings.

Although fighting was widespread over many areas of the country very little was reported in the papers, for the vernacular newspapers had long since been banned under the emergency laws. Scraps of information were handed out over the radio, but this source was denied to the forest men. Therefore, although they feared the unknown, each man was determined to prove his prowess, and as zero hour approached their fears grew stronger. This was their first planned fight for the Cause, and the consequences of failure were too terrible to bear consideration. Mrefu too feared for them, and that morning he had visited the camp to find out whether everything was going according to plan. He realised far more than they the implications and possible consequences of such a fight. It was then that he "gave the green light" to the Witchdoctor, and advised him to perform a very formal blessing ceremony which was to be their last comfort before the assault.

Toga had been requested to return home immediately after his arrival at Naro to continue his work. Therefore his advice, which would have helped to raise the morale of the men, was not forthcoming and Kifaru for one missed his steadying influence. The nearer the time came, the more apprehensive was Kifaru, and he wished more than ever that Toga could have been there. Although Kifaru had fought on his own, he was not all that self-confident when it came to total warfare, and expert advice like that which Toga gave was very hard to come by. But it was no real use relying on anyone else — this was his show. Njogu was not there either for, following instructions from Nairobi, he had been transferred to another district. Truly Kifaru was on his own, and lonely is the man with the power.

In an almost blind panic, Nundu decided to change his plans completely at the last moment. He divided his company into six groups with ten men per group. Three were to remain on guard at the caves which were daily being stacked with ammunition. Kifaru had decided to lead the group which was to attack the Police Post. Two more groups were to guard the entrances to Cook's farm, one was to attack Cook's house and the other one was to guard the major road to take care of any security forces which showed themselves. Each group commander had orders to start operations at 1 a.m. sharp. They were to remain in the middle of the groups at the major road and gate, and the major road group was to fire at the last vehicle to pass, and the gate group was to wipe out the enemy and cause complete panic. The group which was to attack the Police Post were to tie branches of trees around themselves for camouflage purposes.

Kifaru ordered all the group leaders to be in their respective positions at 1 a.m., and warned them sternly that any premature firing would mean extermination of them all. He summoned his group leaders to detail the new tactics of the battle to them — which included the names they were to use, the routes each group was to follow, and the positions of their men. In case of defeat, they were also told in which direction to escape and where they should meet after dawn. This meeting lasted for three hours and, as usual, dispersed after prayers to Kiranyaga. Whilst Kifaru was wishing each of his leaders every success, he noticed the gloomy faces of the fighters and the nervousness and uncertain atmosphere that pervaded the gloom. He therefore decided to address his men before they left, for he foresaw possible desertions which would not only make a mockery of his plans, but which would also cause certain death to others.

He called them together in the cave, and they crowded around him eager to hear him speak.

"Listen, my brothers, my comrades in arms, you have seen all our preparations for the battle tonight — a few changes of plan have been made, but your group leaders will brief you — and I have looked at your faces and seen that you are afraid. Believe me, I understand your feelings.

138

The message I have for you tonight as you prepare for your first battle is very important and you must listen carefully to my words. Our forefathers have died for this soil, and we shall wet it with our blood ... remember, a house which is not built with concrete will not stand. Our blood, perhaps yours and mine, perhaps that of many of our comrades, will have to be expended in building this firm house, our country, and in taking it away from the white man. All peaceful demands have failed, so now we have taken up weapons to force them to return our land. It is not an easy task for any of us. We all have homes and families, but it is because of them that Kirinyaga has entrusted this task to us; because he hears the desperate cries of our countrymen begging for freedom. I have been commanded to lead you in the name of Kirinyaga, for our mission is a sacred one, and our leaders have also been so blessed. So our laws are those of Kirinyaga, and therefore I must give you a stern warning. Desertion means death, and if any of you desert, Kirinyaga will find you and the longer it takes to find you the more horrible your death will be. You must fear the words of Kirinyaga spoken through your leaders far more than the white man. There is the death penalty too for anyone who loses his gun, or leaves it behind him. If you are wounded and you feel that your last hour has come, lie still and eat a little soil and Kirinyaga will find a safe place for you. He is the god above all gods, and we are his children. But this he will only do for you if you die honourably. Fight hard. Take all the guns you see, any uniforms that you can find. This has been ordered by our supreme commander. We must chase the white man off our soil. This is our land — Kirinyaga has spoken. Now, I wish you every success. Prepare yourselves for you will start in about two hours. Death to the white man is what you must say to yourselves when you fight. I must leave you now, for I too have to prepare. I will see all of you again when the time draws nearer. Rest awhile and do not fear." So saying, Nundu went into his personal cave which was reserved solely for him, his visitors and his secret papers. It was guarded

139

twenty-four hours out of the twenty-four, and so he had no fear of gate crashers interrupting his solitude which he needed so badly to try and stifle his ever-growing fears.

His followers gazed at one another in silence, never dreaming how frightened their leader was, each wishing in his own heart that he had never joined the Movement. Wenye, who was sitting quietly in the corner, whispered to one of his friends:

"Look, brother, there is no point worrying about the outcome, for even if we don't go and fight, after this strong warning from Kifaru, we will have nowhere to go and no one to turn to. We will be hunted like dogs and killed likewise. Apart from this, the people at home, especially the young men, are being shot on sight or sent to work in detention camps and treated like slaves. Believe me, that would be a hell on earth. What on earth is the use of us walking into it? Do you want to be tortured with electric shocks and beaten by rifle butts? I don't think Kifaru really needed to have warned us about deserting. Who would want people who never shave, never wash, who have long unkempt hair? They would know immediately that we belong to the forest, that we are the sons of the soil."

"You are right," replied his companion. "Here we eat and drink in peace; we are masters of the forest. But I feel nervous when we are expected to go and fight a well trained army, carrying only a few guns and daggers and stones. Well," he sighed. "I came here because there was no better place to live. Let's go and make ready."

They all dressed themselves and made sure that their knives were sharp, and a few of them tried to eat some meat, although few felt like food. Each group assembled and the silent night became full of frenzied whisperings and an occasional shout. Eventually, they fell silent and waited for their leaders to appear.

Mrefu visited the camp in the evening to brief Nundu on the latest moves of the troops and to give his blessing. He again stressed that the element of surprise was their greatest hope. Then he left them, very afraid of what might happen, especially after hearing that Nundu had changed his tactics at the last moment. The group leaders were then summoned into Nundu's cave. After about half an hour they reappeared, each holding an automatic rifle, their pockets bulging with ammunition and a few home-made guns. Every man present braced himself and the groups started out, each following a different route.

Nundu was the first to move. He and his band followed the line of the valley until they crossed the river and stealthily made their way over the plains that led to Kiko's farm and the Police Post which they intended to demolish. They moved in single file, each man twenty yards away from the first. They kept near to the main road for they feared meeting one of the many wild animals that prowled the bush at night — if they did it would mean premature firing and an immediate alarm. They were also afraid of losing their way for it was very dark. The only light they had was that of approaching cars and that meant they had to dive for cover every few minutes.

The four miles that normally took less than an hour was completed in one and a half hours because of the care they took. As soon as they reached the predetermined spot near the police post, they were ordered to crawl around the post and surround it. This had to be done in utter silence. Even a cough would have revealed their presence. They could do nothing but await the signal. Kifaru had already reminded them once again that each man was responsible for what he himself achieved; that the aim of all was to kill as many of the victims as possible, and to seize all the uniforms, weapons and ammunition that were available. He had told them too that if this raid was successful, their reputation would spread and that the whole country would hear and praise their courage, discipline and loyalty.

At five minutes to the hour Kifaru, who by this time had lost all fear of death in his determination to conquer, and his two closest friends, walked boldly towards the main entrance of the post. He was dressed as a Police Inspector and the two others were wearing askari uniform. Immediately came the expected call, "Halt! Who goes there?"

They halted smartly without hesitation and Nundu answered, "Inspector James on night patrol. I wish to see the Inspector in charge. Open up immediately."

"Yes, sir!" replied the constable, and with a firm salute he opened the barbed wire gate and saluted again as Kifaru and his "constables" marched in, Kifaru saluting as he passed the guard. Once inside, they quickened their pace and hurried to the duty office. "Where is the Inspector?" asked Kifaru of the duty officer. "Hurry man, hurry, where is he?"

"He's in Naro, sir, and hasn't returned yet, sir," the man stuttered.

"Well, what kind of place is this? Fetch me his deputy," Kifaru ordered peremptorily.

"Yes sir. He's asleep in his house — I will wake him up and bring him."

The duty officer rushed out of the office, leaving Nundu free to do his nefarious work. He ordered one of his guards to look for the key, but he could not find it. They found a six-round pistol which they took. Kifaru stood ready in the shadow of the door to shoot the officer at 1 a.m., praying that he would arrive in time. For this was the signal and he knew well that his men waiting so patiently outside in the bush would annihilate the fleeing policemen.

At this moment, the duty officer came running back and Kifaru, swearing under his breath, concealed the pistol under his coat, keeping his finger firmly on the trigger.

"Excuse me, sir!" the man gasped, breathless with running, "he is just coming. I found him awake because

one of his guards has just seen a crawling object outside the fence and they are wondering whether it was an animal or a human. Did you come across anything out there?"

"You fool!" spat Nundu, who was beginning to feel extremely afraid again. "If I had seen anything worth reporting I would have roused the camp. Now stay where you are. This post is useless and the men idle. Instead of fighting the enemy, some of you go to bed and others chase dark shadows that come with the night. I am going to see you punished for sleeping at the desk. That is how I found..." He broke off as he heard heavy footsteps approaching and saw the tall figure of the Sergeant Major looming out of the darkness.

The Sergeant saluted. "Yes sir, I have . . ." and Kifaru shot him five times, the shots echoing through the still night. His guards shot the constable and then immediately took shelter to fire on any who dared to approach them. Kifaru laughed exultantly. "They are all running!" he shouted. "Quickly fire the light mortar and we shall see." The sudden blaze of light showed uniformed men streaming through the gate and being met by Kifaru's men, who were quickly despatching them. Very few got away. A few of the constables who were guarding the towers started sending up distress rockets, but these too were soon stopped. Kifaru, in true military style, crept around the barracks and shot the few askaris that were hiding, and then he and his men, moving quicker than lightning, removed the uniforms and guns from the dying and dead men, raided the armoury, set the post alight, and rushed through the unguarded gate to make their way more cautiously than ever back to the caves with their spoils.

Once the urgency of the fight was over Nundu's mind turned again towards Kiko. Exalted by victory and inflamed by the sight of the dead and the smell of blood, he felt that he must find out as quickly as possible what had happened to his arch enemy. Life was not to be borne if it had to be shared with Kiko a moment longer. He should have led the raid on the house himself, not left it to others. At last, he could bear the anxiety no longer and, telling the rest of the gang to go back without him, he struck across country to investigate. When he arrived in sight of Kiko's house, he was alarmed to find no sign of any raid and a number of cars parked in the driveway.

"Had his men been surprised on the road?" he wondered in terror. He hid in a clump of bushes growing close to the door, determined to wait until the gathering dispersed so that he could listen to what was said, sure in this way that he would discover what had happened to his comrades. After about an hour, the door opened and several Europeans came out on the porch.

"Goodnight, old man," said one. "Mind you watch out for yourself. Remember you're number one target to these black swine."

"They won't venture in here," growled Cook's voice. "They know I'm armed and can take care of myself."

With that, the cars were started and Cook went back inside.

Kifaru breathed a sigh of relief. It was clear to him now what had happened: his men had seen the cars at the house and had either given up the venture for the night or were lying low somewhere in the vicinity. If the latter were the case, they would certainly wait until the victim had settled down for the night. They were not foolhardy enough to run blindly into gunfire.

Kifaru's heart beat furiously with excitement and the blood pounded in his ears like drumbeats. His chance had come! He would dare anything to get his hands round his enemy's throat. He waited till the porch light was off and then, silent and skilled as a game tracker, he began circling the house to find a means of entry.

All the windows were fastened and guarded by wire

and the curtains were closely drawn; but, a surprising oversight that filled him with evil joy, the windows were not shuttered. At last he found a small gap in the curtains of what proved to be Cook's bedroom. Crouching outside in the utter blackness of the night he looked through. Nobody was in the bedroom but the door beyond was open and a light shone inside. This, Nundu concluded, must be the door of the bathroom. Evidently Kiko was preparing for bed, washing his face, clothing his disgusting body in the orange and black pyjamas which he affected, and doing whatever it was he did do with the false teeth which closed the gap in the front of his mouth.

Soon he would come in, and then at last the time of reckoning would be upon him. The watcher was trembling with impatience as if with an ague and he felt as if his pounding blood was on fire. He was determined not only that Kiko should die, but that he should know that the moment of his death had arrived, and by whose hand his fate should be administered.

At last a shadow appeared on the bedroom floor thrown by the light in the bathroom behind. His enemy was coming! Nundu waited in a fever of impatience until Kiko was in full view, crossing the room towards the bed. Kiko's gun, he had already observed, was not in sight; probably it was under the pillow. With his own gun he smashed the glass of the window to smithereens. The noise of the splintering glass shattered the dead silence of the night and brought Kiko to a sudden halt. In that single instant of immobility, Nundu shouted, "Kiko! I've come for you!" and immediately fired five shots. Cook staggered and fell, but now the bed was between him and his killer, and Nundu was unable to see if his aim had been accurate enough for his purpose.

He simply must get inside! His thirst for vengeance could only be slaked and his hate satisfied if he could get his hands on his victim and wreak physical violence upon him, smashing his hated face to pulp. He crept round the side of the house and shattered the lock of the kitchen door with three shots from his gun. The door creaked open. Kifaru knew that no staff slept in the house at night for fear of treachery. He was also certain that the sound of gun shots would keep any of the shamba hands away. Kiko was not the sort of man other men risked their lives for. Nundu crept into the house as silently as possible, just in case Cook had been able to get at his gun and so take a shot at him as he approached. But when he reached the bedroom door, he saw that his caution was needless. Cook was not dead, but was evidently very near it. Three of the five shots had hit him: one in the neck, from which the blood was pumping like a gusher, another had smashed his shoulder, and the last had lodged in his chest. Oblivious to everything but his burning blood lust Nundu sprang upon his victim, slashing the hated face again and again with the panga until it was nothing but an unrecognisable bloody pulp. He slashed until from pure exhaustion he could slash no longer . . . his savage joy, now that his long cherished desire was achieved, left him so weak and shaky that he was obliged to rest on the floor beside the man he had mutilated and killed, now so still and silent. So still and silent indeed that a cold chill began to creep into Nundu's blood.

At last he rose and left the house as silently as he had come, hiding again in the garden to wait and discover if his comrades had abandoned the raid altogether, or only been delayed by the sight of the cars in the driveway. As soon as he heard the others coming, he made off into the night.

When the group to attack the farm house arrived they were astonished to find their quarry dead on the floor. However, they followed their instructions and they broke open Cook's safe and took all the money and three guns, a pistol and clothes before setting the house on fire. They didn't wait to watch the flames, but took to the forest without delay.

The groups who were at the main gate trapped three Police lorries, but after firing on them they took fright and

147

ran. However, even this part of the raid met with success for two of the lorries were set on fire and the third was left deserted. Many dead and dying policemen were left on the roadside whilst their companions had fled into the bush. The group hurried back to the caves before signals could be sent to fetch the dreaded Johnnies.

As a matter of fact the security chiefs refused to send the British soldiers to the area immediately, as this first-ever attack and complete victory was something that had to be analysed and investigated before they could commit the army to fight against well trained and armed forest fighters. The Chiefs were completely out of their depth and, as a result, troops were not sent until dawn.

Immediately the members of the various groups arrived back at the caves, they started bragging about their feats and talking about Kifaru's evacuation plan which had to come into effect immediately before the Johnnies came to hunt them down.

Kifaru spent precious minutes deviating to Mrefu's house, where he regaled him with the news of their success. This was no surprise to Mrefu, however, for the reflection of the blazing buildings in the sky could be seen for miles. Nundu was looking extremely pleased with himself, and indeed he had quite forgotten his blind panic.

"Well done, brother," said Mrefu. "I knew our faith in you was not unfounded. What will you do now?"

"It rather depends on how many of my men have survived this venture," he replied. "We intend first to hide our booty and, oh brother, you should see what we have got! As soon as we have done this, we must take to the thick forest for surely the Security Forces will start searching for us at first light." He touched Mrefu lightly on the shoulder. "Never fear, we shall be safe and as soon as we have found a good hiding place I will let you know. The details of our grand victory can wait to be told then. I must hasten now. Farewell, brother."

"Take care, Kifaru, please take care. Remember you are as a son to me." Mrefu stood watching the reflection of the flames for a long time after Kifaru had left, shaking his head sadly at the terrible times on which his people had fallen. Eventually, with a sigh, he turned back to his house to spend the rest of the night tossing and turning sleeplessly, for he feared swift and fierce retribution.

Meanwhile, Kifaru sped swiftly through the darkness, unhampered by any grim thoughts and full of elation. To his great surprise, for he had forgotten that his men had arrived at the caves before he did and had missed him, cheers resounded through the glade, and many of his followers caught his legs and lifted him high in the air sobbing for joy. "We thought you dead, oh Kifaru, Kifaru our saviour. Thanks be to Kirinyaga for bringing our leader safely back to us."

The extent of the damage, and the number of dead was made known in the newspaper headlines the following morning — "Major Cook Brutally Shot And Slashed To Death By Terrorists — Police Post Wiped Out After Fierce Battle With Terrorists" — The newspapers gave varying reports — not all strictly true, for the numbers of dead given were a hundred terrorists and ten policemen. Kifaru and Mrefu knew that they had lost five men and that three more were seriously wounded, and that the number of Policemen killed totalled over fifty. However, the paper reported quite truthfully that two hundred of Cook's cattle had been slashed, his dog killed and fifty sheep burned to death, so this was some consolation. That they troubled to print the details at all showed the state of shock into which Cook's terrible death had plunged the reporters.

As the first light of dawn struck the sky, the first batches of troops arrived on Cook's farm. They immediately took up the search. Spotter planes buzzed low in the sky like bees. Naro was turned overnight into an Army camp. War had been declared and the occupants of the district were to bear the consequences. Most of the African population were too scared to venture from their huts, but for Kifaru it was a different story — it was he and his men who were the hunted. Bomber planes were out in full force, and they were bombing the forest area indiscriminately. The sound of continuous heavy mortar fire filled the air and numbed the senses. Overnight, Naro had become a hell on earth.

Nundu and his comrades travelled very speedily, but even so daylight had found them only four miles away from Naro. Another six miles before they were in the outskirts of the great forest, and another ten to twenty miles after that before they were safe. They therefore had about twenty-six miles to cover under heavy mortar fire and the many bombs which were exploding all around them. "Hurry, Hurry!" gasped Kifaru. "Or we will all die." He stood unheedingly waiting for the stragglers of the party to catch up, and to whisper a few words of encouragement. He then took his place at the front of the party again and soon they were out of immediate danger. They walked a little further and stopped at the foot of a small hillock. Kifaru held up his hand and crept forward. To his amazement, he saw convoys of lorries travelling along the main road, which was quite near their hiding place, and one convoy was turning off into the forest using a road frequented only by big game hunters.

He turned back and slid down the hill to where his comrades were anxiously awaiting him, fear and exhaustion written on their faces. "Thank our god of Kirinyaga — there are many lorries full of Johnnies on the main road and on the white hunters' road. He has shown them to us, and if he had not, we would have been caught. You know we had planned to follow this valley and that road, and nothing else could have prevented us from meeting. I only wish we could attack them, but after a night such as we have spent, it would not be wise . . . Duck down! A spotter plane is coming."

They listened to the plane's engines roaring overhead, their hearts beating frantically. They breathed a sigh of relief as the sound faded away in the distance. Nundu cautiously raised his head and looked around. "O.K., brothers, safe for the moment. Now, we have been forced to change our plans, and I think we had better make for the trees over that side — spotter planes are coming over now every five to ten minutes so we must hurry. If you hear one, for heaven's sake don't hesitate, throw, yourselves down. Look out, here's another one!"

They threw themselves on the earth, and the plane flew so low that they were sure they had been seen. "Let's get out of here," said Kifaru. They steadied the heavy bundles on their backs which contained their personal belongings, and started running towards the thick forest. They had divided themselves into two groups, one consisting of those carrying the ammunition and the other to follow behind in case a fight broke out. This rearguard Kifaru commanded personally. Altogether, they had about a mile to cover before they could consider themselves safe once again, with very little cover under which to travel.

Soon enough they were spotted, and the mortar fire, for the first time that day, was directed on live targets. As soon as they realised they had been seen, every time the mortars fired they ducked to the ground, lay still, then ran again, rather like hares running from the hounds. They ducked and twisted and eventually reached the cool safety of the trees.

Immediately the Johnnies ordered an advance party to follow them, whilst Kifaru ordered his men to scatter along the outskirts of the forests to cover those who had gone before. They positioned themselves and waited silently, relentlessly, watching the approaching soldiers. Kifaru heard a sharp order to "Halt!" and watched the soldiers drop back under cover. "Something's up," he muttered to himself. "What are they doing now?" He rubbed the sweat off his forehead with a grimy hand and tried desperately to keep his eyes open. He was so tired. They were all so tired. What was going to be the end of this? He listened in horror at the sound of approaching planes. "Find yourselves good cover, they are going to bomb . . ." It was all he had time to say, for the next minute the forest shook as bomb after bomb was dropped. Boom! Boom! Was there going to be no end to it? They hugged the ground fiercely as tree after tree crashed and stones and earth showered from the air. The whole ground shuddered in agony at the onslaught, and when the bombs had stopped falling, the pilots strafed the forest fringe over and over again. Then, after two hours, silence, blessed silence . . .

Kifaru hastily gathered his much depleted band around him, but there was no time to count casualties for the soldiers were approaching once more. He looked at them, and to his fury spotted several white settlers egging them on. His fury knew no bounds and so, instead of running, he pulled his dispirited men back into battle formation. "Fire until you can fire no longer. If they fall back, then run, for the bombs will be dropped again. If they don't, then stand and fight until you drop. Wait until I give the word and then start into them. Now go, and Kirinyaga be with you all."

They hastily checked their weapons, and once again waited silently for the command, their weary faces ablaze with hatred. Kifaru waited until the first line of soldiers was nearly on them and then shouted, "Fire! Fire!" To his great delight, he saw the leaders drop to the ground together with about five others. The platoon was thrown into confusion; some of the soldiers threw themselves on to the ground, others ran back. Scattered rifle fire answered their fierce effort, as the soldiers in charge of the mortars did not dare fire for fear of wounding their own comrades who were spread over the battlefield. The platoon was taken completely by surprise, and after a few minutes' engagement, the bombers came roaring back. This gave Kifaru the chance he needed, and he and his men rushed deep into the forest, following the tracks of their advance group. Planes bombed the forest for the rest of the day, and Kifaru could still hear the explosions until as late as six-thirty in the evening. They had lost another ten men in an unfortunate engagement which cost them dear. Several were wounded, and this slowed their progress as they had to be carried. At nightfall, they had covered fifteen miles and they decided to change course and find hiding places. Kifaru advised them to find safe places the following morning after they had slept. Each man therefore found a good tree and, after eating a small piece of meat which they had carried with them, they climbed up their respective trees, settled themselves as comfortably as possible, and slept the sleep of the dead. The next morning, Kifaru sent off four men to find a suitable hiding place, with instructions to report back to camp within two hours. He picked four other men to back-track and obliterate any traces they had left of their journey the previous night. Soon one of the searchers came back with heartening news. He had found a small bowl-shaped valley surrounded by thick forest, the sides of which were honeycombed with caves and steep rocks. It was practically inaccessible, for the only way into it that he could find was down a jagged rock side. Here they would be safe. Wearily they gathered their bundles and made their way to this valley of paradise. One of the trackers went

153

F

to search for the advance party who, luckily, were not far away, and as soon as they had all gathered in the valley, Kifaru spoke to them.

"My brothers in war, you have truly displayed courage and tenacity and I am proud of you all. We will be safe here, and can relax. The only duty I require is that two men shall be on guard at all times by the cliff path. Rest now." His words had gone practically unheeded, for his men had collapsed where they stood, apart from two "old faithfuls" who saluted feebly and staggered up to the path and stood there nodding over their guns. A few hours later, after they had all rested, Nundu selected the youngest man there to go to Naro to report to Mrefu and make arrangements for food and more recruits to be sent. He was also to find out all the news possible, especially the reaction to Kiko's death. This lad was chosen as he had not yet grown a beard, which was the mark of forest men, and was therefore less likely to be detected.

The security chiefs were astonished and disgusted at the quick thinking and thorough discipline displayed by men whom they considered little better than savages. At Major Cook's funeral, which was held with full military honours, the Provincial Commissioner promised to take even sterner measures in the area to make sure that no more such raids would take place. He admitted that, for once, the Security Forces had been taken by surprise, and he warned those present that the time had gone when they could relax comfortably in their homes, thinking that the terrorists were just an unruly crowd inexperienced in the ways of war and armed with primitive weapons. He requested them all to spare no effort to wipe out the terrorists and informed the public that one battalion of British Troops was to be stationed permanently in the area to protect the white citizens and their property. He begged the farmers not to leave, stating that an economic crisis could not be averted if they did. He stated that no one could forecast how long the "dirty war" would last, but that H.M.G. was determined to exterminate the trouble-

154

makers and bring peace back to the land. A huge crowd of settlers and soldiers, who had come to pay their respects to an old companion and friend who had lost his life for them, heard this oration and swore vengeance and death to the terrorists.

The next day, troops started to settle in on the farm which only a week previously had belonged to Cook. They came with their tanks and light cannons, their lorries and their camp equipment. They surrounded the camp with barbed wire, and, within a fortnight, had made a rough landing strip for their small planes and had widened the road to Naro. They were men with one aim in common — to find Cook's killers, dead or alive. They went many times into the forest, but not knowing the country and not possessing tracking skills, they found nobody and eventually had to give up hope.

Due to the difficulties of forest travelling, Kifaru's messenger took five days, travelling at night only, to arrive at Mrefu's house. He was terrified of being caught, as any stranger was whipped off to a detention camp if seen. He was only a young lad and trembled at the thought that if he was caught no amount of reasoning would stop them torturing him until he had to talk. His fears were somewhat alleviated when he actually sat down in Mrefu's house, after a heartening welcome. He gave Mrefu a note from Kifaru and sat back wearily, watching him read it. He could not understand why Mrefu was laughing so happily, for boy-like he had read the letter, but was most puzzled by its contents of which he could not understand a word. It read as follows and was, of course, in code.

"Dear Mrefu,

I have arrived safely and only lost ten of my bags on the way. Is water still flowing through the pipe, or was it cut by the wagon on that day near the border?

I want more stuff for my stomach so tell the dresser, and inform him when he comes back where and at which shop to collect.

He has his mouth full.

That evening, Mrefu cried for joy to know that his beloved "son" was still alive and that although the going had been hard, so many of his band had survived. He told the messenger how there was complete military rule in the town now that the Johnnies had moved in.

"They have killed about ten people, and raped over a dozen of our women. There is one thing to be said, however, and that is we can get what we want out of them in the way of ammunition and guns, for our women are playing their part magnificently and we are increasing our armoury daily. I am arranging for many of our followers to work in the camp, and they too will prove worth their weight in gold. I have a few recruits who will join you soon, for I know that you will need some. They are running away for fear the Johnnies catch them. Oh, by the way, take this letter to Kifaru. It is his appointment as Field Marshal. He has been promoted for his wonderful leadership in the raid. His battalion, of which you must be proud to be a part, will now be known to the world as *Ngwa* (lightning) because of its quick action in battle. This is now, of course, a Special Area and many more people have been taken away for interrogation. I myself was taken but my employers, who trust me, managed to obtain my freedom. Even so, I was very badly beaten by a son of the settler who lives across the road. They took me out in the bright moonlight and used rifle butts on me. Never mind, I said nothing, and the pain will go. I am thinking very seriously of taking revenge and making his father pay. Anyway, tell the Field Marshal that he can work from his new hideout as he pleases — he does not necessarily have to ask my permission. Of course, I would like to be kept in the picture. Food will be brought to the edge of Naro Valley, just on the forest verge, and it will be hidden under fig branches. We shall endeavour to keep up a regular supply every Monday, Wednesday and Friday. Ask him to make arrangements to collect this at dusk on each of these days. Make yourself at home, and you can leave here sometime tomorrow evening. I must sleep now, for the pressure of work now that so many of our brothers have been detained is almost impossible. Never mind, we will win this war soon and all the toil and heartbreak will be over."

The following evening the young messenger and the food carriers crept stealthily out of Naro, many times only just avoiding discovery. They followed the river valley to the edge of the forest and the carriers showed how and where the food was to be hidden. After they had gone, the young man fled into the forest. He was no longer brave now that he was alone once more, and the cries of the many wild animals which seemed to follow him almost petrified him in his flight. He eventually climbed a large tree and settled himself fairly comfortably in its "v"-shaped branches and slept. Much braver in daylight, he boldly hurried over the last few miles, full of pride and joy not only at the news he was bearing, but at the success of his mission.

He was almost smothered with questions when he arrived at the camp, but swaggered triumphantly through the curious, expectant group refusing to speak to any but his leader. Kifaru drew the messenger into the solitude of his cave to hear his news. He could not contain his joy at his promotion, and jumped up and down like a little boy who has been given the toy of his dreams. He listened avidly to all the news his messenger had brought. For once he seemed almost human. Too soon, however, his aggressive nature reasserted itself and he spoke almost brusquely to his adoring follower.

"You have done well, brother, and I will see that you are suitably rewarded. Go now and tell my band to gather outside the cave for I wish to speak. Tell no one what has occurred. Let them hear it from my lips only." His breast swelling with pride, he strutted out of his cave like a turkey cock and held up his hand for silence.

"My brothers in war, oh hear what great news I have for

you!" A hush fell over his men, but they crowded round him rather as sheep round a shepherd.

"I've now been promoted to the rank of Field Marshal. . . ." He could go on no longer for his men, cheering and shouting, lifted him shoulder-high, promising him a leopard headress and jacket befitting his rank, as a token of their happiness at his success.

"But hear me!" Kifaru roared above the din. "I have yet more to tell you." They reluctantly put him down and were quiet once more.

"From now on, our Company is to be known as *Ngwa* — and that is to your credit, for every man has to co-operate with the other to make a success of our task. Hush! You may talk after I have finished. For the rest, the news is not so pleasing. The Johnnies have overrun Naro and are looking for us but without success. We are safe here so never fear. Our food supplies are at this very moment awaiting collection, and from now on, every Monday, Wednesday and Friday at six o'clock in the evening, four of you must go to this place" — he pointed to a rough map on the cave wall behind him — "to collect them. I will ask our messenger, who brought us this wonderful news, to go with you and show you exactly where and how it is hidden. Tread carefully, for you might run into a patrol, or perhaps someone might betray us. Celebrate tonight, and rest to-morrow, for it is nearly time for us to make another raid. We must not rest on our laurels." He disappeared inside the cave, his heart overflowing with happiness and apprehension. A peculiar mixture of feelings, but he knew that it was time for him to plan another attack to justify the honour that had been poured on him — never mind his band. In a way, however, he was reluctant to do this, for the valley had proved a Shangri La for himself and his men, a state of affairs that could so easily be shattered.

Meanwhile, Naro was still full of fear and unrest. The area that had already been declared a Special Area was in a state of terror for it was widely known that the terrorists were in the five-mile strip of forest nearby. The forest was therefore considered to be a "specially special area" and anyone found in it, or even on its outskirts, was to be shot without warning by the Security Forces. Since Cook's death, which had almost paralysed the neighbourhood, no effort was spared to arrest or kill the terrorists. The night patrols intensified door to door checking and people were not allowed to stay in their friends' houses overnight as it was known that oath-taking ceremonies were held at these seemingly harmless social evenings. As a particularly stringent measure to prevent food reaching those hiding in the forest, many houses were burned down and the occupants were compelled to build new houses and form villages isolated from the rest of the community. Many families were forced to live under trees for many weeks during the completion of this project. They were closely guarded and the builders, who were forced to gather their materials for supports and thatching from the forest, were also watched by home guards. One suspicious move — and the suspect was ruthlessly shot. Fear reigned supreme. The Government loyalists, for there were some, were issued with guns and ordered to patrol at night. The home guard posts were built on the same lines as the police posts, and their administration was somewhat similar. A specially selected headman, or tribal policeman, was put in charge, and the old headmen and chiefs were dismissed. This, of course, was to enable these specially chosen men who were always particularly sadistic to administrate as well as fight.

Kifaru, once again the strategist, was busy making plans for his next appearance. He decided that once each week he, together with a couple of specially picked men, should hide on the side of any major road that was not too far from the forest and ambush any army vehicles that passed by so frequently, and harrass them with strong gun fire before once more disappearing into the darkness of the forest. If no lorries were available, the target was then to be the loyalists who refused to join the freedom fighters. They were a great danger and had to be wiped out as quickly as possible. This presented a bigger problem, however, as they were escorted by guards at all times.

The Field Marshal swooped again and yet again on these unfortunates with complete success. The only setback to these manoeuvres, and a serious one, was the retaliation of the Johnnies. They arrived almost immediately on the scene of the fight, arrested all the adults in the vicinity, and took them with their children to the nearest police or home guard post. They were beaten and tortured and the more stubborn ones shot for revenge. Many gave way to this form of treatment and told who had fought, and who had supported them. The law was that of the jungle; no courts were needed to pass judgement or sentence of death.

This swift action left very little choice to the people. Either they had to run for their lives and join one of the forest gangs, or become loyalists. As the latter at least they would be safer. However, the fire of hatred burned too strongly in their hearts for them all to choose this comparatively safer way out and many of them joined Mrefu. Mrefu, although proud of his protégé, Kifaru, was becoming rather envious of his frequent successes and therefore decided to form a group of his own. His power had much diminished since Kifaru had become his second in command, and he was determined to show the fighters who was the most powerful and influential of the two. Apart from this, he still suffered considerable pain from his damaged leg which now had given him a permanent limp, and he was full of bitterness against the young settler who had treated him in this way. He worked out a watertight plan for raiding this settler's farm. In his way he, too, was a supreme strategist. However, he was not to know that one of his seemingly dependable supporters was in reality a police spy, and that all his plans were immediately relayed back to Frank Jones.

The farm was to be raided at three in the morning, and so just after dark two truck loads of soldiers were sent to prepare an ambush on the would-be raiders. However, they had to traverse a rickety wooden bridge and this gave way just as they were passing over it. Reinforcements were sent to help rebuild the bridge — which was ten miles from the farm buildings. The security forces fretted and fumed at the delay and some of them set out across country in an endeavour to protect the settler and his family from certain doom. Mrefu, unknowingly, very nearly succeeded in his venture, for impatient as always, he had decided not to wait until the pre-arranged time, but to attack at midnight. The small group of security forces arrived just as the raid was beginning, and managed to hem the raiders in cross fire until reinforcements arrived. They surrounded Mrefu and his men and shot down all those who attempted to escape. Wenye, one of Kifaru's brothers, died thus, and one by one, most of Mrefu's band were killed. Mrefu managed to escape, but due to his injured leg, was unable to run far.

He cowered in a ditch where, at dawn, the soldiers found him and dragged him to the detention camp. They knew he was the leader, and once more he was beaten and interrogated. All the raiders' firearms were captured, and for the first time the Security Forces found some home-made guns. These were made with half-inch steel piping tied with wire to a stick. A bolt was fixed firmly to close one end of the piping with strong rubber and the bullet, placed in the mouth of the piping, was hit with the rubber, thus giving it a great firing velocity. The police eyed these weapons with horrified surprise and suspicion — for what had seemed to be just a small uprising was obviously something far greater if the terrorists were able to make their own weapons. It was all very well checking their own armoury and finding out what guns were missing, but when it came to home-made guns, no one knew how many were available or even where they were being made. They then realised just how much they had under-estimated their opponents.

They therefore intensified Mrefu's interrogation for, being the leader, he was bound to know where these weapons came from and how many there were. They stopped beating him, fearing that he would die before they extracted the information they required as he was so weak. They hoped that they could persuade him not only to confess, but to agree to fly in one of their aeroplanes over the forest and appeal to his friends to surrender. But many weeks passed and Mrefu, steadily growing weaker, refused to give in. A more staunch supporter could not be found anywhere. He had, of course, lost his job, and all the Kikuyu employees in the railways were dismissed as the administration felt that they were using the trains for their own purposes — which of course they were.

Field Marshal Kifaru's blood turned to water when he heard the news, for in his own way he had loved Wenye, and of course Mrefu had become a father to him, apart from the fact that Mrefu was his only contact with the outside world. He had relied on Mrefu's practical help and guidance to such an extent that the news was a blow almost worse than death. Impetuous as always, he immediately summoned his camp leaders to a meeting and told them that he planned to attack the detention camp where Mrefu was held and release him. The group leaders were quite naturally not keen to embark on such a hairbrained scheme, and firmly made Kifaru aware of this. However, Kifaru had turned into a dictator and what he ordered to be done had to be accomplished under pain of death.

The Security Chiefs began to relax their guard again after Mrefu's arrest. They were lulled into a sense of false security especially now that the Field Marshal had ceased his sudden swoops in the vicinity. They did not know that Kifaru was planning a much greater and more important raid than ever before, and were consequently caught completely by surprise one night by a rain of bullets on the camp. Confusion reigned and, although the askaris managed to organise a defence of sorts, Kifaru's well disciplined army carried away the laurels without much effort. Many of the detainees escaped, and Kifaru who feared little, crept under the hail of bullets coming from the defence posts, into the camp to look for Mrefu. He found him fairly quickly, unable to walk from sheer weakness and maltreatment, so he threw him bodily over his shoulder and once again braved a hail of bullets, this time from his own men, and ran to safety completely unscathed. His men followed him jubilantly, leaving a stunned, half-wrecked detention camp behind them. The death toll amongst the enemy was great while they themselves had lost only two men, and had gained thirty.

Not a man in Naro could believe that one of the hated terrorists could accomplish such a feat. The settlers gathered agape round the remains of what, to them, had symbolised their security and safety. They bitterly mocked the security chiefs who had now been defeated twice by a gang of terrorists. They, with all their skill and experience, had allowed a bunch of "uneducated natives" to wipe the floor with them. Headquarters hummed with shame and embarrassment and the telephone lines were abuzz with the news. The Commander of the camp was dead, so he could not be courtmartialled. They summoned all the Europeans to plan retaliatory action in the area, and to lay down even more stringent security measures. The tide had turned in favour of the terrorists — what was going to happen next?

8 FOREST WAR

After the raid on the detention camp, Kifaru, who had achieved the complete success of his wildest daydream, discovered to his surprise that he was capable of fighting in the open, although even he was cautious enough to realise that they had to remain near the forest in case of defeat. In the forest, the gang reigned supreme. Therefore, he decided that he and his men should wait in ambush in broad daylight for a security patrol about a mile from the forest, hidden in some small bushes on the top of a hill which gave them hardly any cover. From this point, they could view the countryside without obstruction for about three miles on all sides, and thus have plenty of time to prepare themselves to meet the oncoming security forces. They had eagerly watched Carey and his patrol and, being stimulated by the *bhangi* which they had consumed and which they wholeheartedly believed made them "bullet proof", agreed enthusiastically when Kifaru proposed that they should stand and fight, even though they were but a few and the security patrol many. Kifaru's band was much depleted at this juncture as most of his men had gone into the forest to escort the newly-freed prisoners to their hideout.

Carey Milton had been put in charge of the combined security forces in the district — a mistake on the part of the Administration, for he was a District Officer, not an Army Officer. He was young and inexperienced, but could not really be blamed for underestimating his opponents, especially in view of the fact that he had never encountered them on the battlefield. He had read in the newspapers that some of the braver soldiers had, after fierce battles with the terrorists, discovered home-made arms and ammunition and he determined to capture some of these treasures himself with which to decorate his office walls. It was true that he desired to boast about his achievements to his District Commissioner but above all, he wanted a Commendation in the New Year or Birthday Honours. Many officers, both administrative and army, had received decorations for their heroism in the battle against the terrorists and he also wanted to gain an honour. He therefore brooked no interference or advice from the army, and on this, his first patrol, he failed to ask either the army or the Police Air Wing to keep his men covered. Instead, he called together the Tribal Police askaris unknown to their chief. He had been issued with an automatic rifle with which he went shooting game at will without question from anybody. He took the whole affair very lightly as far as the fighting went, for who but an utter fool could be defeated by a few wild natives armed with spears and arrows and a few stolen guns and bullets, the supply of which could not last for ever?

When Carey met the police sergeant that morning, he was wearing the new battle dress that had just been issued to senior officers. The askaris crowded round him eagerly, fingering the helmet and material. The Sergeant saluted smartly and gazed at him in admiration. Carey preened himself, and condescendingly answered the Sergeant's query as to whether these uniforms were to be issued to the lower ranks.

"These were promised to us by the Chief Native Commissioner and you will receive them shortly. We used these in Malaya when we were fighting the Communists and their green colour is supposed to help you to hide in the bush. You tie these strings here, and you will be warm at night. It is the perfect garment for guerilla warfare. Now, what have you got to report?"

"*Effendi*, I have heard that the gang who raided the detention camp are but ten miles away. My men are ready and we would like to try to follow them into the forest to see where they have gone. I can then come back and tell the army so that they can lay an ambush."

"Yes, call your men straight away, the sooner we leave the better."

165

The Sergeant and Carey rode in the Administration Landrover, collected another group of askaris from a camp further afield, and then left the vehicle and started their patrol. Carey began talking to the Sergeant and, since they thought that the terrorists had returned to the forest, they failed to keep a sharp look out while they pushed their way through the trees and elephant grass. The Sergeant was quite overwhelmed, for never had an *Effendi* deigned to talk so freely to him. He gazed at Carey, who was explaining rather volubly how the terrorists would eventually fall.

"With courage and determination, we shall succeed in restoring what our fathers have built, and in many cases, have died for," Carey pronounced. "We know what clever fighters the terrorists have proved themselves to be and what heavy casualties they have inflicted on us — in many cases we have been so taken by surprise that we have been unable to defend ourselves. But I have heartening news for you. Many other districts have got material and information that will prove very useful to us. We shall have to change our tactics, and will do so as soon as this information is rec . . . ." He stopped dead in the middle of a word and staggered backwards. "Help me," he stammered. "I've been shot!" and he collapsed on the ground, blood trickling from his back and elbow. The only thing the Sergeant remembered was Carey lying unconscious on the grass, whilst he threw himself down beside the inert body in sheer panic, his gun dropping from his nerveless fingers.

Kifaru knew how to play his ace cards. He had waited until the patrol had almost passed before firing the first shot. The askaris, following the example of their leader, had kept little or no look out, and the one shot came as such a surprise that they thought one of their own men had run amok. Many of the askaris threw themselves down, afraid to move, and a few others turned tail and ran. The Sergeant, who was cowering in terror beside Carey, was too paralysed with fright to give orders, and they all lay motionless.

In that split second Kifaru, who had hidden many of

his men in antbear holes after placing a large rock in front of each of them thus making them even harder to detect, thought that a large force of askaris was creeping up towards them. As he was completely outnumbered, he immediately ordered his band to retreat and they fled back to the forest so quickly that no one saw them.

"*Effendi! Effendi*, are you all right?" The quivering Sergeant gazed in horror at his prostrate superior. He lifted his head cautiously, looked around, and beckoned the others to come to him. He tried in vain to administer first aid, and then ordered some of the constables to lift Carey gently and carry him to the Landrover. They all gazed at the Sergeant both stunned and terrified. Who had done this terrible thing? No one had seen any terrorists.

The Sergeant heard the whispers and it was obvious that his men were afraid to come near him. Surely they did not think he had shot the *Effendi*? His heart thudded and its beats seemed to rise up and strangle him. What was he going to tell them? He himself had no idea where the bullet had come from, but he had been standing beside Carey when it had happened. What would they do to him? He staggered, and had to be half carried to the Landrover where they put him in the front seat beside the driver, and an askari sat beside him to give him support. They drove immediately to Naro, but the Sergeant was too frightened to report to the Police Station, so he made the driver stop at the Police Barracks, stumbled out of the car, and made his way to his room. He huddled under his blankets, cowering with terror, to await the dreaded summons from his chief.

Meanwhile, a furious Police Officer was bawling at the patrol group which had just arrived at the Station. They stood huddled around the Landrover unable to answer the spate of furious queries. The Police doctor arrived, examined the motionless Carey and immediately asked that a Police Aircraft take him to Nairobi, where he would receive proper medical care. Frank Jones summoned one of

167

the Corporals from the Station and ordered him to guard the unfortunate men who had been on patrol and see that they did not discuss the incident amongst themselves. He also sent a Corporal to guard the Sergeant.

"I'm going to find out the truth!" he shouted. "And until I do, you are all placed under house arrest and are to talk to no one. If you dare to disobey my orders, I will take the severest of disciplinary action!" He glared at the cowering group. "Corporal!"

"Yes, *Effendi!*" The Corporal stood smartly to attention. The Bwana was truly in a very bad mood; he had never seen him like this before. Better to keep on the right side of him, for he didn't want to lay himself open to his wrath.

"Send those men into my office one by one. When they come out they must be escorted to the barracks and closely watched — that is, if I haven't discovered the truth." He swung round and hurried into his office.

One by one, the frightened men went in for their interview, and in all cases the questions and answers were the same:

"Why did you go on patrol without air coverage?"
"I don't know, *Effendi.*"
"Were you keeping a careful lookout?"
"Why yes, of course, *Effendi.*"
"Did you see any terrorists?"
"No, *Effendi.*"
"No one?"
"No, *Effendi.*"
"Where was Bwana Carey?"
"Leading us, *Effendi.*"
"Who was with him?"
"The Sergeant, *Effendi.*"
"Were you near him?"
"No, *Effendi.*"
"Who shot the Bwana Carey?"
"I don't know, *Effendi.*"

"Did you see the Sergeant shoot the Bwana?"

"No, *Effendi*."

"Are you lying to me? If you are I'll have you horse-whipped."

"No *Effendi*, I *swear* I am not lying."

"Wait outside . . . Next!"

After he had interviewed them all, he sat in his office wondering what to do. He fingered the Doctor's report thoughtfully. Carey would be all right, given time; the bullet had bypassed his backbone and had lodged in his right elbow. An inch further over and . . . Frank sighed. "I've never been at a loss to know what to do before," he muttered. "The Sergeant always seemed so loyal, even blindly so, but so many of these terrorists were thought to be loyal." He sighed deeply and picked up the telephone. The Commissioner had to be informed — perhaps he should have contacted him earlier . . . "No, let him wait awhile. I'll rush over to the Barracks and see the Sergeant. I must be sure." He pushed his chair back with such vigour that it smashed against the wall. He picked up his cap, rushed to the door, jumped into the Landrover and drove off to the barracks. The askaris whispered anxiously amongst themselves. The news had spread like wildfire, and the *Effendi* looked red and angry — just like a half boiled lobster.

The Sergeant heard his Chief coming and made a poor effort to stand to attention, a dutiful smile quivering on his lips.

"Sergeant!"

"*Effendi!*" replied the Sergeant, saluting smartly.

"Now listen to me. I have come to see you as I have been told that you and the Bwana were talking to each other when he was shot. Is this true?"

"Yes, *Effendi*," replied the poor wretch, shivering uncontrollably.

"Did you shoot him?"

169

"Effendi! Effendi, I did not! Please believe me . . ." The stalwart face crumpled like a baby's at this accusation, and tears rolled down his cheeks.

"Well, tell me what happened," snapped Frank, feeling that this situation was getting completely beyond him. In fact he was quite sure by now that this man was guilty — he looked guilty, and anyhow, someone had to be blamed. No native could be trusted at any time. Make an example of this one and that would be the end of it.

"Sir, I was talking to the Bwana when a shot rang out and I fell to the ground. I looked round for the Bwana and he was lying terribly still beside me . . ."

"Did you see any terrorists, did you fire any shots?" interrupted the Chief impatiently.

"No, No, *Effendi,* you must listen to me . . ." gabbled the poor man in terror.

"How dare you speak to me like that! Get into the Landrover and come to my office — you must make a statement."

The terrified Sergeant could barely walk to the car, he was shaking so much. The penalty for shooting a Police Officer was death, and he knew the *Effendi* well enough to realise that he didn't care whether it was true or not. All the *Effendi* wanted to do was to finalise the whole matter — the *Effendi* wouldn't mind if he was unjustly charged. He hated anyone with a black skin — there was justice only for the whites.

Frank pushed the Sergeant roughly out of the car, abusing him at the top of his voice. The Sergeant had been so absorbed in his fears that he hadn't realised that they had arrived. He endeavoured to pull his wits together, marched to Frank's office, and stood to attention there whilst the European officer who was to witness his statement prepared his papers. Frank stalked in and sat down at his desk.

170

"Come on now, and make it as brief as possible. I must warn you that anything you say may be used in evidence . . . come on! I've got work to do; I can't waste all day here with you . . ."

The Sergeant looked at him hopelessly. What was the use of saying anything? They wouldn't listen to him. They didn't care what happened to him — he was only a black man. He gazed at the hard faces in front of him, searching vainly for a spark of sympathy, of belief. He shrugged his shoulders. No, it was no good. He had seen his people condemned unjustly so many times — why should he be different? He took a deep breath and mechanically murmured his story. It was recorded officially that the Sergeant was talking to the District Officer when he heard a shot, and as he threw himself to the ground he saw the District Officer lying prostrate beside him. He was too stunned and frightened to fire back and when, a few minutes later, he had the courage to lift his head there was nothing to be seen or heard. It was also noted that he had tried to administer first aid and had stated that there were no signs of a mutiny. He signed his statement and was then removed and placed in the Police Cells. He then fully came to grips with the fact that all hope of salvation had gone and stoically prepared himself for what he knew would inevitably follow.

That evening, Frank and his second in command thoroughly reviewed the case for, as Frank said, it didn't matter what happened to the Sergeant as he was only a native, but the records had to be fully complete. They therefore interrogated all the patrol members one by one again, and were greatly relieved to find that the evidence still remained the same. The Chief therefore contacted the Commissioner and obtained his permission to charge the Sergeant on two counts: that of firing in an endeavour to incite a mutiny, and of shooting at the District Officer with intent to kill. After an even more thorough investigation by the Police, it was decided that, owing to the extreme gravity of the case and the bad example it had set to the security forces, apart from the publicity it was being given, the Sergeant should be sentenced immediately and executed within a week of his "mock" trial. The European public was howling for his blood and so, guilty or not guilty, there was nothing else to be done. In complete secrecy the poor Sergeant, hapless victim of both fear and circumstance, was sentenced to be shot the following day. Early in the morning at first light, he was executed, and now that the inevitable had come, none faced death more bravely than he. All the askaris were petrified at this arbitrary treatment of a colleague whom they respected so highly. They mourned his passing and wondered who would be the next.

A man named Kamau, who had been posted to Naro to act in Carey's post as District Officer until Carey was fully recovered, came that afternoon. He had not followed the example of his former classmates — Nundu and the others — but had carried on with his education until he had succeeded in obtaining a bursary to a university abroad. On his return, he had joined the Administration as a District Assistant and had been promoted fairly rapidly to a District Officer. He was tall and handsome, and his skin was a light coffee colour. He was intelligent and dependable and had a charming personality. He was extremely sensitive, and as it was his first assignment to a "troubled area", and success could lead to promotion, he was very anxious to make a go of this new challenge. Unfortunately, to do this he needed the help and co-operation of the settlers and he was met with hatred, fear, and, in some cases, loathing. They spurned him and refused to acknowledge his existence. A spate of bitter complaints rained down on the Chief Native Commissioner in Nairobi, and a petition for the removal of this native whose very kith and kin were forest fighters was sent to the Governor.

Fortunately, the machinery of Government moves very slowly at times, especially when an awkward situation arises, and in this case there was no European available to take charge. So, by the time the Government had been forced to sit up and take notice, Carey was sufficiently recovered to return to Naro and work half time. Kamau was then only allowed to act under immediate orders and the closest of supervision. He was utterly humiliated, for in all his life he had never met with such treatment. To him, racialism was something unknown. He had been brought up by white missionaries, and at his university had been treated like everybody else. Even in the Administration he had met with a rather patronising kindness which he had mistaken for the hand of friendship, and until his transfer to Naro, he had worked entirely "in the field" with his own people. He was a true Christian and expected to be treated as such. For the first time in his short career, he began to doubt the sincerity of the white man, and bitterness and hatred flooded his soul. He suffered many agonies from this internal conflict which was intensified by the settlers who completely ignored him and indeed looked through him as if he were a piece of furniture. He was not allowed to enter their club or any of their houses. He, a better educated man than nearly all of them, had no one to talk to on equal terms — no friends to turn to. His own kind called him, sometimes to his face, a stooge of the white man and spat at his feet as he passed by. He was in a cleft stick, for there was nothing he could do. How could he overcome a situation such as this when it was his own people who were fighting the Government?

He had discovered to his great consternation that many of the prominent fighters were his old classmates and that Mrefu too was probably deeply involved, although as yet this had not been proven. He knew too that he had to hide this fact from Carey whom, incidentally, he was forced to call Bwana, for if this was found out he would be dismissed from the Service — nay worse, the fate that befell the hapless Sergeant would perhaps be meted out to him, and who was there to protect him? This thought made him determined to confide in no one and treat no one as a friend ... but what had become of the European's God — was he in their hearts no longer? This internal conflict was in no

173

way lessened by the fact that one ill advised move would put him in front of a firing squad.

Meanwhile, the forest fighters were themselves extremely disturbed, for several of their band had quite unexpectedly surrendered to the enemy and had been received with open arms. They were compelled to build many more hide-outs and camps in which to hide their supplies, for fate seemed to be turning against them. Their hide-outs were in most cases caves which had been used by their ancestors. These presented serious problems, for they belonged to the dead and, by custom, all houses of the dead were burned down and caves left uninhabited for fear of evil spirits. The fighters, however, had no alternative, for a great number of their hide-outs that had been barely obvious to a careless passer-by had been discovered and obliterated by the security forces and several of the men captured.

Many of the caves contained skeletons, bones and utensils which no doubt would have been of great interest to archaeologists but which petrified them. The more superstitious swore that they could hear the evil spirits moaning and moving about at night and that the bad luck that seemed to be dogging their footsteps was entirely due to their presence. The number of young people who had fled from the fury of the security forces had increased one hundred fold and disunity was growing. The youths resented obeying orders given by the young, experienced fighters. When information was received that forest fighters had been in any villages at night, the security forces would swoop at dawn, remove all the young men and girls and take them to the nearest security camp, where they were beaten with clubs and whips and tortured in lurid ways to force them to inform on their kinsmen. The forest fighters were wont to descend on any village, force the villagers to gather food and carry it into the forest, and remove some young girls for their enjoyment. This newly developed practice, started through sheer desperation, had made life in the reserve unbearable and the only sanctuary seemed to be the forest under a company leader, where they could pretend they were the lords of creation — the alternative being to acknowledge openly that they were on the Government side. The result of this would be that their families would be subjected to merciless humiliations by the freedom fighters and they themselves would be completely ignored by their friends. Unfortunately, when they went to the forest, they found that there was little or no accommodation, life was extremely unpleasant, they were forced to obey men in some cases younger than themselves, and discipline was enforced stringently and without mercy.

Many hide-outs were constructed in large trees, but these were impracticable on a long term basis. A sudden gust of wind or a tropical rain storm would leave them bereft of all secrecy. Poisonous snakes and various wild animals lived in these trees, and they could only afford shelter for three or four men. The caves could be purified by sacrificing lambs to Kirinyaga with special incantations. These sheep had to be of one colour only, preferably black, but if pitch black sheep were not available, the witchdoctor was allowed to choose another colour at his discretion. He was therefore entrusted with any sheep stolen on raids and used as many as possible for this purpose.

In the centre of the forest, about a mile away from the caves, there was a bowl-like valley with very steep jagged sides, extremely inaccessible. They entered this valley, which was about a hundred feet deep, by means of strong ropes, which meant that should the security forces discover and surround it, they would be hemmed in and completely defenceless. The houses they built were of a special nature. They first constructed the roof out of branches, and then supported it at an angle of 45 degrees on three or four posts on a raised edge, depending on the size of the house. Only one "wall" was built, also of branches, and they were situated only in the thickest bush. All who lived there had to be careful not to reveal their presence by footpaths leading to the houses. They slept facing the opening, so that if an emergency arose they could immediately camouflage the whole structure with creepers and forest plants to make it unidentifiable from the sky. The houses were built at intervals of two hundred yards and each camp formed a circle with all the openings on the outside. Each circle possessed its own commander. Eventually the caves were surrounded by these camp circles, which afforded them very necessary protection as they housed all the stores of food and ammunition. All the cooking was done there to prevent the smoke being seen by the spotter planes. Cattle, goats and sheep had to be kept in the valley not only for breeding purposes but also to feed injured, disabled and ageing people who were considered as retired, and prisoners awaiting trial. The young women who entertained the soldiers were also allowed to eat meat. One man was placed in charge of the herd, and dire punishments were meted out to those who disobeyed the rule and tried to steal livestock with which to feed themselves. A Field Marshal, Nundu in this case, was in charge of the whole camp. Camps like this one, varying in size, were scattered over many suitable sites.

Whilst Field Marshal Kifaru was engaged in implementing these new arrangements on orders from Nairobi, there was a brief respite for the security forces, for no one had time to go out and fight. During this period the security forces believed that the terrorists had been wiped out by the almost continuous mortar fire and bombing on the forest.

This was the time that Kifaru and Toga decided to increase their food supplies, for it was clear that due not only to the dry weather but to the many deserters, they were being forced into a defensive position. Unless great efforts were made to store food before the coming of the rains, when the security forces would be unable to reach them, they would be in no position to guarantee food for their men, which at this juncture could be disastrous.

Toga, the Chief's son, who had always admired the Cause and given it his full support, was entrusted, together with his wife, with the organisation of a steady food supply whilst Kifaru was busy laying out his new camp. He was in a very advantageous position to do this, for being a

Chief's son, the Chiefs having assumed such arbitary powers, it was unthinkable that anyone from the Security forces or the Tribal Police would dare to question him. The Tribal Police whom his father commanded, interrogated suspects as they were Kikuyu too, and reported their findings to the Chief, who then forwarded the information received to the Police or the District Officer.

The fact that Toga had lost his wooden leg in the fire was also a blessing, for he was obviously unable to move around and who could suspect a man hobbling on crutches? His wife was young and energetic, and in her own right had become a leader of the village women. Toga used her legs instead of his own and sent Njambi on all his missions. Before long she was renowned for her organising capacity. She organised loads of food, raw or cooked, but preferably cooked as in the tropical heat uncooked food very rapidly became uneatable, to be carried from village to village. Village A took it to Village B, B to C, and C in its turn to D, which was the village nearest to the forest. Here it was hidden in antbear holes, or covered with foliage, from which the forest fighters collected it. This was a method of transportation devised with much care for the Government had acquired such a great knowledge of their plans that all new faces in any village were reported to the nearest Home Guard Post, for it was alleged that the strangers would bring trouble on the village concerned.

The foothills of Kirinyaga over which these women had to travel are divided by rifts and valleys, tributaries and rivers, bush and tropical forests, far surpassing those of Mount Kilimanjaro which would have been a picnic in comparison. They had to labour and strive, pretending to carry water in four-gallon *debes* under the pretext of travelling to and fro from their shambas. They were no ordinary women, for the hardships of daily life were of no consequence when compared with these strenuous duties and, apart from this, discovery meant maybe worse than death. It was no wonder that in such a short time Njambi's name became a household word, for no one could believe that

177

these complicated manoeuvres could be carried out with so little fuss.

By this time, however, the tide had turned in favour of the Government. The security forces had captured many of the fighters and had killed many more, with the natural result that their morale was ebbing fast. At one point they had all started to smoke *bhangi*, believing that it made them bullet resistant, but alas! even this desperate resort did not work as expected. The leaders began to bicker amongst themselves, accusing each other of weakness, toying with the camp women before battle, losing faith in Kirinyaga and so on. The Government now possessed enough information to excise this abscess in their protectorate. Very few of those captured could withstand castration, electric shocks, immersion into cold water, disfigurements, beatings and the hundred and one other things that were inflicted on them. Rumours were rife that detainees were kept without food or water until they confessed and informed on their comrades, but this was the least of their sufferings. They were expected to answer in the affirmative to the charge of being terrorists, give the names of their friends, where they were hiding, where they had taken their oaths and when, and many other queries. The security forces also had competent spies whom they sent into the forests and the information these spies provided proved invaluable. The demoralisation of the forest fighters progressed at an alarming speed for even the most prominent citizens, who so far had seemed above reproach to the public, were being betrayed. In sheer desperation they admitted many people into their ranks who were insincere and comparable to bounty hunters. Their stern rules of admission were relaxed as more and more defected or were captured or killed and soon enough the spies had learned every detail of their movements — how they received their food and equipment and where they lived.

Manpower became so scarce, especially as the young village men were fast losing interest in a dead cause, that where two Field Marshals were living close together, they joined forces to avoid duplication of effort. Njogu, Nundu and Mrefu were the first to adopt this procedure and they grouped their men sadly together. Very few of their old comrades were left, but Muta, cheerful as always, still entertained the men in the evenings to take their minds off the inevitable end. Many of Mrefu's former pupils were engaged in this holy war and they all regarded the forests of Kirinyaga as their heaven on earth, regardless of conditions. Alas, they were of the minority. Most of them were by now completely unrecognisable, and indeed Nundu's beard had grown so long that it impeded his eating and drinking which made everybody laugh heartily — there seemed to be little else to laugh at. Njogu's hair looked like black quarter inch ropes about eighteen inches long tied in bundles over his head and falling behind his shoulders. They made futile attempts to disguise the gravity of their situation, which only a few months previously had been so very different. Victory had slipped out of their grasp although none would admit it.

There was no alternative but to stay in the forest, for if they ventured out into the reserve the security forces would swoop on them like a pack of wolves. No one even dared to confide his fears to his closest friend in case he was suspected of treachery in such critical times. But the worst was yet to come: Njambi had been caught redhanded and detained. Rumour, that enemy of all enemies, had it that she had been seriously wounded and was not likely to live. She had been seized whilst settling a dispute over the contribution of food. Some villagers were complaining bitterly that their food resources were finished and that they had donated more than their share. The villages nearest to the forest had had to shoulder the responsibility of producing more food than those further afield as it was becoming practically impossible for them to transport food as formerly under the hawk-like eyes of the security forces. No forest fighter dared venture from his hide-out for fear of discovery, and even if he was brave enough to slip out of the forest, he was unable to shoulder more than a very light load of food.

179

Njambi was always called to settle disputes, which were numerous, and this led to her downfall. She had just left her home after being summoned to settle an argument between two village groups, one refusing to hand over food to the other. Some women very unfortunately chose the time of her arrival to prove their loyalty to their men fighting in the forest by bringing extra food. The security forces had previous knowledge of this meeting and had followed these women, so even before they had started their *baraza*, they were fired upon by automatic rifles. Njambi fell instantly to the ground to cover her four-month-old baby, and her leg was shattered. The Security Forces ruthlessly killed all present, regardless of sex or age, except for three women. Many children were slaughtered and no quarter was given.

Njambi, whom they now knew was the women's leader, was removed and taken to hospital. When she regained consciousness she found her hands tied to the bed frame and two stalwart policemen standing guard over her. She cried with joy however to see that her young baby was alive and well beside her — nothing else, not even the worst of treatment, seemed to matter.

This terrible news spread like wildfire in the forest, and many of the men sat down and wept. This meant the end of their sustenance, for she had organised her women so efficiently that whilst nearly all the other battalions were starving or receiving only very irregular food supplies, they had been kept well fed and it was through her that many of them were still alive. The only one who dared to comment was Kifaru, who was in a state of complete despair, and all he said was "What a tragedy! May the God of Kirinyaga help her and her husband."

No one knew better than Kifaru that his days of power were drawing to an end and it was only a matter of time before his friends started to desert him. Even the information, volunteered by one of the Police defectors, that the Sergeant was shot because of the District

Officer's injury, failed to arouse his apathetic spirits. Normally, news like this would have made him strike back blindly to revenge such an injustice, but Nundu had changed irreparably, and in him his men now saw only a fierce brute who had taken to living the life of a recluse. They had lost hope to such an extent that even seeing Nundu in difficulties with his beard no longer raised a spark of hilarity.

A matter of great concern to Nundu was that since the reorganisation of their forces, a bitter struggle for power between the leaders was becoming intensified daily; in fact even the lower ranks were beginning to wonder who was in command. As far as he could see, he had every right to command the battalion for it had regrouped in his area. Apart from this, he had proved his supremacy over the other leaders so many times with his endless succession of daring ventures and victories. Traditionally, however, he could not command men like Njogu and Mrefu who were senior to him in years and who had joined the Movement when he was but a lad. Everyone knew these older men lacked the initiative and dynamic vigour required, and indeed they feared that if tradition was strictly followed they would lose their war for no other reason than that Nundu was not in supreme command. Nundu writhed under the orders of these older men for he knew that their inferior strategic ability, apart from galling his pride, could lead to utter defeat. Even the ordinary fighters preferred to fight under Nundu and the other Field Marshals knew this but they, being ambitious and only human, refused to admit the fact that a young man could have superior ability; and so they prated of tribal customs and traditions and kept him firmly under their thumb.

Nundu decided to call a meeting of the heads of the battalion — three Field Marshals and six Generals — in order to thrash out their differences once and for all and to decide who would be the overall leader of the battalion. Although he was but poorly educated, he was a genius when it came to organising and this talent had found fertile ground on which to develop. After they had eaten their morning gruel, he sent his aide-de-camp to ask the heads to come and see him. They arrived one by one and sat on the grass just outside Kifaru's house which had been built on a raised part of the ground. The atmosphere was tense, and it was not long before the curious soldiers saw their leaders gesticulating furiously. At one point Kifaru and Njogu, who were once such comrades, stood up to fight each other, but Mrefu, still the conciliator, intervened and persuaded them to be calm and sit down again. The sound of loud angry voices rang through the glade, and Njogu and Kifaru eventually stalked away, leaving the whole battalion gazing silently after them.

One of the generals stood up and faced the horrified group. "Brothers," he said, "Field Marshal Kifaru summoned your leaders here this morning in an effort to resolve our differences and nominate a supreme leader for the battalion. We thought this to be an excellent idea, but unfortunately they could not find a solution and the whole meeting as you saw was a sad failure. They all want to be supreme commander and, as far as we, and I believe you, are concerned Kifaru far surpasses them all. Unfortunately, tribal custom forbids him to command us whilst there are older men here of the same rank. Field Marshal Kifaru asked them to prove their organising ability, to speak of their prowess and leadership in war, to prove that they were more capable than he of commanding this battalion, and they refused to answer. As you see, they have left the meeting and we are still at discord. Go about your various duties and keep calm. This rivalry will be settled one way or the other."

The fighters wandered disconsolately away, discussing this new trend of events. It was more than clear that they wanted Kifaru to command them, but even they realised that if an exception was made and custom flouted, a dangerous precedent would be created. The whole battalion was in confusion for it had no leader. The security forces had become so powerful that they could no longer swoop in night raids and come back triumphant, but for the most part the general feeling was that it was better to stay where they were and die in the forest, which was their home, rather than return to the reserve which was a very hell on earth.

Kifaru tossed restlessly on his pallet that night, and as he smoked his *bhangi*, he decided that the only course was to take his men and with them any others who wanted to follow him, and cut themselves off from the endless bickering and confusion by organising a daring raid on the reserve. In other words, his band could either follow him or remain in the camp. Thus, and only thus, would he know where he stood.

The following day he summoned his closest friends and told them that they were going to make a raid in the reserve and requested them to spread the news as unobtrusively as possible amongst all those whom they considered would be eager to follow him. Without question they agreed to these proposals, and chuckled amongst themselves at leaving the other Field Marshals in the camp to continue their quarrelling. They whispered the news to their friends, and nearly the whole battalion volunteered to follow Nundu, who drew his main support from the younger men to whom he was an inspiration. The secondary reason for these raids was that they were desperate for food and they agreed to operate between the forest and the reserve and collect as much food as possible. They also wanted to fight the security forces with a new "hide and seek" method for they believed in action rather than in words.

Kifaru's first attempts met with outstanding success. He had chosen an area which had been relatively peaceful and in which the security forces were not expecting him to operate. He had decided against the Naro area where he was too well known. He and his band swooped on a village fifty miles from Naro on a dark, moonless night. This was to their advantage for they could see like cats in the dark, and indeed their senses had developed, due to their forest life, far beyond those of normal people. Because of his success, Nundu decided that instead of returning to the forest he would press onward until perhaps he could sweep the security forces out of his path and capture Nairobi. If he was still alive by then, he would become the king of the whole country.

On the day following the fourth raid he ordered his men to rest in a conveniently situated valley where the women and children could bring them food. This particular valley, where water flowed in abundance, had a very wide basin-like swamp which never became dry. Maize and arrowroot, that stood five feet high, and many banana trees made it an ideal hiding place, and best of all it led right back into Kirinyaga forest: a quick getaway could therefore be made should they be attacked. Unfortunately this decision conflicted with that of the witchdoctor, who had predicted evil happenings that day. Nundu brushed the witchdoctor's advice aside with a scornful laugh, partly because so many things had been predicted that had never come to pass, and partly because Nundu, in his desperation, had determined to forge ahead regardless. He only allowed the witchdoctor to accompany them as his presence and guidance comforted the older fighters.

When he informed some of his men that they would be resting in this valley for a short time, they were not over enthusiastic as they had raided a village only twenty miles away the previous night. But this band was so strongly disciplined that they had to comply without comment. They lay there for the whole day, enjoying a freedom of spirit that somehow was completely absent in the forest. They watched the villagers and looked at each other's untidiness and filth with disgust, full of envy at the normal decent lives the villagers were pursuing. The quiet beautiful green countryside bewitched these hard relentless men, and they wished that they could return freely to their own families and firesides.

Nundu was awakened abruptly by his guards at about three o'clock that afternoon, and together they watched a middle-aged woman being roughly escorted along a footpath by a Tribal Policeman and three Home Guards armed with rifles taking her, so they supposed, to her nearby shamba. A recent Emergency Law was that no woman should go to her shamba unescorted if it was more than a few feet from her home — in many cases, these plots were anything up to five miles away. They watched this group anxiously, for though they had been fed by some small children in complete secrecy, it was quite likely that the escort would stumble upon them by chance. They lay motionless ready to silence these intruders if necessary, when the guards, looking around and, finding no one in sight, started to beat the woman with rifle butts, chuckling with glee. There seemed to be no one near enough to hear her heartrending pleas for mercy, and the three men knocked her down and one of the men raped her whilst the others roared with laughter. Kifaru hastily resorted to *bhangi,* and as soon as he felt its stimulating effects, he could keep silent no longer. By the time the second man had begun his evil deed, Kifaru ordered his men to mow the guard down. What an error he made, for his efforts were answered by a spate of rifle fire from all sides — they were surrounded by security forces. Someone had betrayed them, and the men they had mistakenly assumed to be guards, were soldiers who had arrested the women and were using her as a decoy.

Field Marshal Kifaru had made the blunder of all blunders. He had misjudged his position on the battlefield. Instead of proving that he was infallible, he had, for the first time, proved himself to be but human. His men, although doubting the wisdom of this order, had obediently surrounded the guards and opened fire. It was Nundu who had second thoughts on the probable close proximity of the security forces, and he was also afraid that one of the guards would get away and reveal their presence. Could they reach the forest in time should this happen? How could they traverse the necessary distance in broad daylight without being spotted — their very appearance would give them away. They were completely unknown to the population on this side

185

of the forest. Even the few who might co-operate only did so from fear and were liable to betray them. But these thoughts came too late — he ducked automatically at the unexpected burst of bullets and heard the groans of his men. Karoki, his dear friend, was crying out in agony about thirty yards away from him. Kifaru lost his head and ordered his men to fire, fire, fire. Again they were answered a hundred fold and, without orders, the men who were left crawled on their stomachs, amidst a hail of continuous bullets, towards the river and those who could swim dived in. All had but one thought — to get back to the forest before they were captured or killed. Kifaru crawled after his men, swearing profusely and urging them to hurry before all was lost. By using the water as a cover, they managed to break through the cordon and, although the security guards were quick to find this out and to follow them, the fighters started to run, dodging through the trees and firing behind them, and this kept the guards from getting too near.

Unfortunately, the security chiefs, visualising this possibility, had laid another cordon about six miles further on where a bridge had been built over the river and the scrub had been cleared. Kifaru, once more at the head of his men, spotted the Johnnies and changed course to a thicker part of the forest which lay a little further away. Mortar bullets rained down on these hapless men, and army planes dropped bomb after bomb. Each man was fleeing for his life, but even so, they formed a strong bodyguard around Kifaru. As they drew nearer to the Johnnies the planes stopped bombing, but the mortar fire became even more intense. They dropped once again on to their stomachs and crawled silently and unobtrusively towards the enemy lines. When they were all within range, they began singing independence songs and fired with all the guns they could muster. Their brazenness and sheer effrontery took the Johnnies completely by surprise, and thus they forced their way through the enemy lines and sped to the safety of the forest. They burned all the houses, grass and crops lying in their path, and even when they reached the forest they could see the pink and red glow in the sky. Not one villager had dared to oppose them. The Johnnies followed close on their tail and bullets still whined around them. It took the survivors three hours to cover five miles, and when mother nature spread her protective cloak of darkness around them, the security forces did not pursue them any further.

The depleted force travelled about three miles into the forest interior and when they were quite certain they had evaded their enemies, they collapsed on the ground and begged their god of Kirinyaga to help them and their comrades lost in the battle. Field Marshal Kifaru was impotent with rage at his mistake, and as soon as they had had a brief rest, ordered each group leader to take a rollcall of his men and to submit a list of the missing. He wept unashamedly when he heard that two of his former schoolmates and lifelong friends, Karoki and Iru, were dead. Very few answered to their names and indeed, it made no difference whether they were wounded or dead to the survivors. They sat in complete silence unable to believe that such a thing could have happened and many of the men wept. The death of Karoki and Iru was, to Nundu, the straw that broke the camel's back and he shook with grief.

Although Kifaru had lost most of his men in this unhappy collision, the security forces had also suffered heavy casualties. They had thought that they were going to meet a few half-starved natives, weak and defenceless from lack of food, but they had encountered an alarmingly well organised battalion who retaliated with astounding courage. News of the combat spread far and wide like a bush fire, and many secretly praised their people for such an effort. Unfortunately, the captured fighters revealed for the first time Kifaru's name, his rank, that he had commanded the battalion and that he had a good store of guns and ammunition. They revealed every detail and the news was given headline prominence in the newspapers. The Government offered a reward of 5,000 shillings to anyone who could help the Police capture Nundu.

187

After this raid, Kifaru's name became known over the whole country and although he had very foolishly lost so many of his men, it was soon forgotten, for the widespread publicity that he was being given angered the other Field Marshals and the struggle for power reached its climax. His followers refused to reveal how many were missing for they too had their pride, and they were determined to show that their company was the best and to recruit more supporters to their ranks. The other Field Marshals accused Kifaru of contravening tribal customs and demoted him to the rank of general, after which action they refused even to acknowledge his presence.

Kifaru could barely contain his anger and shame at this unjust treatment and the whole battalion was on the brink of mutiny when he called a hasty meeting of his supporters to inform them of the position.

"My faithful brothers, truly it is a sad day for us all. You must all know by now of the ignominy that has been thrust upon me, your leader. You have all known for some time how these Field Marshals of ours have been bickering and quarrelling and that only I am fit to lead you. Why should I, and all of you, suffer and maybe lose our lives because these men try to enforce customs that we know are outdated and futile in circumstances such as these? We all respect our traditions, but you must not forget that they came into being many, many years ago. When our forefathers created these customs, how could they have visualised what was going to happen? Are they here now, or are we? Will they suffer, or will we?" He paused and looked round at the hope dawning on the faces of his men.

"I cannot impress upon you too greatly the importance of a well organised army," he continued. "We have been forced into a defensive position, and why? Because some muddle-headed old idiots who couldn't even organise a relay race are so keen to better themselves that they could not care less how they do it. What a feeble excuse for this behaviour! My friends, would I be speaking to you like this if I were incapable of leading you? Would I sacrifice you all for my own benefit? We must get ourselves back into our former position. We must be on the offensive, attack and kill." He regarded his silent audience, who were hanging on his every word with rapt concentration.

"You are not children, you are men! It is up to you to decide which path you are going to follow. I can organise you. We can move mountains together, and maybe even capture Nairobi! There are no limits to what we can do. On the other hand, you can stay here and vegetate with our wonderful Field Marshals and eventually die like rats in a trap. The survival of every one of you depends upon your fighting skill and your leader. Tomorrow, I leave this den of weaklings, and if you stay, you stay without me." He turned abruptly away and walked towards his cave followed by resounding cheers which echoed through the valley. No one noticed that Nundu had omitted to mention the crushing defeat that was so recent.

The following day, as he had promised, he summoned his group leaders and told them to collect all those willing and follow him to another area many miles away where he could command them once again. The other Field Marshals tried desperately to prevent them going, for they knew how highly Kifaru was revered and they waited anxiously to see the outcome. They begged Kifaru to stay, but Kifaru who, as was now his habit, had boosted his spirits with *bhangi*, refused to compromise, and by mid-day, three-quarters of the men were on their way to a new hideout, they did not care where, as long as Kifaru was with them.

They travelled swiftly, resting during the night and moving during the day, as the forest was too thick in this part to reveal their presence. They trekked fifty miles before they found a suitable place to build a camp. When they arrived, they despatched their spies to encircle the area and find out how far they were from the reserve, to make tentative contacts with the local people. They were also instructed to learn the layout of the land, for they could not settle

189

comfortably in a new base until this was done.

*   *   *

About six months later, Nundu was both horrified and angered to hear that it had been his brother, Heho, who was the traitor that had revealed their hide-out to the security forces and who had even acted as their guide on that fatal day. Kifaru had sent word to his mother, whom he had not seen for several years, to come and see him, and the messenger had warned her not to speak of this to anyone. She, however, was overjoyed at the news and, ignorant of the strategies of war, had told Heho in confidence, never dreaming that one brother could betray another. Nundu was so furious that his first reaction was to wish he could shoot Heho, who had not only betrayed the Cause, but had wanted him, Nundu, his very own brother to be captured.

Edward Heho, for he was now so called after his baptism, had promised to collaborate fully with the Security Forces. He had been captured, had confessed and a few months later had become converted to Christianity. Nundu had misunderstood his motives, for Heho wanted him to be captured so that his soul could be saved, for fighting and killing were mortal sins. Heho had told his mother that he intended to betray Nundu, but told her, much to her bewilderment, not to seek the riches of this world but to wait for the riches of heaven — it was better to suffer in this world than to bear the torments of hell fire.

Nundu's nights were once more restless. His plans seemed to be failing continually. Their source of water had dried up, and the people in the new area were very hostile and persistently spurned his efforts to convert them to the Cause. The hopeless task of rallying them to his side was made even more impossible by the mere fact that he looked like a wild beast and that there was a very large and tempting price on his head. He knew too that Heho, whatever his motives, would keep up the search for him. Maybe the 5,000 shillings' blood money would tempt his own men to turn against him. What could he do? The nearest friendly village was over twenty miles away, food supplies had come to an abrupt end, and who could fight on an empty stomach? He felt a pang of guilt. "These men, who are my comrades and who have been with me for so long, what have I done to them? Will they all die because of my foolishness? Oh, god of Kirinyaga, help me!" There was not even one bullet left with which to shoot an antelope, let alone fight their way back to safety, to their friends.

He roused himself from his reverie and sent his A.D.C. to the camp to summon the group leaders immediately. "Warn them that they will have to obey my orders without question," he muttered, and gazed after his A.D.C. He sat motionless — what was he going to tell them?

9 INTO THE HORNET'S NEST

A few months later, the European section of Naro held a grand party for Carey Milton to celebrate his full recovery. Carey was not a very happy man for he guessed who had shot him, and he knew too that the Sergeant had been unjustly condemned to death. He realised that he could not have prevented this miscarriage of justice, but felt that he should exonerate the Sergeant for the sake of his wife and family. He came to the party with every intention of telling his associates the truth, but when Frank Jones, the Police Chief, in his welcoming speech informed the gathering that Carey had been commended in the New Year's Honours List for an M.B.E. for his bravery and the work he had done in the District, he was too overcome with joy to worry about a native family, and decided to shelve this unpleasant subject indefinitely.

He was hoisted shoulder high amidst enthusiastic cheers, and all his comrades, most of them bristling with weapons, clapped him on the back, drank his health and shouted the words of that well-known song, "For He's a Jolly Good Fellow!" Carey felt himself bursting with pride, and was unable to reply adequately to the compliments and praises that showered down upon him. If this was what happened after a miscarriage of justice, he thought, then so far as he was concerned there could be many more! The voice of his conscience was thus stifled very effectively.

This joy, however, did not resound in the forest. Mrefu himself had turned into a recluse. He missed Nundu, whom he still regarded as his son, and missed too the aura of security that Nundu seemed to carry with him. He had turned into a desperate man. The power struggle was not yet resolved and as a result the remainder of the battalion was a shambles. Still more men had deserted, there was little food, and their supply of ammunition was practically non-existent. The Army planes were dropping their bombs deeper and deeper into the forest, and it was only a matter of time before the camp would be obliterated and they with it. It was after many nights of sheer mental agony that he decided to escape and give himself up to the security forces. "Maybe," he thought, "they will allow me to go back to my work, but if not, I can go to the reserve, to my home." He knew that even his own men would shoot him without mercy if they discovered his intentions, apart from what they would do to those who agreed to go with him. He therefore summoned Muta and Kato, his former pupils, whom he trusted completely, and cautiously confided his thoughts in them. They respected his judgement highly, and although they were horrified that such a faithful fighter should consider deserting, they agreed to go with him and to try and recruit their closest friends. This was all done in the greatest of secrecy, and indeed from that time on they were never seen in public together in case the other men grew suspicious.

One evening they grouped together in a thicket a mile away from the camp. One by one they crept in, and Mrefu was happy to see that Kato and Muta had recruited three others. They glanced around fearfully, terrified that their moves had been detected. The safest time for this rendezvous was in the late evening, for the members of the battalion often wandered out of the camp at this time but they had to return by the time darkness fell.

Mrefu looked at these men and wondered what was in their hearts. "I cannot condemn them for what they intend to do," he thought, "for I am going to do it myself — how low can a man sink?" He sighed and beckoned them to gather near.

"My comrades," he whispered, "I cannot say I am happy this night. I hope you all realise why you are here, and what a dangerous venture we are contemplating. One word out of place, and our own friends will kill us. We all have our own reasons for wanting to go, and these must remain

193

personal. What we must plan is how to go. I must warn you that it is too dangerous to take any equipment with you. Anything you own must be left here: that is obvious. I would suggest that we group together as if going on a hunting trip, or on a routine patrol, and then, when we are clear of the camp, we'll make our way out of the forest. You have all read the pamphlets the planes have dropped and heard the loudspeakers, telling us how to surrender. Remember? We are all to surrender now, and the security forces will not rest until all the terrorists have surrendered. Bring your guns and ammunition, and hold a large tree branch over your heads to indicate surrender, and keep it there until you meet the security forces and no harm will come to you. My own personal feelings as your supposed leader are that surrender is the only sensible solution, and my decision was cemented by the power struggle that is causing a sheer waste of human beings and their resources. If we remain here, we shall die, either from starvation, as Njambi can no longer bring us food, or from the bombs that are being dropped daily nearer, apart from the severe cold we have to endure at these heights. What we really have to decide is where to die. In my opinion, it is better for us to die in the reserve where our people will know that we are dead; and it is possible that we may save our lives by surrendering. After all, we've killed all the buck and the rabbits nearby, and we are being pushed farther and farther up Kirinyaga, and in a short while we shall die of exposure on her snowy peaks." He paused, and looked sadly at his comrades. "My friends, a building divided amongst itself must fall, and great is that fall."

They discussed many methods of escape, and eventually decided that Mrefu's suggestion that they go on a hunting trip was the best. So they agreed to lose no time but to start out the following morning. Mrefu, for the first time in many months, asked them all to kneel and pray to their God of Kirinyaga. They prayed that he would help them to reach the reserve safely and allow them to see their wives and children and parents, if they were still alive. They prayed too that they might be helped safely through the forest and not meet any wild animals or security forces, and that they might be spared so that future generations would have someone to tell them the truth of the forest fighters. They then dispersed, promising to meet early the next day in the camp.

Mrefu watched them go, and then made his way back to camp. He lay on his pallet but could not sleep. "I hope I didn't do any harm this evening," he thought, "but I'm sure that we will never win another battle. We never go on fighting patrols now and what is the use of vegetating here until we die?" He wept silently, his face writhing in anguish. "Oh why, why did I ever stop teaching?" he moaned. "Why did I take the oaths in the first place? What a misbegotten and worthless dream it all was, and now I too have become a traitor. I, Field Marshal Mrefu!" He blindly reached for his *bhangi* — the last of a well hidden bundle which no one knew he had, and which he smoked secretly by himself in the early hours of the morning — and a few minutes later, the effect of the drug made him justify his defection. "Why, I ate this morning after starving for four days. It's too much to expect. I'm not going to stay here and starve for any man, and I'm not going to chew hides to keep myself alive any more. We never receive news of our other bands, or our relatives and families. I don't know how long I've been in this place, and although it is true that we had many victories in the beginning, the god of Kirinyaga has closed his eyes to his children. Perhaps we have made mistakes in his sight, and so we win no longer. There was plenty of food too, at the beginning," he murmured wistfully. "Whenever we fought, we brought back food and ammunition in plenty, suffered few casualties, and certainly food was brought into the forest past the security forces as if our god had blinded them. This was a holy war but . . ." he spat scornfully. "If our god turns against us, what are we to do? He has even let us kill all the wild animals here after Njambi was captured, and no wild life survives any higher up the mountain. He doesn't even bother to look after his own any more with his usual benevolence. We are on the run, and the security forces are pushing us further and further up the mountain. It's too cold for anyone to live up there, especially now that we are half naked because we can no longer steal clothes. Oh why did we have to bicker about leadership? Why didn't we let Nundu take charge; surely we would have been in a better position with him to lead us. He was such a wonderful man, and we are all such fools." He paused, and then began to whimper pitifully, rocking back and forth in his grief.

The security forces had gained all the knowledge required to defeat the terrorists, and they had changed their tactics to this end. They had made quite certain that no food supplies were being smuggled into the forests, and slowly and relentlessly they were driving the fighters nearer and nearer the snowy slopes of Kirinyaga, and the heights of the Aberdare Range, where no wild animals lived, thus ensuring that they starved to death if they did not surrender. Constant bombing attacks followed up by inter-forest patrols that engaged the fighters in damaging skirmishes demoralized and divided the fighters so much that they quarrelled amongst themselves and gave up hope. Mrefu, unknowingly, was therefore not alone in his decision. But he was ignorant of this, for the persistence of the "propaganda" pamphlets led him to believe that, even in this time of frustration, the masses remained staunch. The lack of information also made him believe what the loudspeakers said, for he had worked with the Government and he believed implicitly that it was just and true to its word. He never realised that he and his comrades had been in the forest for almost three years, for he had long lost count of the endless days. Apart from this, he forgot to take into account the vicissitudes of war.

Mrefu had very little sleep that night and, as the first rays of dawn crossed the sky, he dressed hurriedly in his scanty skins and crept round the camp to wake up his comrades. They grouped themselves together, laughing and talking, and marched up to Mrefu, who was waiting for them beside the caves. A few ribald comments were made by the remainder of the men, and bets were laid on the probability or otherwise of the hunting party bringing back some food. As soon as they were all ready, they marched to Njogu, saluted smartly, and Mrefu, grinning, hoping that the thump, thump of his heartbeats which were almost choking him could not be heard, said:

"Request permission to go hunting, Marshal." — these formalities were observed even more stringently after Kifaru's disappearance, and everyone was expected to show blind loyalty and discipline, even Mrefu himself.

"Permission granted — General Mrefu!" replied Njogu. "Report back at noon, and good luck."

These two friends continually joked about their rank, Njogu good humouredly, Mrefu because he had genuinely lost interest, but no one knew this as he was so reticent.

The group turned, and made their way out of the camp. None of them knew how far they had to go, what route to take, or even in what direction to travel. They had been so relentlessly chased by the security forces that they were utterly lost. They chatted about Kifaru, voicing their regret at his absence, agreeing wholeheartedly that out of them all only Kifaru was fit to take command for, although ruthless, he took the right decisions at the right time. They talked about many other things whilst they were within earshot of the sentries, but as soon as they had traversed about half a mile, they fell silent and stood back to allow Mrefu to take the lead. They looked around them at the huge, silent trees, the almost impassable undergrowth and the giant liana creepers. Mrefu shrugged his shoulders, much perturbed.

"It makes no difference which way we go," he whispered. "We have no compass and know not where we will find ourselves."

They stood helpless for a moment, when Muta said, "I have an idea, Marshal. See that massive tree over there? Couldn't one of us climb to the top and try to see over the forest? Perhaps we could locate our position, especially if we can see Kirinyaga."

Mrefu looked at the younger man rather benevolently, as if at a wayward child. "Yes, it's a good idea," he said, "but I'm too tired and weak to attempt such a climb, and I don't think you can do it either!"

Muta picked up the gauntlet without hesitation, weak as he was. "I'll do it, just let me try!" he said enthusiastically. They both felt that any slight disagreement could lead to an argument, which would have been disastrous, and to keep themselves united, they had at least to simulate friendship, and so Mrefu agreed.

"Try," he said, "but if you find it too difficult, we can abandon the idea."

Muta grinned and immediately set himself to conquer what looked to him like Mount Everest. The tree itself had a diameter of about two yards, and although its lower branches were more accessible than those of the other trees surrounding it, it was almost twice as high. His friends gave him a sharp boost up the tree, and from then on he was on his own. He climbed slowly, his arms clinging to the tree trunk, and hoisting himself up with a movement rather like that of a frog. He painfully climbed half way, and then sat on a great branch to rest, his breath coming in short gasps. The others gaped up at him, sub-consciously comparing him to a monkey; for who but a monkey could climb so high? He struggled on, and then, to the horror of the onlookers, he seemed to lose his grip and suddenly toppled downwards. Regardless of the danger of revealing their presence, his comrades screamed in terror at Muta's rapid descent that ripped noisily through the branches and leaves. They held out their hands in a vain effort to catch him, but at the last moment he became entangled in the thick branches near the bottom of the tree, and they sobbed with relief. Only these searching branches had saved him from certain death. Mrefu and Kato climbed gingerly into the tree and, during a breathless silence, lowered Muta to safety.

They examined a shivering Muta carefully, and found that although he had sprained his arm and was severely bruised, he was not seriously injured. They sat and rested for five minutes and Mrefu, abandoning this plan that had nearly caused the death of a close comrade, decided that they should use the sun as their "compass" by day, and the stars by night.

By midday, they had covered about five tortuous miles. The liana creepers tripped them, almost strangled them, and they felt that an eternity was being spent hacking and hewing their way through them. The only sound was the whoosh of the wind through the top branches of the trees, the continuous rustle of the bamboo, and the constant whine of the crickets. Mrefu called a short halt, and they flung themselves down, gasping for breath, only too glad to rest awhile. Until now, they had encountered no wild animals, much to their relief, but when they resumed their *safari*, they met a herd of baboons, who chattered and shrilled excitedly at the presence of humans.

"We look so like them that they won't even run away!" remarked Mrefu ruefully.

The whole forest trembled with the uproar, and the group quaked in terror once again, for thus could their presence be revealed. The undergrowth almost choked them and began to impede their progress to such an extent that they decided to rest again. They were too terrified even to whisper, apart from Muta who started to complain bitterly, and loudly too, his voice magnified in the silent surrounds, that his leg and arm hurt him and that he wanted some food and water. A day dream indeed! For they had neither, nor had they seen any water on their journey, even though they had travelled several miles — deep into the unknown. Mrefu snarled at Muta.

"Shut up you fool! Where do you think you are, heaven? Or are you just a baby? We must try to hurry. At the rate we are travelling we shall never see our homes and families any more. Perhaps tomorrow after we have

199

rested it won't be so difficult. Perhaps we may find a buck, or maybe some water. Your leg will probably be better as well." He turned to the others. "Deploy yourselves at twenty yard intervals," he ordered. "We start at dawn tomorrow, so get as much sleep as you can."

Accustomed to such orders, they unhesitatingly shinned up the thicker trees and settled themselves down for the night, apart from Muta, who was still moaning from his injuries. Kato broke a few branches from the bottom of his tree, and helped Muta to settle down on them, lending him a skin cloak to keep him warm.

Unfortunately, but perhaps naturally, very few of them slept that night. It was bitterly cold, and the wind howling through the trees chilled them to their marrow bones. In their hearts, they doubted the wisdom of having embarked on such a venture, and wondered if they would ever reach the outskirts of the forest, let alone their homes. But, as they had spent a night away from camp, they could not go back. Apart from the fact that they did not know where the camp was, a stern rule had been enforced that no one should stay out of camp during the hours of darkness. The reason for this was that a man could easily spend the night with a woman who could bring them all bad luck and who could also betray their position to the security forces. Any man who did rejoin his battalion the next day risked execution or, at the least, a purification ceremony with very unpalatable rites performed by the witchdoctor.

Next morning, very early, they climbed down from their trees and sat down near Muta whilst Mrefu tried to verify their position.

"To my right is the East, where the sun rises," he said. "And now, my right hand is pointing directly at Kirinyaga. My left hand will therefore be pointing west towards the Aberdares. I must be facing the North, and Naro Township, and behind me is the South, which is the direction which should lead us approximately to our homes." He stood thoughtfully awhile, and then turned abruptly to his comrades.

"As far as I can ascertain, we must travel due south, which is this way. Come, we must make haste and start without delay."

Kato, who was standing beside the still sleeping Muta, shook his shoulder to rouse him. "Come, Muta, we must be on our way," he said.

"I can't walk Kato, what am I going to do?" Muta whined. Kato relayed this information to Mrefu, who swung furiously around.

"Use your common sense, you fool!" he snapped. "Can't you ask some one to help you pick him up and support him by his shoulders until he is better? I'm not waiting any longer. You'd better make up your minds quickly." So saying, Mrefu stalked away from them, knowing full well that at such a time sympathy, with which his heart was overflowing, would turn them soft.

Although Kato did not reply, he was extremely annoyed with this treatment from his friend. He swallowed his chagrin for the sake of their continued unity, and without a word to Mrefu, he asked one of his comrades to help him. They gently helped Muta up and slowly made their way after Mrefu.

They followed Mrefu very closely, and Kato began to regain his temper for Mrefu, as the pioneer of the party, was breaking down thick bamboos and bush and clearing the undergrowth with a large stick as he had no panga. The forest was even more impenetrable at this point, for the liana creepers, thick and sturdy, had entangled so closely with the bamboo and the thicket, that it required a continued superhuman effort to break through. Muta chuckled to himself as Mrefu toiled and sweated, whilst he followed with comparative ease. His leg was beginning to feel a great deal better, but he felt it was easier to travel this way than any other. Mrefu lost his footing many times, and was bruised and buffeted by the strong plants. His comrades laughed quietly, but could not restrain their merriment when he was stung by stinging nettles; but he too laughed, although grimacing with pain, and thus good relations were once more at their peak. Despite these hindrances, Mrefu was determined to achieve his goal. He could not change course, for the occasional glimpses he got of the sun told him they were still on the right track. If he wavered, they would be lost and he would have to shoulder the blame. Muta hobbled along, supporting himself first on one friend and then on another, until they found a dry stick strong enough to support him. A little later on, they sat down to rest. They were growing feebler by the hour, for it was their second day without sufficient food. They had all managed to carry a little food with them when they had set out, but it was each man for himself and the little that was left was given to Muta, who had to gain more strength if he was to keep up with them. They did not want to abandon him, but were quite prepared to do so if he became too much of a nuisance.

They had chosen a very cool spot in which to rest. A gap in the huge trees allowed the sun's rays to filter in, and as a result, the grass was lush and green. They listened happily to the cacophony of sound from the trees above, caused by the hundreds of birds that were flying from branch to branch. The baboons chattered overhead, and the monkeys swung to and fro on the creepers, peering curiously from time to time at the weird objects below. The crickets shrilled, and honey bees buzzed peacefully around their hives. It was obvious that they had descended quite a way from the heights, and they praised Mrefu for his leadership. They chatted about this and that, telling old tribal tales, describing their homes — it was as if they had sworn an affidavit not to mention their experiences in the forest, or talk about the journey that they were undertaking. The past was taboo.

After an hour's rest, they started on their way once again, Muta still limping badly and stumbling over the smallest obstacles. Mrefu continued hacking a rough path, but with an enthusiasm and determination that was wavering considerably. Later on in the afternoon, they came upon an elephant track on which was fresh spoor. Mrefu almost broke down and wept.

"Look!" he shouted. "Look — we are not alone any more; here is life. We have disturbed this elephant, and if we travel another mile or so, we shall find something to eat. Where elephant are, there are buck and rabbits and numerous other animals which we might be able to snare. This will give us an incentive to travel a little further."

Kato was pessimistic. "Even if we do get that far, how will we be able to slaughter an animal? We have no knives and no means of making a fire — we shall die with the food looking at us!"

"Shame on you!" Mrefu replied scornfully. "Have we not a few bullets left? Our forefathers had no fire and no knives, and yet they lived — they had not even one bullet or knew what a bullet was! Here, take this rifle, and take one of your comrades and go and find us something to eat!"

Kato regarded him doubtfully.

"Come on!" Mrefu snapped. "That's an order, and we are hungry! A faint heart never succeeds — are you going?"

"Oh yes, Marshal, but — what do we do if we run into some security forces?"

"Concrete thinking on your part, for once," replied Mrefu sarcastically. "From now on, we must all carry a green branch of a tree in case we meet them, and when we do, we shall wave them in the air, signifying our surrender."

They tore down sufficient branches and waved them triumphantly in the air, and then Kato and his friend reluctantly made their way towards the expected buck, whilst Mrefu and the others made their night camp — a few green branches carelessly heaped round a small clearing for the fire, near which they would have to sleep, not only to keep themselves warm but to protect themselves from any of the larger game that might be near.

Kato crept through the undergrowth, which was now easier to traverse and, as he had been taught in such circumstances, to avoid getting lost he broke branches to mark his way back to camp. They walked about two miles but found nothing and heard nothing, except the singing of the birds and the chitter chatter of the baboons, who were settling themselves down for the night. On their way back, they saw a baby elephant which they tried to shoot, but the first shot missed, and to their horror they realised that its mother was grazing nearby with a great herd. The sound of its terrified squeals rent the air, and the bull elephant and the mother with one accord turned and charged. They scrambled up a large tree with seconds to spare, as the elephants thundered past them. They were marooned in the tree for about an hour until the bull elephant, tiring of standing underneath it, made his way slowly back to the herd which had wandered away, trumpeting his displeasure. They slithered silently down the tree and crept away from the danger, quaking at their narrow escape, and felt their way back to the camp, for darkness had almost fallen, and it was only by feeling the lower branches of the trees to find the broken ones that they succeeded.

Mrefu laughed to hear their tale, but was very upset to find that they had returned empty handed. They were all suffering from severe starvation, but there was nothing left to do but sleep. They huddled together in an effort to keep themselves warm — they were too dispirited to attempt to make a fire — and gazed sympathetically at Muta, whose leg and shoulder were rapidly swelling, and were obviously causing him a great deal of pain. The fact that he was both hungry and thirsty did not alleviate his suffering. Indeed, he looked as if he was in the last stages of elephantiasis, and his swollen shoulder gave him the appearance of a hunchback. He groaned continuously from the pain and at times screamed out, waking his comrades, who eventually lost all patience, and shouted and railed at him to stop his nonsense. They were afraid too that his screams would attract any wild animals nearby. However, they soon slept again and were in such dire straits that they even forgot to post guards round their camp.

Just after dawn, at the time when the early mountain winds would surely freeze the marrow bones of a polar bear, they heard a sound like thunder, comparable to a big diesel tractor without an exhaust pipe, rushing towards them. In utter confusion, and forgetting poor Muta who was unable to move, they flung themselves into the bush, and ran blindly from the scene. Muta screamed with terror as he saw a huge male rhino charging towards him. He felt himself hoisted into the air, and heard the roots of the bush beside which he was lying being torn out, and they were both flung several yards. He screamed with panic as he thumped to the ground, and hid his face in the soil, not daring to look up. The others, who had sufficiently regained their composure to peep through their cover, saw the rhino charge away in the other direction leaving Muta entangled in the uprooted bush. They rushed out to help him, but to their surprise and joy, the sharp horn had missed him and they could only surmise that the rhino had not seen him at all but had been annoyed with the bush! They all knew what peculiar whims rhinos suffered from due to their excessive shortsightedness! If it had charged Muta, he would have died a speedy death. Even so, the toss had shaken Muta's bones, and he whimpered with agony. They looked at him helplessly and prayed to their god of Kirinyaga to help them and to keep such dangerous wild animals out of their path.

On Mrefu's orders they searched for suitable material out of which to construct a rough stretcher, after a heated argument as to whether they should abandon Muta or not. Mrefu, however, could not stomach leaving such a dear friend to the mercy of the forest and its dangers, and his authority eventually swayed the reluctant men. After a search taking about three hours, they found two long and two short sticks, about one and a half inches in diameter, and made a rectangle out of them, just big enough to carry Muta comfortably. They covered the stretcher part with tree bark, weaving the bark in and out in basket fashion.

They laid Muta, none too sympathetically or gently, on the improvised stretcher and took turns to carry him. Apart from Muta's weight, although he was but light, they staggered almost uncontrollably, for it was their third day without either food or water. Their resentment mounted at this unwanted burden, and indeed they would have left him by the wayside if it had not been for Mrefu's repeated orders that he should not be left. Mrefu travelled in front of the stretcher bearers, clearing a pathway of sorts. They moved slowly and when, at what seemed to be midday, they came upon an animal track, from sheer desperation, weakness and hunger, they decided to follow it. A few miles further on, they found a stream rippling merrily over pebbles and rocks. They dropped the stretcher and, like desert cattle, they rushed with one accord to drink their fill, and it was not until they had had enough that one of them thought of the groaning Muta a few yards back. He, also in desperation, had crawled off his stretcher and was making his painful way to what seemed to be his salvation. They carried him to the stream and allowed him to gorge himself with the fresh, icy cold mountain water and watched him happily, once more laughing and talking about their good fortune. They sprawled on the river banks, their nostrils quivering in ecstasy at the fresh river scents, when suddenly Mrefu jumped to his feet in horror.

"Look," he stammered. "Let's get out of here, now!" The objects of his sudden panic were two big leopards asleep in the scrub by the river.

"Not another sound," he whispered. "You know full well that leopards lie in wait for their prey beside water. Quickly, we must go!"

They carefully lifted Muta back on to his stretcher and crept away from the leopards which, as a matter of interest, had not even noticed the intruders! They followed the course of the river, cursing now and then at its weaving banks, but even the most ignorant knew that all rivers flowed down the mountain side towards the reserve. Had not the god of Kirinyaga arranged this so that his people on the reserve could gain full benefit from the mountain waters? Therefore, there was no argument as to the course they should take, and their hearts once again full of joy, they followed their leader without question. A few miles further down stream, Mrefu halted and gathered his comrades round him.

"My brothers," he said. "Truly our god is with us once again. Look, for the first time since we left the camp, after three days without any food, I was about to lose hope, and look what blessings have fallen on our heads. I have had it at the back of my mind that if our brothers back in the camp suspected that we had escaped, they would have followed us, and they, being stronger than we, would easily have caught us. We would therefore have died, either from starvation or from the hands of our own. Now, with pure water running at our feet — unlike the filthy water in the bamboo shoots which is full of *dudus* and which never quenched our thirst — we shall be able to attain our goal. May the god of Kirinyaga bless us. Now, let us rest awhile."

They sprawled themselves out on the river bank, and Mrefu looked at them reflectively. "I very nearly lost my control over them," he thought sadly. "I really thought that they would refuse to carry Muta, and then what could I have done? He has been such a headache. If it hadn't been for him, we would have been miles away from here, and safe by now; maybe even in the reserve." He sighed pensively, got up and started to walk away from the others.

"Why, Field Marshal, what's wrong?" queried Kato.

Mrefu looked at his questioner, knowing that he could not reveal his true thoughts. "Oh," he said, "I was just thinking how glad I was that Muta is progressing so well, and that we have got so far. Why, after we have bathed him in the cold water, his swellings should go down, and perhaps he will be able to walk by himself very soon — but hush, look at those water buck over there! Quietly now, and we will be able to have some food!"

He stopped abruptly, and the others, without being told, quietly cocked their rifles and took aim. Bang! Four shots rang out and resounded in the glade. The immediate silence was broken by the shrill of frightened birds, and the thud of hooves as the water buck fled blindly from the scene, leaving four of their kind writhing on the ground behind them. Regardless of the possible proximity of the security forces, they left Muta lying on the river bank and ran towards the dying beasts. They were overjoyed at having found food at last, and indeed Kato and Mrefu had already started to drink the blood that was pouring from the bullet holes. Kato, hearing his friend's frantic pleas, plucked a water lily leaf, folded it into a bowl, and allowed the blood to fill it, upon which he took it to Muta, who drank greedily. It was almost sunset by this time, and they had to hurry to make full use of their quarry before the scavengers of the night swooped on their prey. Two of them collected firewood whilst the others searched for sharp pieces of wood suitable for skinning the animals, and liana creeper to use as rope to hang them on the lower branches of the trees. Mrefu was determined that they should have a real feast, not only to make up for their suffering, but to enable them to gain enough strength for the rest of the journey.

They had no artificial means with which to make a fire, and so Mrefu whittled two pieces of dry wood, boy scout fashion, and eventually caught a spark on some dry grass from which they made their fire. The others soon returned with sharp sticks, and efficiently they skinned the animals and removed all the innards. This had to be done first for, as in all tropical countries, meat goes bad much more quickly if the offal is not immediately removed. They forged a chain; first cutting a chunk of meat and placing it in the centre of the glade, then going to collect firewood, then resting from their exertions. Kato collected branches with which to make a rough hut under which they could sleep, when Mrefu called them all to him.

"We are fools!" he said. "Here we are, in the open and completely defenceless, when in the middle of the river is a small island covered in scrub that could surely harbour us for the time being. Come, use your last ounce of strength to remove all traces of our presence here, and let us cross the river and rest on the island. There, we shall be safe."

They wearily did as they were told and followed Mrefu, who was carrying a lighted torch, across the river to the island. Kato, who for some unknown reason, had more strength than the others, made several trips back and forth to bring the remainder of the meat and firewood. It was he who remembered that they had forgotten Muta in the excitement, but soon he too was safely installed on the island, a happy grin curling his lips at the succulent smell of roasting meat. Kato, who took care of Muta as they had been at school together, roasted Muta some meat, and together they sat discussing their schooldays. Had they not joined the fighters together, and run away together? Their bonds of brotherhood were growing stronger daily.

The others were far too greedy to wait for the meat to cook. They gulped down the raw meat as if they were animals and, fully gorged and lulled into a sense of security from the warmth of the fire and the ripple of the waters, they sank into a deep sleep. Muta ate more slowly, but soon he too was satisfied and, after drinking a good deal of water, he too slept. There was not a breath of movement on that island until about ten o'clock the next day, when Kato lazily pulled himself together and put some small logs on the fire, which had burned all night and which was just about to flicker out. He cooked some more meat, and the men stirred at the delicious smell. Once again they gorged themselves until they could eat no longer for who knew when they would eat again? Kato, with permission, gently lowered Muta into the stream. Mrefu felt that the cold water would relieve Muta's pain, and perhaps lessen the swelling. Muta was greatly helped by this, and slept once again, relaxed and almost pain free.

They rested in this camp for about four days, mainly to ensure Muta's almost complete recovery before they attempted the final part of the journey. After the first day, which they spent eating and sleeping, they were less relaxed, and Mrefu ordered that, in case of surprise attack, only Muta and the man roasting the meat should remain in the centre of the island. The others were to deploy themselves at six hundred-yard intervals along the shore, being fed by the camp cook. In the evening they gathered together on the island, which they christened "Safety Island" and, without bothering to post guards, slept. On the second day, Muta showed great signs of improvement, and indeed walked a few steps. Mrefu was very pleased, for this proved to the others that his prediction that Muta would regain his health was true.

Here again, they did not discuss their past experiences in the forest. They were all fully aware of the danger hanging over their heads from both the security forces and their own people, and they knew full well that their comrades would already have started to look for them, fearing them dead or even captured by the security forces.

Indeed, their fears were not unfounded. Njogu was extremely disturbed when Mrefu did not return on the first night, but he decided to wait a little longer in case they had lost their way and were unable to find the camp. Two nights later, he summoned his group leaders and informed them that five of their comrades and Field Marshal Mrefu had not returned to camp although this they knew already. "They could either have defected or died of starvation," he said. "Perhaps they have been captured or molested by some wild animals, but as I am not sure what has happened to them, and I have heard nothing, ensure that the camp is well guarded at all times and that no one has the chance to slip out. Now, you and you," pointing at two of his group leaders, "are to make a search in the surrounding area and report to me twice daily. Move!"

They hurried away from Njogu's cave, murmuring amongst themselves. Obviously the Field Marshal was seriously worried at the disappearance of such trusted men and thought that they might have gone to betray the whereabouts of the camp. Even if this was not their intention they would be made to do it if they were captured. A surprise attack on the camp at this stage, with the men weak from lack of food and with very little ammunition, would be fatal.

The scouts reported at mid-day and in the evening to Njogu who ordered them to scout further afield, but still to no avail. After four days of searching, he ordered them to continue until they found a sign of either their spoor or perhaps their bones — which would be all that was left of them if they had been eaten by wild animals. He decided that there were only two possibilities remaining — either they had run away or they had missed their way back to camp, which seemed extremely unlikely. Mrefu was a hardened and much experienced campaigner. Njogu frothed and fumed, and intensified the sentry guard on the camp. He spent a week at the look-out post waiting for news from the searchers. Had they deserted too? At last he espied the two weary men making their way back and, regardless of the composure he was supposed to show as Commander, he shinned down the tree and ran as fast as he was able to meet them. He listened avidly to their report.

"We found a stretcher, sir," gasped one man.

"And a hut on the island on the river a few miles from here," chimed in the other.

"Calm yourselves," Njogu begged, "and tell me lucidly and clearly what you found."

"Well, sir, we found these things, and we gathered from a few traces that some people, one of them very sick, had stayed on this island for quite a long time. But the

211

long rains have just started and the island is almost covered by water. We had the greatest difficulty in reaching it. The traces we found were several days old and now the river is a raging torrent. I think that all the men on the island were drowned. We found no traces of anyone having left it."

"Congratulations on your efforts," replied Njogu, smiling broadly and patting them on the back. "You have done well and have proved yourselves to be true brothers of the forest. Go now and rest, but tell no one of what you have seen. I will make a public announcement later on in the day."

Njogu watched them wearily dragging their feet over the last few hundred yards, grinning with exultation. "I'm sorry they are dead," he reflected, "but, my goodness, far better dead than captured. I'm sure they must have been on their way to give themselves up — they deserve whatever death they got. It's lucky for them I didn't find them first! Maybe they are not drowned, but I must ensure that the rest of the men believe they are. Morale is low enough in this camp already, so perhaps a tale such as the one I will tell them will raise it a good deal." Chuckling to himself, he made his way back to camp and ordered his men to assemble.

He assumed a solemn mien, and gazed at his depleted troops.

"My brothers," he said, "we have waited a long time for news of Field Marshal Mrefu and those that went with him. I have noticed the tension building, and the looks of sorrow on your faces. Although I am happy to report that we have news of them, I am sad at the tale I have to tell. Our search party found their traces on the banks of the river. No doubt they had gone too far afield in their search for food and were caught by the torrent sweeping down from Kirinyaga. You all know the rainy season has set in, and the river is dangerously high now. I'm afraid that they all must have drowned. I order you all to go into official mourning for them by not eating an evening meal for four days. This will show our God how much we respect our comrades and how much we mourn their sad fate. I must say how grieved I am at having lost such a valued comrade and friend, apart from the men who were with him, in such a senseless way. I will take the earliest opportunity to inform their relatives, and tomorrow I will send a scout to search for Field Marshal Kifaru to give him the sad tidings. I'm sure that he will mourn too, for they were as father and son. Let us stand with bowed heads in silence for three minutes and pray that they are safely with our God." He turned away abruptly, rather to hide the expression of triumph on his face than to hide his sorrow, and went into his cave.

The next day he despatched a scout to find Field Marshal Kifaru. He hoped that this news of Mrefu would heal the breach between them and bring Kifaru back into the fold. He needed Kifaru badly, and saw this news as a means to draw them together once more, and cared not that the tidings might be false and that they would probably break Kifaru's heart. He had pondered for many sleepless nights on how to make peace with Kifaru and knew that his chance had come. He gave the scout a brief note saying:

"It is with great sadness that I have to tell you we have lost Mrefu and four others who were drowned on a hunting trip." — He did not dare mention Muta or Kato, whom Kifaru had known so well, for he knew that Kifaru would not believe any such story about their fate and would think that he, Njogu, had conspired against them and had shot them. — "We greatly mourn the departure of these dear comrades, and hope that you will join us in this unhappy hour.

"May the God of Kirinyaga keep them in a safe place, Njogu."

The scout returned a week later triumphant, for he had contacted the elusive Kifaru and bore a message from him. For the first time since they had parted, Kifaru wished Njogu every success and sent his sympathies over the tragic death of a man he had known and revered for so long. So Njogu's plan had indeed succeeded.

Meanwhile, after their stay on the island, Muta had almost completely recovered and was only limping slightly. He still suffered slight pain from his shoulder but this was hardly noticeable. Indeed, he had been so well fed and looked after that he looked physically far healthier and stronger than the others! It was he who, much to their surprise, broached the proposal that they should continue their journey, but Mrefu, always cautious, recommended another day's rest.

On the fifth day, Mrefu looked at the rising waters with an appraising eye and, realising that if they tarried much longer they would be marooned, gave the order to move. They waded through the deep angry waters with great difficulty, and made their way down the river bank. They covered ten more miles that day and surprised countless herds of buffalo, rhino, elephant and various types of buck coming to the water. They gazed longingly at their tracks, but did not dare venture from the river in case they lost their way again. The rain was now coming down in floods, they were cold, again hungry, and very miserable. They were forced to cross many tributaries leading to this now great river, and they too were swollen and angry. They made their way through thick swamp covered in papyrus grass which cut their feet and legs and dripped cold water down their necks. Muta began moaning with pain once again and began to lag behind. They were too frightened to sleep on the ground as they had encountered several prides of lion, so instead they slept in the trees, making the same arrangements for Muta as before.

The next morning dawned in a cover of thick swirling mist and barely a bird was stirring. They dared not move until the thick mist had cleared for a radius of a hundred yards in case they ran into the security forces. Mrefu was sure that their journey was nearly at an end. But hardly had the hope stirred within him before they heard the explosions of bombs — the security forces were still bombing the outskirts of the forest. Apprehension written on their faces, they looked to Mrefu for guidance. He listened a moment, and then grinned.

"Never fear," he said, "they are about ten miles away to the south of us. You know how sounds echo in a forest! Still, they will serve as a reminder to us that we are not as safe and secure as we might be — we must tread carefully now, but first let us pray that we arrive safely."

They once more followed the river, which was growing bigger at almost every turn. To their surprise and fear they saw fish that were accustomed to go upstream to spawn. They knew then that their journey was nearly at an end. An hour or so later, Mrefu's sixth sense warned him that danger was at hand and so he halted the party and ordered his men to hide in the thick river reeds. As they crouched, half immersed in the cold water, Mrefu wistfully remembered the traditional custom of keeping a log burning in the house every minute that the master was away, a custom which had been passed from generation to generation, and he wondered if his wife and mother had kept a log burning for him all this time. For a short while, the only sounds that could be heard were those of the croaking of the old bull frogs and the snorts of the hippo which abounded in this part of the river. Then they stiffened: no animals could make that noise! The crashing in the undergrowth and the sound of breaking twigs grew louder, and suddenly a large group of Johnnies broke through the bush surrounding the river bank and, laughing and talking, they knelt to drink water, completely unaware of the shivering freedom fighters so near to them. Mrefu and his party froze where they were. A sudden move would mean, at best, a bullet in the head. They heard desultory pieces of conversation and watched, their mouths watering, the soldiers pull what looked like small cooked chops from their knapsacks and start to eat them. At a command, they grouped together again and marched, to the best of their ability, although much hampered by the forest conditions, towards the edge of the forest, throwing the finished bones away. One of them struck poor Muta on his sore shoulder and it was only Kato's quick thinking that saved the day, for he immediately clamped his hand hard on to Muta's mouth, thus preventing the scream of pain from escaping his lips.

They heard the bomber planes coming nearer and cowered in the reeds, but fortunately they changed course. For a few moments all was still. Mrefu stood up and looked around.

"All's clear, brothers," he whispered, "come on out!" But no sooner had he spoken than they heard sporadic bursts of machine gun fire. They dived back into safety, shivering with terror, and waiting to hear the whine of bullets and feel them thudding into their bodies. However, even the noise of the fighting faded away at last and once more they stood up and looked round. Mrefu began to wonder whether it was really worth while surrendering. "If our people are still fighting," he thought, "surely we should be fighting with them and not hiding here like a bunch of rats. Maybe our final victory is at hand. But even if we did join our comrades, they would think we were Government spies. Would they really welcome us with open arms? We cannot give our reasons for leaving our battalion. If only I could think of a good excuse for us being here — something that they would believe. If they didn't believe us, why our fate would be far worse than that meted out by the security forces. Even if I could withstand their pressure, what about Muta? He is weak and in great pain. They would only have to hit him a couple of times and he would blurt out the whole truth. But why should I bother with these thoughts now that we have come so near to securing our goal?"

He turned to the others. "Come now," he said cheeringly, "we are nearly home now. But from now on all of you keep those branches ready and wave them in the air should you see the Johnnies. They will know that we are surrendering and will not shoot us. They will just make us prisoners of war like they did the Italians during the great war."

They sat on the river banks in the sun to dry themselves. They were shivering uncontrollably — not from the cold but from fear and Mrefu, seeing their state of mind, began to talk to them reassuringly, rather like an elder advising his sons beside the fire.

"Now my dear, dear brothers, my comrades in adversity, we are about to reach either the reserve or the areas where the security forces are operating," Mrefu said. "It is understandable that you are afraid, for we have all seen that there is still a fierce fight going on, and indeed we will meet our fate in the very near future. Now, I must warn you again about these branches," indicating a pile of branches that they had torn off the neighbouring trees. "Carry them with you all the time and the Johnnies will know that we are coming to surrender. When the time comes, you must not panic. Oh yes," he laughed, "I understand that it is not easy to stand still and put your hands up when you are at the wrong end of a gun, but that is the way it must be. Now rest awhile. As you've heard, there is a big fight going on in front and we don't want to run into it. We must therefore wait here and sleep until tomorrow. Eat all the meat you have left, and then choose your trees as usual."

By this time the group regarded Mrefu as their father and, childlike, relied on every word he spoke. They therefore slept peacefully, leaving Mrefu in a state of mental agony that none could relieve. He still doubted the wisdom of leaving Njogu, and remembered, particularly on this his last night of freedom, the oaths he had taken never to betray his country or the Cause for which he was fighting. He remembered too that he had sworn never to surrender his gun or betray his comrades. He groaned aloud in agony. "But that is exactly what I am intending to do," he whispered. "I feel, deep within me, that I can best help my country by coming out of the forest and working with and for my

217

H

people. What use am I to anyone by allowing myself to stagnate uselessly in the forest? I can do so much good out in the open. I know I can — so am I really betraying them? Can't I serve the Cause as I think fit? I am an intelligent man, not a fool. I can work underground — perhaps form a political party. Oh God help me, what am I to do? I can't go back and answer the barrage of questions that Njogu will ask me." He looked at the trees which sheltered his comrades. "I know not, nor care, what their motives are, but how can I take them back with me to certain death? They are but children and follow me as if I were their father." He wept brokenly and prayed that he had taken the right decision. Now there was no turning back. They were on the threshold of betraying all they had fought and lived for. Mrefu slept very little that night.

Dawn broke the next day to find them preparing themselves for the final encounter. Mrefu had aged many years during that one night and, although he had persuaded himself yet again that he had taken the right step, part of him revolted at what he intended to do. But stoically he hid his feelings from the men and ordered them to go immediately on their way so that they could bring the inevitable suffering to an end one way or the other. The going was still very tough and they crossed tributary upon tributary, each one seeming angrier and more swollen than the other. They had covered another ten miles by the evening. They knew that they were nearly at journey's end for they had spotted the imprints of soldiers' hobnailed boots in the mud near the river, and the bush was becoming less impenetrable. They also noted with horror the numerous bomb craters around them. They gazed and gaped, and indeed all but turned to run back to safety. Again, it was Mrefu's fatherly, reassuring voice that brought them to their senses.

"Look at them and look well," he whispered, "but do not be afraid. They bombed here yesterday but not today. They do not waste their bombs in the same spot all the time. Eat the meat you are carrying and then rest in the trees.

I do not know how far we have yet to travel, but it is not very far. We cannot shoot any buck now, or light a fire: it is too dangerous."

Mrefu again spent a night of mental agony, even though his common sense told him that it was useless to continue fighting against such heavy odds in such a way. He gazed at the semi-obscured stars and breathed a prayer that "All our fighting and suffering might not have been in vain. Oh God of Kirinyaga, give us our *Uhuru*. Have we not fought for it? Do we not deserve it? Forgive us for surrendering, but surely you must understand that we are but human and we did our best. I want to continue fighting but in a different way. You must understand my motives. Oh give us our freedom! Free us from the bonds of slavery — let your people go! Do not let all our suffering count for naught!"

They gathered around Mrefu for directions the next morning, their eyes glazed with hopelessness and fear. The mist was heavy, giving them the appearance of mysterious and weird ghosts. Mrefu looked around him and once again waited for the mist to clear before he gave the order to move on. They had followed the river so closely that they had not noticed it led into a deep gorge, with sides that became more steep and sheer with every mile that they travelled. Mrefu, seeing that they would soon be trapped, sighed, and gave the order from which there was no return.

"We must climb up the sides of this valley," he said. "The rocks are not so sheer just over there and there are plenty of bushes and trees that will help us. This must be our final day of freedom. We will soon meet the security forces. Today is the day. If you want to go back, make your choice now."

They looked at each other fearfully and grouped even closer around Mrefu. "We will go wherever you go," whispered Kato. "We cannot turn back now."

With one accord they turned towards the cliffs and slowly

219

ascended them with the help of the numerous liana creepers and trees. Muta was unable to climb it by himself as his foot had swelled yet again, so Mrefu helped him out of the valley. They reached the top with little difficulty and gazed at the thick forest which they had just left. Looking ahead, they saw contours that they knew; contours that meant home. They drank in the scenery with a mixture of hope, happiness and sorrow in their hearts, for none of them knew what the immediate future would bring.

They travelled towards the forest verge, closely following the line of the valley, and by midday they came upon a large clearing that stretched for several miles. They feared to cross this for they felt naked away from the protection of the forest that had clothed and befriended them for so many years. Mrefu told them that this could be one of the special areas where they were waiting for the fighters to surrender, and so, bravely lifting their green branches high above their heads, they crossed the clearing and reached another forest — one of pine trees which had been planted by white men on the land that they had stolen. The Forest Department, they remembered, had planted these trees several years ago and the group was aghast at the height the trees had attained. It was only then that a growing realisation came upon them that they had spent many years in the mountain forests. They grew more confident, and indeed began to chat happily about the freedom that was so near. They had not been molested, so why should the security forces attack them now? Mrefu strolled ahead of his friends, marvelling at the height of the great pine trees. It was an enormous man-planted forest. The other side was considered to be a special area, but this they did not know. They dodged around the trees until suddenly Mrefu, pushing aside a large bush, came face to face with a huge crowd of people, perhaps numbering ten thousand, men, women and children, who were sitting apathetically, obviously resting from their labours, sprawled round a huge trench which, to Mrefu's eyes, seemed to measure ten feet by ten feet and was visible as far as the eye could see.

Several askaris, both white men and Africans, were standing guard with guns pointed at the group.

This crowd of people had been forced to dig the trench, and every man and woman who could stand, and every child over the age of eight, were forced out of their houses at three o'clock every morning and made to dig, with short periods of rest, until seven in the evening. Embedded thickly in the bottom of the trench were sharpened sticks. There were two purposes to this trench: one was to keep the people fully occupied and under close guard so that they could not take food into the forest, with the desired effect of making their hatred, resentment and discontent direct itself at the forest fighters rather than towards the white man; and the second was to keep the fighters hemmed in the forest. It was intended that this trench should eventually surround the whole of Mount Kirinyaga — a length of approximately two hundred miles at the least. At any rate, it served the purpose of keeping the people fully occupied and under the Government's direct eye. They had been digging for months and had nothing to look forward to but more digging. They had covered many miles and had many more to go. These people were being treated like slaves and they blamed the forest fighters for each day of slavery that they suffered, for placing them in this predicament. Those, and there were many, who sympathised with the fighters and would have done anything to help them given the chance, did not dare to express their feelings.

Neither Mrefu nor his colleagues had ever heard about this venture, and they walked boldly out into the open. Many of the people, who had turned almost into beasts, waved their arms to attract the guards, screaming and shouting frenziedly. Kato and Mrefu did not run but stood their ground. Muta, limping badly, and the others turned to flee back to the welcoming trees, dropping their green branches in panic. The askaris opened fire, and bullet upon bullet poured into their defenceless bodies. Mrefu and Kato were seized by the angry crowd, each person endeavouring to hit them to satisfy his anger at the cause of his ill treatment. The askaris, grinning at each other, strolled over to push the mob away, but when the District Officer arrived on the scene both Kato and Mrefu were more than half dead. He threw them into the Land-Rover and drove away. He stopped the vehicle half way up the hill, and drove back.

"Attention all of you!" he shouted, and listened to the sullen, angry murmur fade away. "You have done well this day, and for your good deed you will be allowed to rest for a full hour starting now! I thank you for the service you have done the Government. When these two," he glanced contemptuously into the back of the Land-Rover, "die, I will display their bodies in the market place. Askari! Take those bodies over there and put them on show near the market, so that all can see how they suffered for their crimes."

He drove away in a cloud of dust leaving the people, no less sullen and resentful, resting silently under the trees.

Mrefu's wife was amongst those working and she had recognised her husband, but did not dare cry out for fear of being arrested herself and maybe making things worse for him. Her heart overflowed with anguish. "Will he live?" she moaned to herself. "What will they do to my man? The man I have not even seen or heard of for years? Will he not even be allowed to see me and his children, who are now fully grown, before he dies?"

10 REUNITED

Mrefu was kept in the hospital for a month. He was allowed no visitors: even his closest relatives were unable to see him. Two askaris maintained a twenty-four-hour guard by his bedside, and they were so frightened he would escape that, sick man as he was, they tied his hands and feet to the bed rail to make him completely immobile. He was perpetually bothered by crowds of curious spectators who crowded round the windows of his room to gape and stare, and their comments on his filthy, rope-like hair and straggly beard made him writhe. He knew full well that he looked like a wild animal, and had begged the hospital staff on many occasions to give him a bath, cut his hair, and make him into a decent human being once more, but to no avail. They gave him a rough "lick and a promise" a day, and left him severely alone. They fed him, but only with sufficient food to keep him alive. Many of the more important Europeans of the rank of Commissioner and above had come to interrogate him, and the District Commissioner always accompanied them on their visits.

Mrefu, however, refused to speak, and they did not dare to treat him roughly in case he died before they were ready to execute him. He felt that indeed his surrender had been in vain, and he mourned the loss of his close companions, blaming himself for their deaths. He knew that they were keeping him alive for the gallows, and he prayed that they would make an end of him quickly. He had seriously pondered on whether to betray his comrades or not, and whether he should take the security forces to their camp, but he had come to the conclusion that he had done enough damage; he was traitor enough, and had descended low enough without committing the final sin of betrayal. He determined therefore not to talk unless he was tortured to such an extent that he could not help himself. He suffered extreme mental agony, and his isolation made him wish he could commit suicide, but the chance was never offered to him. He could not believe that the Government for which he had worked would treat a prisoner of war so badly, especially after all the promises it had made. What distressed him even more was the people who were making him a figure of fun, especially the askaris' families. He recognised many of these people, and thanked God that they did not recognise him.

He breathed a sigh of relief on the day when the doctor said he could be released from the hospital. "At last," he thought. "My time has come. Now they will hang me and I shall soon be with my ancestors." He was pulled roughly out of bed, and, as he was too weak to stand, they dragged him out of the ward. Askaris armed with cocked automatic rifles stood guard outside the hospital in case any attempt was made to rescue Mrefu. He blinked at them, and tried to hide his eyes from the bright sun. A crowd of onlookers jeered at him, but he barely registered the fact. He was bracing himself for the inevitable end, and was determined to meet his death bravely. They blindfolded him and pushed him roughly into the prison van standing directly outside the main entrance. He did not know where he was going, but he knew they were going to shoot him, for he had heard many tales of how people were being taken into the bush and shot in cold blood by the security forces without any questions asked, and indeed without even the Government's knowledge. He again asked himself why he had been fool enough to believe what he had read, and the broadcasts he had heard; why he had trusted a Government to keep its word. It employed me, he muttered over and over again; it never lied to me before; what is wrong with me? Have I been condemned to die like an animal because I listened to them? I wanted to come back, and because I did, they are going to kill me. Is this the way I shall leave the soil of my forefathers, the soil that is already soaked in blood and reeking of the rotting bodies of those that have died for their fatherland? Am I not even to be allowed to say goodbye to my wife and children? My children! He paused.

Why they must be grown up now. I don't think I could even recognise them. His reverie was broken abruptly by an askari shouting at him.

"Move up there! Move up there!" the voice bellowed. Mrefu screamed uncontrollably at the agony of a whip laid mercilessly across his back. He crawled blindly away from his persecutor, quivering with pain. Even slight movement exhausted him, and he stopped only a few feet away, thinking he was well out of reach. Thwack! The whip shrilled down on to his defenceless back, and a rifle butt landed squarely on his shoulder.

"Move up, you fool," the voice repeated impatiently. "I told you to move up!"

Tears of agony blinding his eyes, he crawled across the van, guiding himself with his hand against its side, until he reached what he thought was the furthest corner away. There he cowered, waiting once more for the feel of the lash. He heard more orders given, people coughing, and the sound of shuffling in the van.

"They are not beating them," he murmured. "Why persecute me? I was only trying to free my country. I wonder what they are going to do to them — are they to die without trial too, or for some reason unknown to anyone, are they going to merit better treatment than I?"

He felt hot bodies pressing against his, and shrank back in his corner in an endeavour to protect his flaming body. He then heard footsteps approaching his corner, and felt a sharp chain being shackled round his wrist with a fierce brutality that electrified his already overstrung nerves. He stoically bit his lips to prevent himself uttering any further cry of pain. After all, he had brought this senseless suffering upon himself — he should never have left the forest in the first place, never have trusted the white man's words. He lifted his shackled hand with much difficulty, and found that it was joined to someone else's. At a sharp order to "Sit!", he forced himself into a squatting position, groaning with the effort, but not before a truncheon landed on his head because he was not moving fast enough. He tentatively stretched out his hand to feel the figure next to him, and was most surprised when it shrunk away.

"Jambo, who are you?" he whispered. "Don't be frightened, I won't hurt you." But, meeting with no response, Mrefu sat quiet once more.

"He doesn't even seem to understand what I am saying," Mrefu thought. "Who is he? What have they done to him? Ah well," he sighed, "perhaps I shall never know — maybe I should think about myself. Will that make things any better?"

The mysterious nonentity seated beside Mrefu was Nundu. Yes, poor Nundu had been captured at almost the same time as Mrefu, but, as he was not wounded, he had met with far worse treatment than his former school teacher. He had suffered all the worst forms of torture that his jailors could devise. Electric shocks, burning his eyes with bright lights, immersion in icy cold water, constant beatings, were all in the order of the day. His mental agony was even greater than all he had suffered physically, if this was possible, for he had watched many men suffer, and had seen them killed and thrown into graves and buried without any rites. He wondered who was sitting next to him, but did not dare respond because he knew the methods of the askaris, and what they would do to him or to the unknown stranger at the least provocation. Before they had bound his eyes, he recognised one of the askaris as being the man who had continually led him out into the forest to meet the firing squad and then led him back, still alive but a quivering wreck, after having witnessed each time the death of some of his comrades, and waiting for the bullets to tear into his own flesh.

Kifaru had received the message that his beloved Mrefu was dead, and he had wept bitterly. But Mrefu, still surmising who could be next to him, could never, in the wildest stretch of his imagination, have thought him to be Nundu. He fell to thinking about his adopted son, his heart full of affection, and he remembered bitterly the reason for the break between them. Anyhow, he thought, at least Nundu was clever enough to keep himself out of this predicament. I wonder what he is doing now, and what will happen to him.

In all, there were about forty detainees in the prison van, all of whom had suffered, in varying degrees, from the hands of their captors. They were from different camps and Police Stations, and had been rallied together to catch the monthly aeroplane to take them to the big detention camp situated on Kudu Island, about six hundred miles away. Kudu Island was one of the largest islands in the Great Lake, and considered the most inaccessible from shore, and therefore escape-proof. They knew not, nor cared, where they were going, and the fact that they were all blindfolded, either to prevent them from knowing where they were going, or from personal animosity or pure sadism, did not raise a spark of protest.

The van stopped with a jerk that made Nundu's already sensitive body burn like fire, and he bit his lip desperately, to prevent himself from screaming in agony, knowing full well that if he did, the whip would descend on his already raw shoulders. They were all herded roughly out, and were forced to march, military style, towards the waiting plane. For the first time, Mrefu realised that he was accompanied by a great many people, a realisation which helped him to conquer his agonizing pain, and the cramp which cruelly bent his body after sitting in one position for so long. Once more, he fell into an almost self-protective reverie, and winced as he remembered the way the crowd had booed and jeered at him, and quite unintentionally he faltered, bringing the wrathful, ever ready whip once more on his already bleeding back.

"What do you think you are doing?" spat the wielder. "This is not the forest where you are free and get fat and order people around! This is another place, son of a dog!"

227

Thwack! "Get a move on, you will soon learn!"

Mrefu came back to harsh reality with a painful awareness of his situation; he would remember the sound of the whistling whip and the bracing of his muscles in anticipation of the blow, and the actual blow itself, for the rest of his life. He grimaced. How long will that be? he wondered. He felt his companion pull him forward, and cursed himself for faltering. Kifaru knew what treatment to expect and forced his aching body forward, almost as if in a dream, to prevent the askaris using him as a target for their cruelty. Still blindfolded, he tripped over the gangway — which he did not know was there — and a rifle butt descended unhesitatingly upon his back. He was told to climb up it, and so he did, pulling Mrefu up behind him. Mrefu knew now that he was going to his death for, when but a child, he had been taught how the white men hanged people, first making them climb up steps, and when they reached the top, they stepped into a gaping void and then they were no more. He held his head up bravely, and murmured long forgotten prayers that he would not disgrace himself or his people by faltering at the end. He said "Amen!" so loudly, that all those behind him stopped in panic, for he made them think they were going to die also! He felt the sides of the plane with his hands, and wondered what was happening. He went through the door, and was forced to sit on what appeared to be a very hot, hard floor. He braced himself, waiting for the floor to cave in under him, when only seconds later he heard the door bang shut with such a force that most of them jumped up in fright.

He heard an engine start, and a voice saying very loudly, "All set for Kudu Island — Roger! . . . . Captain Macshort taking off in two seconds time. Will arrive in three hours. Over and out!"

Mrefu immediately realised where he was and what was happening, and he breathed a sigh of relief and began to enjoy his first ride in an aeroplane. Not so the others; they began to scream and shout for mercy, with the inevitable punishment. He heard the engines screaming into a roar, felt the plane move faster and faster and eventually they were airborne. "I've never heard of this strange Island," he thought exultantly, "but at least I am still alive, alive — oh the joy of being alive!"

One of the detainees started shouting once more; there was a sickening sound of a rifle butt crashing on to a skull, and then silence, deathly silence. No one dared move, and Mrefu, although longing to remove the cloth that bound his eyes never lifted a finger but, unbeknown to him, the others, many of them prisoners of several months' standing and hardened to the treatment they received, had removed theirs. They had become openly rebellious and defied everybody and everything, and indeed this type of prisoner had become nicknamed "Charcoal" (hardcore) by the authorities. When the journey was nearly over, amidst roars of laughter, one of the detainees uncovered Mrefu's eyes, but he, blinking at the bright light, hid his head to ward off any reprisals. He groped for the cloth and was just about to replace it when he came to his senses and realised that everyone was looking at him. He laughed shamefacedly, for he knew he had made an utter fool of himself. He looked curiously at the man who had been shackled to him all this time, but still could not distinguish his features as his head was turned away, and he obviously had no intention of making any overtures.

Mrefu looked out of the plane window, and saw the Great Lake below him and realised they were descending rapidly. An island, which at first looked small, grew bigger and bigger, and soon he could distinguish row upon row of what looked like army barracks, and many many people looking up at the aeroplane. So this was Kudu Island? He heard the pilot flick on his radio.

"Calling Kudu Island! Calling Kudu Island — Over!" .... "Get your guards ready, we have a load of charcoal on board. Landing in five minutes, over and out."

Mrefu watched the land taking shape outside the plane

and felt the slight bump as they touched down. He gaped at the trees whizzing past, in amazement. Were they really travelling so quickly? Would they be able to stop? To his great relief, slowly everything came back into perspective and they ground to a halt. The plane was immediately surrounded by prison warders — who looked very strange to Mrefu, who had never seen the uniform before. He wondered what kind of people they were, and certainly hoped they were better than the strange people who had guarded them all this way. They could not even speak Swahili correctly, and their ears were pierced and their ear lobes dangling, in some cases, almost to their shoulders — a custom he had thought used only by women. They were tall and cruel-looking, and certainly seemed manly enough, but no man would be seen dead with his ears pierced. Mrefu could not understand it at all, but he had soon forgotten these details when he, together with the others, was forced to line up, descend from the plane, and walk towards the camp.

The fresh lake winds played softly on his face, and he could hear once more the welcome chirrupings of the birds in the little clump of trees beside the airfield. He braced himself; this didn't seem half so bad! All the detainees were naked, except for shorts; it was too hot to wear anything else. The camp itself, upon closer inspection, consisted of many roughly built mud huts, with twenty men per hut. The inmates crowded curiously around the latest arrivals, pushing and shoving to obtain a better glimpse of them. Some were still eating their lunch. "At least we get food here!" Mrefu thought, and he obediently fell into line and marched with the others. He looked again at his still silent comrade with much curiosity. Surely he had seen him somewhere before? Who was he? Mrefu felt a pressure on his arm and, wise already to the normal maneouvres called upon in prison life, looked straight ahead, but unobtrusively bent his head nearer to his comrade.

"Mrefu, Mrefu!"

It was someone who knew him, Mrefu thought. It almost

sounded like — no, that could not be. He is still safe in the forest.

"Mrefu!" The whisper became more persistent and the pressure on his arm was quite painful.

"It is Nundu, oh my father . . ."

Mrefu stopped short, and tears of joy began to pour down his face.

"Nundu, my son!" he whispered.

"Go on, go on. Do not stop or look at me, or we will be separated and punished," whispered Nundu. "My father, I thought you were dead." He broke off, too overcome to say any more.

Mrefu pressed Nundu's arm. "Yes, it is I, my beloved son, it is I, alive and not so well. But what have they done to you? You have surely suffered?"

"Yes . . ."

Nundu broke off as the contingent came abruptly to a halt. They both watched the warders unlocking the shackles, and listened to them clinking as they fell to the ground. Mrefu held up his hand eagerly.

"Not so fast, my friend," growled the hefty Sergeant. "Your turn will come all in good time."

The Sergeant unlocked their fetters, and Mrefu gratefully rubbed his arm in an effort to get the blood circulating freely once again.

"Now listen, all of you!" came the gruff voice of the Prison Commandant. "I want no nonsense here from any of you. You will do as you are told without comment and follow the prison routine implicitly. Any insubordination, and the troublemakers will be beaten. You will be under close guard all the time, but, I warn you for your own sakes, do not try to escape. This island is fifty miles from the nearest land. No doubt you could build yourselves small canoes from the driftwood that is so frequently washed ashore — others have tried that and indeed, we have watched them sail away. For your information they have never reached the mainland. They were either drowned — squalls blow up so suddenly on this lake that they even sink large dhows — or they were eaten by crocodiles. The hippos have a nasty habit of edging under canoes and turning them over, and then the occupants become crocodile meat. I personally will help you to build the canoes if you so wish." He burst into raucous laughter. "No, this is the island from which there is no escape. But," and his voice took on a warning note, "you will do as you are told, or it will be the worse for you. My warders will allot you your cells, and the inmates will tell you what to do. I want no nonsense from any of you." He turned abruptly away, leaving his subordinate staff to marshal the prisoners to the mess.

"Don't let on you know me," whispered Nundu through his teeth as he was led away, and they both determined to get a bunk in the same cell from where they could talk to each other. They both knew that if they were found to be friends they would not only be separated, but would be tortured to give details of how their friendship came about. They were issued with tin mugs and a tin plate, two thin blankets, a spoon, and a pair of shorts and rubber sandals each. After eating they were shepherded to their quarters.

Kudu Island was situated in the middle of the Great Lake. It was a God-forsaken place, ideally suited to the restriction of dangerous convicts, for none had escaped alive from its precincts. It was about two miles square, sandy and desolate. Palm trees grew on its shores, and until the detention camp was built there, it was completely un-inhabited apart from the swarms of mosquitoes that still lived there. The sun shone down relentlessly on it all day, and the heat was unbearable. During the lake storms, it was battered and beaten by the waves, and it turned into an unpleasant mire. Indeed it was the true concept of a desert island, for even the grass was sparse and only unhappy looking cacti and aloes, apart from the odd palm tree, eked out an unhappy existence there. The only part of the island which could be termed healthy was in the centre, where a small fresh water spring trickled out of some rocks, and here the vegetation was quite green and healthy. The contours of the island rose gently in the middle, leaving a wide valley between the hills, and it was here that the airfield had been laid out and the camp erected. Two large watchtowers, in which were two warders with automatic rifles, had been erected on each hill, and from this viewpoint the whole island and the activity on it, could be watched without hindrance. Two powerful spotlights, working from a large generator, could be switched on and off at will, and these shed light on the camp and could be used if there was any disturbance. There was a small jetty at one point, where the water was extremely deep, and here the cargo boat stopped once a month and docked to stock the camp with the necessary supplies of food and other items. When this boat came, stringent security precautions were enforced, and the prisoners who were not helping to unload the cargo were locked in their cells. A rollcall was held before the boat docked and after she went.

The view from the island was desolate but beautiful. Miles and miles of unbroken water — azure blue on a fine day, and grey and forbidding during the very frequent storms. The other side of the island was planted with vegetables, irrigated by the waste water used in the camp, and although the prisoners toiled over these plants, treating them almost like children, they met with little success. The actual camp was about a mile long, and had been built in a straight line, with the askaris' houses at each end. The toilets were of the bucket type, and were very seldom emptied. This of course brought flies, and many of the inmates eventually died of dysentery. A doctor only visited the camp once in every three months, and there were no other medical facilities available apart from the normal First Aid Kits. The washroom was constructed of four sacks, supported by sticks at both top and bottom. The one redeeming feature was that the lake water was fresh, and therefore there was an abundant and never-ending supply of fresh water.

233

Unfortunately, Nundu and Mrefu were separated, although their cells were very near. However, they had been paired together for working duties, and therefore ate together. No one had guessed their relationship, and they behaved as a couple of strangers would behave to each other in such strange circumstances. After eating a sparse meal of posho and beans, which was to become a never varying diet, they saluted each other courteously, and went to their cells. Mrefu eyed his room mates with great suspicion and cordial dislike — they certainly looked a lot of ruffians, and any one of them could be an informer, but he had no choice of selection, and so he rolled himself up in his blanket and soon slept, feeling happy that out of all this mess he had found his son. That was enough consolation for all he had suffered and would suffer. He thought of Muta before he slept, and thanked Kirinyaga for taking him and therefore saving him all this suffering. "He was but a child," Mrefu mused, "and I loved him dearly. He was very brave on our journey, and indeed I feel it was really worthwhile to have saved him the way I did. He could never have withstood all the suffering that I have had to bear. God knew this and took him away before he disgraced himself in front of us all. Now, we will all have a fond, affectionate and proud memory of him. He was a grand boy, and it was no waste that he died when he did. He had done his job, and done it well. He's happy and well now, and must be very proud of his achievements as I am also. I am proud to have been associated with him. But what about Kato? I've been so full of my own troubles that I've hardly thought about him. He's a grand boy too, much fuller of stamina than my Muta. I wonder if he's still alive — but it's no use mourning over the dead; perhaps he will turn up yet. No one knows what's happened to him. I can but pray that he's still alive. Oh, I'm so tired, I must sleep . . . sleep . . ."

The following morning, after rollcall, Mrefu was summoned to the Commissioner's Office. His heart sank to his boots. Here it comes, he thought, and holding his head high, he marched as smartly as he could, his body still aching from the treatment he had received the previous day, into the office. He was immediately surrounded by a group of European officers who began to interrogate him. What was his name? How old was he? Where was his family? Where was he working before he became a forest fighter? How many raids had he led and how many people had he killed? Where was his camp? Where was the rest of his battalion? How much food and how many arms had they? and so on and so forth until Mrefu could have screamed from pure exasperation. He answered the first few questions which he considered irrelevant, but when it came to betraying his comrades, he fell dumb and refused to speak. They followed this line of questioning for four days before giving up all hope of obtaining information. However, they followed it, on each day, with brutally devised persuasive methods; on the first day they forced Mrefu to lie on the ground, and making him support his body by his right forefinger, they twirled him round and round until he collapsed.

But worse was to follow. On the second day, they tied two sticks, one against his forehead and one against the back of his head, as tightly as possible; twisted them tighter, rather like a tourniquet, and then hit them with a hammer. Mrefu screamed out in pain, and mercifully soon lost consciousness, but they revived him time and time again by pouring buckets of cold water over him, but still to no avail.

On the third and fourth days, they beat his private parts with solid sticks, making him curl in agony, and then they stuck needles in his nails and worked them round inside the flesh and flailed his whole body with a cat o' nine tails; but when the wrecked body still lay before them mute and unflinching, they gave up in disgust and threw him into his bunk and left him there to lick his wounds, more dead than alive.

They questioned Nundu severely, but as his body was

235

already so bent and emaciated from previous treatment, they did little to him. The other new inmates of the camp were also put to the test in varying degrees, and then they were all left to the elders who were charged with the task of seeing that they remained alive.

The camp routine was that of a normal prison camp. The prisoners were awakened at six o'clock every morning, and after they had tidied up their cells and made their beds, they partook of a porridge breakfast and then swept the compound. They were supposed then to empty the toilet buckets, but seldom did, and then they worked in the prison warders' gardens and in the shambas. At lunch time, they ate posho and beans and in the afternoon they were drilled, and did physical exercises until they were exhausted. Only in the late afternoons and early evenings were they free and then, before supper which again was composed of posho and beans, they played cards or draughts, or even slept. They were encouraged to hold debates, but although this attracted a large number of interested onlookers, few were brave enough to take part, as they were afraid of talking in front of the prison guards. This was the time that Nundu and Mrefu seized their chance, unnoticed, to renew their relationship, although it took Mrefu well over a month even to recover partially from the severe treatment he had received. Nundu had visited him on several occasions, and they had agreed that once Mrefu could walk, they would play draughts together, and like condemned men, they lived for the day when they could do this.

Once Mrefu was well enough, Nundu played draughts with him constantly, much to the amusement of the warders, who chaffed them continually about their lazy habits. Nundu, who was always rather a lone wolf had, since his capture, grown into a complete recluse. His conversation and habits verged on the peculiar, he seldom ate or talked much, and avoided company like the plague. Whilst Mrefu was convalescing, Nundu spoke to no one unless it was absolutely necessary, for he felt there was no one else in the camp worth talking to. Mrefu chafed at the bit

during his seclusion, for he too wanted to find out what
had happened to Nundu and the others, and he dared not
speak to his cell comrades in case one turned out to be an
informer. Although he had been a Field Marshal in the
forest, his appearance had been something of a mystery to
the authorities; although unkempt, his manner had an
indefinable bearing of authority and dignity; but all their
attempts to find out who and what he was were in vain.

As Nundu was almost completely illiterate, Mrefu
offered to teach him and to read to him; this also gave
them a chance to talk to each other. There were numerous
magazines in the mess, and it was quite a normal sight to
see them, in their free time, detach themselves from the
others and sit under a lonely, small palm tree, much the
worse for wear, where they pored either over the draught
board or the magazines. Neither of them were interested
in these ostensible occupations, and Mrefu not only wanted
to know what had happened to Nundu and his comrades,
but wanted to obtain Nundu's approval for his action. He
knew in his heart that he had betrayed his oaths, and
desperately wanted to hide the fact that he had been caught
on the brink of surrender and it was only due to unforeseen
circumstances and utter confusion that his plan had failed.
He knew too that the others had been killed, but was
completely uncertain as to Kato's whereabouts, or whether
he was dead or alive. He feared that Kato would probably
tell the truth if he was still alive, and this increased his
worry and uncertainty, and he felt that the only hope left
was to gain Nundu's support. He almost hoped that Kato
too had been killed so that he would be the only man left
alive who knew the truth. He trembled to think that one
word from Kato could ruin the reputation which had been
built over the course of so many years, and reveal that it
was he who had not only blundered, but through that
blunder had sacrificed the lives of his closest comrades,
through his plans going awry.

Nundu and Mrefu, as soon as Mrefu was partially
recovered, collected the draughts board, picked their small

tree, and sat down. Nundu started to talk, stammering at first and unable to find the correct words, as he had remained silent for so long that he had almost forgotten how to talk.

"How lucky we are, Mrefu," he said, "that we are really together again. We can say what we please here without danger of being overheard; it gives a bit of excitement to this dull life, apart from anything else. We must just remember to move the pieces around a little and watch out for the guards." He stopped, in an endeavour to explain as briefly and lucidly as possible how he had been influenced in his decisions by the trend of events, omitting completely to tell Mrefu that he had been listed as dead.

"You know I had to leave the battalion because of that terrible power struggle; the frustration and inactivity was too intense to bear." Nundu took a deep breath and continued, "That was where I made my mistake, and I regretted it deeply later. If only I had stayed with you . . . I'm sure that neither of us would have been here. If only, instead of losing precious time, we had united ourselves even more strongly; instead of fighting our enemies, we fought amongst ourselves; because of greed and ambition, we forgot that unity is strength. Oh, Mrefu, I never thought it would end up like this. Why, why did we do it?" He broke down, overcome by emotion. Like Mrefu, he wanted someone to stand by his side in case events turned out for the worse; and Mrefu, overcome with joy to find that Nundu was suffering in the same way, nearly embraced him openly. If they stood together regardless of each others' mistakes, surely they would be safe.

"Look, Nundu," he answered consolingly, astonished that his surly and reticent son should speak thus, "you mustn't take all the blame on your own shoulders. I'm certainly to blame myself, for if I had used my intelligence instead of opposing you, I could have stopped the whole thing happening — time is, time was. There is no use in crying over spilt milk."

Nundu looked at him and smiled. "Let's play a little now, Mrefu, or maybe the guards will suspect us."

Nundu bent over the board, completely disinterested in the game, in an endeavour to hide his facial expression in case it betrayed him. He knew that Mrefu, knowing him so well, would read his thoughts, which would jeopardise his whole reputation for heroism, which made everyone who came into contact with him admire him. It was bad enough to be a nonentity identified only by a number, but it would be worse if, when he was freed, Mrefu did not support him.

"Field Marshal, you know . . ." Nundu stopped, a look of horror on his face. If any of the warders heard that title, both of them would be hauled back into solitary confinement and torture, and although he felt very inferior at this juncture because of his actions, this would give him notoriety of the opposite kind. He could not bear the thought of the man he regarded as his father being dragged back for another round before he was even fully recovered from the first.

Mrefu gaped at him, utterly astonished. "You fool!" he gasped, "You know . . ."

"Yes, I know," interrupted Nundu. "I'm sorry, it just slipped out. It just seemed like old times talking together apart from the others like this, and I forgot myself. I swear in the name of Kirinyaga that I will not repeat this mistake. Please forgive me," he begged, almost sobbing.

Mrefu, realising that tension was running dangerously high and that they might give themselves away, bent even closer to the draughts board saying, "Forget it! I don't blame you for your mistake. I too allowed myself to be carried away."

They dropped the subject, and began to play seriously as one of the warders strolled towards them.

They played countless games, day after day, during which

Nundu, hestitantly at first, related his own experiences to Mrefu. It must be noted here that it took Nundu over six weeks to tell his tale, but for the sake of clarity it is related as in one sitting.

Mrefu patiently endeavoured to get him to open out, but it was not until they played their seventh game that Nundu really volunteered information.

"Listen, Mrefu," he whispered, "we must be careful. They, the warders I mean, have never seen me talk, really talk, since I came. They've grown used to seeing us chatting a little here, but if we really talk and forget about the game, they'll creep over and listen."

"Calm down, Nundu," said Mrefu soothingly. "Nothing will happen. I'll keep a look out. You just trust me." He said no more, although agog to hear the news, in case he petrified Nundu into silence once more, as he had done before when Nundu thought he was over-eager.

"I was stupidly caught," muttered Nundu bitterly. He leaned forward. "Do you know, Mrefu, it almost seems as if someone betrayed us that day. We'd planned for some time how to capture some recruits for my battalion, which rapidly became depleted through various causes once I left you. We decided that the best place was that enormous, stupid trench the white men are making our people dig. There we could find many young, able bodied men, and young girls too." He sighed wistfully. "The girls could fight as well, but they could also have given us that extra spurt of encouragement, and boosted our enthusiasm. It was so long since any of us had even touched a woman. My battalion had lost all its verve and vigour, and there was just no morale left at all. So I decided, mine of course being the final decision, that we should go and hide during the night in the nearby Government forest, and in the early morning, as soon as the people had started to dig, I intended that we open fire on the soldiers and askaris and cause a panic. Surprise has always been our element. Anyhow, in the confusion, many of the people would have run blindly away, and we could have seized them and made them our captives as they ran through our ranks. We were going to drive them back to our camp and train them to fight for their country. My group leaders thought it was an excellent idea." He paused, and Mrefu dared not speak lest the spell was broken. Nundu gazed pensively at the board for a few minutes and then continued:

"So we started a journey which was to take us a week. Funnily enough, we passed only three miles away from Njogu. I knew this, because Njogu sent a scout to inform me that you and a few others were drowned in the river, and that you had probably been washed away whilst trying to get from that little island to the shore. The scout told me where Njogu was hiding . . ."

Mrefu was severely shaken at this information, for he had never realised Njogu's men had come so near to finding him, but again, he dared not speak.

"But when I saw you in daylight in the plane, very much alive, if not very well, I could not believe my eyes, and I nearly wept for joy. But you must tell me your experience when I've finished; please don't interrupt me!" Mrefu, who had no intention of doing anything of the sort, just looked at him, his face devoid of all expression, terrified that he would reveal his guilt.

"Anyhow, I welcomed the messenger, and sent brotherly greetings to Njogu, but I did not reveal our plan because we were rivals. I led my men on that long trip, and we reached the forest verge just at dusk. We lay down beside the trees, making sure that none had seen us; but somebody must have done, otherwise how would they have caught us like rats in a trap?" Nundu groaned aloud — then quickly, in case a warder had noticed, he pretended he had made a stupid mistake in the game. Once he was sure he had not been overheard, he went on with his story. "But I must finish. Long before first light we crossed that wide open expanse between the two forests. I thought it was very small, but found it so large that we had to hide another

241

day in the Government forest. Perhaps we were seen there? We walked four miles, and then nearly ran into a group of askaris. We crept back about half a mile, and then covered ourselves with tree branches — they make a good camouflage — and slept for most of that night. We again crept forward, and I commanded my men to fire only when I gave the word, and only at the soldiers; they were not to harm any of the civilians, old or young, whether we needed them or not. At dawn we watched the people, our people, being herded to their work, and not gently either. Many of the small children cried bitterly from the cold, and the old men who could hardly walk, and who had barely sufficient strength to wield the *jembes,* tottered to the trench and started work. They were grouped in together by location, and each group was closely guarded. You know . . ." He bent forward, and grasped Mrefu's shoulder almost desperately, "I told my men to rout the soldiers, capture as many guns as possible, and drive as many prisoners as we could get back to the camp. We weren't going to hurt them — they are our people." He relaxed his grip and gazed vacantly across the prison compound. "The soldiers patrolled up and down, occasionally hitting those who weren't working with rifle butts or whips; and they were the old, and the babies. The young men and women just worked and worked; they were too scared to speak to each other. We waited a while to strike at the appropriate time — perhaps this was what caused our downfall. I had a lot of men, and I was captured as if I had been a drunken guinea fowl, but how it happened is still a mystery, and I hope someone will be able to elucidate for me if I ever survive to see our country free. Anyway, as I ordered my men to open fire, perhaps a split second before I gave the order, I thought the whole place was exploding around me; perhaps they were using sten guns, I don't know, but bullets whined around us and the whole forest vibrated with the noise. I threw myself to the ground deafened, and even now my hearing is still impaired. Then they stopped firing, and we were ordered to get up by the Johnnies in English, at least that's what I thought they said, for I do not speak their beastly language. Amidst terrified screams I climbed to my feet, hands held high in the air, and gazed in helpless horror at the scene before me. Many of the workers had fled in panic, some had thrown themselves down and others — that was what the screaming was about." Nundu shuddered, and hid his face in his hands, trying to shut out an ever present sight. "There were so many wounded there, so many writhing in agony and screaming pain; young children too. They didn't care who they shot; I saw all this in a split second, and then tried to turn round to see what had happened to my own men, but they fell upon me, like vultures on a lion's kill. They wrenched my gun out of my grasp, and then started to beat me and hit me with rifle butts, and when I fell to the ground, they stamped on me with their nailed boots and ground them into my face." He leaned forward. "Can't you see how disfigured I am now?" Mrefu didn't answer, and Nundu shook him angrily. "Can't you see . . ." Mrefu, who was barely listening, jerked to his senses with a shock. "Shush, you ass! Look at the warders, they'll be coming over in a minute. Why do you have to make such an exhibition of yourself?"

Nundu, once again sullen and very subdued, moved a draught on the board. "I'm sorry, brother, I forgot myself again, but you must hear me out or I shall go mad with keeping it all to myself. I'm calmer now." He stopped a minute, took a deep breath and then continued. "My whole body was a mass of pain and I lost consciousness."

Mrefu once again dropped into a brown study, unheeding Nundu's tale. "That's why the patrol of Johnnies was in the forest," he thought. "That'll also explain why our people were so hostile to us, why I was mistreated by them so much . . ."

Mrefu, with a supreme effort, shook himself out of his reverie and tried to listen to what Nundu was telling him.

". . . the Police then came and visited me in the hospital, and talked to the doctors in their barbaric language. I was told that I was going to the Police Station

243

because I was better and ready for questioning." Nundu spat in disgust. "More like a cow ready for slaughter," he muttered. "They half-dragged, half carried me to the Police van, and I was taken under heavy escort to the station. I didn't even know where I was, because they took me in the dead of night and threw me in the cell without even a light or a blanket. I shivered there until the next morning when they hauled me out for questioning. My whole body was already aching from the beating I had had. I wouldn't speak to them, for I knew whatever I said would be used against me. They offered me a reward if I gave them information that would lead to the capture of others in the forest; they promised to release me, not to detain me, and to give me police protection against those I would betray. It sounded like a lot of wishful thinking to me, and so I still didn't talk. Oh, they promised to give me lots of money too, I'd forgotten that — but when I still refused to speak, they beat me as if I was a horse, with rhino whips, and then they hit me with rifle butts. The rest they did I think it's better for me not to mention, you've just come through it and are not yet fully recovered. I don't want to remind you . . ." He fell silent again and pondered awhile on his misfortunes.

They shuffled draughtsmen round in a very desultory fashion, Mrefu once more back with his dear Muta in the forest, Nundu quivering with impotent rage at the terrible treatment he had received.

"I lay unconscious for a long time. But you know, I'd lost all count of days and dates, and even my memory is not what it used to be after being in the forest so long. When I regained my senses and started to totter, very painfully, about my cell, I found there was no window, that the only light I had filtered in through a tiny grille at the top of one wall, and that the door had four locks on it. There was a peephole in the door, so that my two guards could watch me continuously. I nearly went crazy at being cooped up like that, and when I heard my guards talking about the sun and trees, I begged them, and believe me

Mrefu, with tears streaming down my face, to let me go outside for just a short while. They pitied me and let me go out, but my eyes were so badly injured that I could not see. I heard many people shouting rude things at me and jeering, and I learned that I was something of a seven-day wonder. The warders told me that I was 100 miles from home and that everyone in the town knew a terrorist was in the prison, and every day many of them crowded round the prison in the hope that they would see me; a terrorist in this part of the country — and I still don't know where I was — was something to be viewed. They'd never seen one before. I think they must have been one of the tribes that live near the small lakes. The shouting got louder, and they obviously started throwing stones and sticks at me, for I could hear them hitting the wall behind me. I was taken in and locked up once again, and the crowd was dispersed. A short time later, they ordered me out of my cell, blind-folding me first, so I don't know whether it was night or day, and I was pushed outside. I heard people marching beside me, and I thought it was a firing squad. When they stopped, I panicked and started to run. Run!" Nundu roared with laughter, tinged with more than a little hatred.

"Do whisper," said Mrefu. "I'm listening so intently that I can hear every word, but we don't want the askaris to hear too. Now do go on!"

"Well, they caught me easily enough, and I felt myself being picked up and thrown into something, and gathered that it was a van. They whipped me, and indeed I nearly bit my tongue in two to prevent myself crying out. I crawled blindly away from those whips, what little blood I had left pouring out of my body, and then they caught me and chained me to two askaris. I was forced to sit between them, and I didn't dare move. The thing jolted up and down, every bump bringing its own exquisite twinge of agony. I don't know how long we were in the van, but when we did arrive, they didn't remove the cloth around my eyes until I was in another cell. I think I must have stayed there about sixteen days. It was a peculiar place, but it suited

245

me, because I feared the company I was given so much. Food was passed to me through a tiny hole in the wall, and the bucket was removed every morning and emptied by someone else who always woke me because he jangled his keys, almost making them play a tune. He opened a small door in the wall to remove the bucket — do you know, that place was so small, the bucket and I filled it. When they opened the door, the only thing I could do was to sit on it. But when they eventually took me out of there, they were so kind to me. I wasn't beaten — they lifted me gently into the van and chained me up to someone else, and that someone was you! Anyhow, you know the rest. I've talked too much! I'll see you at roll-call tomorrow. Listen, there's the food bell — let's go."

They joined the throng of hungry prisoners and made their way to the mess to collect their rations. Mrefu was still too deep in thought to notice the normal buffeting around the food bin, and Nundu had once more retired into his shell. And so, daily, they followed the normal prison routine, and in the late afternoons Nundu retailed his experiences, never noticing that Mrefu was not in the least forthcoming over his.

The following day, they were confined to their cells whilst the army aeroplane arrived. They watched eagerly through the bars and saw many more detainees descend from the plane, together with their guards. A medical team followed them, and many important prison officials, and together they toured the camp to inspect its condition. This, as Mrefu learned later, was a regular part of the monthly routine. The Head Dresser examined each inmate, closely guarded, and it was not until the plane had left, after selected prisoners had unloaded its supplies, that another roll-call was made, and the prisoners were allowed out of their cells. They eyed the new intake curiously, and with pity, but they did not dare make any gestures of open friendship until they had been interrogated. The cells, which formerly housed two to three inmates and even then were over-crowded, were filled to overflowing. Some of them had five men, some six and others even seven. The dining room was so small that they had to eat in groups and life became yet more unbearable. They were cooped up like sardines in a tin, and it was rumoured that even more detainees were to come.

Mrefu and Nundu kept apart for a week after the new inmates had arrived. They feared to be seen together in case one of the new arrivals recognised them, and indeed they felt that if they were seen together too much, the hand of authority would descend in suspicion upon them. But they soon realised that others had paired off and that no one seemed to mind what the prisoners did as long as they obeyed the prison rules without question. The screams of the latest inmates echoed over the camp as each one was forcibly interrogated, and it seemed to be wicked to enjoy any leisure whilst comrades, though strangers, were suffering in this fashion. They quaked in their shoes too, in case one of them gave information that would lead to more severe interrogation of the old inmates. During that week, both Mrefu and Nundu looked eagerly for one of their own comrades, Mrefu especially for Kato, but they recognised none.

After there were no more screams, and the camp was peaceful once more, Mrefu and Nundu wandered off to their usual place. By this time, Nundu had related all he had to tell, and was eagerly waiting to hear what Mrefu had to say. He had become Mrefu's shadow, rather pitiful in one who had been so independent, and followed him wherever he went, when it was possible. Even during the week they had been apart, Nundu had kept close to Mrefu.

Mrefu also felt the urge to tell his story, and had taken advantage of the past week to compose a tale that would conceal all his misdeeds and his desertion. They sat down under their tree, and before Nundu had time to set out the board Mrefu, eager to get the ordeal over, said, "After you left us Nundu, everything toppled completely and it became very difficult to find food."

"Excuse me, Mrefu," Nundu interrupted; "let me prepare the board before you start . . . Now, I'm ready — fire ahead."

"Well, we spent most of our time sitting in camp or hunting, and we got no information at all. Of course we heard the bombs dropping occasionally, but that was all. Njogu would not let us leave the camp except to hunt, and we never went out to fight."

Nundu was dismayed. "Do you mean to tell me that since I left you, you never went out to fight? I can't believe it. Why, we have fought numerous battles since we left you, that is why my battalion got so depleted. Honestly, Mrefu, I must blame you for such womanly behaviour. Even if Njogu was a coward, you had the same rank. Why didn't you take over the whole command? If you intended to behave like a lot of old women, it's just as well I left you sitting there . . ." He glared at Mrefu, who was inwardly chuckling with joy — "I've got Nundu just where I wanted him," he thought.

"Now listen, brother," Mrefu interrupted, "why do you think I was caught? You just keep calm and listen. You know that ever since my days in Naro, I never was a power seeker, and I had no wish to bring the struggle to a head. For this reason, I decided to select my very best men and start my own battalion like you did — and I too was caught in the process."

"Ah Mrefu, you misunderstood me," explained Nundu. "I didn't mean what I said. I've worked with you so long that I know how courageous you are! It is only because you were so disinterested in taking full command that you made me into what I am. You gave me every assistance and how can I forget how you stood behind me? I know that if it had been just you and I in the forest, without Njogu, we would have stayed together. But Njogu is a difficult man who stops at nothing, and sometimes I wonder if he knew why he was even in the forest. But that's all over now. Continue your story and forget him. He has made us suffer enough."

Mrefu gazed at Nundu, glancing occasionally at the draughts board, making no effort to hide his pretended anger at Njogu's behaviour.

"I think it's your move, Nundu," he interrupted, and bent down over the board to reassemble his thoughts. "Well, I don't blame you for saying these things," he said. "I too am furious, which is probably why I started telling my story so badly. I must control my feelings, and tell you the whole thing lucidly. Oh, by the way don't forget that this week we are in the first shift and there's the supper bell. We must hurry."

"Here, you take the draughts board and I'll follow on. I've got a thorn in my foot," replied Nundu.

Mrefu was thrilled at the timely interruption. Now he knew just what approach to use. He could play on Nundu's dislike for Njogu and he would be believed, whatever he said. The only setback to this was that Njogu was perhaps still alive and might be sent here. What about the message he sent to Nundu about my death, he thought. I'll have to make up a story that Njogu can't refute. I'll have to work it out tonight.

"Mrefu!" Nundu shouted. "It's really a long thorn, but I've got it out now — I suppose I'll have to wear these bloody sandals now." All the prisoners wore sandals made out of car tyres, and they chafed the ankles of people like Nundu who were accustomed to walking barefoot.

Mrefu did not answer, for he had reached the mess, and the quicker he got his food the better it was. The food was served from a forty-gallon drum, and the scrapings from the bottom were never appetising. Apart from this, as the inmates increased so did the rations allotted decrease. They had to wash their plates when they had finished, and there was only one tap available. There was therefore always a pushing and shoving around the food bin. After they had

249

finished their suppers, Nundu and Mrefu went to their respective cells, promising to continue their game the next day.

Next afternoon, as usual, they met under the tree, and Mrefu, who had spent a sleepless night, immediately continued his tale.

"I'm sorry I couldn't tell you more last night, Nundu," he said. "Being on first food shift leaves us very little time. These newcomers have put our daily routine out of balance. Anyhow, in our camp there was no discipline, no orders, no food, and confusion, quarrels and fights were all in the order of the day. So, as you did, I discovered I had no part to play in such stupidity, and I realised that I had not gone to the forest to sit around, but to fight for my country. So I took Muta, Kato and two others to help me recruit some men. When I eventually persuaded them to see things my way, I went to Njogu and told him we were going to hunt for some food, and he agreed. So in the morning, we took just the normal hunting equipment with us and set out. Indeed, if I'd known what kind of a journey it was going to be, I would have never attempted it. I never realised just how far we had been pushed into the forest. We must have been in the densest part, with huge trees, creepers and clumps of impenetrable bamboo. We could find no water except the nasty liquid in the bamboo stems. We couldn't see which way to go, so Muta climbed an enormous tree to try and locate our position. But he fell out of it, from sheer weakness, and injured his shoulder and ankle, and became a burden that grew more and more cumbersome as we went on. Then we came to the river, after having found no food at all. We were half starved. We saw a huge herd of water buck and shot four of them, and we had *kimandi* for five whole days. I reckon we deserved it. We rested, and indeed Muta benefited highly. After that we decided to follow the river to avoid getting lost. We heard sounds of firing and bombing. Perhaps it was you getting caught? We were nearly caught ourselves by a patrol of Johnnies, but we hid in the reeds in the nick of time. They talked of someone big having been captured. Of course now I know it was you. From there, we continued along the same river in the hope that as soon as we could see the edge of the forest we could penetrate it for about ten miles and establish a training base where we could be really independent of Njogu. A little further down, I discovered some boot marks in the mud which were obviously those of a security patrol. After that, we decided it was too dangerous to stay in the valley, so we climbed out of it and continued along its line. After a few more hours, we crossed what I had never seen before — the natural forest planted by the Government. Before we could regain our bearings, we came face to face with a huge crowd of people, all digging an enormous trench. Before I could do a thing, I was struck. The people seemed to rise up and fall upon me. I heard rifle fire, and the only thing I remember before I lost consciousness was Muta falling down with a cry — he'd been hit, and from the way he fell, I'm sure he is dead. The next thing I remember was that I was in a hospital bed, my hands and feet tied to the bedposts with two askaris sitting on either side of me. I saw a crowd of people peering in the windows, and they never dispersed until I was taken away. Some police officials asked me stupid questions, and I decided not to speak to them. They pestered me continually. My body was aching all over. The crowd had beaten me horribly."

Mrefu paused and shuddered at his recollections. "When I was taken out of the hospital," he continued, "I was blindfolded and led to the van where I was chained to you. They beat me because I stumbled, and I've never met such rude people before, apart from their brutality. I couldn't see where I was going, or where to sit, so they showed me with rhino whips and rifle butts. I still ache even now from their treatment, leave alone that room . . ." Mrefu pointed at the interrogation office. "You know all about that."

This story was also told over a period of a few weeks. Prisoners were flooding into the camp, as a result of which spare time was becoming more and more limited. When Mrefu and Nundu had told their stories, they took oaths that they would never repeat what they had heard, and they promised to remain friends and stand together and work together for the sake of themselves and their country. "We will support each other through these days of difficulty and suffering until our country is free from foreign oppression," they swore, and each ate a handful of soil to seal the oath. They decided to honour "their" tree, the tree that listened to all their secrets, by placing a few stones at its base to support it until it fell from old age, and they prayed that the God of Kirinyaga would keep it alive until after Uhuru so that they could come back and visit it. They decided to continue to play draughts under this tree but, in future, only to discuss current camp affairs.

The influx of new prisoners was still continuing at an alarming rate. Detention Camps on the mainland were slowly being emptied of recalcitrant prisoners, for the authorities felt that the "charcoal" was far safer on Kudu Island than anywhere else. Safer, as far as detention was concerned, that is, for they were blindfolded and knew not where they were, and their friends who were still free were unable to make plans to rescue them. Many important, well known people, whose sympathies were veering in favour of the suffering patriots, made many attempts to find out where they were being taken. But the arm of the Government stretches far, and none were able to discover this well kept secret, nor did they dare to complain or oppose this move. This ideal island, where the prison officials reigned supreme, was redesignated as a punishment camp, for the Government was determined to wreak its vengeance on those who had caused so much trouble. Conditions went from bad to worse, and the prisoners were forced to work, on meagre rations, continually the whole day. Gone was the semi-kind treatment that Mrefu and Nundu had received. The Government had lost its temper, and everyone had to suffer. A permanent airfield of concrete had to be built. This was the first item on the programme. After this, all buildings, starting with the warders' houses, had to be rebuilt with concrete so that the camp would become a permanent institution. Many extensions were to be built too. Cargo ships docked at the island's jetty to unload the raw materials for many days, and then the prisoners were set to work, regardless of their physical condition. No amenities such as cement mixers or bulldozers were provided. All the work was to be done with bare hands, and the minimum of tools. A contingent of prisoners was set to chipping the enormous boulders that had been provided into chips suitable for concrete. Others were set to level the airbase and clear ground. Every man was working from six in the morning, with half an hour's break for lunch, until seven in the evening. If one faltered, he was whipped mercilessly by the prison warders, who were enjoying being little lords of creation. The suffering became intense. With sadistic pleasure, the Chief Warder decreed that, apart from being whipped, if a prisoner hesitated over his work, he was to forfeit his food ration for the day, and as a result conditions went from bad to worse, and indeed many of the detainees died from this treatment.

The few educated prisoners fared far better. The Administration decided that those who could read and write were to be taught to become overseers and liaison officers, and perhaps coach the more intelligent of their illiterate friends. A message to this effect was circulated throughout the camp, and Mrefu, doubting its veracity, remembering what had happened to him before when he believed the Government, went to discuss with Nundu whether it would be wise for them to go for an interview. They decided that not much worse could happen to them and so, the following day, they joined a few others and took their turn in the office.

Mrefu had no trouble in answering the few questions in English that were asked of him, and he was only required to write a line of English. Ironically enough, he was the most highly educated person in the camp. Unlike the others, including Nundu, who were sent back to manual labour, he was given a chair, told to sit down and questioned as to his ability and experience for about thirty minutes. He explained readily that he had been a teacher and a high grade railway clerk, and when he was asked why he had ever joined the forest fighters and wasted his brain away, he answered simply that it was because he wanted to see his country free from the yoke of colonialism. They pressed him no further, and informed him that he had passed with flying colours.

The Head Warder escorted him around the camp, explaining the building plans. He was given confidential instructions on how to deal with the detainees and their grievances. Mrefu was astonished when he was shown a thick file containing many complaints, many of which had been presented whilst he and Nundu were talking by themselves, and he was extremely surprised to learn that just before he had arrived, the detainees had gone on strike.

The following morning, at roll-call, Mrefu was called in front of the lines of prisoners and introduced as their leader. To his dismay, and that of the prison officials, there was no response whatsoever, and not a prisoner blinked an eyelid. After roll-call was over, however, they grumbled and groused so loudly that the warders feared they were going to have a riot on their hands. Mrefu's new appointment was shortlived, for he was unable to convince his fellow inmates as to why he had agreed to accept the position of liaison officer. They had regarded him with suspicion previously as he had kept so much to himself, and now they believed that he had publicly declared himself a stooge of the Government.

One evening a couple of weeks later, the detainees, in a top secret meeting, decided to send a letter to the British Government in London to complain at the death of thirty of their comrades through dysentery. Even on an island such as this, they had ways and means of sending letters without the knowledge of the officials. When Mrefu heard of their plan, he immediately reported to the Chief Warder who instituted a search of the whole compound. Luckily for Mrefu, he was well liked by the officials, who protected him against the now openly hostile prisoners. They composed a song about the "Traitor" as he was nicknamed, and several of them started to pelt him with sticks and stones during the search, and soon a serious riot shook the camp. As a result of this riot, ten detainees were killed, several wounded and one warder also was killed. Much stricter discipline was enforced and Mrefu was hated even more.

By this time, the detention camp accommodated about six thousand men, and every hand was up in arms against Mrefu. They made life so unbearable for him that the Authorities gave him the task of supervising the stone breakers as they were very near his cell. Compound No. 1 was a hundred yards to the east, No. 2 a hundred yards to the west, No. 3 to the north and so on. From the air, the island had an appearance of a honeycomb filled with thousands of buzzing, busy bees, and as the detainees increased so did the numerous day to day tasks which had to be carried out. This was really what saved Mrefu from death or complete isolation, for many convicts were elected as cooks, storemen, overseers, liaison officers, and he was put in charge of them all. Although out of favour with the men, he was greatly liked by the warders, and they trusted his judgement implicitly. He was the man that had nearly lost his life for them, and they regarded him almost as a saviour, for if a letter of that nature had ever been sent to the high authorities, they would have all been summarily dismissed and even perhaps detained as collaborators. They felt that their debt of gratitude could never be too highly repaid and treated Mrefu accordingly. Mrefu was always quick to seize a chance and so, after the immediate uproar had died down, knowing just how unpopular he had made himself, he quietly approached Nundu, who had given him the information in the first place, and promised that he would help him to better his position in the camp if he would give him his support. He asked Nundu to tell the others that he would never betray them again, but only wanted to help them, and then sat back to await results.

The increasing number of detainees presented many more problems to the worried warders. More were dying of dysentery, more mouths had to be fed, and the general behaviour of the detainees had deteriorated to an alarming extent, for the camp was seriously understaffed and needed many more warders to enforce law and order than they had. Soon a serious epidemic of dysentery and malaria broke out. The food became practically uneatable, and the men hardly slept at night because they were packed into their cells like sardines. A few extra buildings that had been erected did nothing to alleviate this crush. Each block had its own secret leader, and one night, after a meeting, they decided to form a committee to draft letters to certain members of their organisation in Nairobi, who, as far as they knew, had not been detained, to see if they could help. Unfortunately certain of these leaders had played a prominent part in the betrayal of most of the detainees in the camp, but this they did not know. Nundu represented his block and Mrefu, forgiven for his errors because he could write the letters for them and would therefore prove a valuable asset, was summoned in front of the committee, sworn to secrecy, and quickly briefed as to his task. He and two others were told what to write, and the next day, under cover of the workers unloading the cargo of a ship that had just docked, and under the very noses of the askaris, they wrote the letter amidst the hustle and bustle around them.

Mrefu, who received preferential treatment, and was given better blankets, better food and even allowed to stroll outside the prison bounds, had no difficulty in obtaining the paper and pen. He presented the letter to the committee during the lunchtime break, thus proving his loyalty, and he was forgiven for his previous mistakes. One of the men passed it to a member of the cargo boat crew in the late evening, instructing him to pass it to a certain taxi driver who travelled frequently from the main port of the lake to Moka.

Unfortunately, the letter never reached its destination. The committee never realised the stringent precautions that were being taken and that all persons entering and leaving Moka were thoroughly searched by security forces.

The taxi driver hid the letter deep in the inside pocket of his leather jacket, and it would never have been found had he not panicked. When the police stopped him and searched him, he felt so uneasy that he betrayed himself. He remembered the instructions that he had been given — to give it to a certain person in a hotel in Nairobi, and to that person only and if the police caught him, he was to destroy the letter immediately. The sweat started to pour down his face as they searched the car, and he twisted his hands in such obvious panic that a plain clothes constable summoned him away from the others on to the side of the road. He was very well known, and as far as the police were concerned, it was a mere formality to search the car as he travelled on that particular route three times a week. However, as soon as he was called aside, he immediately reached for his inside pocket. Like lightning, the constable pulled out his gun and told him to put his hands up. They fell on him like a pack of wolves, thinking he had a gun, tore off his jacket and stripped him bare, regardless of his horrified passengers. Satisfied that he carried no firearm, they went through his papers. Soon enough, they found the envelope he was trying to hide. It was not addressed to a person, but to the hotel concerned. The European officer tore the envelope open, and to his astonishment found that it was addressed to no one except "Our leader in Nairobi" and contained a message to the effect that the leader was to call a meeting of the heads of the organisation, tell them of "our difficulties," and to please do it quickly before hunger, disease and hard work killed the prisoners; and it was signed by "Kudu Detainees." On another piece of paper inside the envelope was a comprehensive map of the Kudu Detention Camp, and suggestions as to the best way of invading the island and freeing the prisoners there.

The taxi driver was immediately handcuffed and he was dragged down to the nearest police station for interrogation. He was beaten severely before he gave them the information

257

they wanted. They immediately took him to the main port where he was told to point out the member of the crew who had given him the letter and his instructions. As the ship had once again set sail for Kudu Island, he was taken there in a Police Aircraft and escorted to the jetty. He failed to identify the man, upon which they called the mainland for extra men to help the prison warders interrogate everyone in the camp. As soon as reinforcements arrived, they laid about them with bayonets and whips. They cut the prisoners' rations to a quarter and made them work at a frantic pace, without rest, for several days. Many of them died from hunger or from diseases, or maltreatment, before one of them told the Police who had written the letter.

Mrefu was immediately arrested and flown to the mainland to face charges, leaving behind him many dead and dying. The taxi driver was kept as a witness, and also the warder who had given Mrefu the writing materials. Mrefu had told him that he wanted to write to his parents, and so the warder was to be one of the main witnesses for the prosecution. But all believed Mrefu guilty of subversive activity, and as he once again refused to betray his comrades, as he had done so long back, he and he alone bore the brunt of the charge of subversion, the penalty of which was death, if proven guilty.

Nundu, left behind on Kudu Island, wept bitterly and retired even further into his protective shell. The Head Warder told them all that he would keep them informed as to Mrefu's fate, and warned them what would happen to him for inciting them to betray the Government. Mrefu had won his way back into the hearts of the detainees, and had paid back his debt in full. As a result, tension grew and soon afterwards, the warder who had volunteered to bear witness against Mrefu was brutally murdered. The murder weapon, a piece of wood with six-inch nails driven through it, was found beside him.

11 "AT THE GOVERNOR'S PLEASURE"

The murder on Kudu Island shook the Authorities, and desperate attempts were made to find out who had committed this terrible crime. The incident never became known to the public, neither did the treatment of the prisoners after it happened. In the interests of security, partly because of the panic the news would have caused, and partly because the Authorities did not want to reveal the lack of discipline and law and order in the camp, it was decided that the matter would be treated as top secret, and top secret it remained. But the anticipated panic should the news leak out was nothing to the actual pandemonium that broke out in the camp immediately after the event. Security forces were flown to the Island in their hundreds, until they outnumbered the prisoners, and only then did they begin their search for evidence that might incriminate at least one prisoner.

The inmates were marshalled forcibly into lines, and a roll-call was made. Upon finding no one missing, the soldiers went from cell to cell, practically tearing them apart. This took them several hours, and during this time, the detainees were forced to stand to attention in the blazing mid-day sun, and indeed, many of them fainted from the over-exposure, and were left lying where they fell. After the fruitless search was over, the Chief Warder informed the group, now closely surrounded by guards with cocked guns, that no stone would be left unturned to find out who had committed this terrible crime. He advised them to speak out, and warned that if no information was forthcoming, they would all suffer until it was. He was met with a sullen, unbending silence and so, after discussions with his officers, it was decided that each prisoner should receive a quarter of his food ration every two days, and that water should be issued every three days — one glass per man. The Commandant hoped that this near starvation, plus the fact that it was the hottest time of the year — 90 in the shade — would soon break down the barrier of stubbornness. Someone was bound to collapse under the strain, and come forward. However, when, a week later, he had still met with no response, he ordered that the men be made to work even harder than previously; the weaker a man was, the heavier work he was to be forced to do. The whip, which had become a common feature in the daily life of the camp, was laid with even greater vigour on flinching backs, and many more men died from this severe treatment.

The Commandant, together with his senior officers, was seriously worried; indeed many of the prison officials feared for their lives. They had never encountered such a stubborn, unflinching number of prisoners in their lives, and many of them had worked in the Prisons Department for over twenty years, and were old campaigners. They called for Nundu, feeling that as he had been a personal friend of Mrefu's, he was probably the culprit. They interrogated him again, but remembering their previous failure with him, they soon left him alone. Nundu, although miserable at Mrefu's sudden forced departure, soon found that because he had been Mrefu's close friend, he was regarded as a hero by the rest of the prisoners. He was asked to be their leader, and to advise them how to behave in these terrible times. In many small secret meetings, he told them all to keep on fighting and not to give in (nearly all the inmates of the camp knew who had committed the murder, for the news had spread like wildfire) and he encouraged the weaker members when he felt their strength might fail them. It was entirely due to Nundu's efforts and encouragement that the warders never did find out who had committed the murder, and after three months of treating the prisoners like oxen, in conditions no different from a German concentration camp, they decided that they were wasting their time, and allowed the prison to return to something like normal. The Commandant knew, from the beginning, that it was a useless endeavour, for when they had buried their comrade on the island, with full honours, not a detainee had attended the funeral; but he felt that it was his duty to prove to the authorities that he had done all that was possible. Indeed, all the officers in the camp were severely reprimanded, and he himself, a couple of months later, was removed from the Island and sent to command a small detention camp in the Frontier District, a position which commanded little authority.

Mrefu, who was being held in custody in the Police station near Nairobi, overheard the warders discussing the events on Kudu Island about six months later, and was absolutely horrified at what had befallen his comrades. He himself was utterly bewildered at the justice that was being meted out to him. Every month his case appeared in the Magistrate's Court for mention; every month, the prosecution asked that he be remanded in custody to enable the Crown Counsel to procure more evidence. He had no idea that one of the main witnesses had been murdered, and he could not understand why neither the taxi driver nor the warder appeared at his hearings. He had been informed many times that he would be sentenced to death, and, for the first few months, was tranquilly awaiting this event. He had again given up all hope of remaining alive, and had stoically prepared himself to die bravely. However, as time went on, he slowly lost his self-control; when were they going to kill him. Why wouldn't they try him? After nine months of appearing in court, and returning to his cell still not knowing what was going to happen, he began to weep bitterly, and refuse his food.

"If you are going to kill me, why not do it now?" he would shout. "Why torture me in this fashion?"

He was kept in solitary confinement, and although he was treated fairly well, this did not compensate for the mental agony he was undergoing. He attempted to commit suicide by hanging himself with his blanket, and after this, the peephole in his cell door was kept continually open, and the warder on duty was instructed to look at him every five minutes, both day and night, and the light in his cell was left on all night, thus making his already poor eyesight

261

much worse. He was kept in this way for months and had completely resigned himself to remaining in the Police Station for the rest of his life, when one day the Officer in Charge, accompanied by two askaris, entered his cell and sat down on the bed. Mrefu gazed at him with apathetic eyes and huddled in the corner as far away from him as possible. This was the end, and he was not really sure whether he cared any more.

"I am ready to die now," he said. "I've been ready to die for the past year. Just get me out of here and get it over with . . ." Mrefu broke down and started to sob.

The Inspector looked at him, shaking his head sadly. Perhaps it would have been better if this man had been executed, he thought. I pity him for what he has suffered, even knowing him for what he is, and now he will suffer still more. He leaned forward and put his hand sympatheically on Mrefu's shoulder.

"No, my friend, we are not going to kill you, we are not enemies," he said reproachfully. "No, nothing of the sort. I have news for you at last." He paused, but Mrefu gazed at him wordlessly.

"I have just been informed that you are to be held at the Governor's pleasure," he continued, and waited expectantly for Mrefu's reaction.

As Mrefu still gazed at him vacantly, he tried to explain what this sentence meant. "Listen, Mrefu, you are going now to Moka Central Jail. No one is going to kill you! Don't look at me like that. What it really means is that our Governor has decided that you should be sent to prison, and when he thinks that you have changed your ideas and are no longer a dangerous political prisoner, he will have you released. Come on, you must leave here straight away. You have been a model prisoner, and I am sorry to lose you."

Mrefu gaped at him: was he being sarcastic or not? He watched the Officer walk to the door, and nod to his escort who pulled Mrefu rather roughly to his feet and took him out of the cell. He was taken to the office, where he was allowed to collect his pitifully meagre belongings before leaving the station.

Mrefu, whose mind had been affected by the treatment he had received, had not really grasped the meaning of what had been told him. He could not understand the obvious sympathy on the faces of the officers, and indeed on those of the few inmates of the police cells, who considered that this sentence was worse than death, for Mrefu would probably remain all his life in Nairobi Central Jail. Apart from this, British justice had failed sadly in its judgement of Mrefu. He had not even had a trial. However, Mrefu, still completely dazed, did not understand the intricacies of such a sentence. He realised that he was still alive and was probably going to remain so, although he did not trust any Government officer after his previous experiences, and still felt the shadow of death hovering over his shoulder. He obediently climbed into the Police van, and just as obediently entered the dark, forbidding precincts of Nairobi Central Jail and went through the formal motions as did every prisoner who was brought to this prison. He made no murmur of protest when he was locked in a cell, barely noticing it was bigger and more comfortable than the one he had just vacated. The old inmates, as also the prison staff, had gathered surreptitiously around the corridors to watch the newcomer arrive. The prison grape vine was always avid for news, and quick to discover anything out of the ordinary; and although Mrefu barely noticed the looks of sympathy on their faces, he sensed a friendly atmosphere, which seemed to rise up and enfold him in its protective cloak.

As soon as he heard the door lock behind him, he sat down on the bed, his mind whirling round to such an extent that soon he began to feel physically dizzy. "What was that the warder said to me when I came in?" he thought . . . " 'Never mind, brother, when you've been here a year or two, you'll forget you've got a name. You'll only be a number. Then it won't be so bad. What could he have meant?" Mrefu

263

thought perplexedly, as he mulled these words over in his mind. "I know I've got a number, what was it — 007984, yes, that's it, but I'm still Mrefu, or am I? I must be! That was the name my parents gave me. How can I forget whom or what I am?" He shrugged his shoulders. "At least it means that I shall still be alive in a year or two's time, and that's all that really matters." He pondered awhile, until he was brought sharply to his senses by the grating of the key in his door, and simultaneously, the penetrating clang of a huge bell.

"Come on, 7984," said his jailor. "Don't look so frightened — it's lunch time! We haven't put you in solitary confinement here, you know. You are a privileged prisoner — the Governor very seldom deigns to detain a man, you know. In a few days, when you've got used to the prison routine, we'll be giving you some work to do. You are not alone any more. Do you like your cell?"

Mrefu looked astonished. Was this man asking, yes, asking him if he liked the cell? Was he trying to make him happy, was he going to be well treated at last? He looked around him for the first time, and realised just what a nice room he had been given. Although the door was thick and strong, and the one window, yes a real window, forbiddingly barred, the cell itself was rather pleasant. He had a real bed, with a comfortable mattress and two blankets, and there was a stool too.

The warder, seeing Mrefu glance at the magazines on the floor, laughed. "Yes, you are allowed to read, and I can easily bring you some more magazines and books too if you would like them. You are allowed to write one letter a month, and if you want to make any particular request, you can do that too. You can keep the magazines here until you've finished with them— we're not sadists here!"

Mrefu gaped at him. This treatment, after all he had suffered, was beyond his comprehension. "Thank you," he murmured. "Yes, I like it very much," and he stopped abruptly, unable to say any more. He meekly followed the warder to the great dining room, and barely noticed the sudden hush as he entered. He was placed at a little table at the top of the room, next to the warders' tables, and he was served with plenty of good, wholesome, appetizing food, which he ate with enthusiasm.

Once Mrefu fully realised that this was to be his life, and that he would probably never know any other, he came to terms with himself and determined to become an indispensable asset in the prison. His mind was slowly beginning to function properly again, and he realised that if he behaved well, he would receive better treatment. Perhaps in time, if they thought him fully converted to their ways, this would lead to his release: who could tell? As soon as he had become used to the prison routine, and had made friends with many of the inmates, he was summoned to the Chief Warder's office. No longer fearful, he went readily. Here he was told that he was to be the prison storekeeper, a task only given to the most privileged and well behaved prisoner. He accepted this task readily enough, and soon learned how to issue the posho, beans and various other rations and stores to the warders themselves, the cooks, workers, supervisors and all the others who took part in the smooth running of the prison. He soon learned too how to sneak out extra posho for the warders without being caught by their Chief, thus making himself even more popular. He buried himself in this work and indeed tried to keep away from his fellow prisoners as much as possible — he liked them well enough, but could not bear to hear them talking, as they always did, of how long they still had to serve time, how they were counting the days, and what they were going to do when they were released. He watched, with an aching heart, prisoners come and go, and wished, with a pain that was almost too great to bear, that he too could cross off the days as they passed by, that he too could anticipate the day when those ominous gates would open to let him pass through, and close for ever behind him.

Unfortunately, his position of storekeeper made it impossible for him to remain in isolation. It was his duty to check all stores issued once a week, and the prison was so large that this took him the best part of four days to accomplish. During this check, he associated closely with not only the overseers and helpers, but also the normal inmates, and he found it hard to keep his composure when he heard a sudden hush when he entered a room, for he knew that they were discussing pending departures, and out of respect for him and his plight, they did not want to hurt his feelings by mentioning this subject in his hearing.

Very soon after his arrival, he was allowed to enter all the places forbidden to other prisoners. His cell remained open all day, and was only locked after "lights out" at night. All the inmates of the prison, old-timers, newcomers and officials, did everything they could to make him happy. They liked and respected him, and mobbed each other for the privilege of speaking to him and working beside him. The prisoners were not jealous of Mrefu; they pitied him for the way he had been treated and, in their own rough way, became his comrades. But Mrefu was a different man when he thankfully escaped to the solitude of his cell. Here he pondered again and again, and there was the rest of his life to ponder in, on what had happened to him, and how events had forced him to be where and what he was. He remembered vividly and always painfully how he had deserted from the forest, how he had been responsible for the death of one of his dearest friends, how he, Njogu and Nundu had fought amongst themselves to the detriment of their men. He wondered often whether Nundu had been shot, Njogu captured, what had happened to Kato. And then his mind would turn to his family. Although he had written to his wife every month since he had entered Nairobi Central Prison, he had had no reply. Where was she? Where were their children? Was he alone in the world? The other prisoners were allowed visitors once a month, and so was he, but all the efforts he made to trace his wife had been fruitless. He had asked those who were leaving to go to his home and tell her where he was. He had questioned those who had come, but with no result. He was utterly alone in the world. He could not even obtain word of Nundu, his dear son. It seemed as if all his relatives had also disappeared off the face of the earth, and his friends too had deserted him.

As the months went by, so any hope he may have had of being released slowly disappeared. He determined to stop grieving over his own misfortunes, a practically impossible aim to achieve, and endeavoured to turn the prison into his home. He had changed greatly over these past few years, and the treatment that he had received, detrimental physically, had also affected his mind, and he became rather confused. He found it hard to assemble his thoughts correctly; they became muddled and vague, and his memory hardly functioned at all. He resigned himself to die in prison, feeling that it was no use grieving over what he would never see again, and grieving too that he would not be buried in the land of his ancestors. He was completely isolated and yearned for his forest, if not for his home and his people, and try as he could, he could not blot them out of his heart.

One day over three years later when he had, as the warders had predicted, become just a number, he had just finished issuing stores when he saw the Prison Commandant, accompanied by two askaris, walking across the quadrangle in front of this store. He immediately hurried behind the counter, grabbed the broom and started to sweep the floor. The Prison Commandant was seldom seen, and conducted inspection tours of the prison only once every quarter. Mrefu was puzzled. Something extraordinary must have happened, for the Commandant had toured the prison only a few days previously. He peeped cautiously through the window and realised to his consternation that the group was coming along the verandah to his store. Mrefu, who by now had lost all fear of being suddenly executed, began to wonder if the Commandant had found out he was giving certain warders more than their quota of rations, or maybe the Commandant had just been passing by and had seen him idling, which would perhaps be worse. If he had, Mrefu would surely be punished severely. He started to quiver, and dropped the broom in sheer terror as the great man stalked into the room. Mrefu stood to attention, perspiration dripping off his face. "Good morning, Sir!" he stuttered, and then stood with bent head to hear sentence pronounced.

"7984," barked the Commandant, grinning broadly,

"Sir!" whispered Mrefu, who did not dare lift his head, and therefore missed the Commandant's expression.

"Get me a chair, I want to sit down here and talk to you a little!"

"Sir?" queried Mrefu, who hurried to do as he was told, almost falling over his own feet in panic.

"Do you see this envelope?" asked the Commandant, as he brandished a large, very official looking envelope in the air. "The contents of this, 7984, have told me that you are to be released immediately! As it is a bit late to release you now, the gates of my prison will open for you first thing tomorrow morning. But from this moment, you are a free man. How does it feel?"

Mrefu grinned feebly. "This man is mad," he thought. "What a beastly cruel way to amuse himself. But I must humour him, or I'll be punished."

"Yes, Sir!" he answered. "I feel all right!" Mrefu felt tears stinging his eyes. Why did the man have to joke with him over this? Everyone knew that he would never be released, and that he would die in this place!

The Commandant looked puzzled. "Listen, 7984, or, forgive me, Mrefu, I'm not playing. I mean it. This letter," he tapped the envelope with a bony finger, "is from the Governor. It tells me I am to release you forthwith. Why, I was so happy when I read it that I came personally to tell you." He leaned forward and patted Mrefu's quivering hand. "You must believe me, it's true! Listen — you can read. Here, take it and see for yourself."

Mrefu obediently took the letter, but was unable to read a word, as the sentences danced up and down in front of his eyes until he was dizzy. "It can't be true, it just can't be," he thought. "I have to die here. The Government ruled so. This is just a trick, I don't believe it, I mustn't believe it!"

"Well, have you read it?" demanded the Commandant.

"Yes, Sir, I have," replied Mrefu automatically.

The Commandant roared with laughter. "And you still don't believe I am telling you the truth? Never mind, I can understand how you feel. Let me be the first to congratulate you. Tomorrow, when you are on the train speeding home (for I have ordered that a seat be booked for you, and paid for) you will know I spoke the truth today. You have been a model prisoner, and a great asset to us. You have made no trouble, and that is the reason our Governor has decided to release you. We'll miss you and all the help you have given to us — but we know that you will be happy and that you deserve your release, and that's all that matters. Farewell, Mrefu, and good luck!" The Commandant took Mrefu's hand and shook it enthusiastically, and still meeting with no response, he laughed again and left the store.

Mrefu stood stock still, tears pouring down his face. He still did not believe that he had been released. He watched, almost as if in a dream, his prison comrades streaming across to congratulate him, followed by the warders. They clapped him on the back and raised him shoulder high, but still he could not believe it was true. Gifts showered down on him as if from heaven. Many of the prisoners uncovered their secret hoards and selected various precious items, wallets, socks, razor blades, handkerchiefs, and even in some cases, a little money, to give to him; items that had been secretly collected in anticipation of their release over a period of years, and obtained from no-one knew where. One of them even produced a small suitcase. The Warders clubbed together and gave him all the clothes he would require in his new life, and they collected a few pounds which he was told to use as pocket money. The whole prison, except Mrefu, was jubilant, and merrymaking went on far into the night: even the strict rules regarding "lights out" were side-stepped. A triumphant procession escorted Mrefu back to his cell, all his friends fighting and pushing to carry his belongings. When they eventually left him in peace, he sat down on the bed and wept. Even after all these demonstrations, he still did not believe that he was free. He heard the jailor coming round to lock the cell doors, and when he heard him pass by his cell, he called the jailor to tell him that he had forgotten to lock "7984". The warden burst into roars of laughter, and his only reply was, "You are a free man now — if I lock your door, I will be detaining you unlawfully. Good night, Mrefu!"

"Mrefu? Mrefu? They never called me Mrefu before," thought Mrefu. "I am just a number, a nonentity. Why are they doing this to me? Perhaps it is true, perhaps I am a free man at last." He got up, crept to his door, and tentatively tried to open it. It swung open readily at his touch. "It is open! Perhaps they are not teasing me. Well, even after all this, I won't believe I am free until I am out of those evil gates, holding my train ticket in my hand!" He climbed into bed and gazed blankly at the ceiling, his mind in a turmoil — "Is this true, or isn't it? Am I freed or not? Can any of this be true?" and so on, until he fell into a restless sleep.

The following morning, his jailor helped him to pack his things. He had a hair-cut and a bath, and dressed himself in civilian clothing. He had a hurried breakfast, was given his railway ticket, and after hasty "goodbyes" almost as if in a dream, he heard the prison gates clang shut behind him, and he climbed into the waiting van. Half an hour later, he was sitting in the train — bound for home.

EPILOGUE

. . . . Mrefu heard himself yelling, "That will teach you . . . !" He awoke with a start as the train roared under a bridge, and he sat still for a moment, bewildered at his surroundings, blinking in the strong sunlight that shone through the carriage window.

"What's that?" he muttered, "Oh, I must have been dreaming. But what a dream! I could have sworn that I was back in Ngorano Primary School. Oh, I was a beast in those days. It's funny that those boys I treated so badly somehow gravitated back to me. I remember that day vividly now. They all ran away and then I was sacked. What did I do then? Oh yes, I went to Naro and started to work as a railway clerk, and it was then that I got involved in the Freedom Movement. Yes, I soon became a changed man. That reminds me of that brute Cook. He met a deserved end, and from Nundu's hands too. That served him right for treating those boys' fathers like that!" He burst out laughing. "Swine that he was! He suffered in the end, my goodness he did. We worked so happily in those days. Nundu, oh yes, there was Heho and Wenye too, his brothers. Funny that Heho turned into the kind of Christian that would betray his own brother. He didn't succeed, although a lot of good men were lost on that day. I remember those boys growing up beside me. How Nundu blossomed out when he started to love me." Mrefu smiled proudly. "What a son to have! He is magnificent. The others? Well, none of them were of Nundu's calibre, although I loved Muta. Poor Muta . . ." he paused. "Well, it was my fault that Muta and the others were killed. I wonder what happened to Kato? Are Nundu and Njogu still alive? I hope that when I get home I'll be able to find out. What fights we used to have in those days and how victorious we were. I'll never forget the day those askaris came to question me after the raid on Cook's farm; the day the young settlers took me out and beat me! I never let on, but I do remember

271

chuckling even with all that pain, at the consternation and worry on their faces. It was really amusing to watch the white men panic! It was then that Nundu first went to the forest, yes, that's right. I went to visit him so many times. Oh, what a great leader he turned out to be: much greater than I had ever hoped. He well surpassed his old school teacher! Funny too, the bond that grew up between us, especially after he had run away from school solely because of me. If I'd been different, would all this have happened?" he wondered. "I suppose I would still have been teaching." He shook his head. "No, even if I had not taken part in the fight, Nundu would have done. He was, or, I hope is, belligerent. He always looked for trouble, or perhaps trouble always sought him out, I'm not sure which!"

Mrefu was almost jolted off his seat as the train lurched to a stop. He looked out of the window, and sank back into his seat with an impatient sigh. "It's only Kija Station — I've still got another 100 miles to go. Won't be home for hours. I wish this train would hurry up," he thought, and while the train was in the station, he paced impatiently up and down the platform and indeed, not hearing the guard's whistle above the *mêlée*, he caught hold of the guard rail and clambered into the train with much difficulty, as it was leaving the station.

Once safely back in his compartment, he started to roar with laughter. "That reminds me of the time Nundu banged his leg against the rail when he was running away from me! He often told me that story. But it was a good deal later on when he ran to the forest, and then, oh yes, then eventually I had to flee myself. It wasn't a bad life to start with; not when we had plenty of food and plenty of victories too — it was when we started to lose that things went wrong. No, not even then. I think the trouble really began when we teamed up, and of course Njambi's capture made things far worse. My memory must be getting very rusty. I can't remember which happened first." He stopped and rubbed the back of his head thoughtfully. "No," he whispered. "I can't remember. But what happened after that?

My home village was burned down, and Toga had his wooden leg burned — ah, but that was months before we broke up, surely? But what I remember so vividly is my desertion. Can I ever forgive myself for that? Can I ever justify my action in my own eyes, let alone those of the world? Yes, I think I can now." He gazed at his reflection in the window as the train went through a tunnel. His reflection grinned back at him, and the lines on its worn, now old, face seemed to picture pride and achievement rather than suffering and failure. He stood up and stretched himself. "Well," he said to it, "as far as I am concerned, and if I may dare to venture an opinion, I think I have exonerated myself, and paid my debt." His reflection nodded and grinned back at him, obviously in complete agreement, and then he dozed off again.

He pulled down the window as soon as he woke up, leaned out, and for the first time enjoyed breathing in the fresh air and looking at the view. "My goodness, we must be nearly home. I must sleep again; makes the time pass very quickly!" He was soon lulled by the rhythmic movement of the train, and after a short time he was woken up by the train steward, who informed him that he had arrived at his destination. Mrefu blinked at him, and then realising what he had been told, he sprang up and leaned out of the window. Was this Zebu Station? It looked so different, but yes, there was the signboard, still in the same place. He shook his head to clear the fog on his brain. The whole station must have been rebuilt, and over its roof he could see huge buildings that were certainly not there in his time. He collected his baggage and climbed down on to the platform, and was immediately engulfed by the hubbub of humanity which was either trying to get on or off the train, or to sell the numerous vegetables and fruits which abounded in this area.

Very shaken, and feeling almost frightened at this unexpected difference, he made his way to the District Officer's office to report his presence. Fortunately this was still in the same place as it had always been, and because of this Mrefu managed to regain a certain amount of his self-confidence. Whilst he was waiting to see the District Officer, he found, rather to his consternation, that Kamau, the former District Officer at Naro, had been promoted to the rank of District Commissioner; and far worse than that, Carey Milton had become a Permanent Secretary. "I wish I had had the chance to kill that white swine," he muttered. A Permanent Secretary indeed! What is this country coming to? The more brutal a man is, the more he is able to better himself, in Government Service anyway. After his interview, which was rather unpleasant as the District Officer treated him as if he were sub-human, which brought back vivid memories of the past, he left the town towards home. He looked around him in bewilderment. What had been happening during his absence? All these little plots, all these strange faces; where were all the villagers he had known, had grown up with? The hills and valleys remained the same, but that seemed to be all. When he reached his home, he found that it was a shamba. The huts had been pulled down and there was no sign of his wife or children. He gazed round him aghast. Where were they? What had happened to them? All his old fears flooded back and almost engulfed him. He supported himself against a tree, horrified and helpless: had he come back to this?

He shuddered uncontrollably, and with an effort walked over to some nearby huts, dreading to ask, but realising that he had to know the truth. He tentatively asked for news and, obtaining no help, he walked back to what looked like a camp to find the Headman. He waited for over an hour before the Headman could be contacted, and then, his surprise and joy when he saw Toga limping towards him cannot be imagined.

"Toga, my dear friend, is it really you?" Mrefu could not believe the evidence in front of his eyes.

"Mrefu! Ah, Mrefu! How wonderful to see you . . . I thought you were dead!" They embraced, tears running unashamedly down their cheeks, to the great interest and curiosity of the passers by.

"Toga! I thought you were dead too, and now you are Headman! You, of all people! You, who fought so hard. What happened? Have you changed your ideas?" replied Mrefu.

"Shush Mrefu, it is too dangerous to talk here. Come into my house and I'll tell you why — I can give you a good deal of news of our comrades too, and I'm sure you have plenty to tell!" Toga took Mrefu's arm, and started to lead him towards his house.

"Just a moment. Toga, I must ask you this before I go any further. What of my wife and family? What of Nundu? Are they all . . ." Mrefu stopped, unable to say the dreaded word.

"Dead?" finished Toga, laughing merrily. "No, dear friend, they are not dead, they are safe and well."

"Well, where are they? Don't keep me in suspense. Where are they? Tell me, tell me," Mrefu begged.

"I suppose that means you have already been to your old home and found nothing? Well you see, Mrefu, the Government has laid down this enormous Land Consolidation programme. Thousands of people are being shifted off their old shambas and forced to go to new ones. That's all that has happened. Your wife and family are now living on a small plot about ten miles from here. Unfortunately, brother, they've got the worst part of the bargain — their shamba is full of stones and rocks; but even so, they are managing to eke out a meagre existence. Listen, I'll send one of my men to bring them here, and whilst he is doing that, let's go and have a real heart to heart talk."

Mrefu, tears of happiness, joy and relief once more making themselves more than evident, agreed readily and followed Toga to his house.

Toga produced some pombe, turned his wife and children out of the room and locked the door. "I have to be very careful," he explained to a bewildered Mrefu. "You see, if they hear us talking you'll be whipped back into detention, and I will accompany you!"

275

"Oh yes, yes, I understand that, but where is Njambi, your wife — was she killed too? The last I heard of her . . ."

"Oh no, she's alive," interrupted Toga. "We were divorced. She told me not to accept the post of Headman, and when I did," he shrugged his shoulders, "she upped and left me. I believe she is somewhere in Moka now." He shook his head sadly. "She just refused to understand my motives."

"Yes, we have all suffered greatly," replied Mrefu, "and I'm sorry to hear that. She was such a standby during those terrible days. I'm telling you, that it was she who saved us from starvation, and she alone."

Toga regarded him pensively. "I think what really happened was that she received such terrible treatment it turned her brain. The Njambi of old would never have left me after I had explained everything to her. She just seemed to be incapable of reasoning things out. Anyhow, that's over and done with now. Tell me about yourself: what happened after you left Kudu Island? You must have suffered pure hell."

"Me?" Mrefu grimaced. "Yes, I suffered all right, but before I tell you all about it, tell me: what has happened to Nundu? What is he doing now?"

"Nundu? He's almost become your son, hasn't he?" asked Toga. "Well, he too is battleworn, but like all of us still fighting — but not with weapons this time. I'll tell you all about that later. He is a semi-invalid at the moment, and he's living with your family."

"But what of Njogu, Kato and the others: are they all dead?" asked Mrefu eagerly, but dreading the answer.

"Njogu?" Toga shook his head sadly. "I don't know what has happened to him. When did you last see him?"

"I left him in the forest — it looked as if he had settled down there for the rest of his life. He had quite a lot of men with him. He showed no wish to fight further . . ."

Mrefu nodded, "Yes, he's probably still in there — a very likely solution."

"Yes, you could be right. Anyhow we've heard nothing of him, although we have tried to trace him. I think Choti must be with him, for I've heard no news of him either. I do know that my brother Muta was killed. A terrible loss. Tell me how it happened. I believe you were there at the time?" replied Toga.

"That, my friend, is all tied up with my experiences, and I'd rather leave them for the time being. Let me settle down a little first. My memories are so vivid, and I don't want to destroy my joy at coming home," pleaded Mrefu.

"No, Mrefu, it was very unkind of me to ask this of you. I understand how you must feel." Toga gazed at him compassionately. "Forget it for now, and let's have some more pombe." He got up and went over to the cupboard. "You asked about Kato," he said over his shoulder. "Kato's fine. He's working for a butcher in town; doing pretty well, I believe. I think he's busy saving up all his hard-earned money to buy a small shamba, but I'm not sure about that. He's turned very sullen; I think he frets after Muta, you know. There was Karoki too; they were such good friends — we've never seen nor heard of him since his sister was raped. Do you remember? The security forces killed his grandfather, and took Karoki away . . . Oh God, how we have all suffered!" Toga sighed, and gave Mrefu another bottle of beer. "Drink up! We can be happy that you are home. I was never more surprised in all my life when I saw you standing outside my office!"

"Nor I, when I saw you limping towards me," laughed Mrefu. "We must be thankful that we are still alive."

"I've remembered something that might interest you, Mrefu," said Toga. "You must remember Kara, the shepherd's son? Yes, I thought you did. Well, he is now a Tribal Policeman. He married Njambi's great friend, Mary. Do you know, he's still as ignorant and inquisitive as ever! How on earth he ever wangled his way into the Tribal Police Force,

I shall never know. I consider him to be absolutely un-employable!" They both burst into roars of hilarious laughter, and Mrefu nodded his head in agreement.

"That reminds me of the good old days, when I beat the life out of the lot of them! You know, that's where it really all started; when I whipped young Kimu that day. I think I literally half killed him!" Mrefu looked perturbed. "I was a young swine in those days — I could never do such a terrible thing now. Talking of Kimu, have you heard what happened to him?"

"I think he's working as a farm labourer somewhere near Naro. It's funny how you all gravitated over there, and how the youths you beat so sadistically worked and fought beside you. I bet when you went to Naro you thought you'd got rid of them completely!" Toga grinned happily and took another swig of beer. "And you seem to have followed most of them back here! What a small world we live in!"

"Yes, that's true," replied Mrefu. "Listen, I don't want to interrupt, but shouldn't my wife be here now? Are you sure she's still alive? I mean, your messenger seems to have been gone for hours!"

"You, my friend," said Toga, regarding Mrefu affection-ately, "can have no brains left in that thick head of yours. I told you your family is living over ten miles away from here. There are no buses at this time of day — I sent my chap on the bicycle, but you know what hilly country it is. When he gets there, he's got to bring your wife back with him. Supposing she's gone to see a friend of hers? Ah no, they won't be back for at least another two hours, if not more. Just settle down and relax!"

"I deserved that, didn't I?" laughed Mrefu. "It's only just that I've been through so much, and lost hope so many times that I can't believe that everything is really going to be all right — after all, I was only released from prison two days ago!"

They sat silent for a few minutes, Toga pondering over the past and where it had led them, and Mrefu reliving his experiences, and wondering what Kato and Nundu had told Toga.

It was Toga who eventually broke the silence. "Do you remember Mwangi?" he said.

"Mwangi? Which Mwangi? I know so many," replied Mrefu, rather puzzled.

"Oh, you remember, the Mwangi that was Cook's servant."

"That one! Oh, he was a funny character, scared of his own big toe! I remember him now, he used to do a little spying for us, like Nono did; and then used almost to flee for his life," Mrefu remarked. "What's he gone and done now?"

Toga roared with laughter. "That's a perfect description of him! Well, do you know what he did? After you people raided Cook's farm and razed it to the ground, Mwangi braced himself and stepped in — he pinched a few cattle. This wasn't noticed in the furore, but after Cook was killed, why, he pinched a whole lot more. The Police apprehended him, and the fool admitted to having done it before they had sufficient evidence to convict him. If he had kept his mouth shut, I don't think they could have proved anything! Anyhow, he's in jail, and likely to remain there for a good time longer!"

"Silly ass! I told you he was scared of his big toe!" said Mrefu. "Have you got any more beer? I'm terribly thirsty!"

Toga produced the beer, and then continued, "You know, that fool Monckley got such a fright at Cook's death that he left the country forty-eight hours later, and good riddance to him!"

Toga paused and looked at his watch. "They should be here any time now. Listen, I must tell you this before they arrive. We've re-grouped ourselves. The fight for freedom isn't over yet, as you well know, and we intend to fight until the last. We're trying different tactics, and have nearly everybody behind us. I tell you, Mrefu, we've won far more support now than we ever did before — everyone's absolutely sickened at the treatment of our people. Anyhow, that's getting off the point. We are now fighting underground — little bit of sabotage, go slows, and most important of all, we are educating our people to fight through the medium of politics. We are forming another political party — it's still secret, but it won't be for long. I'm telling you, Mrefu, pressure of public opinion, which we intend to make, and have started to make, world opinion, is what will bring us our Uhuru. The world is already horrified at the way the Colonial Government has treated our freedom fighters, and those not even remotely connected with them."

"But what has all this got to do with me?" asked Mrefu in sheer bewilderment.

"Those experiences of yours must have turned your brain!" said Toga. "We have just begun holding Committee Meetings once a week — the next one is to be held in a couple of days' time. We meet, funnily enough, at your house! But that isn't why I told you. I want you to join our Committee. You are an educated man, you will be able to help us so much and give us so many new ideas. This society of ours is but an embryo; we want to nourish it until it grows up and enfolds the whole world. You have fought, and fought bravely; do you want to give up now? Is all your suffering, and that of your comrades, going to count for nought?"

"Truly, Toga, I am not thinking straight," replied Mrefu. "No, I too will fight until the day I die for what is rightfully ours. You know, our physical fight wasn't a complete failure. You wait and see. In the years to come, our fight for freedom will be known as something noble and worthwhile; and this fight, which we have sadly lost at the moment, will prove to be the decisive point, the point where the white man started to think about our Uhuru — wait and see, they won't admit it, but it will be true. For the time being, we shall still continue to fight in the way you suggest. I predict now that world opinion, within the next few years, will force them to give us our freedom." He bent forward and took hold of Toga's shoulder. "I must repeat," he continued, "our blood has not been spilt in vain . . ." A deep silence fell, and the two men gazed at each other in complete unity and friendship.

"Mrefu, my brother, before you come to the meeting, you must tell me what happened to you — Nundu has told us everything up till Kudu Island — I must know what happened after that! I'm dying of curiosity!" said Toga, a few minutes later.

"Toga, you also have suffered! I don't know how you got here yet, do I? Yes, we must have a get-together — come up to my house tomorrow night so that we can tie up all the loose ends. Listen! I heard voices! Have they come at last?" Mrefu sprung up, opened the door and peered into the gloom. "Look, they're coming, they're coming!" he shouted, and rushed out to meet his family, his cup of joy now filled to overflowing.

What a joyful family reunion! Mrefu's wife started crying, and began ululating—forcing the sleepy town to wake up and peer round its doors to find out the meaning of this disturbance so late at night. Mrefu gazed in awe at his children, now almost grown up — who gazed in equal awe back at a father whom they could barely remember. He wept shamelessly with joy, and soon many of his old friends had surrounded him, and welcomed him back with open arms. He could barely distinguish their faces in the gloom, and indeed recognised few; but what did that matter? He was home . . . "Home." He spoke the word aloud, allowing it to linger on his tongue, almost as if he never wanted to speak another word. Home indeed. Amidst all the bustle and excitement, he heard a voice, such a dear voice behind him.

"Welcome home, my father," it said.

He swung round and saw once again the face of his Nundu, a face he thought he would never see again. They embraced, and Mrefu gazed eagerly at him, fingering the lines on Nundu's no longer boyish face. "Nundu, my son — truly I thought we had parted for ever!" Mrefu stopped, too overwhelmed to say any more, and swung round again at a persistent tugging from the other side. "My wife," he said gently, "I agree with you, we must go home now. I am here, back safe and sound. Once more we shall live together in love, harmony and peace. Maybe we shall even have more children; who knows!"

"That is true, my husband," she answered contentedly, "but all that matters now is that you have come back to me. I have wept for you for many years, and I have begged our God of Kirinyaga to give you back to me. Now you have come." Her sweet face lit up with excitement. "My husband, we shall have such an *ngoma* at our home as has never been held in the whole country." She turned and shouted, "Do you hear that, my friends, we must celebrate Mrefu's return with full honours and kill a goat — with the Headman's blessing and permission, of course! We shall have merry-making and laughter, and none will be so happy as we."

Mrefu's friends roared their approval, and his wife arranged that this grand feast and party should be held two days hence. "After all," she said coyly, "I have to have a little time to prepare! But now you must forgive us: we must return home, for we have a long way to go."

Toga insisted upon finding them some means of transport, and he held a collection to raise enough money to pay for it. He met with no difficulty and so, ten minutes later, Mrefu, his wife and family and Nundu climbed into a lorry and left in a cloud of dust.

It was not until the next day that Mrefu found out that his grandmother had died a few months previously. He was very upset, for he had loved and respected the old lady, and he missed her gruff, cheery ways badly. His wife soon turned him out of the house, declaring that she had too much work to do preparing for the *ngoma* to have men lounging around and getting under her feet! Mrefu and Nundu therefore went into the shamba and walked down to a little stream nearby, where they dabbled their toes in the water and talked. They discussed their experiences from the time they had parted, and Mrefu was very happy when he found that Nundu had been released less than a year after he had been taken off Kudu Island. They sat there and talked for the whole day, completely reunited. At dusk they grinned sheepishly at each other.

"We must be getting back home," said Mrefu, "or my wife will never allow us to come into the house!" He paused. "Nundu, you must stay with us now. You are my adopted son, and have the same right to live in my house as have my true sons . . . that reminds me: what's happened to your two brothers? I remember one of them was killed, but what about the other? Heho, yes, that's right, Heho."

Nundu looked at him in astonishment. "Why, haven't you heard? Heho went off his head. I think when he realised the consequences of his betrayal of me (you remember that time when we were ambushed and had to fight tooth and nail through two groups of soldiers to get back into the forest? We lost many men that day) he went crazy and started to beat his head against the wall. They took him away and put him in a mental home, where he has been ever since. I don't think he'll ever be allowed out. I went to see him a few weeks ago, and he shouted about how he had betrayed me, and frothed at the mouth. I don't think he even recognised me. Oh well, now you know. I'd rather leave the subject alone. Don't say anything about it, please!"

Mrefu patted his shoulder sympathetically, and together they walked back to the house, to find Toga there waiting for them. He had been pushed into a corner by Mrefu's wife, who was still far too busy to take any notice of mere men! Once more they grouped together and began to talk —

there was so much to talk about that they could have gone on for ever! Toga stayed so late that he had to accept Mrefu's offer of a bed for the night. He could not possibly manage to catch a bus at that time of night.

The following afternoon, people began to turn up for the party, bringing with them gifts of all kinds. The hero of the day, Mrefu, was fêted by all, and indeed they clapped him on the back and shook his hand so many times, that his arm began to feel as if it was going to fall off, and his back, even now still tender, began to ache! The men built a huge fire in the garden — there was no room to accommodate all the guests in the house, and the pombe was circulated freely. Mrefu greeted his old friends enthusiastically. Kato arrived early, but had no time to recall his adventures, as Mrefu was immediately surrounded by jubilant villagers again, and although he managed to give a special welcome to his comrades, none of them had any chance to speak to him in private. The feasting and merrymaking went on far into the night. Mrefu, although enjoying himself, was thoroughly puzzled and disturbed. Half-way through the evening, he had seen Toga, Kato, Kara, Nundu and several of the others, go into a little huddle on the outskirts of the party. His last actions in the forest came back in a rush, and he wondered if Kato was telling the real story of what had happened to them when he had decided to escape. He shrugged his shoulders. Even if Kato did, it could do him no harm; he had paid off his debt in full, and could easily prove it. He entered into the party spirit with zest, and joined the dancers who had started cavorting at dusk and looked like continuing until dawn; but even so, he kept on glancing curiously towards the little group, and was much relieved when it dispersed about half an hour later.

After about three in the morning, one by one the reluctant villagers began to stagger away to their homes. Mrefu watched them, grinning. "I wonder how many of them will sleep on the roadside tonight," he said to Toga, who was standing next to him.

"I don't know," replied Toga. "All I do know is that I've never seen so many gallons of *pombe* consumed in one night in all my life! I expect the garden will be dotted with inert bodies until tomorrow evening, and boy, what a hangover they will have!" He laughed. "Anyhow, Mrefu, I think the time has now come . . ." He paused and glanced at Mrefu.

"The time has now come?" queried Mrefu. "I don't understand what you mean!"

"You soon will," laughed Toga. "Here, come with me".

Toga beckoned to Nundu, and led Mrefu away from the still blazing fire until they were standing by themselves. Mrefu looked utterly bewildered. "Do tell me what this is all about," he said.

"You'll see in a moment," said Toga. "Don't be so impatient. Wait until the others come."

Mrefu soon realised that the "others" were all those who had been talking with Toga in that mysterious little group earlier on in the evening.

As soon as they were ready, Toga turned to Mrefu. "Sit down, Mrefu, and all of you. I have something to say." He waited until the little group had made themselves comfortable, and then continued, "I think Mrefu is the only one amongst us who doesn't know why we have gathered here. Mrefu, I think you saw us talking earlier, but you didn't know what we were discussing. We have decided, now that you are back, to ask you if you will do us the honour of becoming the Chairman of our Society . . . No, don't interrupt," for Mrefu had jumped up and was obviously intending to speak, "I want you to know that we respect you as a man, and love you as a friend. No one has done more for our Movement than you, and it is the least honour we can pay you. This decision was quite unanimous; we need your guidance and experience, and we need it badly . . . Well, don't just gape — for heaven's sake, say something!"

They all began to laugh at Mrefu's obvious confusion, and it was not until five minutes later that he had sufficiently collected his thoughts to answer.

He stood up and looked at his friends, completely overwhelmed. "I — I don't know what to say," he stammered. "I feel that I am not worthy of this great honour you have offered me. I just can't believe that you all feel this way — I've done nothing to deserve this." He stopped, and looked at the blurred faces in front of him. "I can hardly see you," he said. "My eyes don't seem to want to focus. Listen, please. Give me a little time to think. It's not that I don't want to help; of course I do — I'll fight with you until the day I die. It's not that, it's just that I feel so unworthy. Please give me time to think, time to come to terms with myself, and then I will give you my answer. I cannot accept this responsibility unless I feel I deserve it. Forgive me, and please understand." He turned abruptly away, and walked back to his house. He heard Toga say, "I know Mrefu, he'll do it!" and heard his friends respond by clapping and cheering him. He went into his room and slammed the door. He leaned against it, his mind awhirl.

"What have I done to deserve such an honour?" he thought, as he prepared to get into bed. He lay down and stared blindly at the rafters. "I? No, not I. Have I got the character to see this thing through? I've been a failure all my life; everything I've touched I've never finished, although I must admit that I have paid for my sins, and paid generously. I must forget that day in the forest. I've paid my debt," he smiled, "yes, the God of Kirinyaga must agree with me, or he would never have offered me such a wonderful chance. Yes, I've been forgiven, and now I can start life anew, but with the same purpose — to free my people. We'll have to do it differently this time. Yes! Find a loftier, better, gentler way. No one people can keep another people in chains of bondage for ever! Our names will go down in history as those who fought to free their country, and who, through untold hardships and suffering, more than should be borne by any man, succeeded, heads still held high and spirit unquenched through days of disappointment and defeat as well as days of victory. The suffering of my people will become known throughout the world, will be emblazoned in the history books. True patriots, who fought unflinchingly for their beliefs, and won."

Mrefu tossed restlessly on his bed. "But how mixed up we all are," he thought. "Myself, for instance! What have I done during my life? How much have I changed from that big-headed schoolboy who decided to take up teaching as a career? Teaching? Oh yes, I failed at that, hopelessly. I still can't understand how I could have been so brutal — perhaps I was just conceited, and wanted to show off. Then? Then I became a railway clerk — I was a good one too. I bet they missed me when I ran away to the forest! How I deceived them!" Mrefu laughed. "Yes, I was a model employee, and look what I got away with!" He fell serious again. "I certainly had my head screwed on straight when I joined the Movement. Everyone seemed to be so mixed up, going first one way and then another; I had to steady them up, and that I did and did well. But now they've started again. Like reeds in the wind, they don't know which way they are being blown, but desperately want to control the wind. If I join this committee, if I become its leader, I will be able to help them. I am older, wiser, better educated and more experienced than they; they need someone like me to steady them up and to prevent them doing anything hasty . . . hasty? Yes, like my action in the forest when I deserted. And yet was it so foolish? Now I can do what I have prayed to the God of Kirinyaga that I might do — help them, be an active member who is free, not confined to the forest or cooped up in a beastly detention camp. Perhaps I was right, for Kirinyaga has guided me back here, back to start fighting again. Then, after I deserted, oh yes, all that pure hell I suffered. I tried to kill myself more than once, I remember so well the mental agony that I suffered, apart from the physical pain . . . I made a mess of things on Kudu Island too, but I made up ten thousand fold for that. I was given another chance, and although I suffered a great deal for writing that letter, it was well worth it. Then? Then I was sent to prison and then home; here is my home, my people. They are so muddled, so uncertain of what to do. They have become as my children and are crying out to me to help them, to lead them to victory. I should be very proud, and indeed am, but how confused they are. Yes they are, we all are, a confused generation . . . a generation of confusion." The words jingled in his mind . . . A . . . generation . . . of . . . confusion . . .

    Mrefu slept.

GLOSSARY

Askari	A soldier or policeman
Baraza	Public meeting
Boy	Employed to mean male servant. Originally spelt 'Boi' and confused with 'Boy'. Widely rejected as a discriminating term
Bhangi	Indian hemp
Bwana	Either a white man, an employer, an important person, or a substitute for Mr.
Calabash	A bowl or basin made by cutting a large gourd in half, usually lengthwise
Chui	A leopard, used here as a name
Dawa	Medicine, a dye, or other similar preparation
Debe	A can or tin, usually of 4 gallons
Dudus	Insects
Duka	A shop or stall
Effendi	Officer; title of respect from a junior in rank; high official or person of rank
Godown	Store or warehouse
Hapa	Here
Ihii	Uncircumcised young boys
Ihurura	A ground creeper, like a pumpkin
Irio	Special Kikuyu dish of meat, maize and vegetables
Jambo	A Swahili form of greeting
Jembe	A digging tool, rather like a heavy broad hoe
Kaburu	European, especially of Boer stock
Kaffir	A Boer word for African, used as a term of disrespect

289

Kazi	Work, employment
Kifaru	A rhinoceros, used as a nickname
Kiko	A smoking pipe
Kimandi	Feasting
Kirinyaga	The Kikuyu name for Mt. Kenya where God is believed to live
Kuja	Come
Lete	Bring
Lima	Dig, cultivate
Mabati	Sheets of metal, usually for roofing
Manyatta	A Masai dwelling or village
Mboga	Vegetable; often used colloquially to indicate something to eat with ugali (posho) — even meat
Memsahib	A European woman
Mrefu	Long or tall, used here as a name
Mwalimu	A schoolmaster, teacher
Mzee	Old, ancient. Also a title of respect
Na	And or with
Ndio	That is so
Ngoma	A drum, a party or a dance
Ngwa	Lightning. Here used as a complimentary title
Nyoka	A snake
Panga	A heavy broad cutting tool used for such rough work as cutting grass, hacking wood, etc. It makes a formidable weapon
Pombe	Beer brewed from maize
Posho	Maize meal
Reserve	A district set aside in colonial days for one particular tribe
Shamba	A farm or homestead; arable land
Shauri	Business, affair, court case, or matter for consultation or advice
Simba	A lion. Here used as a nickname

Twiga	A giraffe. "Long necked one"
Ugali	Maize meal cooked to the consistency of bread
Uhuru	Freedom or independence
Upesi	Quickly
Wote	All
Ya	Of

Published by the East African Publishing House Ltd., P.O. Box 30571, Uniafric House, Koinange Street, Nairobi and printed by The English Press Ltd., P.O. Box 30127, Reata Rd., Nairobi.